AUDEN AND ISHERW

Also by Norman Page

A. E. HOUSMAN: A Critical Biography
TENNYSON: An Illustrated Life
SPEECH IN THE ENGLISH NOVEL
THE LANGUAGE OF JANE AUSTEN
E. M. FORSTER
MURIEL SPARK
A DICKENS COMPANION
A KIPLING COMPANION
A CONRAD COMPANION
A BYRON CHRONOLOGY
A DICKENS CHRONOLOGY
A DR JOHNSON CHRONOLOGY
AN OSCAR WILDE CHRONOLOGY
AN EVELYN WAUGH CHRONOLOGY
WILKIE COLLINS: The Critical Heritage
NABOKOV: The Critical Heritage
D. H. LAWRENCE: Interviews and Recollections
BYRON: Interviews and Recollections
TENNYSON: Interviews and Recollections
DR JOHNSON: Interviews and Recollections
HENRY JAMES: Interviews and Recollections
THOMAS HARDY

Auden and Isherwood
The Berlin Years

Norman Page

St. Martin's Press
New York

St. Martin's Press, Scholarly and Reference Division, 175 Fifth Avenue, New York, N.Y. 10010

First published 1998
Reprinted 1998
First paperback edition (with new preface) 2000

Published in the United States of America

This book is printed on paper suitable for recycling and made from fully managed and sustained forest sources.

Printed in Great Britain

ISBN 0–312–21173–2 clothbound
ISBN 0–312–22712–4 paperback

The Library of Congress has cataloged the hardcover edition as follows:
Page, Norman.
Auden and Isherwood : the Berlin years / Norman Page.
p.   cm.
Includes bibliographical references (p.   ) and index.
ISBN 0–312–21173–2 (cloth)
1. Auden, W. H. (Wystan Hugh), 1907–1973—Homes and haunts–
–Germany—Berlin.   2. Isherwood, Christopher, 1904–   —Homes and
haunts—Germany—Berlin.   3. Auden, W. H. (Wystan Hugh), 1907–1973–
–Friends and associates.   4. Isherwood, Christopher, 1904–   –
–Friends and associates.   5. Berlin (Germany)—Intellectual
life—20th century.   6. British—Travel—Germany—History—20th
century.   7. Authors, English—20th century—Biography.   8. Berlin
(Germany)—History—1918–1945.   9. Berlin (Germany)—Biography.
I. Title.
PR6001.U4Z765 1997
820.9'00912—dc21
[b]   97–35010
                                                                      CIP

For Kamal

Contents

List of Plates

Acknowledgements

For advice and assistance of many kinds I am grateful to the following: Don Bachardy, Neville Braybrooke, Sally Brown (British Library), Katherine Bucknell, Mrs Mireille Burton, Jane Callander (BBC), Humphrey Carpenter, Mrs Alethea Constable-Maxwell (née Turville-Petre), A. T. Cornwell (Hon. Obituarist, Oratory Society), Ralf Dose (Magnus Hirschfeld Gesellschaft, Berlin), Loren Driscoll, Wayne Furman (New York Public Library), Robert Golding (Free University, Berlin), Rainer Herrn (Magnus Hirschfeld Gesellschaft, Berlin), David Luke (Christ Church, Oxford), J. R. Maddicott (Librarian and Archivist, Exeter College, Oxford), Francis O. Mattson (Curator, Berg Collection), Luke McKernan (British Film Institute), Professor Edward Mendelson (Literary Executor, the Estate of W. H. Auden), Mr and Mrs Konrad Muthesius, Peter Parker, Renata Stepanek (née Muthesius), A. J. Tinkel (Archivist, Oratory School), Professor Thorlac Turville-Petre, Edward Upward, Rick Wandel (National Museum and Archive of Lesbian and Gay History, New York).

The Leverhulme Trust generously granted me an Emeritus Fellowship for research on the subject of this book.

Quotations from W. H. Auden's 'Berlin Journal' are copyright by the Estate of W. H. Auden and reproduced here by kind permission of Professor Edward Mendelson and the Henry W. and Albert A. Berg Collection, the New York Public Library, Astor, Lenox and Tilden Foundations.

Preface to the Paperback Edition

Auden, Isherwood and their circle are most closely identified with a decade early in the century that is now drawing to a close; but the interest shown in this book since its first appearance a few months ago is further evidence (if any is needed) of the wide interest they are still capable of stimulating. There is a phenomenon familiar to students of literary history whereby writers who have enjoyed popularity in their lifetime commonly suffer disparagement and neglect in the years that follow their death; but, whether or not it proves the rule, the present case seems to be an exception. Isherwood's Berlin stories continue to undergo metamorphoses into different media – surely a sign of their inherent vitality – and not long ago Auden enjoyed that rarest of distinctions for a modern poet, that of best-seller, when copies of a selection of his love poems were to be found, like bags of confectionery in a supermarket, cannily placed near the cash desk in leading bookshops. On a more academic level, editions of Isherwood's diaries and Auden's early poems have recently appeared, and both writers continue to receive attention from biographers.

The Weimar Republic and the rise of Nazism, now as remote from us as the French Revolution was to the Victorians, exerts a similar fascination, for somewhat similar reasons: in that distant period may be discerned some of the origins of the world we have inherited. Auden and Isherwood themselves were born nearly a century ago, but, so far from joining the revered and respectable ranks of the Mighty Dead, they seem to retain, in their lives, their ideas and their work, a perennial freshness and youthfulness. This is of course particularly evident in the early chapters of their lives that are explored in this book: the crucial phases of self-definition as individuals and writers.

Just as the closing years of the Weimar Republic contained the seeds of much of the history of the rest of our century, their time in Berlin was for these writers deeply formative. Both as a chapter of public history and a phase in the lives of individuals, the period covered by this study remains of absorbing interest.

Norman Page

xi

Prologue:
Looking for Berlin

Like many of us, this book originated in chance and accident rather than forethought and planning. Not long after the *Wende*, the coming down of the Wall, I happened to be in Berlin, and, as I wandered through the newly open city, it struck me (as it doubtless struck many others at that time) that after some sixty years – roughly the span of my own lifetime – Berlin had returned to a state it had not known since the Nazis came to power. This brought to mind the group of English writers who had, briefly or not so briefly, made Berlin their home in the last years of the Weimar Republic, and I wondered idly how much in a merely material sense had survived two generations of destruction and rebuilding, partition and reunification: how far the physical fabric of the Berlin that Wystan Auden, Christopher Isherwood, Stephen Spender and others had lived in and written about could be, historically or sentimentally, recovered or rediscovered.

So I went home and did a little biographical and topographical research and, the next time I was there, wandered the streets again, only this time with a 1930 map of Berlin in one hand and a modern map in the other. Not surprisingly, I found that a lot had disappeared. I found, for instance, that the neat lawns of a public park now cover the site of the busy, fashionable, dignified neighbourhood of tall houses, theatres and restaurants where Isherwood stayed when he first settled in the city, and the tenement where he lived briefly but (from a literary point of view) productively with the family of his working-class lover has likewise vanished. But I also discovered that an unexpected amount has survived. The two houses where Auden lived in 1928–9, one in a smart suburb, the other in a former working-class district, still stand, and while there is no trace of the various lodgings that Isherwood occupied during the earlier part of his time in Berlin, the more celebrated house which provided him with the primary setting for his Berlin stories remains intact, its interior not much changed since that time. Of all these sites only one is commemorated by an official plaque – bearing, as it happens, erroneous information.

Particular bars, cafés, dance-halls and cabarets have long ceased to exist: many of them, indeed, barely outlived the Weimar Republic itself. Notorious squares, streets and alleys have become respectable when they have not been entirely swept away. Of 'the Passage', the alley off the Friedrichstrasse frequented by homosexual pick-ups and widely celebrated in fact and fiction, not a trace remains. A once famous political theatre, after being for a time a 'porno' cinema, is now a disco hall and a venue for rock concerts. But the shape and pattern of the city, the streets that are perambulated in getting from one place to another, even the street names, have changed surprisingly little. The hidden skeleton of the U-Bahn or subway and the visible one of its elevated counterpart the S-Bahn are still there to convey us on the same trips that Auden and his friends made. Landmarks like the Zoo Station and the Kaiser Wilhelm Memorial Church still stand, though the latter only part-ially, its stately spire snapped off like a broken tooth and officially transformed, like the bombed Coventry Cathedral and the deva-stated dome in the centre of Hiroshima, into a faintly self-conscious symbol.

When a city is smashed to pieces by natural or unnatural disas-ter, there are two options open to the rebuilders. They can take the opportunity to plan and build a new city. Or they can rebuild the old one so that what they end up with is very like what has disappeared – sometimes so like it that the ignorant visitor may be seduced into according the modern structure a deference appro-priate only to the antique. Just as some of the baroque churches of Munich were scrupulously restored down to the last lick of gold paint, the new Berlin rose in the postwar years along familiar lines, and the spatial feel of the present-day city, when due allowance has been made for new buildings and changes in traffic flow, may not be so very different from what it was around 1930. Certainly, one can still, for instance, walk the route that Spender took when he stepped out of his lodgings and went to visit Isherwood in his, or the even shorter route that led Auden from *his* room to the famous Cosy Corner bar. One can also, if so disposed, in the spirit of the literary pilgrim exploring Dickens's London or Hardy's Wessex, tread in the footsteps of Sally Bowles, Mr Norris and other fictional or semi-fictional characters whose literary lives are largely confined to this city.

My interest growing, I moved on from topography to less tan-gible aspects of the past, asking myself what had taken these young

Englishmen to Berlin and what they had found to fascinate and detain them there, making Auden, for instance, feel 'homesick' for the city after he was obliged to return to England to earn his keep, and a little later impelling him to write poems in bad German to express his nostalgia and longing to return. The biographer's trade nourishes any natural tendency that already exists towards scepticism, and I was not prepared to take at face value the well-publicised boasts by both Auden and Isherwood that they had gone there purely and simply – well, simply – for sex. Berlin around 1930 was not just an enticing destination for sex holidays or fieldwork in the study of decadence. It was the most exciting city in Europe, perhaps in the world, for anyone sympathetic to experiment and innovation in a wide variety of art forms, high and popular, pure and applied: a vital city that in a surprisingly short time had become a magnet for gifted young artists and artistes.

When Auden, in the last line of one of the best known of his early poems (written, incidentally, in the first month of his stay in Berlin), expressed a wish for 'New styles of architecture, a change of heart', he may have had the Bauhaus specifically in mind but was surely not speaking only of architecture. The line expresses the mood of a whole generation for whom Berlin seemed to offer the promise of artistic and social tolerance. The tragedy, it goes without saying, is that the heyday passed so quickly – was, indeed, already under serious threat at the point at which this book begins, though many of those with whom it is concerned came to recognise this grim reality only with the passing of time.

The number of talented Berliners had been swollen by others who, like Bertolt Brecht and Kurt Weill, had come from other parts of Germany, as well as by an international crowd of writers and others, actual or aspiring, who headed for the German capital just as, a few years earlier, their slightly older counterparts had headed for Paris. To read the biographies, autobiographies, letters, journals and memoirs of those who were young or youngish during that period is to encounter many accounts of expeditions to and periods of residence in the city – by, for example, Paul Bowles and Aaron Copland, Francis Bacon and Aleister Crowley, William Plomer and Harold Nicolson, Robert McAlmon and John Lehmann. Auden and Isherwood differed from these, however, both in staying longer and in absorbing their Berlin experiences more thoroughly into their lives and their art.

This book begins with an account of the time spent by these two young writers in Berlin, its boundaries being the arrival of Auden, aged 21 and a brand-new Oxford graduate, in October 1928, and Isherwood's final departure a few weeks after Hitler came to power early in 1933. Its immediate chronological span is thus about four and a half years, though Isherwood was not the only English visitor who went on writing about Berlin long after he had left the city for good. The second chapter looks at the city they found when they stepped off the train: its history and its contemporary ethos; its historic landmarks and newly erected public buildings; its places of entertainment and also certain private dwellings, usually notable only because they were once the homes of writers; its social life by day and night; and some representative creative talents who were active in the city during the period with which we are concerned.

Chapter 3 presents portraits of a number of figures who seem to me to be interesting in two respects. All of them impinged in one way or another on the lives of one or both of the writers in question, and in addition they help to exemplify the kind of personalities and life-styles to which Berlin at this time was hospitable. Not all of them are Germans, but some would be hard to parallel in, say, London or New York at the same period, and since they tend to flit like shadows through other biographies of Auden and Isherwood (understand-ably enough, given the much larger scope of these undertakings), it has seemed worthwhile to try to recreate them in as much detail as possible, especially since most of them are remarkable individuals in their own right and by any standards. A conspicuous absentee from the list is Jean Ross, the prototype of Isherwood's best-known char-acter, Sally Bowles, who has been so exhaustively investigated by other writers as to leave little or nothing to be added to the record. In Chapter 4 the cinema, an art-form that flourished in the Weimar period and has a special bearing on the work of Isherwood, is given separate treatment. Finally, since the reason for investigating the lives of the young men who stand at the centre of this study is that they were writers, there is a chapter that considers the literary out-come of their Berlin experiences: the poems, plays, autobiographies and fictions that exploited and transformed (often more than is read-ily realised) elements from the lives they had lived there, the places they knew and the people they met.

Among other things, this book may also, in its small way, lay claim to being an experiment in biography. At a time when fiction and most other literary genres have been radically 'made new' by a century of innovation, all but a very few biographies still resolutely follow the nineteenth-century model by offering a chronological birth-to-death narrative of a single life. Not a few, indeed, seem, technically speaking, to represent little advance on the annalistic method of the Roman historians, conducting the reader through the subject's life (and the author's files) in the unshakeable belief that what gives shape and meaning to experience is the fact that Monday is followed by Tuesday and February comes after January. Sometimes, though, there may be a case for limiting the focus to a crucial or formative phase of a life, as (to cite two rare exceptions to the general rule) James L. Clifford does in his *Young Samuel Johnson* and H. C. Robbins Landon in his *Mozart's Last Year*. But in any case we do not live alone but very largely through our relationships, so that sometimes lives, including the lives of writers, need to be seen not monolithically but in juxtaposition to each other.

Though many other figures are introduced, the emphasis in this book is on two writers, Auden and Isherwood, who not only talked, ate, wrote and slept together but between them spent the last four and a half years of the Weimar Republic in Berlin. It may therefore be thought of as an attempt to write a biography, or microbiography, of two men and a city during a period which, though brief, was of considerable, even crucial, importance in the lives of all three. That Berlin, and Germany, could never be the same again after the Nazis came to power will hardly be disputed. That going to and living in Berlin involved far-reaching choices for Auden and Isherwood, affecting the course of their future life and work, may be less immediately obvious but is, I believe, fully borne out by the evidence.

1

Two Young Englishmen

In the summer of 1928, Wystan Hugh Auden, aged 21, left Oxford with a third-class degree in English literature, a considerable quantity of poems, and a nearly finished play, *Paid on Both Sides*. His Oxford had been, among other things, the Oxford of Evelyn Waugh (four years older than he), Harold Acton (three years), Henry Yorke, who became the novelist Henry Green (two years), Brian Howard, later a friend of both Auden and Isherwood (two years), and John Betjeman, who entered the university in the same term as Auden himself. The young men of this generation had been schoolboys during the Great War, in which the fathers of many of them had fought and, not infrequently, died.

In the immediate postwar years the atmosphere of Oxford had had an unmistakably military flavour. As Christopher Hollis points out in his memoir of the period, the majority of undergraduates came from military service and some took shortened courses: 'Military life was still the life they thought of as normal and they referred to Hall as the Mess' (*In the Twenties*, p. 17). By the time Auden got there, however, efforts to revive the carefree and hedonistic glories of prewar days and to combine them with the new freedoms of the Jazz Age were well under way. As Martin Green has shown at considerable length in *Children of the Sun*, mid-1920s Oxford witnessed the glittering rise of the New Dandies, and though the group that formed around Auden was 'entirely separate from [Harold] Acton's and quite hostile' (p. 333), regarding Acton and his poetry as frivolous, Auden himself developed a personal brand of non-Etonian aestheticism. As Green aptly says, he cultivated the 'eccentricities of dandyism' and became 'a phenomenon of self-stylisation' (p. 334), and this was a personal style that was to last, with modifications, for the rest of his life.

It was, says Betjeman's biographer, Bevis Hillier, 'the Oxford of plus fours, verandah suits, violet hair cream, batik or Charvet silk ties and open sports cars' (p. 130), and of more or less illicit visits to the London theatres and nightclubs by the train familiarly known as the Flying Fornicator. More sourly, Henry Green recalls in his

6

not unsnobbish autobiography *Pack My Bag* that on entering Oxford he and his contemporaries were 'either to become money snobs or too sensitive to the difference money makes... I was to court the rich while doubting whether there should be great inequalities between incomes... We played at being gentlemen' (p. 195).

This wasn't, however, entirely Auden's style, sartorially or otherwise. During the General Strike he had driven a car in London for the Trades Union Congress ('out of sheer contrariness', as he later said), and the resolve to be unfashionable and nonconformist, which later in life developed into an instinctive and comprehensive eccentricity, is revealing. His first publication, the *Poems* of 1928 (privately printed by Stephen Spender), had been an altogether more serious affair than that of his fellow member of Christ Church, Harold Acton, who was proud to be thought of as an aesthete and who as a schoolboy had brought out, with Brian Howard, a pink-bound volume titled *The Eton Candle* and quickly dubbed *The Eton Scandal*. Auden was not averse to schoolboyish high jinks or to flying his sexual colours from the mast: the private mythologies or fantasy worlds shared with Isherwood and prominent in his early poems and plays suggest a nostalgia for a pre-adolescent, private-school world of privileged irresponsibility. But the camp glamour of the Harold Acton set, which sought to perpetuate in the postwar years the vanished world of Wilde and the Decadents, and perhaps even the earlier blue-china atmosphere of Wilde and Pater's Oxford, did not seduce him. Industrial archaeology and the Icelandic sagas were more to his taste than Japanese prints or 'the Hellenic ideal', and his vision looked to the bracing north rather than the relaxing south.

Born in York in 1907, he was the youngest of the three sons of George Auden, MD, who in the following year became school medical officer for Birmingham. Dr Auden had interests in Greek, Latin and psychology, while his wife, a trained nurse and a High Anglican, had an enthusiasm for music. Long before his Oxford days Wystan had made up his mind to be not just a poet but a great poet, which necessarily meant an original poet. Poetry, though, is a vocation rather than a profession, and sooner or later he had to earn a living. A year after leaving Oxford, he was to imitate another Oxford contemporary, Paul Pennyfeather in Evelyn Waugh's *Decline and Fall*, by drifting into that traditional refuge of the highly educated and totally unqualified, private-schoolmastering. But first, with what seems like extraordinary generosity, his father offered him a year on the Continent. During the summer he fell ill, and in August spent three weeks recuperating at the Belgian resort of Spa; it may have been there that he had some sessions of psychoanalysis. But by October he was fit enough to travel to Berlin, where he remained, with some interruptions, until the summer of the following year.

Why Berlin? It was a time when many British writers and artists, still following the eighteenth-century tradition of the Grand Tour as modified by Byron and by such Victorian escapees from intolerance and repression as John Addington Symonds, instinctively turned south, especially towards the Mediterranean regions. It was a fashion that had recently received a boost from the great popularity of Norman Douglas's *South Wind* (1917). But Auden was proud of his Icelandic name and looks, and took delight in unfashionably preferring the north. A more practical consideration was that, being extremely fair-skinned, he burned easily and painfully when exposed to the hot sun. Isherwood came to share and perhaps imitate his refusal to conform: indeed, he held out much longer, since while Auden later in life made a home in Ischia, Isherwood had turned fifty before he even set foot in Italy.

Paris, since the late nineteenth century the inevitable destination for many aspiring artists and writers, and in the 1920s a refuge for Prohibition-fleeing Americans, was by now past its palmiest days even for those less inclined than Auden to Francophobia. Berlin, moreover, was the place where some of the most progressive movements in painting and theatre, architecture and cinema, and other pure and applied arts were located. Even more enticingly, it had a richly deserved reputation for sexual permissiveness and for the diversity of its sexual underworld. A joke current in Berlin at the time said that, if a lion were sitting outside the Reichstag and a virgin walked past, the lion would roar. Stephen Spender recalls the joke in his introduction to Thomas Friedrich's pictorial history of Weimar Berlin, and was probably also recalling it when he made the character based on Isherwood in *The Temple*, his *roman à clef* partly set in late-1920s Berlin, declare solemnly that it was ' "a city with no virgins. Not even the puppies and kittens are virgins" ' (p. 185).

Thanks to this dual reputation, the city was attracting an international crowd of artists and writers as well as tourists, as a sentence from Robert McAlmon's memoirs makes clear:

I went to Berlin, and there, or soon to be there, were Thelma Wood (sculptor), Marsden Hartley (painter), Djuna Barnes (writer), Berenice Abbott (photographer), Harriet Marsden (dancer), two musicians whose names I have forgotten, Isadora Duncan, and quantities of others....

Even though these are not now names to conjure with, the mood of excitement created by these incessant international comings and goings is unmistakable, and the 'quantities of others' might have included, for instance, Francis Bacon, Paul Bowles, Aaron Copland, Aleister Crowley, William Plomer, and Beatrix and John Lehmann, of all of whom something will later be said.

Moreover, and not least important for a young man living on an allowance from his father, the exchange rate was such that for anyone with sterling or dollars to spend it was a cheap place in which to live. As McAlmon puts it, 'No one knew from one day to the next what the dollar would bring in marks, but everybody knew that, whatever happened, the dollar bought in Berlin as much as ten or twenty dollars would buy elsewhere.'

Of the ten months between his departure for Berlin and his reluctant return to England and job-hunting, Auden spent a total of only about seven in the city: the rest of his time was passed in other parts of Germany and in short visits home. But it was to be in many ways a decisive choice: nothing less than a turning-point in his life, which might have turned out entirely differently if, say, he had got a better degree and remained at Oxford. He was to write some of his finest early poems in Berlin and to embark on his first collaboration with Isherwood. He was also to recognise and come to terms with – indeed, eagerly embrace – his own sexual identity: before Berlin he had been engaged to a Birmingham girl who was training to be a nurse and had cheerfully described himself as 'ambidextrous'. A letter of this period tells how he went to a wedding, got 'decently drunk', and fell in love with one of the bridesmaids. There appears, however, to have been nothing bisexual about his adventures in Germany, and one of his first acts after returning to England was to break off his engagement. A note in his journal at this time makes the fervent promise to himself that he will never commit such a folly again. He also developed a bohemian mode of existence and acquired a taste for living outside England both of which were to persist for most of his life thereafter. And he became so much of a Germanophile that, when he later came to look around for a place in which to settle, one of the requirements was that the German language should be spoken there. Later he was to make the request that his friends should play the music of Wagner on the day of his funeral.

At first he lodged well away from the centre of Berlin, with a distinguished middle-class family who had probably been found through personal contacts; they were remarkable people, and they and their home will be described a little later. During these weeks he worked on his German, which eventually became fluent but far from accurate, and also on the revised version of his 'charade' *Paid on Both Sides*, which was completed by the end of the year and dispatched on New Year's Eve to T. S. Eliot, editor of the *Criterion*. In December he also wrote the poem that begins 'We made all possible preparations', at first untitled but later given the title 'Let History Be My Judge'. It is one of those mildly obfuscatory poems that Auden liked to write at this stage of his career, suggesting a world of political conspiracy and revolutionary action, of broken promises and betrayed ideals, as if Franz Kafka had engaged in a collaboration with John Buchan.

He went back to England to spend Christmas with his family in Birmingham, and presumably saw something of his fiancée at this time. Certainly he saw his friend Christopher Isherwood, whom he had met three years earlier during the Christmas vacation following his first term at Oxford. Oddly enough, they had been at the same preparatory school and appear in the same group photograph taken there, but the age difference had meant that they had hardly known each other. Isherwood, who was three years older, had left Cambridge without a degree at the same time that Auden left school, and was now a medical student in London, a less than half-hearted venture that lasted only two terms.

Isherwood himself had paid his first visit to Germany the previous May, when an elderly cousin who was British Consul in Bremen had invited him for a holiday. A letter sent from Bremen to his Repton and Cambridge friend Edward Upward conveys the authentic flavour of the trip. Written from Elsassestrasse 42, Bremen, it is dated only 'Wednesday', bears no salutation, and is signed 'Marco Polo' – self-mockingly, or perhaps enviously, for it expresses the desire 'never to remain more than a week in any country' and declares: 'Yes, after all, our later days must be spent in travel.' The envy is more unambiguous in the comment that 'The whole town is full of boys. In their silver-braided forage-caps, mackintosh tunics and green (word illegible) lace-up shirts.' Like his description of the tramp-steamer on which he had sailed, with its Chinese cook, Welsh cabin-boy and drunken captain, this is premonitory of the observing eye of the fictional style he was later to adopt.

This brief visit, though apparently barren of sexual escapades, was of considerable significance in that Isherwood fell under the spell of Germany and received a vision of it as a Promised Land of liberation and fulfilment, a spiritual homeland. (This last word is used in *Christopher and his Kind* (p. 17) when he suggests that, entering Germany in 1929 and asked by an immigration official the purpose of his visit, he 'could have truthfully replied "I'm looking for my homeland and I've come to find out if this is it."' ') The subsequent literary treatment or non-treatment of the brief Bremen trip is instructive. In *Lions and Shadows*, the early autobiography where it chronologically belongs, it is unmentioned, but nearly a quarter of a century later it forms the basis of a whole section ('Mr Lancaster') of a heavily autobiographical work of fiction, *Down There on a Visit*. The author's subsequent judgement (*Christopher and his Kind*, p. 10) is that this version contains 'too much fiction and too little frankness'. In the late autobiography *Christopher and his Kind* the Bremen episode, which might easily have been accorded a colourful page or two, receives just four sentences.

It is not difficult to guess that one of the non-literary topics of conversation during Auden and Isherwood's brief Christmas reunion in England must have been the availability of boys (not necessarily attired in the Bremen style) in the bars of Berlin. It was a subject on which Auden had already made himself an expert, and it calls for no imaginative leap to surmise that Isherwood must have felt and expressed a strong desire to see things for himself. Auden's explorations of the rent-bars that abounded in the city were already well under way, and his wish to have them more conveniently to hand must have been the principal motive for his change of lodgings very soon after his return to Berlin in January 1929.

The cover story was promulgated that his middle-class hosts insisted on practising their English on him instead of allowing him to learn German – which was, after all, his official reason for being in Berlin – and there is no reason to doubt the truth of this. But the truth is not always the whole truth, and other, more urgent motives were at work. A letter written at this time declares that 'The German proletariat are fine, but I dont [*sic*] like the others very much....', 'proletariat' here having sexual as well as social connotations. From all points of view a room much nearer the city centre, and one to which he could take back a 'friend' without awkwardness, was infinitely more satisfactory than being the paying guest of a socially well-placed family in a posh suburb. There was also the excitement of doing something unconventional, a motive detectable in his statement to an English correspondent that from the first of the month he was going 'to live in a slum'. It was an act of modest daring that Isherwood was later to imitate. At any rate Auden liked his new location well enough to remain there until the end of his sojourn in Berlin.

In his 1987 preface to *The Temple*, a version of the novel he had written nearly sixty years earlier, Stephen Spender identifies 1929, a shade facilely, as the last gasp of a dying order, 'just before the Thirties, when everything became politics'. Auden was to become increasingly aware of political issues as the year wore on, but at its outset he seems to have been totally immersed in more subjective and hedonistic matters. And after the evasions and subterfuges and disapprovals of England, it was not surprising that the atmosphere of late Weimar Berlin should have gone to his head.

A glimpse of what the city had to offer during this period to visiting English homosexuals is provided by the experiences of the painter (though not then a painter) Francis Bacon, who spent about three months there in the winter of 1927–8, shortly before Auden's arrival. (Bacon's biographers suggest different dates for this escapade, but the one given here seems the more likely.) Bacon, who was about 18 at the time, in later years provided conflicting versions of the circumstances in which he had been taken off to Berlin by an older man. At one time it was a 'sporting uncle', a friend of his father's who had been charged with the task of making a man of him; on another occasion, the person on whom this ill-defined duty devolved was an old army friend of his father's in London, who promptly fell in love with the lad and took him to Germany. Andrew Sinclair has plausibly and intriguingly identified this latter individual as Sir Percy Loraine, who had married Bacon's grandmother (a marriage that lasted only briefly) but was known to be fond of young men. Loraine was a distinguished career diplomat who soon afterwards became High Commissioner for Egypt and the Sudan and finished his career as Ambassador to Rome; he earns, or at any rate receives, an entry in the *Dictionary of National Biography*.

At any rate, Loraine, or someone equally obliging, carried the young Bacon off to Berlin – a choice of destination that says much for its contemporary reputation in England – and they installed themselves at the luxurious Adlon Hotel, where a waiter would wheel in a trolley ornamented with curving swans' necks at the corners and imperturbably serve breakfast to them in their huge double bed. In the evenings they toured the bars, nightclubs and cabarets, including the Eldorado, the famous transvestite bar that Otto Dix had painted in 1927. Bacon detected in the city, at least in retrospect, 'an atmosphere of tension and unease'; Berlin was, he said near the end of his life, 'a very violent place – emotionally violent, not physically – and that certainly had its effect on me'. Such an atmosphere, decadent, edgy and unstable, is certainly palpable in works as different as the drawings of Georg Grosz and the Berlin novels (for instance, *Laughter in the Dark* (Russian version, 1932)) of Vladimir Nabokov, a resident of the city from 1922 to 1937 and one of a large number of Russian émigrés who helped to enrich Berlin's cultural life in the interwar period. It is an atmosphere brilliantly and unsettlingly conveyed in Fassbinder's film version of another early Nabokov novel, *Despair*.

Auden's new base in Furbringerstrasse was good for poetry as well as sex, for it was there that he wrote a number of poems that were to remain in the canon of his work, including 'From scars where kestrels hover', 'Love by ambition', 'Before this loved one', 'The strings' excitement', 'A Free One', and the first section of '1929' beginning 'It was Easter as I walked in the public gardens'. In February he was briefly back in England to celebrate his 22nd birthday (on the 21st of the month) and to dash up to Scotland to visit his friend Cecil Day-Lewis, now teaching in Helensburgh. Then, in the following month, under the stimulus of their Christmas conversations and no doubt also encouraged by Auden's letters, Isherwood arrived in Berlin for a short visit. It was his first sight of the city in which he was to spend most of the next five years.

At about this time Auden had formed a romantic attachment to a young sailor from Hamburg called Gerhart Meyer, who is mentioned by name, commended for 'Absence from fear ... From the sea', and hailed as 'the truly strong man' in his poem '1929'. Though brief and one-sided, the affair was, as we shall see, intense. His first reaction to the boys of the Berlin bars, readily available and remarkably cheap, had been an understandable euphoria, and in one letter written at this time he confessed – sexual and social liberation proceeding hand in hand – that he was spending 'most of my time with Juvenile Delinquents' and described the city as 'the buggers daydream'.

The same letter adds, probably with some exaggeration, that there were 170 male brothels under police supervision. The figure, presumably derived from gossip rather than published statistics, may be slightly exaggerated, though another account (see p. 63 below) gives a figure not much smaller. Auden also states that he has learned a good many German obscenities; and that his current boy is 'a cross between a rugger hearty and Josephine Baker. We should make D. H. Lawrence look rather blue. I am a mass of bruises'. The wish to shock is transparent, the more especially since the recipient of these confidences was a woman, the fiancée of his friend Bill McElwee. But the hinted taste for masochistic pleasure is confirmed by his friend John Layard, who claims to have witnessed a sexual session between Auden and one of his boys which started with a pillow-fight and proceeded to blows as the prologue to serious sexual activity. 'Wystan liked being beaten up a bit,' observed Layard thoughtfully. When Auden said of A. E. Housman, in his 1938 sonnet, that his 'private lust' was 'Something to do with violence and the poor', he knew what he was talking about – knew about masochism at the hands of rough trade, that is, if not about Housman.

That pillow-fight suggests a reversion to childhood or early adolescence on the part of the young Oxford graduate: one thinks of the apple-pie beds that, in a more decorous and more timid age, Housman and his chums would occasionally make for each other on the occasion of their reunions. Auden's own comment at this time that he was 'having the sort of friendships I ought to have had at 16 and didnt [sic]' suggests a conscious – and, as he ruefully added, 'expensive' – attempt on his part to make good the missed opportunities of his boarding-school days, when many of his peer group would have passed through a phase of homosexual experimentation and in this way, as the saying goes, 'got it out of their system'. The note already cited is enigmatically phrased but seems to indicate that during his early weeks in Berlin Auden still thought of himself as working his way, doggedly though with considerable gusto, through a necessary stage on the road to heterosexuality, respectability and marriage. A letter to Day-Lewis at this time revealingly compares Gerhart's predecessor, his first boy-friend Pieps ('the most elemental thing I have yet met'), to his fiancée. It is clear that as far as Auden was concerned his engage-ment to the student nurse identified by Humphrey Carpenter as Sheilah Richardson was at this stage still a reality.

The turbulence of his sexual and emotional life gave Auden little leisure to acquire knowledge of the wider and deeper realities of the society in which he was now living, and perhaps at this stage he had little desire to do so. As I shall be arguing later, however, his first impressions of Berlin as 'the buggers daydream' was itself something of a daydream. It was an entirely natural response to his liberation that nevertheless ignored both the grim social and eco-nomic realities (there was a vast army of the unemployed in Ger-many at this time) and the sinister political rumblings as expressions and demonstrations of Nazi ideology, including its intolerance of homosexuals and other minority groups, became more blatant and more strident.

If, during his first few months in Berlin, Auden was over-whelmed by the unprecedented freedoms now placed at his dis-posal, what is really extraordinary is the speed with which he passed from the immaturity of his initial responses to an articu-lated self-awareness and self-knowledge. Reading the journal (still largely unpublished) that he kept during the spring of 1929, I found myself repeatedly struck by his mature grasp of the situa-tions in which he and his friends found themselves, his evident desire to understand his own nature and behaviour, and his ability (sometimes, admittedly, a little over-exercised) to extrapolate gen-eral truths from individual experience. Studying his laconic but penetrating analyses, it is easy to forget that this was a young man of barely 22 who had only just stepped off the class-driven conveyor belt of public school and ancient university.

The turning-point at which Auden definitely recognised his own sexual identity and chose his own future may have come around Easter 1929, just after Isherwood's short visit. Isherwood left England on 14 March and recalled long afterwards that the visit had lasted 'a week or ten days'; but he makes an appearance in the first six entries in Auden's journal, and if (as is usually supposed) the journal was begun on 23 March his visit must have lasted a fortnight. (The journal entries give only the days of the week, not the dates, and were clearly written retrospectively.) Quite possibly, however, the first journal entry (headed 'Saturday') refers to 16

March, which would fit in with Isherwood's arrival, possibly on the previous day. It is preceded by the statement that 'Christopher's visit will serve as well as any thing else as the introduction to this journal. Wherever one starts there will be loose threads.' On the Saturday (16 or 23 March) they visited Magnus Hirschfeld's Institute of Sexology, where Isherwood was later to make his home, then went to a restaurant with Auden's English friend, John Layard, and from there to Auden's favourite *Jugendsbar* (boy-bar), the Cosy Corner – an establishment that was to acquire a status in accounts of Auden and Isherwood's Berlin comparable to that of the Café Royal in 1890s London. Layard joined them again the following evening, after which they went (in Auden's habitual phrase) brothel-crawling. No doubt the Cosy Corner, which by something more than a happy coincidence was a stone's throw from Auden's lodgings, was again on their itinerary.

Almost fifty years later Isherwood recalled his first crossing of the Cosy Corner's threshold in terms that present it as a rite of passage, ceremony of initiation or ritual of spiritual rebirth. In the autobiographical *Christopher and his Kind*, which significantly takes 1929 as the starting-point of its narrative, he writes: 'I can still make myself faintly feel the delicious nausea of initiation terror which Christopher felt as Wystan pushed back the heavy leather doorcurtain of a boy bar called the Cosy Corner and led the way inside' (pp. 10–11). Like Auden, though prepared to be promiscuous and to enjoy it thoroughly, Isherwood was really in quest of romantic love, of the Ideal Friend. It did not take him long to discover, and feel 'instant infatuation' for, a youth named Berthold Szczesny who hailed from the German-speaking part of Czechoslovakia and was nicknamed 'Bubi' (Baby). 'To be infatuated,' he observed in *Christopher and his Kind*, 'was what [Christopher] had come to Berlin for. Bubi was the first presentable candidate who appeared to claim the leading role in Christopher's love-myth' (p. 11), and one wonders whether the apparent candour of old age was not actually substituting another, more cynical 'love-myth' for the romantic one here discredited. For all the retrospective self-mockery, the infatuation did not wear off quickly, for four months later Isherwood was still in pursuit of Bubi. The boy is the subject of Auden's poem 'Before this loved one', written in March in response to his friend's 'instant infatuation'. It was a subject on which they were both experts.

The Cosy Corner makes frequent appearances in recollections of this period, and in the mythical Berlin that was created by Auden,

Isherwood and others it looms considerably larger than the Brandenburg Gate or the Kaiser Wilhelm Memorial Church. In due course Isherwood, by then an habitué rather than a candidate for initiation, was able to introduce John Lehmann to the sexual freemasonry of the Cosy Corner, and long afterwards Lehmann too recalled the seismic effect of the experience in a very thinly fictionalised account in which Isherwood appears as 'William' (actually one of his real names):

> One of the first things William did to further my education, was to take me on a tour of the homosexual bars and night-clubs. We started with one of the most popular non-smart *Lokals*, the 'Cosy Corner'. This *Lokal* was a sensational experience for me, a kind of emotional earthquake, and I think William was right to throw me in at the deep end. Things unimagined by me in all my previous fantasies went on there. The place was filled with attractive boys of any age between sixteen and twenty-one, some fair and curly-haired, some dark and often blue-eyed, and nearly all dressed in extremely short lederhosen which showed off their smooth and sun-burnt thighs to delectable advantage....
>   The lavatory had no cubicles. I was followed in by several boys, who, as if by chance, ranged themselves on either side of me and pulled out their cocks rather to show them off than to relieve nature as I was doing. I don't think a drop fell into the gutter from any of them; but many sly grins were cast in my direction. I returned to our bench, shaken by this exhibition into a turbulence of anticipation. William said to me 'Any you fancy?'
>
> (*In the Purely Pagan Sense*, p. 44)

Lehmann's drooling mixture of incredulity and self-congratulation, we can be fairly sure, had also been both Auden's and Isherwood's at a slightly earlier date.

But by the time of Isherwood's arrival, Auden had plainly qualified himself as a knowledgeable guide, and his journal names a number of other bars, some of them more than once, occasionally indicating their particular ambience or clientele. The Hollandais, for instance, seems to have been a high-class and relatively decorous establishment: an advertisement in the gay newspaper *Die Freundschaft* refers to its music, its international flavour and its Sunday tea-dances. Auden's reaction to its denizens was, interestingly, one of moral disgust, and his preference was unmistakably for what he more than once refers to as 'rough stuff'. On 24 April 1929, after an unsatisfying visit to the Hollandais, he went on to the Café Hallesches Tor in the working-class area where he lived, and clearly felt more comfortable for the move.

The Hollandais was in Bülowstrasse, where, picturesquely situated under the arches of the overhead railway and felicitously located at number 69, it was only one of a number of gay and lesbian bars and similar establishments in this busy thoroughfare. Among others, there were the Continental Club at number 2, the Nationalhof (37), the Bülow Casino (41), the Conti-Casino (47), the Dorian Gray (57), the Dede (91), the Hohenzollern Lounge (101) and the Pan Lounge (105). Another neighbourhood patronised by Auden was the Alte Jakobstrasse, not far from his home in Hallesches Tor. (The street still exists, but scarcely a building survived the wartime bombing.) Here, at number 49, was an establishment where, on that momentous Easter Sunday of 1929, Auden met Gerhart Meyer, while at number 60 was the celebrated Eldorado Lounge, much frequented by transvestites. Also near Hallesches Tor, and leading from Alte Jakobstrasse into Kreuzberg, was Skalitzerstrasse, and on one occasion recorded in his journal Auden visited a bar at number 7 and picked up a boy whose name he either never learned or subsequently forgot.

Isherwood made the most of his brief first visit to Berlin and, once discovered, Bubi quickly assumed a central role in his life. The third entry in Auden's journal announces Monday as 'The great Bubi day' and continues:

> Pimping for someone on whom one has a transference creates the most curious feelings. Chiefly I remember Christopher and Bubi playing ping-pong. The sense of bare flesh, the blue sky through the glass and the general sexy atmosphere made me feel like a participant in a fertility rite. . . . In the pine wood I felt the third baboon and a public school one, Sunday walks to be back in time for chapel. In the train all was gloom, reviving a little at tea and later in bed.

As with much else in the journal, there are some obscurities here, but they are not quite impenetrable. 'Having a transference', a recurring phrase, seems to mean having formed a strong emotional bond, though not necessarily being in love. Why 'all was gloom' in the train is not clear: perhaps Bubi had left them by then, or perhaps Auden had had enough of his lover's love, for it certainly seems to have been Wystan and Christopher who were 'later in bed' together.

The course of Isherwood's infatuation did not run altogether smooth, and two days later he and Bubi quarrelled. The subject of their quarrel can be inferred from a scrap of German dialogue reproduced without comment in the journal. Isherwood was evidently anxious to convince the youth that the relationship he desired was that of lovers and friends rather than hustler and client; he felt possessive and was jealous of Bubi's professional contacts with other men, and the next day set off to resume his attempt to transform the rent boy into the Ideal Friend. Coached by Auden, whose conversational German was a good deal better than his own at this stage, he delivered a carefully prepared speech; he had, however, overlooked the Great Phrase-book Fallacy, and was quite unable to understand Bubi's reply. Isherwood's time in Berlin soon came to an end, but Bubi's magnetism, not to mention Auden's friendship and the wider lure of Germany, was strong enough to bring him back again before long.

Auden's reaction to Isherwood's brief visit was an interesting one and is the occasion for a long entry in the journal. Perhaps infected by his friend's excitement, he embarked on a series of sexual encounters: first with his regular boy friend Pieps, then in brothel-crawling and in a visit to the notorious 'Passage' where, after an initial failure of nerve, he made an assignation with one of the boys frequenting that neighbourhood. By the time he came to write the journal entry, self-awareness and self-mockery had been brought to bear on the episode:

> I overcame my fear enough to march up to the boy in the Passage when I saw him again and say, 'Bist Du frei nexte [*sic*] Donnerstag?' ['Are you free next Wednesday?'] He stared coldly at me as [if?] he couldnt hear what I said. I repeated it as he lowered his eyes. 'Ja.' 'Gut, um 4 uhr dann' ('Yes.' 'Good, at 4 o'clock then') and swept off brandishing my cigar picturing myself as the Baron de Charlus [in Proust's *A la Recherche*...]. Actually I was a middle class rabbit....

Isherwood's visit had, however, not merely whetted Auden's sexual appetite but had filled him with a spirit of emulation, and it was only a matter of days before he had found an equivalent to

Bubi. This was Gerhart Meyer, the most important of Auden's
lovers during his time in Berlin. The splendours and miseries of
his brief affair with Gerhart form the heart of the Berlin journal: his
former lover, Pieps, is gradually cast off, though he continues to
make frequent appearances, and Auden continued to feel affection
for and even to have sex with him. Only near the end, after
Gerhart's defection, is another boyfriend, Herbert, taken on. As in
an Olympic medal ceremony, Pieps and Herbert stand in the
journal as significant but inferior figures on either side of the
golden Gerhart, to whom, after more than one promise, attention
must now be turned.

First, though, a word on Auden's reputation for promiscuity will
be in order. Although his reaction to his new-found freedom and
independence was a certain amount of promiscuity and sexual
experimentation – and after all he had, only a few months earlier,
been *in statu pupillari* at Oxford, with home and family nearby in
Birmingham – the scale of his known sexual adventures has been
somewhat exaggerated. This sensationalising of his Berlin sex-life
can have seriously misleading implications, for Auden was at heart
a devout believer in romantic love with a strong desire for a stable
love-relationship and for domesticity. In later years he more than
once expressed a wish to father a child, and seems even to have
considered marriage as a means to this end. The tragedy of his
subsequent personal life is that, even when he seemed to have
formed a monogamous partnership, it turned out to be a delusion.
But in any case the scale of his predatory descents upon the Berlin
bars was less sensational than has sometimes been suggested.

The main source here is a notorious entry in the journal he kept
at this time. This oft-quoted memorandum, which appears right at
the end of the journal and thus constitutes a final reckoning, is
headed 'Boys had, Germany 1928–29' and lists nine individuals.
Five are identified by Christian names – Pieps, Cully, Gerhart,
Herbert and Otto – while the rest are designated 'Unknown',
with some brief indication added (presumably as an aid to memory) to record where they were encountered. Of this latter group,
one had been met in 'the Passage': as other entries in the journal
make clear, Auden often visited this spot but was sometimes too
nervous to proceed beyond voyeurism. Two other boys had been
met in bars, and the fourth had been picked up in Cologne during a
tour of Germany in May; though ugly, this last had, it seems, given
satisfaction.

Of the named boys, 'Pieps' has already been referred to. He had been encountered in a Berlin bar quite soon after Auden's arrival in the city, and is briskly mentioned in a letter to his friend John Layard: 'I like sex and Pieps likes money: it's a good exchange'. There is, perhaps, a pinch of affectation in this no-nonsense cynicism. More revealingly, at his first meeting with Layard he had rejected the latter's sexual advances with the remark that 'I've got a boy named Pieps.' 'Gerhart' must be Gerhart Meyer. (Isherwood later used the names Pieps and Gerhart, the latter spelt Gerhardt, in *Goodbye to Berlin*.) 'Cully' has been plausibly identified by Humphrey Carpenter as Kurt Groote, also named in '1929' and the subject of another poem, 'Love by ambition'. 'Herbert', already mentioned, is known to have been Auden's travelling companion during the tour of Germany in May. And 'Otto' was Otto Küsel, who, as we shall see, accompanied Auden to the Harz Mountains early in the summer and is associated with two other poems, 'Upon this line between adventure' and 'Sentries against inner and outer'. Otto, it seems, was a genuine Juvenile Delinquent, having escaped from a reformatory. Elsewhere in the journal three other boys – Franz, Heins and Paul – are named, and it is clear that Isherwood had a brief affair with the last of these; the absence of their names from the list presumably indicates that so far as Auden was concerned they were no more than acquaintances, though Franz and Heins were on familiar enough terms to visit him at his lodgings and were involved in a highly dramatic episode involving Layard that took place there. Auden saw both of them frequently and on at least one occasion went swimming with Franz.

There is a curiously scrupulous note appended to the list in which Auden puts on record his 'regret' at having associated with one of the anonymous boys picked up in a bar: 'He was not nice and was very dirty; ie Pure lust on my part. All the others were nice.' This repudiation of lust and emphasis on 'niceness' is surely revealing, but is seriously at odds with, for instance, Dorothy J. Farnan's description of Auden as 'engaging in frenetic sexual activity' in Berlin and showing evidence of a 'voracious' sexual appetite (*Auden in Love*, p. 35). The tally of nine partners in as many months, even when those who were not 'boys' but friends of his own class like Isherwood and Layard are added, is perhaps not everyone's notion of the frenetic and the voracious, and hardly qualifies Auden as a Don Giovanni of the boy-bars. (To emulate Auden's scupulousness, it should be said that there is just possibly, but far from certainly, a question mark at the head of the list, and if it is not just a fancy of this bleary-eyed researcher it may point to one or more shadowy pre-Pieps encounters, the memory of which had, several months later, faded almost to vanishing point.)

The really significant point, however, is that with five of the individuals listed something more than a one-night stand was involved. Carpenter is surely right to insist that while 'the length of the list might suggest that Auden was in the habit of "cruising"...he much preferred to have a steady relationship'. The journal indeed reveals that cruising was very much against his nature (which is not of course the same thing as saying against his wishes), for he writes there: 'Feeblesness is a problem. I have often thought I would go brothel-crawling but I can't do it. I become attached to someone, and enter on a relationship at once. Which means of course that I dont want to be free. Complete lechery as Christopher remarked is the end of all pleasure.' Evidently he and Isherwood had discussed the theory and practice of the subject during the latter's March visit. What Auden refers to as his 'feebleness' is clearly a temperamental inability, despite occasional forays, to espouse the kind of large-scale promiscuity represented in his experience by, among others, Francis Turville-Petre.

David Luke has recently suggested that Auden's brief affair with Gerhart in April 1929 was 'more emotionally involving than any of the others' and that the decision to keep a journal coincided with his meeting and falling in love with the young sailor. Although the dated entries begin in March (and continue to 26 April), the cover of the journal bears the inscription 'April 1929', and there is other evidence suggesting that the early entries at least were made retrospectively. If so, Auden may have been enough of a romantic at the time to have selected this means of marking his association with Gerhart as the beginning of a new era, for he had met the youth on Easter Sunday, 31 March, and their first assignation (in Auden's lodgings) had been on 1 April. (With life supplying symbolic dates so lavishly, one hardly needs literature.) As Luke points out, it is Gerhart who dominates nearly twenty pages of the journal, the entries from 31 March to 16 April.

Auden's excitement, emotional as well as sexual, during the first few days of his brief love-affair with Gerhart leaps from the pages of the little book he preserved and carried from place to place for the rest of his life. Meeting Gerhart was something that nearly didn't happen. On that Easter Sunday Auden had wanted to go to the UFA cinema in Alexanderplatz, to see a new film, Joe May's *Asphalt*, but it was sold out by the time he got there. So, at a loose end, he dropped into a gay bar at 49 Alte Jakobstrasse that enjoyed a solid petty-bourgeois clientele and had been recommended by a friend as currently offering a good deal of action. (It became a favourite haunt and is referred to in the diary simply as '49'.) Gerhart walked in, and was introduced with the recommendation that he spoke English. In accordance with time-honoured protocol, Gerhart suggested that the Englishman should buy him a glass of beer, and followed this up with the offer to sleep with him for ten marks. Auden pointed out that he had no ready cash, and that the banks did not open until Tuesday, but Gerhart, perhaps a little unconventionally for his kind, declared himself willing to grant credit. In the event an assignation was made for the next day and duly took place, the youth arriving late and leaving as soon as they had finished in order to look for another customer.

So far, one might think, so commonplace, if not sordid. But the transaction produced in Auden a state of euphoria, and his reaction to it was a curious one, for on the Tuesday (2 April) he called on Layard – ostensibly to tell him about Gerhart, but subconsciously aware that his excitement would stimulate Layard's desire to share the boy's favours. In the journal this subconscious wish has been brought to the surface, and its motives are analysed: altruism (he wants to do his friend a good turn) but also 'sex-snobbery' (he wants his friend to approve of his choice and envy his good fortune sufficiently to want the boy for himself). Perhaps also he wished to revive the curious sensation he had experienced in 'pimping' for Isherwood, though the case now was crucially different. For whereas he had not cared for Bubi he was well on the way to falling in love with Gerhart, and he spent a restless night. It was not the last that Gerhart was to cause him.

Nor was it a night of bliss for Layard, who the following day attempted to commit suicide. Layard's own bizarre story, however, is best reserved for a later chapter rather than being allowed to interrupt the considerable momentum of Auden's affair with Gerhart. On Thursday, while they were having tea together, Gerhart suggested to Auden that they should go to Hamburg, his home town, and Auden agreed to do so that very evening. Dashing back to his lodgings, he left an excuse for Pieps, who was to have visited him that evening, borrowed money from his obliging landlady, and made hasty preparations to set off for the station. The journal catches the excitement of the occasion with its rapid transitions from epigrammatic generalisation and literary self-consciousness to a self-mocking snapshot of Berlin low-life:

> Few things are better than a hurried meal when one is packing to go off to a lover. I wondered what books one takes on these occasions. I took Donne, the Sonnets, and Lear. In the tube I had an encounter with a whore. I stared at her feeling "I'm king of Berlin." She promptly came and stood beside me till I got out. I wanted to make her an 18th century bow and say "Enshuldigen [*sic*] sie, Madame, aber ich bin schwul [Forgive me, Madame, but I am gay]."

In the waiting room at the Zoo Station, where he had arranged to meet Gerhart, Auden thought briefly of Layard, by now in a Berlin hospital, and told himself that he could feel for his friend's misery even in the middle of his own happiness. The journal, however, has no truck with such insincerities and insists that the knowledge of Layard's plight was no more than a sauce to his own pleasure.

In the train Gerhart quickly began to flirt with a girl, and the journal, always eager to swing from the particular to the general, offers a brief analysis of the categories of jealousy. But the most vivid sentences evoke the magic of his lover's physical presence:

> He has the most extraordinary power I have met in any one. He laid his hand on my knee and switched on the current, an amazing sensation. What is odd is that when he could have any woman he liked from the Queen of England upwards, he chooses whores and not the prettiest ones either. I am so jealous with him that I am frightened when he goes to the lavatory that he won't come back ....

It needs no special insight to see little prospect here of a happy and stable relationship, and not coming back was to be a regular feature of Gerhart's behaviour. Even before they reached the hotel in Hamburg he had told Auden that he wanted to visit a 'friend' and could not put it off until the next day since the friend was going away. Auden was not deceived by this palpable fiction, though at this stage he was still prepared to believe Gerhart's promise that he would soon return.

He did not, of course, and a long journal entry for 5 April traces the stages of Auden's expectation, anger and anxiety during that largely sleepless night spent alone in the Hamburg hotel bedroom that had been the anticipated scene of bliss. The diarist's hindsight permits a distanced self-mockery that was surely not available at the time: 'First I posture before the glass, trying to persuade myself but in vain that I am up to his physical level. Then I read the Sonnets to prove my superiority in sensibility. Every time I hear a taxi I go to the window but it's only a whore returning....'

By 5 a.m. he had made up his mind that Gerhart had absconded with his money: how he came to be acting as purse-bearer is not clear. A few hours later Auden made his way to the British Consulate to report that he had been robbed. An impulse to telephone the hospitals to see whether Gerhart had been run over was resisted, and before long he turned up, having got drunk the night before. Kisses and reproaches were followed by lunch, a pub and a visit to the harbour, where Gerhart was sick, and a second visit to the Consul, where, a little puzzlingly, Auden collected his money. (Possibly they had simply cashed a cheque for him.) Gerhart, with his streetwise promptness to turn a situation to his own advantage, was dramatically wounded by the disclosure that his friend thought he had robbed him, and declared it was something he would never, never forget.

Later, for the second time that day, and probably not accidentally, they ran into Rosa, a girlfriend of Gerhart's, and the three of them went to the cinema, where Rosa was understandably upset when the two young men embarked on some heavy petting in the semi-darkness; at any rate she moved to a seat at some distance, from which her sobs were clearly audible. Gerhart, in a symbolic expression of his wish to have his cake and eat it, embraced both of them simultaneously. What the rest of the audience made, or thought, of this off-screen drama is not on record.

When they left the cinema a tearful Rosa continued to pursue them into a restaurant until Gerhart got rid of her and then proceeded to flirt with the waitress and a couple of housewives. When they moved on to a beer-house, Gerhart asked his curiously unsuspicious friend and paymaster to wait outside: getting tired at last of cooling his heels, Auden entered and found him chatting with a girl. At first Auden put on a fair imitation of nonchalance, strolling up to the bar and ignoring the pair, but once outside in the street he and Gerhart had a row: he had, Auden told him bitterly, spent 170 marks on the trip – probably adding that he had precious little to show for it. Gerhart, turning nasty, informed him that, whether he liked it or not, he was going home with the girl, but would be back in an hour and a half. Auden, who by now was learning fast, knew better than to believe him – a scepticism that turned out to be fully justified, for, once again, Gerhart did not return. The next day Auden took the train back to Berlin.

The graphically picaresque recital of the day's events in Hamburg runs to only a few hundred words but conveys not only the rapid swings between joy and exasperation in Auden's love affair with Gerhart but also a process of learning that involved disillusion and a growing awareness of his own nature. In the streets, bars, restaurants, cinemas and cheap hotels, through passion, jealousy, excitement, frustration, anger and self-mockery, Auden was qualifying himself as a great love poet, and the copy of Shakespeare's sonnets he had packed for the trip suggests that such a purpose may not have been far from his own mind.

Two days later Gerhart turned up in Berlin and a reconciliation took place. The journal makes little of this event, which Auden was probably able by now to view with instant as well as retrospective irony, but there is a striking vein of coarseness in his entry for the next day (9 April). In a bar in Alexanderplatz evidently frequented by what Auden elsewhere refers to as 'rough stuff', they inspected the female whores, for whom Gerhart had a taste that was far from fastidious; among the assembled company there were also bargain-price boys and a peroxide blonde who sought in vain to enlist Gerhart's sexual services. (So far from being flattered or tempted, he seems to have given her a black eye.) Auden notes that one of the whores accompanied her highly explicit solicitation by raising her leg like a dog making water. It could all be a description of one of Georg Grosz's more lurid caricatures, and might be supposed to reflect a mood of disgust were it not that the lovemaking with Gerhart that followed earns high marks, and the experience of having breakfast together the next morning even higher. For Auden, even at 22, it was this kind of domesticity (illusory though it turned out to be) that really satisfied.

The cosy breakfast scene was repeated a couple of days later, but it would have taken a larger stock of self-deception than Auden possessed not to recognise that the relationship remained almost wholly one-sided, and there were moments that must have been painful. The night before, for instance, during a tour of the bars,

Gerhart had announced that he was going off to see a client, and was only dissuaded from doing so when Auden promised to compensate him for his loss of earnings. Perhaps there was some consolation in Gerhart's insistence that the only thing that particular client was interested in was being thrashed within an inch of his life.

The journal preserves some vivid scraps of their conversation that morning. First Gerhart asked whether there was any truth in rumours that the Prince of Wales (later Edward VIII) was homosexual, and Auden expressed the opinion that he was not. His comment that everyone is bisexual prompted Gerhart to declare that, being a sailor and therefore 'hot', he liked both men and women – perhaps as close as he ever came to tact and conciliation, though still not very close. Less tactfully, he went on to suggest that they take a woman to Auden's room and both have sex with her – or, if this was not in Auden's line, he could watch while Gerhart performed. It is hard to be sure in what spirit the proposal was made, but in any case it does not seem to have been one that was acted upon.

Thereafter the references to Gerhart become more disillusioned. On the 13th Auden noted that he no longer felt the magic of Gerhart as he had done in Hamburg (only eight days earlier); he might have added that the King of Berlin had lost his throne. There was also an ugly moment when he realised that Layard's revolver, which he had been looking after since the suicide attempt, was missing, and that Gerhart had taken it. Later in the day, perhaps sensing that time was running out, Gerhart asked for a new pair of shoes and a cap, which led to another quarrel. The next day they went window-shopping in Friedrichstrasse, Auden told Gerhart that he could have the cap or the shoes but not both, and Gerhart sulked. After the shoes had been bought Auden was 'ashamed' of himself for spending so much money on his lover: infatuation had yielded place to a sober assessment of the situation, and by the next day he was prepared to admit to his journal that Gerhart's conversation bored him.

For his part Gerhart, having got his shoes, seems to have gone out of his way to be difficult and even hurtful. He told Auden that he used to be a pimp for a female prostitute and enquired whether Auden would like to pimp for him. The wish to hurt is as palpable as the sense that this is a relationship that was very near the end of the road. When Auden, perhaps in a last-ditch attempt to rescue their collapsing relationship, suggested they go to the mountains together, Gerhart retorted that he only liked seaports. Auden's comment at this point, though a shade melodramatic and posture-striking, is impressive in its mature self-awareness: 'This is the revolt of the symbol. The disobedience of the day-dream. From that moment I love him less.'

After yet another argument about money, Gerhart decamped in the middle of the night. As Auden was going out the next morning he met Gerhart on the stairs and was informed that he was going to sleep until two o'clock; according to the landlady's subsequent testimony, however, he was only in the room for five minutes before signalling to a friend from the window and making off. As well as Layard's revolver he took with him Auden's dressing-gown, leaving in exchange a note giving the address in Hamburg to which he was returning.

Auden's summing up of the affair thus concluded is scrupulously and characteristically even-handed:

> In viewing this little history I feel that it is too easy to say "He's a bad egg. I made a mistake." If a person does one an injury one is always half to blame. My dissatisfaction with him during the last few days inevitable though it may have been means that I havent treated him right and this is the result....

But the note of depression later in this entry is understandable. The affair had lasted, from start to finish, little more than two weeks – not long by ordinary reckoning, but long enough for Auden to experience the whole cycle of infatuation and disillusion. The prominence given to Gerhart in the journal implies that it was an experience of great intensity: no other two-week period from either Auden's or Isherwood's time in Berlin is known to us in such intimate and graphic detail. Loutish and exploitative though he was (and though Auden came to know him to be), the handsome sailor exerted a spell beside which the attractions of Pieps and Herbert were superficial. Perhaps his secret was to have come along at precisely the right moment. Conceivably, somewhere, he is still alive, a hale octogenarian.

All we know of Auden's relationship with Gerhart, not to mention Pieps and others, makes nonsense of Farnan's claim that most of Auden's sexual adventures in Berlin involved 'merely an appetite, for his many encounters were usually with boys of the street whom he paid, rather than with equals for whom he felt a romantic passion' (p. 35). Auden himself would hardly have endorsed the facile categorisation implied here: sex with the proletariat for money is mere lust, real love being confined to one's own class. He might also have been surprised by Carpenter's verdict on the affair with Gerhart: 'Auden seems to have obtained some happiness from the affair, though he recorded their sexual encounters in his journal with coolness and a lack of excitement' (p. 98). This both fails to catch the flavour of a peculiarly intense fortnight and to allow for the long-term effect of an episode through which Auden discovered much about his own capacity for loving, including his propensity towards relationships involving unequal affections and pain for himself. One relationship commonly involving unequal affections is that of parent and child, and although Auden seems sometimes to have been seeking an elder brother (he observed with interest his own gratification when Gerhart took charge of buying the tickets for Hamburg), he is more often looking for a son. One of the most striking statements in the entire journal is to precisely that effect: 'With boys I understand what a parent feels. Otto going off in the car. Writing for money.'

Even before Gerhart's departure, when the situation had clearly begun to deteriorate, Auden sought to console himself by reflecting in his journal that, beside an unrequited homosexual attachment, reciprocated heterosexual love was flavourless ('tame and easy'). The 'attraction of buggery', on the other hand, was 'partly its difficulty and torments'. (Like others of his generation Auden consistently uses the term 'buggery' as a synonym for 'homosexuality' rather than as designating a specific physical act.) His conclusions are both general and personal: 'There is something in reciprocity that is despair. How one likes to suffer.'

Once again, in these oddly confused but deeply revealing statements, the potential of heterosexual love as a source of 'difficulties and torments' seems to go unrecognised. In less abstract terms, the comparison was between the still-present Gerhart and Auden's distant fiancée. Uncharacteristically, Auden doesn't seem to have considered the further logical alternative of unrequited heterosexual love being superior to homosexual reciprocation, or indeed the very possibility of a requited homosexual passion. The idea of unequal loving anticipates a fine poem, 'The More Loving One', written almost thirty years later, and the impressive persistence of the idea suggests that this became a permanent element in Auden's attitude towards love. David Luke may be right in seeing these reflections as evidence of Auden's 'romantic emotional masochism', though they might also be viewed as coming from a man anxious to preserve his self-respect and make the best of a bad job. The 'mass of bruises' boast quoted earlier may suggest that the masochistic leanings were not only emotional.

In late April, a few days after Gerhart's disappearance, Auden's brother John arrived in Berlin to spend a few days there en route for Vienna. He was a geologist by profession and had recently seen service in India. Auden's notes on the time they spent together are very brief and indicate that they did not go in for an exchange of confidences, but there is an interesting summary note later in the journal in which he characteristically reflects on the origins of his own sexual orientation and then extends his personal reflections to some sweeping and facile psychological generalisations:

> If [John] was not my brother I could do much more. As it is there is always Joseph and Esau. The interesting question is our different reactions to the same environment and the same mother. Why should one go whoring and the other for boys.
>   Both are a criticism of the mother. Buggery seems an [sic] near unconscious criticism of the mother as a love-object. Whorer a more conscious reaction against her sexual teaching. The bugger presumably though finds his mother more satisfying (she loves me better than John) – ie the bugger gets too much mother love, so shuns off women altogether, the whorer too little, so must always have another.

On the evening of the 26th he saw his brother off at the Anhalter Station. He had spent the afternoon boy-hunting, or at least boy-watching, in the Passage, but this was one of the many things that he was unable to speak about.

Caught up in the rapid twists and turns of Auden's sexual and emotional life, it is easy to forget that he was always a poet, disciplined with regard to his writing if towards nothing else, and during these turbulent weeks the writing went on. A new play, *The Enemies of a Bishop*, was also begun at just about the time that Gerhart and the dressing-gown disappeared in the direction of Hamburg. And since this was Berlin and the year was 1930, with sex and poetry went politics. At the beginning of May there occurred, not far from his lodgings, a confrontation between

Communists and police that led to several days of street-fighting and left 23 dead and some 150 injured. These events are reflected in the second section of '1929', written at about this time:

> All this time was anxiety at night,
> Shooting and barricade in street.
> Walking home late I listened to a friend
> Talking excitedly of final war
> Of proletariat against police....

Perhaps it was these disturbances and this 'anxiety', and perhaps also the wish for a change after the end of his affair with Gerhart, that led Auden, in the middle of May, to leave Berlin for a week or so on a trip that took him to half a dozen German cities. The tour seems to have been decided on at a moment's notice, though the earlier (and ungraciously rejected) invitation to Gerhart suggests that he had already entertained the wish to visit the mountains. His itinerary included Magdeburg (a medieval and baroque city until it was smashed to pieces on a January night in 1945), Kassel, Marburg, Cologne (where he met one of the anonymous boys listed in his journal) and Essen, and he was accompanied throughout by a young man called Herbert (also on the list) as well as an unidentified Dutchman named Dan who evidently shared his sexual tastes. (Dan may perhaps be identified with the D. van Lannep to whom Auden sent a copy of his *Poems* of 1928, though van Lannep remains equally a mystery.)

Herbert had been picked up on 26 April in a well-known homosexual bar, the Adonis Diele, whither Auden had proceeded after seeing off his brother's train to Vienna, and the boy had presumably helped to fill the vacuum recently created by Gerhart's departure. On the occasion of their first meeting, Auden had taken him back to his lodgings and had felt a pang of social conscience when the youth, inspecting the contents of the wardrobe, remarked wistfully, or perhaps with calculation, that he wished he possessed something similar. The relationship lasted long enough for Herbert to be taken along on the six-day excursion, but not much longer, and the journal records the point of no return:

> Köln to Essen. Herbert irritating and I irritated and superior. His behaviour a reaction against my snobbishness.... Herbert's impatience in the train. Odd in someone who must have to put

up with so much.... My relations with Herbert never recovered
after Essen. I must never have anyone to live with me again. It
doesnt work.

It was not a resolution that he was to adhere to, but the self-
awareness, like the careful apportioning of blame, is characteristic.
One of the many places they passed through was the village of
Rotehütte-Königshof in the Harz Mountains, and Auden took such
a fancy to this spot that within a short time he was back there, this
time accompanied by a brand-new boyfriend, Otto Küsel. It was
now June, and he liked the mountain village well enough to stay
there for some weeks – and, presumably, to sing its praises in a
letter to Isherwood, who arrived from England early in July and
recalled the spot long afterwards as 'surrounded by forests. The air
smelled of resin and echoed romantically with jangling cow-
bells.... the whole place could have been a setting for one of
Grimm's fairy tales, except that it had a railway station' (*Christopher
and his Kind*, p. 14). Auden quickly acquired a large circle of
acquaintances among the local people, a dozen of whom are
named, with brief descriptive tags, in his journal, and his unconventional behaviour seems to have provoked interest but not scandal. He is known to have written several poems there, and possibly
he and Isherwood worked together on *The Enemies of a Bishop*.

Soon, however, real drama invaded their idyllic retreat. Isherwood naturally wanted Bubi's company in Rotehütte and before
leaving England had asked Auden to telephone the boy in Berlin
and invite him to join them. Bubi, however, failed to show up,
whereupon Isherwood dashed off to Berlin in search of him. At
Auden's suggestion, in his tour of the bars in quest of information
about Bubi he was assisted by Francis Turville-Petre. Francis was
an English resident in Berlin and a colourful character of whom
Isherwood was later to see much more. For the moment Francis
was useful as an interpreter as well as possessing a profound
knowledge of the bars and the boys. It turned out that Bubi was
wanted by the police and had prudently vanished, so there was
nothing for Isherwood to do but return 'mournfully' to his empty
bed in the mountain village.

Shortly afterwards, having got wind of Isherwood's quest and
suspecting that Bubi might be with him, the police turned up. And
while they were pursuing *their* inquiries, with a remarkable sense
of timing, a letter from Bubi was delivered and read by Isherwood

'under their very noses'. Bubi was in Amsterdam, about to 'ship out as a deck-hand on a boat to South America', and would be glad of a loan. At this point in Isherwood's account in *Christopher and his Kind* there occurs a striking passage that is, in its emotional stance and even in its language, reminiscent of the cloak-and-dagger world of some of Auden's early poems: 'The letter thrilled Christopher unspeakably. As he read, he began to feel that he himself had become an honorary member of the criminal class. Now he must be worthy of the occasion.' That last phrase, so redolent of Isherwood's class and background, of a world of exhortatory headmasters and speech-days, has been subverted by a 'thrilling' act of class-betrayal, like Auden showing solidarity with the workers during the General Strike. Though Bubi was not to be found, the police had not entirely wasted their time, however, for they discovered that Otto was an escapee from a reformatory and took him away with them. Auden, it seems, had not lost his taste for juvenile delinquents.

The quest, that favourite heroic motif of Auden's early writing, was now about to be translated into action, for Auden and Isherwood decided to set off post-haste for Amsterdam. It was a decision in the spirit of the urgent, peremptory concluding line of one of Auden's early poems: 'Leave for Cape Wrath tonight'. With their departure the village must suddenly have seemed much duller, for Auden in particular, whether thumping out Anglican hymns on a piano in the railway station buffet or wrestling naked with Otto in a meadow, had been a source of considerable interest to the local community. The innkeeper, tolerant despite the invasion of his premises by the police, had the last word, observing that he expected ' "a lot of things happen in Berlin which we wouldn't understand" '.

In Amsterdam Bubi was quickly found and duly seen off for South America. Almost exactly twenty years later (one wonders whether some unconscious anniversary-marking was at work) there was a curious coda to Isherwood's love affair with Bubi. In his travel book *The Condor and the Cows* (1949) he describes their reunion in Buenos Aires on 16 February 1949. Bubi, at last publicly identified as Berthold Szczesny, had settled in South America in the 1930s, had prospered, and, on the threshold of middle age, was engaged to be married. The book observes with notable discretion that at an earlier epoch 'The Cosy Corner was ... much frequented by Berthold, Auden and myself'. Well, yes: but then 1949 was still

much too early for Isherwood to be candid about, and take retrospective pride in, his Berlin adventures.

Meanwhile, back in Amsterdam in that summer of 1929, the two
Englishmen enjoyed a day's sightseeing before Isherwood returned
to England. By the end of July, Auden too was back home, his
'year' in Berlin (actually somewhat less) now over. Almost at once
he was writing to Layard that he was 'homesick for Germany', also
that he was breaking off his engagement. The latter was an experiment that had failed and one that, with the greatly increased self-
knowledge that Germany had given him, he did not intend to
repeat.

It was not a good time to be looking for employment: 'Do you by
any chance,' Auden wrote to Naomi Mitchison, 'know of a job for
me? Anything from nursing to burglary...' (*You May Well Ask*,
p. 117). He was to spend the next year as a private tutor, then
five years as a schoolmaster, followed by employment with the
GPO Film Unit and the Group Theatre, journeys to Spain and
China, and, in the last year of the 'low dishonest decade' for
which he became the principal British spokesman, to go to New
York and there to meet the great love of his life, Chester Kallmann.
He was, however, back in Berlin, as we shall see, in the summer of
1930, but from this point the main emphasis of this narrative must
shift to Isherwood, whose own, considerably longer period of
residence in the city began later in 1929.

During the late summer of that year the two Berlinophiles saw a
certain amount of each other in London, where Isherwood was
now living, strictly from motives of economy, with his mother.
Auden, too, was short of money, and soon had to migrate north,
where he could live rent-free in a cottage in the Lake District
owned by his family; a little later he returned to the family home
in Birmingham. On the occasions when the two friends managed to
meet, reminiscences and expectations of Germany must have
loomed large in their conversations, and it was to Bubi and Otto
that they dedicated the play that they worked on together at this
time, *The Enemies of a Bishop*, which was reported, probably in
August, as 'nearly finished'. These were also prolific months for
Auden as a poet, and among other poems known to have been
written at this time are 'On Sunday walks', 'The silly fool' and the
third section of '1929' (in August), 'Will you turn a deaf ear' (in
September), 'Sir, no man's enemy', 'Which of you waking early'
and the final section of '1929' (in October), and 'It's no use raising a

shout', 'To have found a place' and 'Since you are going to begin to-day' (in November).

Their conversations and letters must have kept alive Isherwood's enthusiasm for the city he had so far seen only on a couple of tantalisingly brief visits, and must have confirmed his wish to return for a longer stay. So, on 29 November, he set out once more for Berlin. It was to remain his base until May 1933, a period of almost three and a half years, though his numerous absences during that time add up to about 12 months. Still, it was long enough, and it occurred at the right stage of his career as a writer to prove a crucially important chapter in his life, as it had already done in Auden's, and for him to annex Berlin as fictional territory.

Again, why Berlin? The answer is more obvious but at the same time more complex than in the case of Auden, partly because Isherwood himself did his best to falsify the record. He had seen enough of the city, and heard enough about it from Auden, to be excited by the opportunities it offered for sexual adventures, and in *Christopher and his Kind* he declares that his statement in the much earlier autobiographical volume *Lions and Shadows* that he went to Berlin primarily to meet John Layard was 'avoiding the truth', and that so far as he was concerned 'Berlin meant Boys'. A similar motive is self-imputed in a review Isherwood wrote of Gerald Hamilton's *Mr Norris and I*:

> When I came to Germany in 1929 I was twenty-four years old and in many respects very immature for my age. One of my chief motives for wanting to visit Berlin was that an elderly relative had warned me against it, saying that it was the vilest place since Sodom. For months I had been day-dreaming of it as unrealistic-ally as a child dreams of the jungle; he hopes to meet tigers and pythons there, but doesn't expect them to hurt him.
> (The elderly relative was a cousin, Basil Fry.)

None of this, however, will quite suffice as an explanation, and it certainly does less than justice to his seriousness as an artist. Writing of his Berlin years in the later autobiography *Christopher and his Kind*, he is plainly exhilarated by his own new-found candour concerning his sexual nature: parodying Lawrence, he seems to be declaring to anyone who cared to listen, 'Look! I have come out!' But the old man's candour may be as oversimplifying and misleading as the caginess of the young author of *Lions and Shadows*, and ought to be treated with a similar scepticism.

As far as sex was concerned, his psychological predicament was more complex than the cheerful equating of Berlin and Boys suggests. In the later book he confesses, or claims, that 'he couldn't relax sexually with a member of his own class or nation. He needed a working-class foreigner'. A similar point was made in an interview with Carolyn G. Heilbrun shortly before the publication of *Christopher and his Kind*, where he refers to the 'sexual colonialism' of his early years and admits that the class question certainly entered into the matter. Spender, perhaps partly under Isherwood's influence, took a similar view, suggesting that a homosexual relationship 'would have been almost impossible between two Englishmen of our class.... Men of the same class just didn't; it would have been impossible, or at least very unlikely'. There is some overstatement, and some disingenuousness, here (it would have been surprising, for instance, if Spender had not known that Auden and Isherwood had been lovers), but the implied power of the class taboo is striking.

In the Berlin bars, several kinds of barrier simultaneously collapsed. To make love to a German who almost certainly spoke no English was to simplify the transaction enormously by placing it outside the nexus of class, education and language from which any encounter with an English lover was inseparable, while the commercial nature of the transaction, often reinforced by the age difference, conferred a power that would not obtain with a lover of one's own age and class. Moreover, frankness, both in emotional declarations and in sexual explicitness, comes much more easily to the inhibited when a foreign tongue is being spoken, provided that knowledge of the language is sufficiently rudimentary – as Isherwood's German certainly was at this stage.

In a 1987 interview Spender also pointed to another dimension, remarking that 'sex with the working-class of course had political connotations. It was a way in which people with left-wing sympathies could feel they were really getting in contact with the working class'. A sceptical or snide reaction to this claim comes too trippingly off the tongue: earlier generations had given the poorer classes soup and tracts, or WEA lectures, but the liberated postwar generation could demonstrate their solidarity less patronisingly by sleeping with them. Perhaps E. M. Forster, one of Isherwood's heroes, was the great exemplar here, for had he not, even before the War, made Helen Schlegel sleep with Leonard Bast? Purchased sex could even be viewed as a kind of charitable donation. There is a curious moment in Auden's journal when he deplores the boasting of an American met in one of the bars that he often obtained sex without paying for it: it's so nice, says Auden, to know that you can give a present to someone who needs it ('present' in this context usually meaning, of course, payment in money or goods for sexual services). More seriously, it may be questioned whether the chicken-and-egg question should not be answered the other way round. Quoting Spender's remark in his biography of William Plomer, Peter F. Alexander has commented that 'for writers like Auden, Spender and Isherwood, left-wing politics offered the chance to get close to the working-class that so attracted them sexually' (p. 180).

There were, though, at least two reasons apart from sex that took Isherwood to Berlin. A novelist, unlike a poet, needs a lot of hard information: it is difficult to write good fiction without actually knowing a considerable amount about the external world, and this is especially true if the writer's powers of invention are weak, as Isherwood's certainly were. His experience of life so far had been largely constrained by the rituals of his class: shaped by home, family, public school, university, he had seen little that a thousand other aspiring novelists had not also seen. His early books are, inevitably, autobiographical, and it was a mode that persisted throughout his career (a fact of which he made no secret): his forte was always to be the role of an observer rather than an inventor, the celebrated plainness of his prose indicating among other things the limits of his imagination, and even a late book like *Down There on a Visit* is in effect a sequence of fictionalised memoirs rather than a novel. His invention, it seems, only came into play in the manipulation of material already supplied by life, and that manipulation may have been to some extent unconscious or forced upon him by considerations of prudence.

In Berlin he was to seek, and to find, material for the books that, however lightly he claimed to regard them in his later years, have remained his most widely read. As he moved from one bar or one lodging to another, he was not just answering the call of desire or economic necessity, but seeing life – and filling notebooks and diaries, which was always an important part of his method of work:

I've always kept diaries extensively [he said in 1961], and they give me a great sense of security, because I feel at least this part is factual. Having, however, built on these little islands of fact, I think one goes back and reconstructs everything and changes everything and interferes with everything.

(London Magazine, n.s. 1, June 1961, p. 42)

Perhaps at some level even his homosexuality was explored and expressed as part of his qualifications for the novelist's trade. In his old age he told an interviewer that 'Being gay has given me an oblique angle of vision on the world. Without it, I might never have been a writer' (Scobie, 1975), and the photographic or cinematic metaphor is revealing: angles of vision can be chosen and exploited. Auden had supported the 1926 strikers out of 'contrariness', and there was something of a willed and defiant quality about his friend's sexual role. As he said in another interview at about the same time, 'as long as nearly all the poets, and nearly everybody are going to harp on heterosexuality, I think "No, I won't, I absolutely won't" ' (Heilbrun, 1976). It was a perceptive friend who once remarked to him that if the rest of the world was homosexual, Christopher would make a point of being heterosexual.

There was also a secondary practical and professional reason for a young novelist in the late 1920s to wish to dissociate himself from England and the English literary scene. In the wake of the uproar and legal proceedings that followed the publication of Radclyffe Hall's lesbian novel *The Well of Loneliness* in 1928, British publishers were edgy about the fictional treatment of homosexuality, and in the year that Isherwood settled in Berlin Forster had been impelled to make a discreet plea for tolerance in his contribution to a symposium on 'The Censorship of Books'. Observing that homosexuality 'exists as a fact among the many other facts of life', Forster added that he did not see 'why writers who desire to treat it should be debarred from doing so – always providing that there is nothing pornographic in their treatment' (*The Nineteenth Century and After*, 1929, p. 445). It was not, however, an argument that was quickly to prevail, and in his introduction to *The Temple* Spender goes so far as to say that 'In the late Twenties young English writers were more concerned with censorship than with politics.'

According to Spender's retrospective diagnosis of the mood of his generation, the natural reaction to this repressive ethos was to go to Germany, which offered freedom from censorship along with many other kinds of freedom:

> For many of my friends and for myself, Germany seemed a paradise where there was no censorship and young Germans enjoyed extraordinary freedom in their lives....
>
> Censorship, more than anything else, created in the minds of young English writers an image of their country as one to get away from....
>
> Another result of censorship was to make us wish to write precisely about those subjects which were most likely to result in our books being banned....

'Paradise', like 'daydream', is a word that revealingly recurs in such contexts, but the grim irony of history ensured that the paradise would soon be lost and Germany subjected to a censorship, and even a burning of books, that went far beyond anything known in England. In the event Isherwood, like Spender and others, was to publish his books in England, with all the restraints and limitations that this for a long time implied.

Isherwood's rejection of the values and conventions of his class extended beyond his sexuality and was considerably more complex and deeply rooted than mere cussedness. Near the end of *Kathleen and Frank* (1971), the book about his parents that he wrote in his sixties, is a very interesting page that recalls his return to school, wearing a black armband, after the death of his father in the Battle of the Somme in 1916. He was acutely aware of being cast in the role of 'Orphan of a Dead Hero', a role that carried the full endorsement of Crown, Church and Press; soon, though, he discovered that 'being a Sacred Orphan had grave disadvantages', was even 'a kind of curse which was going to be upon him, seemingly, for the rest of his life'. He began to identify all those who enforced this sense of obligation – 'people he actually met, and disembodied voices from pulpits, newspapers, books' – as 'The Others', and to react against the sense of guilt they imposed upon him.

From rejecting the Hero-Father, he proceeded to a rejection of 'the authority of the Flag, the Old School Tie, the Unknown Soldier, The Land That Bore You and the God of Battles'. Also, he might have added, the sexual orientation expected of a healthy English male, and the marital and dynastic ambitions demanded of a member of the English landed gentry. But ancestor-worship was not, as his revered Forster might have put it, Isherwood's ticket: as he says, not unhistrionically, in *Down There on a Visit*, he had 'vowed to disappoint, disgrace, and disown his ancestors'.

The apron-strings that he so decisively cut were not only tied tightly but double-knotted by obligations to the dead, and in going to Berlin he was both rejecting the past, with its burden of responsibility, and making a gesture of defiance at England and the family. For Germany was not just Abroad but for many English people in the 1920s, especially of the older generation, was still the Enemy. What could emphasise more startlingly and unambiguously his refusal to accept, however metaphorically, the mantle of the avenging son than to go and live among those who had slain his father? By a route that may have begun in his early years, when his adored but somewhat suffocating mother impressed upon him the pride he should feel in the history of his family, and that led through the Flanders mud, he headed for Berlin and a very literal and liberal practice of the precept to love one's enemies.

What 'The Others' had in common was that they were older, representatives of the Past, and the flight to Berlin became a flight from the past as well as from a country perceived as still unrepentantly repressive and intolerant. In Spender's *The Temple*, the hero (based on the author) goes to visit his friend William Bradshaw (based on Isherwood) at his London home,

> his mother's small early Victorian stucco house in a quiet garden-like square in Bayswater. As he was walking up the front steps the door was opened by a lady soberly dressed in the style – though it was ten years since the Peace – of a war widow. She looked at him through eyes as large and watchful as William's but, as it were, in a minor key of sadness and resignation, looking back on the past, where his were in the major key of the future. . . .   (p. 15)

This is echoed in *Kathleen and Frank*, where Isherwood writes that he 'revolted early and passionately against the cult of the Past'.

The refusal to accede to the demands – the moral blackmail – of his country and class informs much of Isherwood's early writing. His first published novel, *All the Conspirators*, completed in November 1927 and published in 1929, had rejected the values of the upper-middle-class family, while *The Memorial*, the novel that he worked on in Berlin and that was published during his residence there, extends the indictment to the British ruling class in general. It was clearly now time to extend his little fictional empire, as E. M. Forster, always a role-model, had done before him. Boys were all very well in their place, but, whatever his claims to the contrary, Isherwood went to Berlin primarily to work, and one of the most revealing moments in *Christopher and his Kind* depicts him leaving his English companion after an evening in the bars in order to get to bed and be fresh for writing the next morning. His comment on this disclosure ('Seldom have wild oats been sown so prudently' (p. 29)) goes far towards subverting the more colourful and more widely repeated claim that 'Berlin meant Boys'.

His English companion was Francis Turville-Petre, who had assisted in the fruitless search for Bubi four or five months earlier, and it was Francis's door that Isherwood knocked on when he arrived in Berlin at the end of November. Francis was the only Englishman he knew in Berlin, and though they were different in many ways they shared, and had both rejected, a similar background and similar expectations on the part of family and class. Francis, though not a Sacred Orphan, was another scion of the landed gentry, another first-born, another soldier's son. At any rate they got on well enough for Isherwood to accept Francis's suggestion that he take a room in the same house, and Isherwood found it congenial enough to remain there after Francis left Berlin. He stayed, in fact, for about ten months, working on the third draft of *The Memorial*.

So far as his social life was concerned, one of his great advantages was knowing very little German. For turning his back on England had set him free not only from family and background but from language and culture. In using a language in which he was still inexpert and in which words were stripped of nuances, implications, connotations and indications of class he felt 'a marvellous freedom'. The phrase is his own:

> Christopher's relations with many of the boys soon became easy and intimate. Perhaps they recognised and were drawn to the boyishness in him. He felt a marvellous freedom in their company. He, who had hinted and stammered in English, could now ask straight out in German for what he wanted. His limited knowledge of the language forced him to be blunt and he wasn't

embarrassed to utter the foreign sex words, since they had no associations with his life in England.

(*Christopher and his Kind*, p. 30)

Revealingly, when he was reunited with Bubi in Berlin some three years after their Amsterdam farewells, he 'found it very odd to be able to chatter away to him in German – odd and a little saddening, because the collapse of their language-barrier had buried the magic image of The German Boy'.

There are also certain advantages for a writer in being in an alien linguistic environment, so that the language of his art remains aloof from the language of banal quotidian experience. It is no accident that many of the most brilliant modern stylists (Joyce, Beckett, Nabokov and Stein among them) have worked under these conditions, and the effect on Isherwood was to endow his English prose with a purity and directness that may owe something to his being distanced from its everyday use. Gertrude Stein's observations in *The Autobiography of Alice B. Toklas* on being an American writer in Paris are to the point:

> One of the things that I have liked all these years is to be surrounded by people who know no english. It has left me more intensely alone with my eyes and my english. I do not know if it would have been possible to have english be so all in all to me otherwise.... I like living with so very many people and being all alone with english and myself.

As a teacher of English, too, he would have had constantly to simplify his use of the language, stripping it free from obscurities, ostentation and modishness. German, on the other hand, was for him not only the language of the daily life of street, market and café, but also the language of sex: as he observes in an entertaining passage in *Christopher and his Kind* (p. 23), whereas a table was 'the dining-table in his mother's house', *ein Tisch* was the shabbier article of furniture to be found in the Cosy Corner.

Isherwood kept a diary in Berlin but seems to have subsequently destroyed it for prudential reasons after the Berlin books had been written, perhaps when he went to America in 1939. It is clear, though, that he quickly made a circle of friends and acquaintances, or rather two circles. One, formed initially through his relationship with Francis, was drawn from the bars and their population of regulars, including young male prostitutes, full-time and part-time, professional and amateur. The other was formed through his friendship with Karl Giese, the assistant and lover of Dr Magnus Hirschfeld, in the premises of whose celebrated Institute Isherwood's room, like Francis's, was located. This was an altogether more sedate world of what Isherwood later called 'middle-class queens', and their characteristic ambience was not the bar or the brothel but the tea-party or the strictly run club where homosexuals could drink and dance together. Through Karl he met a Communist ex-army gymnastics instructor called Erwin Hansen who was to remain a friend for some years and eventually leave Germany with him in 1933.

Residents of the Institute were in the habit of meeting for tea each day in Giese's room, and this was only one item in an often rather formal community life that Isherwood seems to have come to share. Hirschfeld himself was getting on in years, had sober habits and went to bed early, but when he was away the younger residents would organise dinners and parties with dancing. When the master of the house was present, social life would be more serious: lectures were arranged by the Scientific-Humanitarian Committee with social gatherings to follow, and there were also musical evenings and recitations from Goethe and other writers. There is every reason to suppose that, especially as his German improved, Isherwood took part in some of these formal and informal activities, and he must have had a strong sense of belonging to an enlightened community of a kind that could hardly have been paralleled in England, or perhaps anywhere else in the world, at that time.

One aspect of the enlightenment was a capacity for startling unconventionality – startling, at any rate, to one recently arrived from England. It seems that Isherwood took many of his meals at the common table of the Institute, and in a 1977 interview he recalled that 'We all sat down to lunch with extreme politeness and discourse [perhaps a transcription error for 'discretion' or 'decorum']. The only thing was a number of us were in drag, which was never mentioned'. Neither at the time nor some half-century later, it seems, was Isherwood unaware of the comic potential of such scenes, but the novelist-autobiographer's nose for bizarre copy was only the more superficial part of his reaction to the Institute and its inmates. At a deeper level his time there was an education in the open acceptance of sexual identity, the

possibility of community and the need for action. As he told the
same interviewer, Don Douglas:

> It was then that Isherwood got his first insight into what had
> seemed to be a purely private affair. 'I never recognized that I
> belonged to a tribe. Before that I just thought that I had some
> friends who liked boys like I did and others who liked girls. It
> never seemed to be that we were battling against anybody.'

The table-talk at the Institute opened his eyes, transforming secrecy
into community and private tastes into public issues.

His residence in Berlin was interrupted after only two or three
months when, in February 1930, he returned to England for family
reasons. But by May he was back again, and soon afterwards met a
boy who became the prototype of Otto Novak in *Goodbye to Berlin*.
(His real name is unknown and he should not be confused with
Auden's Otto Küsel). It was to be a long-term relationship, for,
despite his initial enthusiasm for the pick-up bars, Isherwood, like
Auden, was attracted by the idea of a stable, loyal and affectionate
partnership. Otto's family came from the Polish Corridor, the area
ceded by Germany to Poland under the terms of the Versailles
Treaty, and, like so many other migrant families then and later,
had settled in Berlin: he was 16 or 17, had Slav rather than German
looks and was not conventionally handsome, was heterosexual,
and cajoled Isherwood into spending more on him than he could
afford.

At the end of June, Auden, who was now a schoolmaster,
returned to Berlin for a two-week visit. It was a great success,
and he left with reluctance, describing himself after his return as
'much too miserable at having to leave Berlin to write a decent
letter', and boasting to his correspondent, Naomi Mitchison, that he
could 'probably exhaust and shock you with Berlin confessions'
(*You May Well Ask*, p. 118). More enigmatically, he told his brother:
'I had a wonderful fortnight.... As usual my heart broke up like a
treacle tart.' Auden, it goes without saying, was introduced to Otto
and in turn introduced him into a poem written for Isherwood's
birthday the following year. Back at his job in Scotland, he wrote
and sent to Isherwood half-a-dozen poems written in German; they
are not precisely dated but seem to have been written in or around
September 1930, and all but one express the pain of his withdrawal
symptoms. One poem makes a promise to return to Berlin in four

months' time – that is, in the Christmas holidays – but however fervently intended the promise was not kept. (More will be said about these poems in Chapter 5.) Isherwood received visits from two other English friends during the summer of 1930. During August he met Stephen Spender in Bamburg, and in the last week of that month Edward Upward visited him in Berlin (the first of two visits paid by Upward). A year older than Isherwood, Upward had been at both Repton and Cambridge with him and, as Allen Chalmers, is prominent in *Lions and Shadows*. In *Christopher and his Kind* he is accorded the accolade of 'Christopher's closest heterosexual male friend' (p. 42); he was also a fellow novelist and a Marxist, though not yet a member of the Communist Party. Politics must have featured prominently in their conversations, for Isherwood dates from this visit an increased awareness of the political realities of the city he had made his home:

> Here was the seething brew of history in the making – a brew which would test the truth of all the political theories, just as actual cooking tests the cookery books. The Berlin brew seethed with unemployment, malnutrition, stock market panic, hatred of the Versailles Treaty and other potent ingredients.
>
> (*Christopher and his Kind*, p. 43)

His 'political awakening' was an important stage in his development that made possible the Berlin stories with their depiction of the intersection of private lives and public events. Within a few weeks, as if to reinforce the lesson he had learned, the Nazis greatly strengthened their position as a result of the Reichstag elections and had to be recognised as 'a major political party'.

Spender, who was soon to join him in Berlin, had been born in 1909 and was hence a little younger than either Isherwood or Auden. He had made his way to Germany partly through Isherwood's example and encouragement. In the preface to his *Letters to Christopher* (1980), Spender states that he 'first met Christopher Isherwood in Auden's rooms at Christ Church, Oxford in 1928'. Auden introduced Isherwood to him as 'The Novelist of the Future', and Spender seems quickly to have fallen under the spell of his personality. More than half a century later he wrote:

Wherever [Isherwood] was seemed to me to be the trenches.
When he asked me to join him in Berlin it was as though some
admired commander had asked me to be his adjutant, and it was
in this spirit that I joined him for months at a time through
freezing Berlin winters and once or twice [twice, actually]
through Baltic summers on the island of Sellin.

(Letters to Christopher, p. 9)

In his autobiography Spender recalled that, at later meetings in
London, Isherwood

simplified all the problems which entangled me, merely by
describing his own life and his own attitudes towards these
things.... The whole [Oxford and Cambridge] system was to
him one which denied affection: and which was based largely on
fear of sex. His hatred extended, though, beyond Oxford. It was
for English middle-class life. He spoke of Germany as the country where all the obstructions and complexities of this life were
cut through.

(World within World, pp. 102, 104)

However, a much more recent declaration by Spender that what
'really' drew him to Berlin was 'the hypnotic fascination of Christopher Isherwood's life' there (*Observer*, 28 November 1993) suggests that it may have been his friend's lifestyle as much as his
personality or his convictions that exerted such a powerful mag-
netic force. As often, different stages of life and different confessional climates seem to have elicited different myths or versions of
the truth from the same source.

Spender did not proceed straight to the German capital, which
Isherwood had not yet made his home, but initially exchanged
Oxford for Hamburg, writing a shade melodramatically on the
opening page of a journal he kept at the time, under the date 22
July 1929, 'Now I shall begin to live.' According to Hugh David,
Spender stated towards the end of his life that he went to Hamburg
because Auden and Isherwood had already annexed or colonised
Berlin (*Stephen Spender: A Portrait with Background*, p. 120). If so, the
wish to escape from under their shadow was a natural one, though
it was not in the event to be entirely accomplished. In Hamburg he
experienced 'a tremendous sense of relief, of having got away from
Oxford and home'.

As with Isherwood's early weeks in Berlin, the sense of what has
been left behind seems almost stronger than the awareness of what
it has been exchanged for. If Isherwood's idealised Germany is
reminiscent of Forster's idealised Italy ('the beautiful country
where they say "yes" '), it is because both were to a large extent
lands of fantasy and wish-fulfilment, and Isherwood's great
admiration for Forster is once more to the point here. But Isherwood, of course, came to know Berlin much better than Forster
ever knew Italy: to know the reality that badly dented, if it did not
wholly destroy, the fantasy.

In the fullness of time, Isherwood turned Berlin itself into a
literary construct, and before the end of 1930 he had moved to
the neighbourhood that was to become Isherwood Country. At the
end of August he wrote to Spender, 'My financial troubles are
worse than ever before': Otto's demands had proved a decided
strain on the modest allowance made by his capricious Uncle
Henry, and he needed to find cheaper accommodation. This inter-
mittently generous relative, who had made Isherwood his heir, is
presumably the model for the elderly, lisping globe-trotter and
boy-chaser in Auden's poem 'Uncle Henry', written in about 1931.

Henry Bradshaw-Isherwood-Bagshawe, to grant him the full
splendour of the name he adopted after his ill-starred and short-
lived marriage, is a figure who seems to have stepped straight from
the pages of the early Evelyn Waugh. The elder brother of Frank,
Christopher's father, he was Christopher's godfather, held the
family purse-strings, took a fellow homosexual's interest in his
nephew's adventures, which he liked to have recounted to him in
detail over a tête-à-tête dinner, and caused consternation in the
family by his late and unexpected marriage, which fortunately
proved without issue.

Impecuniosity was, at least, Isherwood's cover story, though it is
not difficult to guess that there might have been other motives,
both sexual and literary, for his initial move, in October, to the
slum tenement where Otto's family lived. Auden, in exchanging
the rather grand house where he first stayed for lodgings near the
Cosy Corner, had told a correspondent that he was going to live in
a slum, and now Isherwood was following his example. Like
George Orwell's more celebrated descent upon Wigan, this episode
was actually of very brief duration, but the leaky roof, the toilet
shared with three other families (if you were too fastidious to resort
to the bucket in the kitchen), and the washing facilities in the

kitchen sink (unless you made the trek to the public baths) must
have been a revelation to a young man brought up in an English
country house. *Goodbye to Berlin* was, needless to say, to exploit this
material.

Very soon Isherwood moved out, briefly to Admiralstrasse, then
in December to Nollendorfstrasse, where he was to remain until his
time in Berlin was terminated by public events. There, in the
apartment presided over by Fräulein Thurau, one of his fellow
lodgers was an English girl, Jean Ross, who became the model for
Sally Bowles. Spender had arrived in Berlin in September 'in order
to see a girl whom I hope perhaps to marry': this was Gisa Soloweitschik, a 17-year-old Lithuanian, who provided Isherwood with
a model for Natalia Landauer in *Goodbye to Berlin*. Spender took a
room in Motzstrasse, a short walk from Isherwood's lodgings, and
during this winter the two met regularly. From Berlin Spender
wrote to John Lehmann:

> There are four or five friends who work together, although they
> are not all known to each other. They are W. H. Auden, Chris-
> topher Isherwood, Edward Upward and I.... Whatever one of
> us does in writing or travelling or taking jobs, it is a kind of
> exploration which may be taken up by the other two or three.
> (*Christopher Isherwood: A Personal Memoir*, pp. 8–9)

There was some truth in this, though possibly not very much, and
in quoting the passage long afterwards Lehmann commented that
Spender 'was a great maker of legends' and that this 'may have
been largely (his) fantasy'.

One visitor to Berlin at this time was Paul Bowles, the American
composer and writer, who became acquainted with both Isherwood and Spender. Bowles arrived from Paris with his friend,
the composer Aaron Copland, and was unimpressed by the transition, finding Berlin visually and socially unattractive: 'It was,' he
wrote later, 'like a film of Fritz Lang's. The "haves" were going
hog-wild while the "have-nots" seethed with hatred. There was a
black cloud of hatred over the whole east end of the city.' Bowles
had been given a letter of introduction to Jean Ross, who introduced him to Isherwood, who in turn introduced him to Spender.
Bowles, younger than either of the two Englishmen, found them
'overwhelmingly British, two members of a secret society constantly making reference to esoteric data not available to outsiders'.

(This and the previous quotation are taken from Christopher Saw-yer-Laucanno's biography of Bowles, pp. 100–1.) The outsider/insider polarity is prominent in the early work of Auden and Isherwood, and Bowles's comment suggests the ways in which the closed worlds of an upper-middle-class upbringing, including the mandatory private and public schools and ancient universities, could collude with a sense of sexual difference that must to some extent remain covert to generate this 'secret society' atmosphere. Bowles added, with some acuteness, that Isherwood alone was a very different man from Isherwood in Spender's company.

Despite his disapproval and resentment – he objected, for instance, to Spender's 'Byronesque' habit of wearing his shirt open to his chest as being an excessively crass announcement of his status as a poet – Bowles saw a good deal of them while he remained in Berlin. In his autobiography, *Stepping Out*, he describes how they would meet daily on the terrace of the Café des Westens, often joined by Jean Ross and Aaron Copland. But Berlin remained for him 'a strange, ugly, vaguely sinister city', architecturally hideous, and he quitted it without regrets. He did carry away with him, however, and in due course put on record, one vivid picture of the young Spender, blonde and sunburnt, standing in the middle of his room at the top of the house in Motzstrasse with the setting sun streaming through the window, and looking 'as though he were on fire'. Bowles's unintended parting gift to Isherwood was his surname, later appropriated for the latter's most famous fictional character.

Auden, meanwhile, was languishing in a Scottish schoolroom – though, to be fair, he seems to have enjoyed teaching, and was in any case still writing. During the summer holidays he had begun a play, *The Fronny*, which obviously bore some relationship to his Berlin experiences, for its title was the name given to Francis Turville-Petre in the private mythology shared by Auden and Isherwood (it adapts 'Der Franni', the nickname given to Francis by the Berlin rent-boys). The first act was finished by September, and portions were sent from time to time to Isherwood for com-ment. On 8 December Auden sent the complete play to T. S. Eliot of Faber & Faber, who rejected it, but nine months later asked to see it again, agreed to publish it, and then changed his mind. It was also turned down by the Hogarth Press. Subsequently the manuscript disappeared, the work surviving only in a very fragmentary form. Isherwood, too, had been busy, and by the end of 1930 his novel

The Memorial was finished, though getting it published was to take up much of his time in the following year, and it was not to appear until early in 1932.

With *The Memorial* completed, Isherwood worked during 1931 on the first draft of *Lions and Shadows*, an autobiographical work that makes frontier-crossings into fiction in the same way that his fiction constantly strays into autobiography or history. He also began to ponder a vast and never-to-be-completed fictional enterprise, an epic (or at any rate a very long) novel to be called *The Lost*. In March, during the first of three absences from Berlin during this year, he spent about ten days in London, hoping to persuade the publishing firm of Jonathan Cape to accept *The Memorial*. He was unsuccessful, but six months later it was accepted by the Hogarth Press.

He was back in England at the beginning of October on a short visit to his mother, and found himself exchanging one country in a state of turmoil for another. On 21 September Britain had abandoned the gold standard, causing a fall in the value of sterling that was bad news for anyone who was, like Isherwood, living abroad on a small income derived from England. A little earlier in the same month, the British government's attempts to deal with the economic crisis had produced riots in London and Glasgow and a naval mutiny at Invergordon. Aware of the collapse, in the previous July, of the German Danatbank and the ensuing closure of all German banks for some three weeks, Isherwood must have had an unpleasant sense of *déjà vu*.

In July, however, his absence from Berlin had taken him not to England but to the village of Sellin on the Baltic island of Rügen (usually spelt Ruegen by Isherwood). The island had long been a popular resort and is briefly mentioned as such in Forster's *Howards End*. Isherwood had gone there with Otto and Spender, and they had been joined – unenthusiastically, for beaches were not his cup of tea – by Auden. It was this holiday that produced what is perhaps the most familiar icon of British writing in the 1930s: a photograph of the three young men, apparently so remarkably unequal in physical stature that Spender looks like a giant and Isherwood (as he later said) gives the impression of standing in a hole, but all grinning boyishly. The picture was taken by Spender, at this period a shutter-happy enthusiast, with what he called 'a masturbatory camera designed for narcissists'. A less familiar photograph from the same holiday shows Isherwood gazing thoughtfully, even soulfully, at the naked upper torso of Otto, who has his own eyes modestly cast down and appears to be strumming, or at least contemplating, a guitar.

Twelve months later Isherwood and Spender were back on Rügen (which provided a chapter in *Goodbye to Berlin*), though by that time Otto belonged to the past. Isherwood's Jewish friend Wilfrid Israel was with them during this 1932 holiday and duly makes an important appearance in *Goodbye to Berlin*, though not in the section on Rügen.

Looking at these photographic records, it is necessary to remind oneself rather sharply that these were three young writers of promise, or more than promise. For the atmosphere of adolescent high jinks is strong, and in some of the retrospective accounts the idealisation seems remarkably transparent and distinctly naive. In Spender's *The Temple*, for example, his autobiographical protagonist returns to England in a state of gloom:

> London and Oxford towards which he now knew himself being hurled seemed to spell out unutterable grey blankness, a permanent fog. The summer he was leaving seemed more than happiness. It was a revelation. For a moment he thought he had been insane ever to leave Joachim and Heinrich. He should have gone on walking with them down the Rhine for ever.... (p. 132)

Taken all round, the coastal climate of North Germany is not markedly superior to that of London or Oxford, and walking down the Rhine in the winter months could be guaranteed to dampen romantic enthusiasm. This symbolic and subjective use of weather, clumsily introduced into a realistic narrative, points to a more widespread immaturity or irresponsibility. In some of its manifestations it is probably influenced by the emphasis placed on youth, sunshine, scenery and the body beautiful in a tradition of gay sensibility and gay writing that goes back at least to Walt Whitman and Edward Carpenter. In Spender's case one suspects, too, that climate has become a convenient metaphor for sexual permissiveness.

To be fair, it must be added that Spender's journal contains an entry showing that, even on the Baltic beaches and in the copulatory pinewoods, politics could make themselves unignorably felt. There were many young Nazis on the island, enjoying themselves with an earnestness that carried more than a hint of menace:

...the Nazis were doing exercises every evening in the woods....when they sunbathed they would build little forts for themselves on the beach, set up a flagpost, hoist a Nazi flag on it and gaze up in reverence. Whilst they were lounging round listening to the music, they seemed always to be waiting for a patriotic air and when one was played they would stand to attention.

This is paralleled in one of Isherwood's letters written from Rügen to Upward, which first evokes idealised memories of English seaside holidays and then introduces the brutal contemporary images of uniformed, 'hog-necked' Nazis. Before his fictionalised account of the Rügen idyll had been published, the National Socialist Party had opened on the island a vast holiday camp for its members. But by that time Isherwood was far away and felt no obligation to allow his memories to be contaminated by contemporary realities.

In 1932 *Lions and Shadows*, which was not to be published until 1938, was temporarily abandoned, and Isherwood turned his attention to *The Lost*. His vacillation suggests some lack of creative pressure, or at least of a clear sense of direction, and he was not in fact a fertile writer even in his youth: four years elapsed between the appearance of his first two novels, three years between his second and third, even though all of them are short. In August, though, he began the first draft of what became the Berlin stories, and the long-awaited appearance of *The Memorial* in February must have boosted his confidence.

A number of new friendships belong to this period. In the previous year he had met Gerald Hamilton, the prototype of his Mr Norris, and during a visit to England in August 1931, as well as seeing Auden and Upward, he met John Lehmann, who was then working for the Woolfs at the Hogarth Press but was soon to go to Vienna. Other new acquaintances were Gerald Heard and William Plomer. In his autobiography Plomer praises Isherwood as a conversationalist: ' "Amazing" was one of his favourite words, and his capacity to be amazed by the behaviour of the human species, so recklessly displayed everywhere, made him a most entertaining talker' (p. 298). Plomer introduced him in September to E. M. Forster, who had read and admired *The Memorial*; later Forster and Isherwood became close friends, corresponding often, and Isherwood was one of the early readers of *Maurice*. Soon after their first meeting Isherwood wrote to Forster that he was occupied with 'an indecent bumptious stupid sort of novel about Berlin'.

Lehmann's memoir of Isherwood, published after the latter's death, recalls that at this first meeting he was attracted by 'the quality which appealed to me so much in *The Memorial*, an exact feeling for the deeper moods of our generation with its delayed war-shock and conviction of the futility of the old pattern of social life and convention' (p. 11). After Lehmann had moved to Vienna later in the year – for he was anxious to concentrate on his writing rather than on publishing other men's books, and he shared the common urge to escape from England – he visited Isherwood in Berlin. Lehmann had the knack of being in Berlin at moments of crisis: he was there when Hindenburg nominated Hitler as Chancellor, and again when the Reichstag burned down. ('I was in a bar near the Zoo,' he writes, 'when a friend who had been spending the evening at a cinema came in and told us "The Reichstag's on fire!"' (p. 14).) Some vivid pages of his autobiography are devoted to this latter visit, when, 'in the midst of the last agony of the Weimar Republic', he noticed around the city 'huge pictures of Hitler...displayed in the failing light in windows illuminated by devout candles': 'The crucial elections were approaching, and bloody conflicts between the Nazis, the Communists and the Social-Democrats were taking place almost every day in some part of the ice-bound city that was laid out like a patient about to undergo an operation without any anaesthetic at all' (*The Whispering Gallery*, p. 209).

Francis Turville-Petre, whose lifestyle was nomadic and unpredictable, had disappeared from Berlin soon after Isherwood's arrival but reappeared early in 1932. Soon, however, he became bored with the city and conceived a yearning for a rural retreat, settling (more or less arbitrarily, it seems) on a village named Mohrin some distance northeast of Berlin and not far from the Polish border (it is now in Poland and called Moryn). Francis now announced that he had formed great resolutions. He would live in the country, drink less and go to bed early, and he invited Isherwood to join him in this Thoreau-like enterprise.

The affair with Otto was in decline, Mohrin would be cheaper than Berlin, and it would be a good place to work, so Isherwood readily agreed. Francis had already engaged Erwin Hansen to keep house for them, and Erwin had recruited a young assistant called Heinz Neddermayer. On 13 March, shortly before they all set off,

Isherwood met Heinz, who was not only to become Otto's successor as the object of his affections but to share his life for much of the rest of the decade. Isherwood was to stay in Mohrin until late June, though there must have been at least one visit to Berlin during that period, for he was there in April to see Upward, who was on his way back to England after a visit to the Soviet Union. As for Francis, the new regime quickly and predictably palled and he soon began to slip off to Berlin with Erwin for weekends, bringing back with them one or more boys from the bars.

Such promiscuity was not really Isherwood's style, and he quickly fell in love with, and became deeply attached to, Heinz. He was a working-class youth of about 17, slim and with features that Isherwood later described as 'somewhat negroid' and that included a broken nose. He seems to have had no mother, brothers or sisters, saw little of his father and lived with his grandmother. Isherwood's account of their relationship gives an insight into his own emotional needs:

> Heinz had found his elder brother; Christopher had found someone emotionally innocent, entirely vulnerable and uncritical, whom he could protect and cherish as his very own. He was deeply touched and not in the least apprehensive. He wasn't yet aware that he was letting himself in for a relationship which would be far more serious than any he had had in his life.
>
> (*Christopher and his Kind*, p. 73)

Francis, who paid Heinz's wages, demanded that Isherwood should pay half when he learned that they were sleeping together. The relationship was not just a holiday romance, however: it lasted throughout the 1930s, and its centrality in Isherwood's early development is suggested by his remark to an interviewer, after *Christopher and his Kind* appeared in 1977, that the book was 'Basically...the story of my relationship with my friend Heinz, his arrest and its aftermath, and the attitudes I developed as a result of that' (to W. I. Scobie, 1977).

Spender paid a short visit to Mohrin, then, in July, joined Isherwood again on Rügen for the second of the two summer periods already mentioned. This time there was no Otto, but Heinz was there, of course, also Spender's younger brother Humphrey, who later became a well-known film-maker. During this month Isherwood wrote to Lehmann about *The Lost*, his grandly conceived novel about Berlin: 'It is written entirely in the form of a diary, without any break in the narrative. It will have lots of characters and be full of "news" about Berlin.' This suggests an attempt to convey the drama of contemporary events, but as Brian Finney points out, 'This must have been a false start as he dictated a new draft outline of the entire novel to his brother Richard a month later' – that is, when he was staying with his family in London in August. In its recast and slimmed-down form, the book planned to make use of Otto's family and of Jean Ross, and can therefore be regarded as a very early version of the book published seven years later as *Goodbye to Berlin* – in Isherwood's words, 'the very first draft of his fiction about Berlin . . . as crude as his first drafts always were'.

In August and September, as we have seen, he was in England, and towards the end of this visit he seems to have quarrelled with Spender, who decided not to return to Germany. On the last day of September Isherwood left London to return to Berlin, and to a Germany in which public events were moving towards a crisis that had its origins much earlier. In the introduction to *The Temple*, a reworking (in 1986–7) of the novel he wrote in 1929 about the summer he had spent in Hamburg, Spender observes that '1929 can be looked at as the last pre-war, because pre-Hitler, summer, bearing the same relation to February 1933 as July 1918 does to August 1918'. The reality was, however, that those three and a half years – nearly the whole of the period with which this chapter is concerned – had to be lived through one day at a time, and the record of those times is one of gradually mounting tension, anxiety and violence. Behind the world of slum lodgings and rent-bars was a world of politics and power-struggles: behind the personal dramas of Isherwood's love affairs or his attempts to write, the Republic was slowly dying.

In his study of Weimar culture, Peter Gay labels the period from December 1923 to October 1929 'The Golden Twenties' (his terminal date confirming Spender's claim); that from October 1929 to May 1932 'The Beginning of the End'; and the months from June 1932 to January 1933 'Into Barbarism'. The elections of 14 September 1930, held at a time when Isherwood was in Berlin, had seen a campaign that 'plumbed new depths of demagogy and sheer violence' and one that resulted in a massive victory for the Nazis, whose number of seats in the Reichstag rose from 12 to 107 (the much more modest Communist increase was from 23 to 77). 'For many intellectuals,' writes Gay, 'September 14, 1930, marked the death of the Republic.' The world economic crisis, and an unemployment rate in Germany that by the beginning of 1932 exceeded six million, produced serious political instability as well as widespread misery and anger.

This situation was of course exploited by the National Socialists in every possible way. In February 1930, for instance, an obscure Nazis supporter named Horst Wessel had been murdered by the Communists. The son of a Protestant minister, Wessel had kicked over the traces with remarkable thoroughness, living with a prostitute, consorting with pimps and devoting himself to political action. The Nazi propaganda machine quickly turned him into a martyr and folk-hero, and a song he had composed became an anthem of the Nazi party.

Many of the activities of the National Socialists must have impinged directly on the experience of anyone living in the city at this time. Street violence was becoming commonplace, and by the end of 1930 there were signs that the rapidly growing private army of stormtroopers was 'getting out of hand'. The phrase is used by the American journalist and historian William Shirer, who was living in the city at that time and later wrote: 'Its members, even its leaders, apparently believed in a coming Nazi revolution by violence, and with increasing frequency they were taking to the streets to molest and murder their political opponents. No election, national, provincial or municipal, took place without savage battles in the gutters.'

Hitler's personal prestige and the power of his party continued to grow. In the presidential election held in March 1932 he polled over 11 million votes (an increase of some 86 per cent over the previous election), coming second to Hindenburg. Since Hindenburg had failed to gain an absolute majority, a further election was held in the following months, and Hitler again increased his vote substantially (by over two million); this time, however, Hindenburg obtained his majority. Though defeated, Hitler had doubled the Nazi vote in two years and strengthened his personal position immensely. As Shirer notes, a menacing background to these elections was the private army of Stormtroopers, now numbering some 400,000, who stood poised ready to seize power on Hitler's behalf when the time was ripe.

In the Reichstag or parliamentary elections in July, there was a sensational victory for the Nazis (230 seats out of 608), following a campaign 'marked by sanguinary clashes between Communists and Nazis, and Socialists and Nazis'; they were now the largest party in the Reichstag. When new elections were called for in November, the Nazis lost 34 seats but remained the strongest party. On 8 August, soon after the July elections, Goebbels wrote in his diary that Berlin was 'full of rumours', that the Nazis were 'ready to take over power' and that the Stormtroopers were 'leaving their places of work in order to make themselves ready' while the party leaders themselves were 'preparing for the great hour'. The next day he wrote that the stormtroopers were 'throwing an ever stronger ring around Berlin'.

Isherwood was in London at this time, and he had been on Rügen at the time of the July elections, but he spent enough of 1932 in Berlin itself to be well aware of what was going on, and he was back from England in time to witness the campaign leading up to the elections of 6 November, in which the Nazis lost two million votes and 34 seats in the Reichstag, while the Communists strengthened their position. Hitler's personal ascendancy seemed unstoppable, however, and Kurt von Schleicher, who became Chancellor on 2 December, was to hold office for only 57 days and to be the last Chancellor of the Weimar Republic.

On 30 January 1933 Hitler was made Chancellor, and five weeks later, in the elections of 5 March, the Nazis won 288 seats, giving them an outright majority in the Reichstag. Later in the same month an Enabling Law granted dictatorial powers to Hitler. But by then, for Isherwood, as for many others living in Germany who had not yet made their escape, it was time to go.

All of this was the background to the final phase of Isherwood's life in Germany, and sometimes more than the background. On 3 November 1932 he wrote to Spender about the transport strike that had begun that very day, and in *Christopher and his Kind* he recalls that this 'resulted in widespread public violence against strike-breakers and others'. He witnessed a street incident in which a young man was brutally attacked by a group of Nazis on their way back from a political rally, and later made use of it in *Goodbye to Berlin*.

It must be remembered, though, that daily life is not often lived at the fever-pitch attained by historical accounts or fictionalised versions of them, and in mid-January Isherwood was writing to Spender that the political situation was 'very dull':

I expect there is a great deal going on behind the scenes, but one is not aware of it. Papen visits Hindenburg, Hitler visits Papen, Hitler and Papen visit Schleicher, Hugenberg visits Hindenburg and finds he's out. And so forth. There is no longer that slightly exhilarating awareness of crisis in the gestures of beggars and tram-conductors.

(The eye of the professional novelist and the dedicated cinemagoer can be detected in those observed gestures.) When Hitler came to power, Isherwood wrote to Spender that 'we are having a new government, with Charlie Chaplin and Father Christmas in the ministry': it was the more politically aware Spender in England who responded to the situation by exclaiming that 'The news from Germany is awful.'

Even the sleazy paradise of the boy-bars had begun to be invaded by politics, the boys taking sides in arguments and joining one organisation or another. Real life provided one of its symbolic moments when, on 1 April, Isherwood went to make some token purchase at a Jewish department store as a gesture of protest and recognised, standing at the entrance in a stormtrooper's uniform, one of the youths from the Cosy Corner. The transformation of some of the young bar-haunting prostitutes into gleaming instruments of the new regime is presented, though not without tactful evasion, in *Goodbye to Berlin*.

Despite all this, work, love affairs and the comings and goings of friends were perhaps more real, and certainly more interesting, to Isherwood than the reported doings of politicians, though later he expressed regret at not having taken a closer professional interest in the psychology of the members of the Nazi High Command. Lehmann had visited him in October, on his way back to Vienna, and was in Berlin again in late January, just at the time Hitler became Chancellor, and yet again in late February, when the Reichstag was burned. Meanwhile, over Christmas, Auden paid a ten-day visit and discussed plans for his play *The Dance of Death*, not produced until 1934. At this period Isherwood was seeing a good deal of Beatrix Lehmann, John's sister and a well-known actress, who was visiting Berlin, and they spent New Year's Eve together.

Shortly after the mid-January letter to Spender, Hitler's accession to power made it impossible to complain of dullness, and many foreigners, Isherwood among them, either left Germany or began to make plans to do so. Even Aleister Crowley, the footloose poetaster, theosophist, diabolist and self-styled Beast from the Book of Revelation, who had been living in Berlin in 1932, deemed it prudent to depart – despite his claim to have presented the National Socialists with the idea of using the swastika as their symbol, and thereby having presumably earned their undying gratitude. Lehmann's memoir notes that after the Reichstag fire 'Hitler's triumph was complete...and the Nazi terror was unleashed against the Communists and all the known opponents of the new regime' (p. 14). Among the exhibits in present-day Berlin's grim and grimly named museum Topographie des Terrors is a dramatic photograph of police rounding up Communists in a large-scale operation on 22 January.

In addition to known opponents, minorities such as Jews and homosexuals were victimised. Lehmann adds that 'Foreigners who had no obvious affiliation were left alone, at any rate for the time being, but the frequenters of the boy-bars, many of which were being raided, passed some uneasy nights'. Demonstrations of Nazi power took theatrical as well as practical forms: another picture in the same museum shows a *Sportfest* in Berlin's Sportpalast on 17 March in which police with raised rifles were lined up in the shape of a swastika.

Early in April, just a few days after the first Nazi boycott of Jewish-owned businesses on the 1st, Isherwood left for England, taking with him a number of his belongings, including papers and manuscripts. During three weeks spent in London he saw, among others, Gerald Hamilton (whom he had helped to flee from Berlin), Edward Upward and Bubi. He also visited some friends of Forster's at Esher and met Joe Ackerley there: it was to turn out to be a valuable contact, for Ackerley was literary editor of *The Listener* and was later to put a good deal of reviewing work Isherwood's way. It was at this time that Forster lent Isherwood the typescript of *Maurice*, which Isherwood liked and praised.

Back in Berlin on the last day of April, he began to make preparations for a departure that would merely, and perhaps barely, anticipate an official request to leave the country. Francis had bought a small Greek island in the hope (to prove sadly vain) of resuming his career as an archaeologist, and he invited Isherwood to join him there, so to Greece he decided to go. The Berlin dream had turned into a nightmare: there was (as he wrote long afterwards) 'terror in the Berlin air'; and in the end he could not get away quickly enough. During his last two weeks in the city events moved rapidly. On 2 May the German trade unions were suppressed. Four days later Hirschfeld's Institute, with which Isherwood had been closely associated during his first year in Berlin, was invaded and ransacked.

So, on 13 May, he set off for Athens, accompanied by Heinz and Erwin. They took a week over the journey, travelling by train via Prague and Vienna to Budapest, then by river steamer to Belgrade, finally by train again to Athens, where Francis met them. Isherwood spent an uncomfortable three and a half months on Francis's island, St Nicholas, then, still accompanied by Heinz, began the wanderings that were to occupy most of the next seven years. (The Greek episode was put to good account in *Down There on a Visit*.) As for Berlin, the city with which most of those who know his name most readily associate him, it was a long time before he saw it again and he was never again to make it his home.

The relationship of the two writers, and the literary results of their love affair with Berlin (more interesting, after all, than their other love affairs), survived their departure. During the 1930s they collaborated on several enterprises: the plays *The Dog Beneath the Skin*, *The Ascent of F6* and *On the Frontier*, and the travel book *Journey to a War*, based on their visit to China. Isherwood's Berlin fiction also came later in the decade, *Mr Norris Changes Trains* in 1935 and *Goodbye to Berlin* in 1939, so that what had started as a diary ended almost as a historical study. In a later chapter (Chapter 5) we shall consider the ways in which, over a period much longer than that of their actual residence, the experiences of the years 1928 to 1933 were transformed into art.

2
Berlin: Places

PAST AND PRESENT

Although its origins go back to the Middle Ages, and although in 1871 it was promoted from the chief city in Prussia to the imperial capital, Berlin retained until near the end of the nineteenth century an air of provinciality. Like London and other European cities, however, it had been growing dramatically during that century: its population quadrupled between 1800 and 1871, and was already over half a million (521,933) at the time of the first official census in 1861. The symbolic million mark was passed in 1877, and it reached two million by 1905. By this time it had already become recognised as a major international city with a markedly modern flavour: in 1898 it had been nicknamed 'Chicago on the Spree', presumably on account of the number of new buildings that were rising. Later, a 1915 guide described it as 'the most American city in continental Europe'. It also had its share of the problems of modern urban civilisation, including extensive slums and a serious housing shortage. At the same time it was a green city, with nearly twenty per cent of the area within the municipal boundaries consisting of woodland.

The 1931 census, conducted during Isherwood's period of residence, showed a population of 4,288,700, making it the world's third city (after London and New York). It was the most important railway centre in Europe, and already a rapidly developing focus for the new age of air travel, nearly fifty thousand passengers passing through Tempelhof Airport in 1930. Nor was its importance merely a matter of size and economic growth, for after the turn of the century it had begun to compete with Munich as a cultural and artistic centre for Germany, and by the end of the 1920s it had become a serious rival to Paris as a laboratory for creative experiment and innovation.

In a matter of some fifty years, then, from the 1870s to the 1920s, the old Prussian capital had transformed itself into a cosmopolitan city, and as such it had begun to attract a heavy tourist trade.

61

Auden and Isherwood were not the only non-Germans in Berlin, for of the one and a quarter million visitors to the city who registered with the police in 1930 one-fifth were foreigners. Many, of course, came on business, but others were lured by the city's reputation as a centre of the sex industry with a bizarrely and perhaps uniquely varied nightlife. A 1927 guide describes the Eldorado, the transvestite nightclub in Motzstrasse already referred to, which was very close to the quarter that Isherwood was a little later to make his own:

> There is a secret about the place that belongs to the Berlin night. This place, one of Berlin's most popular, recruits its patrons mainly from circles where the arithmetic of love is not without its mistakes. Here men do not only dance with women but with men. And women dance with women. And the nice gentleman from Saxony, who dances with the blond singer, doesn't have the slightest idea that his blond lady is a man....
> (Eugen Szatman, *Das Buch von Berlin*, quoted in von Eckardt and Gilman, *Bertolt Brecht's Berlin*, p. 31)

But this, the guide teasingly continues, is all good clean fun compared with 'the bars that one *really* doesn't talk about...they are known only to the initiated' – a group among whom Auden and Isherwood unquestionably came to be numbered.

William Plomer, a year older than Isherwood and later a friend, was in Berlin in 1930 and detected a more complex, even paradoxical flavour. He refers in his autobiography to 'the then notorious night-life', adding that 'Blatant impudicity on such a scale was certainly exciting to youthful senses, but there was something desperately sad about it – and at times something grotesquely funny' (p. 274). On a more respectable level, the city had an 'air of modernity, open-mindedness and vitality', so that in 1929 Harold Nicolson, who was presumably not thinking on this occasion of the kind of establishments 'known only to the initiated', could speak of 'the charm of Berlin'.

Gerald Hamilton, the 'original' of Isherwood's Mr Norris, found Berlin 'more agreeably mixed and international than London' (*Mr Norris and I*, p. 128). What he meant by 'mixed' is spelled out:

> During the last years of the decrepit Weimar Republic, Berlin outvied Paris with its night life. But though it was supposed to

be gay, there was a sordid element about it which was very
noticeable. There were alleged to be no less than 132 homosexual
cafés registered as such with the tolerant police. Some of them
were used only by ladies as a rendezvous for their Lesbian
friends. Others were exclusively for *Transvestiten*, men and
boys who like to dress up as women. The rest were patronized
by the usual kind of homosexuals who hoped to meet their
destiny at such places. There were weekly homosexual papers,
such as the famous *Freundschaft* which published the most
fantastic advertisements I have ever seen in print. Then
again there were some cafés which specialized in a particular
attraction, such as having a genuine hermaphrodite on the
premises. The height of decadence was reached on the so-called
strich or avenue, where prostitutes offered themselves for
sale. There were girls in men's clothes, often holding a whip,
boys in girl's clothes, and the usual supply of men and women
offering themselves to either sex in return for ample payment.

(pp. 129–30)

Hamilton's air of prim disapproval should not be taken seriously,
since he was a practising homosexual who knew what he was
talking about.

In *Christopher and his Kind* (p. 29), Isherwood suggests that
Berlin's reputation for decadence and perversity may have been
'largely a commercial "line" which the Berliners had instinctively
developed in their competition with Paris': since Paris had for
generations exploited a reputation for easily available straight
sex, it was natural for Berlin to compete by offering 'a masquerade
of perversions'. The roots of the phenomenon seem, however, to lie
more deeply in traditional cultural patterns. The intensely masculine ethos of Prussian militarism may have created behaviour patterns comparable to those generated by the single-sex schools and
colleges attended by the ruling class in England, and the homosexual scandals at the highest levels that rocked German society in
a period well before Berlin's international heyday suggest widespread and well-entrenched practices and lifestyles.

Moreover, the subcultures in question have evinced a remarkable knack of surviving. A whole generation after the years with
which this book is concerned, when the middle-aged Auden
returned to live in Berlin for a time in the 1960s, he would have
found, among so much change and so much eradication of

landmarks, places to enter which was to step back into the earlier epoch. His lines written in February 1965 and titled 'Economics', make the point succinctly:

> In the Hungry Thirties
> boys used to sell their bodies
> for a square meal.
>
> In the Affluent Sixties
> they still did:
> to meet Hire-Purchase Payments.

Loren Driscoll, who knew Auden well and who himself lived in Berlin at this time, has described to me one institution that flourished in Berlin in the 'Affluent Sixties':

> I recall going into Elly's Bier Bar one evening. There, sitting prominently at the bar, was Grandma – actually Grandpa, who had been carefully dressed up by his wife before setting out and was there every Saturday night. Then there was a massive truck-driver, heavily tattooed, with his little boy-friend, and a nice young couple embracing, only a toothless old man had his hand on the young man's crotch. As I entered, the boy looked at me, raised his eyebrows, shrugged his shoulders, and went on kissing his girl. Elly herself was an institution: a lesbian who wore Cary Grant suits and George Raft hats and permitted no hanky-panky in her establishment while she stood there chewing her Havana.

The world of Georg Grosz was still alive and well, it seems, at least in microcosm. And even today, a further generation on, though Berlin has yielded to cheaper and more climatically favoured spots as a venue for the sex-vacation market, by no means every link with the past has been severed, and there is said to be at least one tiny, crowded and smoke-filled 24-hour bar in the neighbourhood of Isherwood's Nollendorfplatz that in decor and clientele bears a strong resemblance to the long-defunct but historic Cosy Corner.

As with many expanding cities, Berlin's centre had not remained constant, but as a result of the upheavals of the last half-century we need to make a double effort of the historical imagination in order to gain a sense of where the hub of the city was situated at various points in its history. Even today, perhaps, for those who have got to know Berlin it is necessary first to think of it as it was before the building of the Wall (the demolition of which has not stopped its citizens from speaking of their city as divided into East and West) to grasp the changes that took place during the period of rapid expansion from about 1924 to 1929: the period near the end of which Auden and Isherwood saw it for the first time.

A glance at a map of Central Berlin in the early 1920s shows the east–west axis of Unter den Linden dividing the area into two roughly equal parts. Near its west end stood the Brandenburg Gate, with the Reichstag nearby, while towards the east were the Cathedral, the Imperial Palace, the Stock Exchange, the National Gallery, Opera, museums and other public buildings. This picture already has an air of looking-glass unfamiliarity to anyone who has known 'West Berlin' in recent decades and for whom the Branden-burg Gate, for instance, has been thought of as lying well to the *east* of the centre.

During the 1920s, however, the centre had begun to shift to the west, rather in the way that, at a less feverish pace, the centre of London had shifted in the early nineteenth century. What had been the 'west end', the area around the Tiergarten, became the 'old west end' as a 'new west end' established itself around the Kurfür-stendamm and the Kaiser Wilhelm Memorial Church (built in 1895 and standing, as its gaunt ruins still do, at the meeting point of six busy streets). The central area now extended itself as far west as the Schloss Charlottenburg, and the Kurfürstendamm ('Ku'damm') developed from a residential street to the brightly lit string of smart shops, cafés, restaurants, cinemas and theatres that it still is. The Zoo Bahnhof (main railway station opposite the Zoological Gardens) became and has remained a favourite centre for rendez-vous and sexual encounters as well as arrivals from and departures to distant cities.

Legislation at the beginning of the decade had created a brand-new municipality of Greater Berlin by adding to the old city seven towns, 52 rural communities and 27 landed estates, and the second half of the 1920s saw the city assuming a new status, and to some extent a new identity, through building and entrepreneurial and technological activity on an unprecedented scale. It quickly became, for instance, an international conference and exhibition centre, with a major radio exhibition in 1924 and an agricultural exhibition in 1926. The Radio Tower, operational from 1926, was described by an official guide in a striking piece of self-conscious symbol-making as 'a masterpiece of modern technology and the symbol of New Berlin'. With the extensive construction of docks during the same period, Berlin became Germany's second largest river port, while the Rummelsberg Power Station, built in the mid-1920s, was the most modern in Europe. The city's largest department store, the Karstadt in Hermannplatz (destroyed in the Second World War), opened its doors in 1929.

Public, commercial and private buildings reflected (and some surviving specimens still reflect) Berlin's growing reputation as the centre of the modern movement in architecture, and thanks to the work of Gropius, Häring, Mendelsohn and others it became 'the uncontested centre of all the most progressive developments in contemporary architecture'. The chronic housing shortage was tackled with the building of new estates and the provision of parks and sports facilities: in 1930 alone, 44,000 new homes were constructed. In 1929 Walter Gropius designed apartment blocks on innovative lines for Siemenstadt, an estate housing employees of the giant Siemens electrical firm.

Martin Wagner, who was in charge of the city's planning department, was responsible for the Wannsee resort, where Auden and Isherwood used to swim and sunbathe. In *Christopher and his Kind* (p. 39) Isherwood relates that he and his lover Otto went to swim in 'the great lake at Wannsee'. This lakeside resort had been established in 1907 and became very popular after its beach was artificially extended in 1929–30. A photograph taken in 1932 shows a large and crowded terrace café with the beach and lake edge full of bathers beyond it, and a view of pine-woods and low hills on the opposite side of the lake. They also visited Luna Park, which is mentioned in both Auden's journal and Isherwood's autobiography. This was a huge and popular leisure complex on the Halensee, on the edge of the Grunewald. Dating from 1904, it had become Berlin's largest amusement park, with attractions that ranged from Expressionist sculptures to a swimming pool with artificial waves. During a visit there on 26 April 1929, Auden was greatly struck by the nonchalance of a eunuch in the showers; it seemed to him an instance of genuine courage that he contrasted with the show-off antics of some of the swimmers.

The public transport system, coordinated by the formation of the Berlin Transport Joint-Stock Company in 1929, was of a high standard. By the mid-1920s the city's rail network covered

53 kilometres, and there was about the same amount of U-Bahn and S-Bahn (roughly, subway and overhead railway) lines, as well as some seventy tramlines and twenty bus routes. Like W. P. Frith celebrating in oils the nineteenth-century railway boom, German artists of the period turned their attention to what the Victorians liked to call the romance of transport. Among the paintings in the Berlin Museum are Jakob Steinhardt's 'Joachimsthaler Strasse und Bahnhof Zoo' (1925) and Albert Birkle's 'S-Bahnhof Berlin-Tiergarten' (1926–7) – the equivalent, say, of titling a painting 'Euston Road and King's Cross' or 'Green Park Underground Station'. All of this implies a busy, bustling city, and Berliners, like Londoners and New Yorkers, had the reputation of being brash, aggressive, dynamic and no respecters of persons.

In the autumn of 1928, at precisely the time of Auden's arrival in Berlin, the electricity companies launched a campaign to turn the city into a *ville lumière* or city of lights that would rival Paris, and Bertolt Brecht and Kurt Weill were commissioned to write a song to publicise this endeavour. According to John Willett's valuable study *The Theatre of the Weimar Republic*, 'the capital now saw an influx of major talents. . . . the attraction of Berlin for composers and conductors was perhaps stronger than for any other class of artist, for it was above all else the city's musical life that most felt the effects of the boom'. Arnold Schönberg had arrived in 1926, Paul Hindemith came soon afterwards, while from 1925 Igor Stravinsky (later one of Auden's operatic collaborators) had made it the principal location for performances of his works. A photograph of 1930 shows five great conductors – Bruno Walter, Arturo Toscanini, Josef Kleiber, Otto Klemperer and Wilhelm Furtwängler – and few cities in the world at that time can have been capable of bringing together such an array of interpretative talent and fame.

Willett's account makes it clear that the theatre, too, flourished on all levels, from productions of German and international classics in the numerous state and private theatres (in 1931 there were 36 theatres with a seating capacity of 43,000) to shows aimed partly at the tourist trade with titles like *Get Undressed* and *Donnerwetter – 1000 Women*. On 7 July 1926 the *Berliner Tageblatt* had reported that nine theatres were devoted to revues and attracted nightly audiences of some 11,000. In the month in which Auden arrived, Max Reinhardt's production of Shakespeare's *Romeo and Juliet* opened, as did Stravinsky's *Histoire du Soldat*, and in the next few months anyone living in Berlin could have seen, among much else, plays by Sophocles, Goethe, Shaw, Maugham, O'Neill and Cocteau. Diaghilev's ballet paid the city a visit in June 1929. This was the age of Hermann Hesse, Thomas Mann and Rainer Maria Rilke; of Georg Grosz and Otto Dix; of Kurt Weill's collaborations with Brecht and Kaiser; of *The Blue Angel*, *All Quiet on the Western Front* and *The Threepenny Opera*. Klemperer was musical director of the Staatsoper and Einstein ran the Kaiser Wilhelm Institute for Physics. As some of the dates already cited indicate, the two young Englishmen came to Berlin when many of the visible symbols of its modernity and prosperity still had the gloss of newness upon them, though the brief period of boom was already past, and the economic crisis at the end of the decade and the political developments that quickly followed were soon to inaugurate a darker era.

HOMES AND HAUNTS

The temporary homes occupied by Auden and Isherwood during their residence in Berlin took them to several parts of the city, ranging from affluent bourgeois graciousness to working-class slum, for periods that varied from a few weeks to more than two years. Auden's first lodging was in the Potsdamer Chaussée, in the suburb of Nikolassee, situated in the beautiful area of lakes and woodland in southwest Berlin. It lies at the southeast end of the long, narrow Havel lake and is handy for the Wannsee Strandbad, a very popular sandy beach a kilometre long whose popularity has already been mentioned. This was both the least central and by far the grandest Berlin house that either of them was to live in – so grand, indeed, that some such genteelism as 'paying guest' seems to be required. For Auden found himself in the imposing home of a prominent and gifted family, and an account of Anna Muthesius, her husband and the house he designed for his family will be given in the next chapter. It was, however, not quite what Auden had come to Berlin to find, and he stayed there for only a few weeks.

From there he moved, at the very beginning of 1929, geographically centrewards and socially downwards, to 8 Furbringerstrasse in the working-class district of Hallesches Tor. This neighbourhood lies at the south end of the major north–south route of the Friedrichstrasse, and in Auden's day there stood, just to the northwest, the magnificent pile of the Anhalter Bahnhof, a mainline station completed in 1870, spared by bombs in the Second World War, but a victim to postwar speculators. It was blown up, for its bricks, in 1952, though its evocative ruins can still be seen across a car park. Auden went there on at least one occasion, to see his brother John off for Vienna after he had briefly visited him in Berlin; as we have seen already, it was an occasion memorable for the words not spoken, the opportunities missed.

Though the neighbourhood of Hallesches Tor has changed much more drastically than the affluent and carefully preserved *rus in urbe* of the Nikolassee, this house too still stands. It lies in the West Kreuzberg district, in what was then the southwest quarter of the central area of the city, and was remembered by Stephen Spender as 'an area of slum tenements'. A stroll round the neighbourhood today, beginning from the U-Bahn station that Auden must often have used, shows that it has gone up in the world and become busier and noisier in the process. The canal and the overhead railway now divide a six-lane throughway with thundering traffic, and around the station, instead of slum tenements, there are modern highrises surrounding public gardens, a public library and other municipal buildings, together with the cosmopolitan and polyglot trappings (a coiffeur, a pizzeria) of affluent modern life.

Just to the east of the station stands the unignorable landmark of a domed red-brick church resembling a Congregational chapel that has got out of hand, and from this point Zossenerstrasse runs south. This too is now a busy traffic route, but to turn left into Furbringerstrasse, where Auden lived, is to be at once in a quieter world. Number 8, on the right, is a five-storey apartment building that, like most of the houses in the street, has been refaced, but number 28, exactly opposite, has its original facade and conveys a very good impression of what the whole street must have looked like in 1929. Despite the chipped and broken, pitted and scarred stonework, as ravaged and discoloured by time as Auden's own face later became, there are still vestiges of the original baroque splendour in the balustrades and the pediments over the tall windows, and the huge wooden doors are elaborately carved. The faded letters of the word 'Kurzwaren' (haberdashery) can still be read above the ground-floor windows, a reminder that the old Berlin houses characteristically had shops or workshops on the street-level and apartments or *pensions* above. If he cared to, or was in a condition to, raise his head, Auden must have seen this facade every time he left his lodgings during the months he lived in Furbringerstrasse.

Returning to Zossenerstrasse and crossing the now busy street, one finds these days a group of commercial premises with (according to custom) the shared number 7: a *Zahnärztin* or lady dentist, a unisex hairdresser, an agency specialising in 'alternative' bus tours and, on the corner, a boutique stocking obviously expensive ladies' wear. Here, in the days when the entire neighbourhood was considerably scruffier, stood the Cosy Corner. This was the rent-bar that assumes almost mythological status in *Christopher and his Kind*, where Isherwood's account (already cited) of his first visit in March 1929 takes on the air of an excursion to the underworld with Auden as his Virgil, and his pushing aside of the heavy leather curtain across the door seems to enact some arcane and hazardous ritual of rebirth. Oddly enough, the opposite side of the street has not shared its partner's transformation: a working-class café-bar, a tiny second-hand bookshop with stock tumbled into the window, a junk shop with the castoffs of other people's lives heaped in laundry baskets and dumped on the pavement – all these, in complete contrast to the modish establishments across the street, seem still to belong to the world in which Auden lived.

The Cosy Corner was no more than a minute's walk from the door of the house where he lodged, a convenient distance in bad weather, or late at night, or with a companion for whom time was money (and money was also money), or when remaining vertical presented difficulties. Presided over by Auden's tolerant landlady, Frau Günther (listed, with her husband, in a directory of the period), the lodging-house in Furbringerstrasse was also a location vastly more suited to his requirements than the handsome suburban home of the Muthesius family. It remained his base until he left Berlin. From his room it was no more than a few minutes' walk, past a graveyard and across the canal, to the U-Bahn station that gave him access to other parts of the city. I was there on a winter morning when, after an overnight snowfall, workmen were scattering sand on the paths by the canal just as they no doubt did in the early months of 1929 – for, although the most familiar images, verbal and photographic, of Auden and Isherwood's Germany are of a land permanently bathed in sunshine in which the normal costume was a swimming costume, Berlin can have a ferociously cold winter.

Where Isherwood stayed on that first visit to Berlin in March 1929 is not known, but it seems likely that he shared Auden's room (they were at any rate intermittent lovers), or perhaps found another room in the same house. By the time he returned to the city in November, Auden had gone home, and Isherwood's first step was to contact the only Englishman he knew in Berlin, Francis Turville-Petre, whose strange life and career will shortly be recounted. Francis's rooms were in 9A In den Zelten, a fashionable street lying between the northeastern corner of the Tiergarten (then a little less extensive at that end than it is today) and the banks of the River Spree, and not far from the Reichstag and the Brandenburg Gate. Although there is still a street bearing the name In den Zelten, not the slightest trace remains of what must once have been a busy and prosperous area, partly residential, partly commercial. Instead, lawns and trees surround an earnest-looking new complex of buildings dedicated to the official promotion of culture.

The neighbourhood had traditionally been a place to which Berliners could escape for relaxation and a breath of fresh air – the name means 'In the Tents', presumably with reference to stalls originally providing food, drink and entertainment – and in the 1920s it still contained many restaurants and an opera house that was to accommodate the German parliament after the burning of the Reichstag in 1933. In *Christopher and his Kind* (p. 32) Isherwood describes a Christmas ball held at 'one of the dance-halls' in the street, a fancy-dress occasion exclusively for men, some of whom wore female attire. In those days the street lay just outside the green and wooded spaces of the Tiergarten, which was extended during the 1950s after the wartime bombing of adjacent built-up areas. As well as being a pleasure-resort, In den Zelten seems in the 1920s to have become something of a writers' and artists' colony. Two expatriate American writers who lived there were Robert McAlmon at number 18 and Djuna Barnes next door.

Possibly, indeed, it had had this reputation even in the nineteenth century, for the famous Hungarian violinist Joseph Joachim, director of the Berlin Conservatory and a friend of Brahms, had lived at number 10. Long before Isherwood's arrival, Magnus Hirschfeld (see next chapter) had established his Institute for Sexual Research in Joachim's former home, a large house on the corner of In den Zelten and Beethovenstrasse. Hirschfeld had also acquired the neighbouring property (9A), had had communicating doors built between the two houses, and had turned the ground floor of 9A into a lecture hall. On the floor immediately above were apartments for the resident medical staff; above that were guest rooms, in which Christopher and Francis lived; and on the top floor were rooms or cells for the accommodation or confinement of those awaiting trial for alleged sexual offences. For it seems that among the Institute's many roles was that of a kind of refuge or sanctuary for offenders of this kind, the police permitting Hirschfeld to assume responsibility for them while they lived under his roof. Contemporary photographs and drawings show Hirschfeld's premises to have been very extensive: the main house is a splendid mansion on a corner site, while 9A, with its five main floors, attics and semi-basement, was on a smaller scale though slightly taller.

Isherwood's room, looking down into a courtyard, was 'dark and cheap'; Francis, who was not short of money, had two rooms that afforded a view of the park. Isherwood spent nearly a year in In den Zelten; although visits to his favourite working-class bars must have involved a journey, it was a good spot for a writer, far from dull but away from the hurly-burly of the city centre. It was there that he worked on the third draft of *The Memorial*, there that he made love to 'Otto', and perhaps there that Auden stayed when he visited his friend in June and July 1930. It may have been their conversations about Francis at this time that led Auden to begin his play *The Fronny* very soon after returning from Berlin.

After leaving the Hirschfeld establishment, possibly for financial reasons, in October 1930, Isherwood occupied two lodgings in quick succession, each for only a few weeks, for by December he was installed in Nollendorfstrasse, where he was to remain until the time came for him to leave Berlin. The two working-class neighbourhoods in which he briefly dwelt have both been swept away by the destruction and rebuilding of the last sixty years. Simeonstrasse, where he lodged at number 4 with the family of his lover Otto, was in the Hallesches Tor district, like Auden's second home in Berlin, but seems to have vanished without trace. In *Goodbye to Berlin* it is renamed Wassertorstrasse, a name that means Watergate Street and was rather surprisingly deemed by its inventor to sound 'more romantic' (*Christopher and his Kind*, p. 43). Admiralstrasse, in the Kottbusser Tor district, where he stayed briefly in November, still exists but has been wholly reconstructed, and there seems to be no sign of number 38.

The Nollendorfstrasse house, however, not only stands but is the only one of the buildings associated with Auden or Isherwood to have received official recognition. Outside number 17, on the north side of the street, is a plaque recording, with more enthusiasm than reliability, that Isherwood lived there from March 1929 to January/February 1933, and identifying him (probably not much to the gratification of his ghost) as the author of the Berlin stories and the inspirer of the musical *Cabaret*. (His residence there began, of course, nearly two years later than stated.) The pre-1914 house itself, on which the corresponding building in the Berlin stories was closely modelled, has a reconstructed facade, though the exterior of number 16 next door gives a better impression of what it must once have looked like. Inside, however, it retains a good deal of the atmosphere it must have possessed when Isherwood pushed open the very heavy doors and climbed the wide staircase, with its massive wooden handrails and banisters and its stained-glass windows on the landings. The rooms have wide doors and high ceilings with elaborate plasterwork; the apartment I was able to visit still possesses a massive tiled stove in one corner, just as in the description of Fräulein Schroeder's flat at the beginning of *Goodbye to Berlin*.

The street, less narrow today than the description at the beginning of *Goodbye to Berlin* leads one to expect, and now tree-lined, has been extensively rebuilt. Like so many other streets and neighbourhoods, it seems to have gone up in the world, and the epithet 'sordid', which Spender applies to it in a rather obscure passage of his autobiography, is now far from applicable to this street of neat small businesses and middle-class homes. In any case, however, Spender's memory may have been at fault and the epithet never have been merited, for Isherwood describes his move there as a move from a working-class to a middle-class neighbourhood: though 'neither elegant nor in good repair', the street was 'middle-class-shabby' rather than 'slum-shabby'. In an earlier generation, the houses, again, followed the traditional pattern of devoting their semi-basements to shops or workrooms (Isherwood refers to them as 'cellar-shops'). Number 17 has five storeys above its semi-basement, the top two of which apparently comprised the *pension* run by Fräulein Thurau, the 'original' of Fräulein Schroeder. If one walks east to the end of the street and crosses the busy Moetzen-strasse to the street opposite, what is now a pedestrian precinct gives a better idea of how the house fronts of the neighbourhood, tall and elegant (and these days generously spray-painted), must formerly have appeared.

Nollendorfstrasse is only a couple of minutes' walk from Nollendorfplatz, the hub of the main routes in that part of the city and the centre of Isherwood's fictional microcosm. Spender describes it in his autobiography as having been 'a grand-shabby square dominated by a station of the overhead railway'. It is today neither shabby nor grand, merely unremarkable. What must have been, especially at night, a very animated scene – it was a favourite resort for homosexuals, and there are said to have been some forty gay bars in the immediate neighbourhood – is now decorously quiet to the point of featurelessness. The cleaning-up of Nollendorfplatz, however, which began as soon as the Nazis came to power, invoked the usual Law of Minimum Displacement of Offending Entities. For in the course of more than sixty years the centre of activity appears to have moved no more than a block or two west – a remarkable testimony to the vitality and continuity of a subculture and the deep attachment it can form to a particular neighbourhood.

Two large-scale reminders of the period have survived these changes. The overhead railway mentioned by Spender still bisects the square. He and Isherwood would have been familiar too with the station entrance beneath it, now a good deal the worse for wear but fresh and bright when Isherwood lived nearby, for it had been built in 1925–6. And on the south side, turning its massive back on the more modest rears of the Nollendorfstrasse houses and presenting a bold, greyish-white, architecturally eclectic front to the square, is the Metropol, though that has not always been its name. Built in 1906, within recent memory a 'porno kino' and now a venue for discos and rock concerts, this was one of the most important of Berlin's theatres in the period with which we are concerned. (In *Christopher and his Kind* Isherwood seems by an odd lapse of memory to refer to it as a cinema.) It opened as the Theater am Nollendorfplatz in 1921, and, as a plaque informs us, Erwin Piscator was Regisseur and Theaterdeiter there in 1927–31. Piscator attracted a constellation of talents to his theatre, and under his direction it played an important role in the development of political and documentary theatre. Asked in a 1961 interview whether Weimar theatre was politically aware, Isherwood replied that it was 'intensely aware' and added that the Theater am Nollendorfplatz was '*entirely* political'.

There is also a third and much less obtrusive reminder of the past in the shape of a small triangular plaque of pink, or at least reddish, marble. This was placed in Nollendorfplatz a few years ago in memory of the victims of the Nazi persecution of homosexuals. Its siting is a reminder of the reputation enjoyed by that neighbourhood in the years before 1933, and a no doubt less conscious acknowledgement of a still vital subculture in the nearby streets. Mounted on a wall near the entrance to the U-Bahn station, just beneath the raised tracks that Spender recalled, its shape and colour allude to the 'Rosa Winkel' or pink triangle that homosexuals imprisoned in the concentration camps were compelled to wear as a stigmatising badge, and its inscription declares laconically:

> Tot Geschlagen
> Tot Geschwiegen
> den
> Homosexuelle Opfern
> des
> Nationalsozializmus
> (Murdered and silenced, the homosexual victims of
> National Socialism).

Beneath, a plaque states that it was in January 1933 that the Nazis began to shut down the gay bars in the square. That was, of course, just two or three months before Isherwood began his own preparations to move out of his home nearby, out of Berlin, out of Germany.

The neighbourhood of Nollendorfplatz has never been the centre of the city, but in Isherwood's fiction it is the point where excursions to other parts of Berlin begin and end. It is perfectly true, though, that it was conveniently situated as a base, lying as it does roughly halfway between the West End and Kurfürstendamm area to the west and the Unter den Linden and Friedrichstrasse area to the east. If one walked northwest from the Platz, one quickly reached (as one still does) the vast expanse of Wittenbergplatz, with the imitation Greek temple (1911–13) that is the entrance to its subway station, and, on the corner, the huge KaDeWe department store (1906–7, rebuilt 1950). From the north side of Wittenbergplatz there was in Isherwood's time a fine view along the broad Tauentzienstrasse, with tramlines down the middle and motor traffic on either side, towards the Memorial Church, looking in contemporary photographs strangely intact to anyone familiar with the present-day ruin. The Lady Windermere, the smartish bar where Jean Ross worked, was just off the Tauentzienstrasse. Another ten minutes' walk brought one to the Zoo Station, so often mentioned in writings of the period by Isherwood and others. Motzstrasse, which ran and runs southwest from Nollendorf-platz, was where Spender lived while he was in Berlin, and his autobiography contains an evocative description of his short journey to visit Isherwood. He would, he recalls,

walk past... grey houses whose facades seemed out of moulds made for pressing enormous concrete biscuits. Then I would come to the Nollendorfplatz, an eyrie of concrete eagles, with verandas like breasts shedding stony flakes of whatever glory they once had into the grime of soot which caked this part of Berlin....   (*World Within World*, p. 121)

Spender's retrospective account makes the whole neighbourhood seem considerably less attractive than it appears in Isherwood's fiction: grubbier, smellier, slipping below the faint line that distinguishes respectable poverty from slum-dwelling. One is left with the choice of believing the fiction that is much closer to the event or the non-fiction that may reflect the process of slow revision to which memory subjects experience, and my own inclination is to believe Isherwood.

All cities, Isherwood's or Spender's Berlin as much as Defoe's or Dickens's or Virginia Woolf's London, are reinvented when they are appropriated by writers, and when the writer is a visitor, like Hemingway or Orwell in Paris, invention is made so much the simpler. Entire facets of the real city can be disregarded, while selected sites can assume symbolic or mythological status. A nice example of this occurs in Spender's autobiography, in which the third chapter begins: 'At the side of a lake there is a city...' The fact is that Hamburg has two dominant physical features, a river and a lake, but it suits Spender, in his account of the time he spent there, to ignore the Elbe and turn the Alster into the symbolic heart of the city. The river, with its docks and adjacent working-class neighbourhoods, represents labour, economic life, domesticity and responsibility, while the Alster is a lotus-eaters' land of swimming, sunbathing and sexual opportunity – or at least it suited Spender to pretend so. Rivers remind us that they have come from elsewhere and are moving on to yet other places, carrying people and objects with them; lakes leave us in peace as if time had ceased to exist. So

Spender's redrawing of the map of Hamburg serves an obvious purpose, but his Hamburg is a subjective city that we can visit only in the text that enshrines it. Much more than Hamburg, and more than most cities, Berlin seems always to have lent itself readily to conversion into symbol. Apart from the writings with which this study is centrally concerned, it has generated a large number of works in literary and other media that have a topographical starting-point. In our immediate period, for instance, there are the films *Berlin, die Symphonie einer Grosstadt* (*Berlin, the Symphony of a Great City*, 1927), a dawn-to-dusk evocation of the life of the capital; *Asphalt* (1929), which appeared while Auden was living in the city and which he had intended to see on the day he met Gerhart; and *Berlin – Alexanderplatz* (1931), based on the 1929 novel by Alfred Döblin. A painterly analogue to these 'city' films is Otto Dix's triptych *Big City* (1927–8).

Individual sites and buildings acquired and sometimes retained symbolic potency. Very soon, the arson attack on the Reichstag was to be seen as an attempt to destroy not just a building but German parliamentary democracy, and the ruined Reichstag was turned into a symbol of great propagandist power – and not only by the Nazis, for in 1945, as the Russians advanced on Berlin, their objective was the Reichstag, a ruin since 1933, furnishing an extraordinary instance of a vast military machine directed at a symbol. One of the most potent photographic records of the period shows a Soviet soldier attaching a flag to one of its towers, thereby proclaiming the fall of Berlin. Today, or rather tomorrow, the rebuilding of the Reichstag (to designs by a British architect), following Berlin's regaining of its capital status, will render it, according to *The Times* (6 December 1994), 'a symbol of democracy rather than German power'. Nearby, in the postwar years, the Wall, Checkpoint Charlie and the Brandenburg Gate became part of the mental landscape of millions who had never visited the city, and not the least potent element in the worldwide reaction to the coming down of the Wall was the fact that a symbol was being dismantled before our very eyes. But symbols are not lightly discarded by a symbol-haunted generation, and a Checkpoint Charlie Museum now stands on the site of the former crossing from East to West.

Another piece of official symbol-making, launched into the world by the postcards of a million tourists, is the ruined Kaiser Wilhelm Memorial Church in the very heart of Berlin, its snapped-off spire as evocative of past splendour and violent destruction as the 'bare ruined choirs' of an English abbey. And as I was collecting material for this book the continuing political power of a symbol was demonstrated by the suggestion (*The Times*, 30 August 1993) that one of the reasons why Berlin would fail to win the 2000 Olympic Games. (as, despite a vigorous and costly campaign, it did) was the existence in a northwestern suburb of the 1936 Stadium – or, more precisely, the association of that building and that event with the Nazis. To visit the Stadium today – so massive, silent and ghost-ridden – would be like visiting a grave-yard no longer open for business, were it not that for anyone who has ever seen Leni Riefenstahl's *Olympia* (1938), given its première on Hitler's birthday, the place is forever inseparable from the images created by that work. In such ways do topography, history and art collaborate.

In his Berlin stories, Isherwood is a topographical as well as a historical novelist. Place-names abound, and it is as easy to trace the movements of his characters on a contemporary map of the city as it is to trace Moll Flanders' wanderings on a map of early eighteenth-century London. In *Mr Norris Changes Trains*, for instance, Norris's flat is in Courbierestrasse, only a short walk from Nollendorfplatz, and the narrator meets him 'by appointment in a small restaurant near the Memorial Church'. Bayer's flat is in Zimmerstrasse, which cuts across Friedrichstrasse and was later the site of Checkpoint Charlie, and his office is in Wilhelmstrasse. The Communist meeting that Norris addresses is held in the district of Neukölln, and a Nazi *Lokal* is placed in Kreuzberg, now very largely occupied by Turkish and other immigrants but then a working-class district where Auden had lodged. After the narrator has first met Norris on a train journey they part on arrival at the Zoo Station, and when he later leaves for England Norris is seen off from the same station, from where Kuno later vainly tries to make his escape. Returning from England, Norris rides in a taxi along 'the dear old Tauentzienstrasse' to his lodgings in Nollendorf-strasse.

Yet this is, after all, the art of the illusionist, and the Berlin that finds embodiment in the work of Isherwood and others is a very personal construct, a carefully modified version of the city they lived in. Certain places, people and events are given prominence, sometimes a symbolic prominence, while others find no place on the maps they draw or in the semi-documentary accounts they give

– for this is true not just of topography but of all aspects of the city's life and history. At the outset, Isherwood and his friends brought with them an image of Berlin that bore only a limited relationship to reality: already there was a darker and grimmer side to the city that seemed to them to extend the bright promise of enlightened tolerance and unrestricted freedom. To cite only a single, though a major, instance: unemployment in Berlin was in 1927 already running twice as high as in the country as a whole, and matters rapidly got worse, so that by the winter of 1929–30, during which Isherwood took up residence, unemployment and hardship were widespread. Many of the 'boys' who were so readily and delightfully available in the Cosy Corner formed part of the statistics, and one of the interests offered by Isherwood's fiction is the balance it strikes, and the compromises and evasions it effects, between a romantic and sentimental *Bildungsroman* and a historically grounded reflection of realities that it became daily harder to ignore.

CULTURES AND SUBCULTURES

Periods of strife and turbulence, as Abraham Cowley pointed out long ago and Harry Lime more recently, are unpleasant to live through but do wonders for the creative arts – and not only the arts. The Weimar Republic was no exception. Defeat, civil war, mass unemployment, stratospheric inflation, then, after a brief interval of prosperity, more economic troubles following the Wall Street Crash, and the tensions and bloodshed that accompanied the rise to power of the Nazis: any German who lived through this decade and a half might well have felt that he or she had supped full of horrors. It was, however, during the same years that Berlin became a centre of innovation and influence across a wide field of artistic, scientific and technological activity – from theatre to photography, from architecture to psychoanalysis, from sexology (Hirschfeld's researches anticipating the later endeavours of Kinsey and Masters and Johnson) to television (the first transmission was made in 1929).

It was as though the political, social and economic collapse that followed military defeat had a liberating effect on art and thought, long-established conventions in the pure and applied arts collapsing along with so much else, including fixed incomes and sexual mores. But the transformation, it goes without saying, was not complete: probably such transformations never are. The old imperial apparatus of power as personified by judges, civil servants and professors to a large extent survived in the new republic. Peter Gay has also argued in his *Weimar Culture: The Outsider as Insider* that although the prevailing tone of Imperial Germany had been conservative and anti-modernist, the modernist opposition – as exemplified, for example, by Expressionism – had in fact begun to flourish during that epoch, and to this extent what has come to be regarded as the Weimar style actually predates the Republic.

In the interwar period Berlin, as we have seen already, became a cosmopolitan city, and Weimar culture has in many of its manifestations the flavour of international modernism. Much of it, however, grew directly out of a highly specific social world at a particular moment of its history. That world and that moment are conveyed to us by some of the enduring cultural artefacts of the age: products, one would add, of high and low, serious and popular culture, if it were not in the nature of Weimar art to blur, challenge and override such traditional distinctions and hierarchies. An artist like Grosz, a dramatist like Brecht, a composer like Weill, all drew on popular sources as surely as media created by new technologies such as photojournalism and cinema offered their mass audiences authentic artworks.

Kurt Weill's career is in many respects paradigmatic. Born in Dessau in 1900, he came to Berlin in 1918 to study composition with Busoni. He was a precocious student whose early works were in the traditional forms: a string quartet (1919), a cello sonata (1920), a symphony (1921). But in 1922 he began to write for the theatre, and from 1926 his collaborations with the dramatists Kaiser and Brecht resulted in a prolific and brilliant seven-year period that ended when he fled from Nazi Germany (he was Jewish) early in 1933.

With Kaiser he produced a one-act opera *Der Protagonist* (1926) and, at the end of his Berlin period, *Der Silbersee* (1933). The latter, his last work for the German theatre, was written after a quarrel with Brecht, who dubbed him (with gross unfairness) 'a phony Richard Strauss'. But it is for his collaborations with Brecht that he is primarily remembered, and between them they were responsible for six works for the theatre, three cantatas and other works. Their greatest success was *Die Dreigroschenoper* (*The Threepenny Opera*, 1928), which was quickly translated into 18 languages, had over 10,000 performances in a period of five years and reached a still wider public through Pabst's 1931 film adaptation, which has become one of the classics of the German cinema. Other notable Brecht/Weill collaborations included *Happy End* (1929) and *Mahagonny* (1930).

After both Brecht and Weill had left Berlin and a few months after the Weimar Republic had ceased to exist, they were briefly reunited in Paris in the summer of 1933 and, their quarrel patched up, the two produced *Die Sieben Todsünden* (*The Seven Deadly Sins*). It was to be their last collaboration, for after settling in America Weill declined Brecht's invitations to work with him again: he himself began a new career, and a highly successful one, composing Broadway musicals. The music of this final period, terminated by his untimely death in 1950, is of a quality that matches the deft and sparkling lyrics of the carefully chosen writers who worked with him, including Ogden Nash and Ira Gershwin, though it substitutes a cheerful optimism for the indignation and protest of the Berlin years, a melodious sweetness for the uncompromisingly harsh, spiky, angular music he wrote to Brecht's words.

Die Sieben Todsünden received its first performance in June 1933 at the Théâtre des Champs-Elysées. Although not strictly a product of Weimar Berlin it is worth considering as a work impossible to fit into any accepted generic category but one of great musical and dramatic power. It was the outcome of a commission for a ballet; what resulted, however, was a mixture of ballet, opera, morality play and fairy tale. Brecht wrote the text, George Balanchine did the choreography and Caspar Neher the décor, while Tillie Losch was the prima ballerina (if that classical term is appropriate to this highly innovative work) and Lotte Lenya, the composer's wife, created the role of Anna.

Or the roles: for Anna is a pair of Siamese twins with the same name, sharing (as a line of Brecht's laconic and acidulous text points out) the same heart and the same savings-bank passbook. In the course of the work, they travel the length and breadth of America in quest of money to build a house in Louisiana (a third Anna/ana) where their family can live happily ever after, and in the course of their wanderings from city to city they encounter in contemporary American life a series of situations exemplifying the seven deadly sins.

The America is that of the earlier *Mahagonny*, half real, half mythical, and the two Annas represent two sides of female, or perhaps human, nature: one is serious, thoughtful and sensible, the other prettier, more impulsive and emotional. They react differently to the seven situations, the former expressing herself through song, the latter through dance. There is also a male vocal quartet representing their family.

Lotte Lenya's vocal style was highly distinctive and created a tradition, still very much alive (in, for example, the performances of Ute Lemper and Teresa Stratas), for the interpretation of Weill's work. The singing often turns momentarily into declamation, and the words are enunciated with great distinctness, in recognition of their parity of importance with the music, while that music incorporates a variety of popular styles ranging from jazz and the cabaret song to the Viennese waltz and the military march. Weill's aim to create a modern international folk music involved the use of popular forms, dance rhythms and instrumentation closer to that of the jazz band than the symphony orchestra. This was a style that had reached its maturity in the Berlin collaborations with Brecht but had already established itself before those collaborations began.

I have begun at the end of Weill's European career, but he was at the time a brand-new refugee and *Die Sieben Todsünden* represents a continuation not only of the partnership with Brecht but of the style defined during the brief brilliant Berlin years. This was a partnership of youth (Weill was only 27 when he met Brecht in the spring of 1927, Brecht only two years older), and one in which not only accepted forms but the very nature of theatrical experience were being questioned and subverted. Highly characteristic is the crossing of generic frontiers or merging of modes traditionally kept separate – by introducing, for instance, song into ballet or drama so as to create a popular opera form. Characteristic, too, is the use of the bizarre and the grotesque for purposes of social criticism: like some of the drawings of Grosz, *Die Sieben Todsünden* evokes a fantasy world that nevertheless bears a disturbing relationship to the real world, and in the process exposes the latter as ugly, greedy, mercenary, unjust and cruel.

Die Dreigroschenoper in particular has often been seen as having a representative quality, of embodying the Zeitgeist. It was the second of the Brecht/Weill collaborations (the first, the singspiel *Mahagonny*, later forming the basis of a full-scale opera). It opened on 31 August 1928 at the Theater am Schiffbauerdamm in Berlin, and was an immediate success with the public, though it was also, predictably, the target of savage critical attacks. Auden, who arrived in Berlin soon after its première, went to see it shortly afterwards. Its reworking of the eighteenth-century English *Beggar's Opera* meant that its origins were both popular and international, and recordings of early performances show how readily it absorbed the jazz idiom of its period while putting all these elements to the service of contemporary political satire. It is hard to believe that Auden did not remember his attendance at the first production of *Die Dreigroschenoper* when, a generation later, he collaborated with Stravinsky on *The Rake's Progress*.

In their youthfulness, their willingness to conduct experiments that involved a rejection of traditional forms and modes, and the collaborative nature of their art, Weill and Brecht were not only representative of Weimar art as a whole but suggestively similar to two other young collaborators, Auden and Isherwood. Auden's plays (three of them written in partnership with Isherwood) and the many poems that represent pastiches of ballads, cabaret songs or graffiti draw zestfully on popular sources in defiance of traditional hierarchies of the 'serious' and the 'light'. It comes as no surprise to learn that during the 1930s Auden not only edited the *Oxford Book of Light Verse* but co-edited (with John Garrett) a highly eclectic anthology of verse, *The Poet's Tongue*, in the introduction to which poetry is defined as 'memorable speech'. Weimar culture favoured the collaborative arts such as cinema and theatre, and it may be no coincidence that Isherwood's fiction was much influenced by the cinema or that Auden devoted much of his creative energy first to theatre and film and later to opera.

Like Weill, Brecht was not a Berliner by origin, having come to the city from Bavaria. Born in Augsburg in 1898, he had studied medicine in Munich, spent much time in Berlin from 1922, and settled there in 1924. *Die Dreigroschenoper* was his first major success, marking the transition from his early dramatic work to *Lehrstücke* or didactic plays, and since he left Germany in 1933 his Berlin heyday lasted barely five years. His biographer Klaus Völker has vividly described the chaotic and near-disastrous rehearsals for *Die Dreigroschenoper*. The première, however, was a huge success and the play ran for nearly a year in Berlin. The choice of Gay's *Beggar's Opera* as a starting-point was not as unikely as it sounds, since the English play had been very successfully revived at the Lyric Theatre in London earlier in the decade.

Brecht's attack on bourgeois ideology and morality has its visual counterpart in the work of Georg Grosz (1893–1959) and Otto

Dix (1891–1969). On a wall of Berlin's splendid Neue National-galerie there hang today three paintings: two of Dix's portraits of successful men, in a violent, almost brutal and Goya-like style, and between them a satirical work by Grosz. The juxtaposition shows very clearly the difference between Dix's harsh realism and the more fantastic, even nightmarish vision of Grosz. The cynicism and misanthropy of the latter, though sometimes recalling Brecht in the exposure of the hollowness and sordidness of bourgeois civilisation, spring from more subjective and emotional origins. Grosz's autobiography tells of a childhood experience that reads like a grim parody of a Wordsworthian 'spot of time': gratuitously pushed into the mud by an older boy, he was granted a vision of 'ein tieferes Gesetz der Brutalität', a profound law of brutality. He had discovered that hell lay about him in his infancy. His depiction of drunkards, prostitutes and madmen owes its force, as Martin Kane has pointed out, to a deeply and incurably personal sense of human wickedness and degradation rather than to any clearly formulated political philosophy. Although he had joined the German Communist Party in December 1918, Grosz was characteristically to speak, through his paintings and drawings, from an individual sensibility rather than with a party voice.

Born in Berlin, he had studied art and then served in the war, suffering a nervous breakdown which led him to attack a hospital orderly and to attempt to desert. He suffered the Dostoevskian ordeal of being sentenced to death and then having the sentence commuted, followed by a period in a mental institution. He had never actually seen active service, hence his battlefield pictures are based on imagination rather than experience. The drawings in the series *Ecce Homo*, executed in 1920–2, evoke the 'brutal and depraved eroticism' (Kane, p. 53) of the bourgeoisie in postwar Germany and led to Grosz and his publisher being prosecuted for obscenity, They were found guilty and fined, while the plates were destroyed and unsold copies confiscated. In court Grosz declared that 'It is clear that my whole view of the world is in complete contrast to that of the State Prosecutor; it is radically more negative and sceptical.... When I behold the greater part of mankind, I see no beauties or delicate forms....' The Swiftian tone of his words is unmistakable, and his work has as close an affinity to the fourth book of *Gulliver's Travels* as *Die Dreigroschenoper* has to its eighteenth-century counterpart.

Grosz was in trouble again in 1928 for his collection of drawings *Hintergrund*, executed for Piscator's production of an adaptation of Hasek's novel *Der Gute Soldat Schweyk*. One of the drawings depicts a crucified Christ wearing army boots and a gas mask. After legal proceedings that dragged on for a couple of years, the charge of blasphemy was at last dropped, with costs being awarded to the defendants, and this outcome was hailed as a victory for the Left. By this date art had become inescapably political, and the trial was given wide publicity and regarded as a political rather than a moral or religious issue. Later Grosz, who fled Germany and reached New York a week before Hitler became Chancellor, found himself on the Nazi hit list. But the horror and revulsion so forcefully evident in his drawings remain very personal: like Swift, he is appalled not by systems but by humanity itself. He returned to Berlin from exile in 1959, just in time to drop dead in Savignyplatz.

What was true of artistic forms and conventions was also true of modes of thinking, feeling and behaving, and if Berlin was, in Robert McAlmon's phrase, 'a city of hyperbole', the life lived by some of its citizens and many of its visitors suggested at times a calculated effort to break with the past by casting off restraints – by going to extremes of personal conduct that matched both the extremes of creative innovation and the extremes of contemporary history.

As Von Eckardt and Gilman's survey of the period shows, the wild 'inflation' was not merely fiscal but extended to drink, dancing, drugs, sex and much else. Not everyone was willing or able to surrender themselves to a life of hedonism: there was large-scale poverty and misery, for this was a society that carried wretchedness as well as pleasure to extremes. As Klaus Mann puts it in his autobiography, for many people the years immediately following the defeat constituted a nightmare that caused violent shocks to their moral standards as well as their bank accounts – and Mann's grim zeugma seems the appropriate device to catch the spirit of the age.

Mann, who met Isherwood in 1931 and became a close friend (they later lived for a time in the same *pension* in Amsterdam), had arrived in Berlin in 1923, found it 'gorgeously corrupt', and 'had the time of my life'. Autobiographical hindsight, however, enabled him to do justice to the violent and absurd confusions of the postwar scene. Eating 'greasy borscht' in 'one of those Russian restaurants which then sprang up at every other corner', he reflects that the waitress could easily have been a Grand Duchess in exile, even 'a niece or cousin of the late Czarina', for Germany was not the only country to be living with the results of cataclysmic upheaval, Berlin was full of refugees, and in terms of the old social hierarchies chaos had come again. For Mann, Berlin was a place that absorbed and magnified whatever tendencies were scattered more thinly elsewhere, its hyperbolical wickedness a parodic equivalent to, and compensation for, Prussia's lost hyperbolical military might:

> Corruptible and always hankering for sensations, Berlin absorbed political and intellectual currents from everywhere. It was its function and force to organise whatever moods were floating throughout the land; to focus and dramatise the desires of a diffuse and inarticulate people. When the general vein was dashingly patriotic, the capital surpassed all other places in vociferous demonstrations. When the vogue was cynical-apocalyptic, Berlin did a great job in displaying misery and vices on a colossal scale.
>
> "Look at me!" blared the capital of the Reich. "I am Babel, the monster among cities! We had a formidable army: now we command the most riotously wicked night life. Don't miss our matchless show, ladies and gentlemen! It's Sodom and Gomorrah in a Prussian tempo. Don't miss the circus of perversities! Our department store of assorted vices! An all-out tale of brand new kinds of debauchery!"   (*The Turning-Point*, pp. 86–7)

For Mann, as for many others, economic disaster and moral collapse, inflation and debauchery, social confusion and sexual 'perversity', were all aspects of the same phenomenon.

One non-German in Berlin, Robert McAlmon, observed that the rate of exchange, so favourable to foreigners, attracted a horde of visitors and 'made for wildness':

> In spite of the poverty-stricken situation of the people there were several smart cafés and one futuristic dance place for tea dancing as well as for night encounters. Otherwise there were joints and dives of every order, and there was no telling whom one might encounter, anywhere. From Russia, Poland, the Balkan States, from Scandinavia, England, France, and South and North America, visitors flocked into Berlin, and even hardened

Berlin night-lifers could not tell with certainty how the tone or quality of any night club might change from week to week.... Dopes, mainly cocaine, were to be had in profusion at most night places. A deck of "snow", enough cocaine for quite too much excitement, cost the equivalent of ten cents. Poverty-stricken boys and girls of good German families sold it, and took it, as they congregated in the dreary night clubs for the warmth not available on the streets or in their homes, if they had homes....

If this social and moral climate entailed much individual misery, it also nourished an intellectual and artistic culture that made Berlin, for many who came from abroad, the natural successor to Paris as the place where Pound's injunction to 'make it new' was being most strenuously implemented. Hence, for example, the Romanische Café, situated opposite the Kaiser Wilhelm Memorial Church and a ten-minute walk from Isherwood's Nollendorfplatz, was 'comparable to the Café de Dome in Paris and the Café Central in Vienna':

It was filled, almost around the clock, with painters and art dealers, writers and publishers, journalists and editors, radio entertainers and broadcasting officials, musicians and conductors, actors and producers, dancers and choreographers, psychiatrists and divorce lawyers, bohemians of all kinds, who seemed to be lost, girls of all ages who hoped to be found, and a lot of cigarette smoke and stale air.

This mingling of painters, radio personalities, actors and the rest illustrates the close contacts between the 'serious', popular and performing arts, the readiness to cross traditional boundaries of taste, so characteristic of Weimar Berlin. And if it also sounds like a natural setting for Mr Norris and Sally Bowles (herself a performer), that may be a tribute to Isherwood's documentary skill.

Klaus Mann's first novel, *Der Fromme Tanz* (*The Pious Dance*, 1925), draws on his Berlin experiences at closer range than his autobiography. Its hero is a young artist, Andreas Magnus, who comes to the city from the provinces. He is both repelled and fascinated by the size and ugliness of the great capital, and descends into a grimy world of sordid lodgings as well as into the nightlife of cabarets and gay bars, hustlers and their well-dressed

clients, transvestites and cocaine addicts. The account of his nocturnal tour of such establishments with two companions has an
Orwell-like quality, if one can imagine Orwell having selected gay
bars instead of doss-houses for his sociological fieldwork:

> But how much bigger the city was by night, when it instantly
> enlarged into a gigantic blazing dream....
>   In the vicinity of the main streets, though at a decent remove,
> naturally, there was some of what they were seeking...: places
> where queerly heightened merriment prevailed and youths in
> alluring outfits tossed paper streamers into the air. With ladylike
> charm, the landlord, white, fat and heavily perfumed, would
> shout out a welcome to them. The young gentlemen would
> burst into shrill notes of rejoicing whenever such old acquaint-
> ances... dropped by the club: their hands made small darting
> movements as if they were tossing their dear guests flowers or
> little balls of silk; they would call 'Hello, sunshine! Just look, the
> three Graces!' – and shake like dancers on the high, uncomfor-
> table barstools they used as perches. But soon they would come
> over to the threesome's table, for they knew them to be well-
> disposed, first to joke a little, to make a great fuss over a silk train
> which, as the great ladies they were now, they pretended to
> wear, to get tipsy on the wine they were treated to. Then their
> eyes would suddenly grow earnest, their carefully painted faces
> would collapse beneath the layer of cosmetics, they would sit
> down, this time with very unaffected movements, and begin to
> talk about money.   (Part II, ch.5)

Subsequently the party, continuing its tour, visits a club, the 'Para-
diesgärtlein' (Little Garden of Eden), 'on the first floor of an elegant
house', then, after two or three in the morning, a considerably less
smart establishment, the 'Sankt-Margaretenkeller' (St Margaret's
Cellar), some distance from the city centre and much frequented
by *Transvestiten*.

    Not all the customers at the Romanische Café or establishments
like those described in Mann's novel were residents of the city.
Some who came to Berlin from other parts of Germany or from
other countries passed through quite briefly, and in the group
of writers with whom this book is concerned Spender, Lehmann
and Upward belong to this class. Others, Auden and Isherwood
among them, stayed longer – indeed, as long as they could.

Robert McAlmon, an incurable wanderer, paid several visits to Berlin in the early 1920s, quitting the city eventually because 'the innumerable beggars, paralytics, shell-shocked soldiers, and starving people of good family' depressed him. His 1925 volume *Distinguished Airs* contains three stories described as 'grim fairy tales' which take as their subject Berlin's celebrated nightlife. One of them, 'Miss Knight', was admired by James Joyce and Ezra Pound. In the title story the narrator is an American who takes a friend on a tour of the night spots, including a 'queer café'.

Much later, in his autobiographical *Being Geniuses Together 1920–1930*, McAlmon observes (with perhaps some of the facile hyperbole that belongs to an oft-told tale) that 'At nights along the Unter den Linden it was never possible to know whether it was a woman or a man in woman's clothes who accosted one'. (*Never?*) As in an earlier passage quoted, he mentions that cocaine and other drugs were widely available, and the picture of a flourishing drug culture is confirmed by other sources.

A more jaundiced, not to say apoplectic, foreign observer was Wyndham Lewis, whose *Hitler* (1931) goes in for Carlylean fulminations: 'No city,' he writes at the top of his voice, 'has anything on it as regards the stark suggestions of being the Hauptstadt [capital] of Vice, the Excelsior Eldorado of a bottom-wagging most arch Old Nick sunk in a succulent and costly rut....' That 'Eldorado', as Lewis must have known but many of his readers surely did not, was no metaphor but a real and notorious place. Interestingly, in locating the nightlife that has 'established itself overnight', Lewis specifies the neighbourhoods in which Isherwood and Spender had made their homes at this time: 'the Kurfürstendamm, Nollendorf Platz, Wittenberg Platz, Motzstrasse, Tauenzienstrasse'.

For Stefan Zweig, Berlin's cosmopolitanism made it 'das Babel der Welt', the Babel of the World, and a city in which

all values were changed... Bars, amusement parks, honky-tonks sprang up like mushrooms.... Along the entire Kurfürstendamm powdered and rouged young men sauntered, and they were not all professionals; every high school boy wanted to earn some money and in the dimly-lit bars one might see government officials and men of the world of finance tenderly courting drunken sailors without any shame. Even the Rome of Suetonius had never known such orgies as the transvestite balls of Berlin, where hundreds of men costumed as women and hundreds of women as men danced under the benevolent eyes of the police. In the collapse of all values a kind of madness gained hold, particularly in the bourgeois circles which until then had been unshakeable in their probity. But the most revolting thing about this pathetic eroticism was its spuriousness. At bottom the orgiastic period which broke out simultaneously in Germany with the inflation was nothing more than a feverish imitation.... Everywhere you looked it was plain that the whole nation, tired of war, actually longed only for calm and order.

There is (once again) surely some exaggeration here (*every* high school boy?), and conceivably less than justice is done to Tiberius and Caligula, but the portrayal of 'the collapse of all values' carries conviction. Many of Zweig's details, including the male prostitutes and the transvestite balls, are paralleled elsewhere as well as serving as glosses to the experiences of Auden and Isherwood. For while his comments refer to the early 1920s, it is clear that much of the ethos he evokes still persisted at the end of the decade. In the period of gross inflation some of those high school boys may have been driven onto the streets by hunger rather than greed – a point that does not seem to occur to Zweig – but even six or seven years later mass unemployment was still causing hardship and desperation that took many into establishments like Auden's Cosy Corner and its many competitors in different parts of Berlin, some of them referred to in his journal.

The emphasis in these passages on cross-dressing is striking, and reminds us that it was an acquaintance of Auden and Isherwood, Dr Magnus Hirschfeld, who gave the world the term 'transvestism'. A later chapter will have something to say on the prominence of this phenomenon in the cinema of the period, but manifestations of sexual ambiguity of differing kinds make an appearance in a great variety of contexts. For the moment, two tiny examples. Germany's most popular vocal group at this time was the Comedian Harmonists, a close-harmony group some of whose members sang in a tenor so light and so high in the register as almost to be a falsetto. Like listening to a counter-tenor (or, presumably, a castrato), the result, though charming, is slightly unsettling, seeming as it does to call into question ingrained expectations and assumptions about male singers. For an even more disconcerting opposite, we can turn to Weill's *Die Sieben Todsünden*, where the role of the mother is performed by a basso profundo whose vocal powers are given full scope by Weill's score.

A more sustained and sympathetic, and probably also a more realistic, account of the boys who took to or were driven to prostitution is given in the 1926 novel *Der Puppenjunge* (translated as *The Hustler*), by John Henry Mackay (1864–1933). Mackay's Scots father died when he was a baby and he was taken by his German mother back to Germany, eventually settling in Berlin and taking out German citizenship. After his mother's death in 1902 he threw himself into campaigning for 'boy love' under the curious pseudonym of 'Sagitta', his identity not being revealed until after his death (possibly by suicide) six days after the Nazis' 'burning of the books' on 10 May 1933. Mackay was a poet of sorts, one of whose effusions is well-known to many who have probably never heard his name, for Richard Strauss set it in his well-known song 'Morgen'. In its small way, 'Morgen' is thus, like Michelangelo's David in its greater, a widely unacknowledged example of homosexual art: just as that well-developed shepherd boy is, for most visitors to Florence, no more of a sexual object than the Ponte Vecchio, Strauss's song must have been sung and enjoyed by multitudes innocent of its disconcerting message. Like many covert homosexual texts, including some of Auden's own poems, the poem is couched in sufficiently vague terms to make it eligible for ready appropriation as an inoffensively 'ordinary' love song:

...stumm werden wir uns in die Augen schauen,
und auf uns sinkt des Glückes stummes Schweigen....
(silently we shall look into each other's eyes, and upon us
falls the peace of quiet joy)

Not many of those who have sung or enjoyed Strauss's fine song will have identified it as a hymn, presumably unconscious on the composer's part, to boy-love. In its linking of pederastic sentimentality with a Romantic view of nature – sunshine, lakeside, woodland walks are all there in its eight lines – it is thoroughly characteristic not only of the *Naktkultur* (roughly, 'cult of nudity') of its period but of a persistent vein of pederastic art, widespread (as Brian Reade's *Sexual Heretics*, 1970, abundantly demonstrates) in Victorian England and far from unknown today.

Mackay also wrote novels, of which the first, *Der Schwimmer* (*The Swimmer*, 1901), is a very early example of the 'sports novel' subgenre, glorifying physical activity. In recent years he seems to have become something of a cult figure in specialised circles: a biography of him by Thomas A. Riley was published in New York in 1972, and a Mackay-Gesellschaft (Mackay Society) founded in Germany in 1974, while some of his writings have been reissued. *Der Puppenjunge* is really two stories in one, depicting male prostitution from different points of view, and in literary terms one of them is greatly inferior to the other. About half of the book tells of a young man's infatuation with a boy he meets in the street, and is almost intolerably sentimental. The other half, depicting the boy's experiences after he runs away from home and comes to Berlin, has considerable dramatic power and documentary interest. It is, moreover, set in an urban jungle as precisely delineated as Defoe's or Dickens's London: in its picture of 'the Passage', which by this time needs no introduction to readers of the present book, Mackay's novel recalls the 'street' films of the same period that rooted the lives of their characters in a specific sordid neighbourhood.

As the boy reflects at one point, 'Everyone comes to Berlin sometime', and his adventures blend the picaresque tradition with the study of his corruption and degeneration. Unable to find employment, he is by slow degrees initiated into the precarious career of hustler, is exploited by clients, fellow hustlers and landlords, and in time learns to exploit others as the price of survival. He frequents the Adonis Lounge, which serves as a kind of club enabling the boys to meet each other as well as customers:

> He opened the door, threw back a curtain, and was in a small front room, bordered on the right by a large bar. In a corner, opposite the entrance, stood a tall stove. At several small tables were seated figures, hard to recognise in the dim light of the room, but apparently juveniles.... They were without exception young lads from sixteen to perhaps nineteen years old....

As the novel's translator, Hubert Kennedy, points out, there are signs that the Adonis Lounge, like much else, is based on an actual establishment. Elsewhere in the novel Mackay gives an address for it, Novalisstrasse 20, which places it at the north end of Friedrichstrasse, beyond the railway station. Either it subsequently moved or (perhaps more probably) Mackay was thinly disguising the real location, for a 1930 guide refers to a spot of the same name but places it at the other end of Friedrichstrasse:

Very promising is the name of a club in Alexandrinen Street near the Halle Gate. Here, where not only the more shady, but also the more disreputable element of Friedrich Street pours out, the evil alliances are more numerous than the good ones. From the white poison (cocaine) to love of all kinds, everything is traded here that can be exchanged for money. Adonis Lounge is the name of the place, in which nothing reminds one of the beautiful legendary figure.

Auden's Cosy Corner – to which, throwing back the curtain just like the boy entering the Adonis Lounge, he introduced Isherwood – may be supposed to have been similar in its set-up and its atmosphere, though located in another area of the city. Auden's journal indicates, however, that he also knew and visited an establishment referred to as the 'Adonis Diele' (Adonis Hall) – as already noted, it was there that he picked up Herbert, one of his boyfriends – and this may be assumed to be identical with the one described in the guidebook, and probably also with the one Mackay refers to.

Near the end of *Die Puppenjunge* Mackay puts into the mouth of his tedious and ineffectual hero an attack on Paragraph 175 of the existing legal code, which criminalised homosexual behaviour: '"There are few human beings who have not become criminals against their fellow humans – not directly, but rather indirectly, in that they tolerate and advocate laws such as this one for example..."'.' Within a line or two this role-reversal – the real offenders are the persecutors and those who tacitly or otherwise tolerate persecution – turns into an indictment of all authority: '... what are all the crimes in the world compared with the ones carried out by those in gowns and vestments, robes and uniforms'.

In the section of *Goodbye to Berlin* titled 'The Nowaks', Isherwood introduces a boy named Pieps who, like Mackay's character, has run away from his home in the provinces to seek his fortune in Berlin. (Whether this character owes anything other than his name to Auden's first Berlin boyfriend, whom Isherwood would almost certainly have met in the spring of 1929, it is impossible to say.) There he lives by his wits and from hand to mouth, picking pockets 'in an amusement-hall in the Friedrichstrasse, not far from the Passage, which was full of detectives and getting too dangerous nowadays'. It is characteristic of Isherwood's caginess and willingness to make compromises with the known and observed reality that the boy should be depicted as a pickpocket rather than a prostitute and that the nature of the Passage's reputation should not be specified. The paragraph ends with a reference to the female prostitutes who plied their trade in the neighbourhood.

A similar protest becomes the central theme of another gay novel of the decade, Bruno Vogel's *Alf* (1929). As Michael Gilbert has said in his introduction to the recent translation, this short novel 'links the repression of gay sexuality to an entire network of oppression extending from the family, school and church (including religious instruction in the Gymnasium), to the judicial, political and military institutions of German society'. This is effected by tracing the hero's progress from home to school, where he falls in love with Felix, a fellow student, and eventually into the army. The second half of the book seems to represent a thematic shift from an attack on sexual intolerance to an exposure of the futility of war; what connects the two is the conviction that both proceed from an older generation of teachers and preachers who have betrayed the youth whose upbringing has been in their hands.

Vogel was born in 1898, the same year as his character Felix, and, like his other main character Alf, served in the war. Returning to Leipzig, he became a journalist and founder of a gay rights group, and in 1925 published a pacifist novel, *Es lebe der Krieg! Ein Brief* (*Long Live the War! A Letter*) which attracted considerable attention and led to his and his publisher's prosecution on charges of obscenity and blasphemy. Among those who successfully came to his defence were Thomas Mann and Magnus Hirschfeld, but when the book was reissued in 1926 and 1928 it was in bowdlerised form, the complete text not appearing again until 1978. Vogel left Germany before Hitler came to power and lived successively in Austria, Switzerland, Norway and South Africa, eventually settling in London where he died in 1983.

Vogel was clearly influenced by the teachings of Magnus Hirschfeld, who is mentioned in one of the letters written from the front by Alf to Felix. Like Hirschfeld, he wrote and worked towards the decriminalisation of homosexual behaviour, and a turning-point in his young hero's experience is the chance discovery, through a pamphlet he stumbles upon in a second-hand bookshop, that 'Paragraph 175 of the National Criminal Code would impose on their love for each other a prison term of up to five years'. As with Mackay, Vogel's disillusion with law and traditional morality, both of which call upon him to disavow his own nature, is extended to a comprehensive disillusion with authority:

They were all just beautiful, grand, empty words: the Law; the Fatherland; Christian culture: the sweet and honourable Death on the Field of Glory; the Best, which is what one's educators want for one, Chastity – oh, one could go on for pages listing such ideals! And how we all fell for the whole swindle – these pedagogical con artists understood perfectly how to dress these words so skilfully with a halo of sanctity so that nobody dared even to stop and think what all the speeches really might mean.

Parents, teachers, lawmakers are all in a conspiracy to entrap the young, and have woven 'the net which we got caught in'. The metaphor is that used by Joyce's Stephen Dedalus, and some of the sentiments are similar, though the ending of Vogel's *Bildungsroman* is bleaker – and his literary art, it hardly needs adding, incomparably cruder.

Outside the smoke-filled cafés, bars and nightclubs, and at a distance from the busy Berlin streets, the young found other ways of developing an alternative culture to that of an older generation tainted by apparent complicity in the war. That the photographs of Auden, Isherwood and Spender taken on Rügen Island and referred to a little earlier should commemorate semi-nudity and beach culture is not surprising, for this was the age of *Naktkultur*, another cultural manifestation in which Germany set the fashion. Valentine Cunningham has reminded us that 'The English varieties of nudism were consciously Germanic imports.... One of Britain's pioneer nudist colonies was actually called *Spielplatz*' (*British Writers of the Thirties*, p. 184). One of the lesser-known events in Anglo-German relations occurred in 1936, when the British government sent a team of observers to Germany to study and report on the Strength through Joy movement. As Auden and his friends must have very well known, *Naktkultur* was also a contemporary fashion with which Rügen seems to have been popularly associated.

Though its origins lay in Romantic nature-worship combined with modern scientific notions of bodily health, it was also a manifestation of the sexual revolution and of rejection of the values of urban and industrial society and the enclosed spaces of home and school. Perhaps it was this subversive, anti-authoritarian quality and its association with romantic individualism as much as its tendency to darken the ideally white northern skin that soon led it to incur the official disapproval of the Nazis. A passage in Spender's *World Within World* offers some suggestive juxtapositions in

the course of a discussion of the multifarious cultural manifestations of Weimar modernism. Remarking that

> Everything was 'new', deceptively so. There were buildings,
> with broad clean vertical lines crossed by strong horizontals,
> which drove into the sky like railroads. There were experiments
> in the theatre and opera, all in a style which expressed with
> facility the fusion of naked liberation with a kind of bitter pathos,
> which was characteristic of this Germany...

Spender proceeds to actualise the metaphor of 'naked liberation':

> Modernism in this Germany was (within certain limits of which I
> was not then aware) a popular mass-movement. Roofless houses,
> expressionist painting, atonal music, bars for homosexuals, nud-
> ism, sunbathing, camping, all were accepted....   (p. 108)

An early Spender poem, the Whitmanesque 'oh young men oh
young comrades', celebrates 'those fabulous possessions / which
begin with your body and your fiery soul', then proceeds to urge
the unconverted to uncover:

> Count your eyes as jewels and your valued sex
> then count the sun and the innumerable coined light
> sparkling on waves and spangled under trees....

Spender's *Journals*, published 34 years later than his autobiography,
make more explicit links between homosexuality and the cult of the
outdoors (the following passage is from a retrospective account
written in September 1939):

> I was 20 in those days, and I was caught up mostly with the idea
> of Friendship – *Freundschaft* – which was a very important part of
> the life of the Weimar Republic. This, if it was frank, was also
> very idealistic. It was not cynical, shamefaced, smart, snobbish,
> or stodgy, as so often in England. It was more like Walt
> Whitman's idea of camaraderie. I admit that I do not feel at
> all easy about this now, but I set it down for what it was.
> Two friends, young men, faced the world together: they
> camped, they travelled, they were happy in each other's
> company....   (p. 26)

The world of Forster's *Maurice* is not far away, with the English greenwood exchanged for a Baltic sand dune or a glade in the Black Forest: Edward Carpenter, 'the English Whitman', had been a significant influence on Forster, and very Forsterian too is the appropriation of an ordinary word, 'friendship', for a specialised and semi-private purpose (Spender must have known that *Freundschaft* was also the title of a leading Berlin gay newspaper). In Spender's *The Temple*, Paul reflects that 'Nakedness... is the democracy of the new Germany, the Weimar Republic' (pp. 36–7). Later, he finds himself 'beginning to tire of the self-conscious insistence of the Germans on their bodies. They worshipped the body, as though it were a temple' (p. 113). In the meantime, Paul has been reading Lawrence's *Fantasia of the Unconscious*, a book that was as important to Layard and Auden as Forster's work was to Isherwood. (Lawrence, of course, had known both Forster and Carpenter, and had written on Whitman.) An entry that Paul makes in his notebook constitutes Spender's fullest endorsement of Weimar *Naktkultur*: '...I confess that till now, whatever I may have pretended to myself, I have always regarded my body as sinful, and my own physical being as something to be ashamed of and to be overcome by compensating and atoning spiritual qualities. Now I am beginning to feel that I may soon come to regard my body as a source of joy....' (p. 54).

Although English writers such as Forster and Lawrence might authenticate such impulses, it was clearly necessary to leave England (as Forster and Lawrence themselves had in different ways done) in order to undergo this conversion. In *World Within World* Spender acknowledges that on arriving in Hamburg he experienced 'a tremendous sense of release, of having got away from Oxford and home' (p. 109). What had been left behind was not only parents and tutors but post-Victorian morality and the prohibitions of English legal and social intolerance. As in Forster's fiction, this transition or release is expressed through contrasting metaphors of enclosed and open spaces, and to the young Spender it seemed that the 'life of the senses' lived by young Germans was 'a sunlit garden from which sin was excluded' (*World Within World*, p. 107). Auden might have claimed to have found his own sunlit and sin-free garden in the rent-bars and cruising grounds of Berlin, but Spender's role is that of an apologist for the outdoor life – a camp culture with a difference – and *The Temple* (a novel of remarkable badness but at the same time a document of considerable interest) is full of images of beaches and pine woods, haunted by bronzed bodies as eternally young and vigorous as the figures on Keats's Grecian urn.

DEATH OF A DAYDREAM

For all their aesthetic shortcomings, novels like *The Hustler* and *Alf* likewise have a documentary force, even at moments a tragic eloquence, that sheds a severe ironic light on the naive lusts of the young Auden and Isherwood. Isherwood had been excited rather than deterred by the warning that Berlin was 'the vilest place since Sodom', and Auden had eagerly inquired, on the eve of his departure, whether the city was 'very wicked'. Auden's boastful early description of it as a 'buggers daydream', like Isherwood's later claim that for him 'Berlin meant Boys', depict the city as a kind of northern equivalent of the Capri of Norman Douglas or the Taormina of Baron von Gloeden. The reality – as Mackay's account of prostitution as a desperate means of survival and Vogel's indictment of intolerance in their different ways make clear – was much grimmer. Or, more accurately, the grim reality lay just beneath the hedonistic surface. Moreover, during the Auden/Isherwood period, public persecution was on the increase, and any guileless joy at the outset at exchanging the prohibitions of England for the freedom of Berlin must have received some hard knocks from subsequent experience. As the American historian Richard Plant has shown in his graphic account of Nazi persecution of homosexuals, *The Pink Triangle*, their elimination was from an early date 'an important aspect of Nazi ideology and action'.

Prussia had a long tradition as the most homophobic of the German states, and various establishment-rocking scandals and sensational court cases did nothing to promote tolerance. But intolerance soon became organised, systematic and official, and Plant has shown that 'the sexual tolerance so often associated with the Weimar Republic began to disappear as rapidly as Germany's economy began to crumble.... The years from 1929 to the end of the Weimar Republic were years of mounting tension' (p. 27). Those are, of course, precisely the years with which the present study is concerned. It was during this period, too, that the Brown Shirts, under the command (by an extraordinary irony) of Ernst

Roehm, a known homosexual later murdered by Hitler, became 'even more brutal and more repressively efficient'.

Even before Auden's arrival a warning signal had been made, on 14 May 1928, in the shape of a Nazi response to a question about its attitude towards Paragraph 175:

It is not necessary that you and I live, but it is necessary that the German people live. And it can only live if it can fight, for life means fighting. And it can only fight if it maintains its masculinity. It can only maintain its masculinity if it exercises discipline, especially in matters of love. Free love and deviance are undisciplined. Therefore, we reject you, as we reject anything that hurts our nation.

This inflexible reasoning led straight to the day less than five years later, and while Isherwoood was still in Berlin, when Hitler, only three weeks in office as Chancellor, banned gay rights organisations; it also led, not long afterwards, to the prison camps and the gas chambers. And it was as early as 1929, the year of Isherwood's arrival, that the official Nazi newspaper launched an attack on Hirschfeld, whose campaign against Paragraph 175 (described in the next chapter) appeared to be having some success:

We congratulate you, Mr Hirschfeld, on the victory in committee. But don't think that we Germans will allow these laws to stand for a single day after we have come to power.... Among the many evil instincts that characterise the Jewish race, one that is especially pernicious has to do with sexual relationships. The Jews are forever trying to propagandise sexual relations between siblings, men and animals, and men and men. We National Socialists will soon unmask and condemn them by law....

Such threats were interpreted in some quarters as being directed exclusively at Jewish homosexuals – an optimism that subsequent events did not justify. Almost before Auden and Isherwood arrived in the city, the paradise – if it had ever been that – was beginning to go out of business, the daydream to turn sour, for anyone who cared to read the signs of the times.

3

Berlin: Faces

ANNA MUTHESIUS

As we have seen, Auden's first home in Berlin was with a family living at Potsdamer Chaussee 49, in the southwestern part of the city. How he was put in touch with them is not clear, but since he seems to have gone straight there after arriving in Berlin, and since they were hardly the sort of people to advertise for a lodger, some personal introduction must have been involved. Auden's biographers pass lightly over the Muthesius family (by one, indeed, they are not even named), merely characterising them as 'bourgeois'. They were in fact unusually interesting people, standing high in the social hierarchy of the capital, having among their friends some of the leaders of artistic and intellectual life, and owning one of the finest and most attractive private homes in the city.

When Auden arrived he found it presided over, in formidable style, by Anna Muthesius, who had been widowed in the previous year. Her husband, Hermann Muthesius (1861–1927), had been a distinguished architect who earned a place in the standard works of reference. He was keenly Anglophile: he had spent several years (1896–1903) in London as an attaché at the German Embassy, and he and his family paid frequent visits to England thereafter. Possibly on one of these visits they had met the Auden family or some of their friends.

Hermann's knowledge of English art and industry had led him, in the early years of the century, to play a leading role in establishing the Deutsche Werkbund, an association of artists, craftsmen and industrialists, with the aim of creating in Germany something analogous to the English arts and crafts movement inspired by Morris and Ruskin. The Werkbund subsequently proved influential in areas ranging from industrial design to architecture. Hermann's particular professional interest was in the English country house, and his book *Das moderne Landhaus* (1905) describes over three hundred examples of country house architecture drawn from England, Germany, Austria and Finland. In Germany, as well as designing estates of model homes for workers, he had built houses for the rich based on a modification of English country house styles. His own home, where Auden lived briefly, still stands and is very much in this style: spacious and imposing, it is set in a large garden with a deer meadow behind. Nearly seventy years after Auden's sojourn there, it remains remarkably dignified and tranquil, though no longer occupied by a single family.

Hermann had been killed in a street accident while inspecting progress on his latest commission: stepping out of a car driven by his son, he had been knocked down by a tram. (The street where it happened now bears his name.) It was thus his widow who became Auden's landlady, though the latter term seems wildly inappropriate for a figure as gifted and dynamic as Anna Muthesius. Born in 1870, she had married Hermann in 1897 and had had five children, of whom one had died in infancy. The remaining three boys and a girl were all living at home when Auden moved in; the youngest of the boys was 24, while Renate, the baby of the family, was 14. The only survivor, she now lives in Munich.

Before her marriage Anna had been a professional soprano, and although she seems to have given up her career she retained her musical interests as well as involving herself in a wide range of social and artistic activities. At the age of 90 (she lived until 1961) she was, according to a newspaper article published to commemorate her birthday, still entertaining her guests by singing to her own piano accompaniment. Accounts of Anna suggest a very energetic individual, perhaps even a little overbearing, with something of the Ibsenite heroine and the 1890s 'new woman' about her. She designed her own clothes as well as window-displays for Berlin department stores. Her feminist convictions led her to write articles attacking the *Fischbeinecorsette*, the whalebone corset that imprisoned the female figure, and she seems to have helped to bring about its demise. Her wide circle of friends included Max Reinhardt, who produced scenes from *A Midsummer Night's Dream* in the deer meadow behind the house, and Albert Einstein, who would pay visits to the Muthesius family from his home in nearby Potsdam.

It was, then, not just any dull bourgeois family but a lively, gifted, artistic and creative household that Auden entered in October 1928. For his part the young Englishman made a strong impression, not uniformly favourable. The youngest son, Ekhart (1904–89), who was only a couple of years older than Auden, often talked about him in his later years. Ekhart's first wife, Miette (born in 1899 and now living in England), can still recall going to dinner at the Muthesius home, meeting Auden, and finding him 'excessively dirty' and 'utterly revolting'. She remembers, too, that the family knew about his sexual preferences and were tolerant of them.

Auden lived there for no more than a couple of months. That the family, as he claimed, insisted on speaking English to him is perfectly consistent with their known Anglophilia, but it has the flavour of an official justification intended for public consumption and was surely not the whole truth. Their splendid house is in one of the most attractive parts of the city, but far from convenient for anyone wishing to savour the pleasures, and especially the night-time pleasures, of downtown Berlin. To reach the Muthesius home involved a longish ride on the S-Bahn, whose timetable would have put an unwelcome limitation on nocturnal adventures. Anna Muthesius's broadmindedness, moreover, might have stopped short at welcoming into her beautiful home her young guest's gleanings from the scruffier boy-bars. Hence the move to Furbringerstrasse, much nearer the heart of the city, where the distance from number 8, the house in which Auden took a room, to the Cosy Corner bar in Zollenstrasse was just seventy paces.

MAGNUS HIRSCHFELD

Chapter 1 has described how, in November 1929, Isherwood travelled to Berlin to begin a period of residence that would last for more than three years and would be brought to an end only by the irresistible pressures of public events. On his first morning in Berlin he knocked on the door of an apartment in one of the tall dignified houses in In den Zelten, in order to enlist the help of his only English-speaking contact. A room was found for him, the establishment being under the care of a sister of Dr Magnus Hirschfeld, whose Institute for Sexology (Institut für Sexual-Wissenschaft) was next door. The Institute was a remarkable place, but not as remarkable as its founder and director, to whom Isherwood devotes several pages in *Christopher and his Kind* and who has come to be regarded, with good reason, as the founding father, saint and martyr of the gay rights movement in Germany, if not worldwide.

Born in Kolberg on the Baltic in 1868, Hirschfeld was one of eight children of a German-Jewish physician who contributed articles on political and social issues to local newspapers. Beginning as a student of literature and philology in Breslau, the young Magnus soon turned to medicine – without, however, completely forsaking his literary interests – and pursued his studies in Strasbourg, Berlin and Munich. After graduating he moved to Paris, met Max Nordau and became deeply interested in Zionism. At this period, during which he worked as a journalist, he seems still to have been wavering between medicine and literature as a career. His subsequent life as doctor, scientific researcher, author and activist was to integrate the two fields with considerable thoroughness and success.

After a couple of years of general practice in Magdeburg, Hirschfeld went to Berlin and became for a time a specialist in nature-cure methods. But his interest in problems of sexuality, and his eagerness to engage in polemic, manifested themselves as early as 1896 with the publication, prudently pseudonymous, of a pamphlet titled 'Sappho und Socrates' and subtitled, with a challenging refusal to prevaricate, 'Wie erklärt sich die Liebe der Männer und Frauen zu Personen des eigenen Geschlechts?' ('How can the love of men and women for those of their own sex be explained?'). As one of his biographers, Charlotte Wolff, has made clear, the pamphlet's origins were dramatically circumstantial and its publication was decisive in determining the future direction of Hirschfeld's considerable energies:

> An officer had shot himself through the head on the eve of his marriage. He had been Hirschfeld's patient for some time before his death, and the day after he died Hirschfeld received a letter from him telling him the whole tragic story which led to his suicide. He called his homosexuality a 'curse' against human nature and the law. He felt unable to marry because of his 'abnormal' desires. He asked Hirschfeld to publish his story as it might help the German people to get a clearer idea about homosexuality.... (p. 33)

One is reminded of the Woolwich cadet whose suicide was one of the precipitating causes of A. E. Housman's poetry, and, as with Housman, Hirschfeld's awareness of his own sexual nature, and perhaps even a sense of how easily he might have shared the dead man's fate lent extra strength to his pity and indignation.

Characteristically, these emotions produced practical results, for Hirschfeld was a tireless activist as well as a vigorous polemicist. In the following year, with two friends, he set up the Wissenschaf-tlich-humanitäre Komitee (Scientific-humanitarian Committee) to work for reform of the laws relating to homosexual behaviour, and in particular the notorious Paragraph 175 of the penal code which made homosexual acts punishable with a prison sentence. Although social life in the capital was reasonably tolerant of homo-sexuals, Prussia as a whole had a long tradition of homophobia: until 1794 the law provided for the burning at the stake of con-victed offenders, and sentences of imprisonment followed by ban-ishment for life were possible until 1837. In nineteenth-century Germany, the liberalism of Bavaria was the exception rather than the rule, and in Prussia Paragraph 143 (the basis, 20 years later, for Paragraph 175) came into force in 1851, providing for a sentence of imprisonment for homosexuality and bestiality alike.

From this time on, Hirschfeld's efforts to promote understanding and tolerance of homosexuals, and to change laws and practices that discriminated against them, were unremitting, indeed lifelong, and were conducted on many fronts. While continuing to practise as a physician he was also a medical and anthropological researcher, a prolific writer of books and pamphlets, the organiser of institutes, committees and congresses, and a lecturer throughout Germany and abroad.

In a society in which homophobia was still widespread, he dis-played an impressive courage as well as extraordinary energy. Unsurprisingly, controversy, opposition and eventual persecution followed. In December 1903, in a pre-Kinsey attempt to chart and quantify the sexual orientation of sections of the male population, he circulated a questionnaire to 3,000 students in a Berlin technical college and to 5,000 metalworkers whom he had recently addressed on the subject of homosexuality. The results were per-haps not entirely predictable. The metalworkers took it in good part and responded willingly, but some of the students took offence and complained; prosecution followed, and Hirschfeld had to pay a fine and costs. It was the beginning of a thirty-years' war between the sexologist and the forces of reaction – what E. M. Forster calls 'the armies of the benighted' – that would end in violence, bloodshed and exile.

Meanwhile, Hirschfeld was earning a considerable reputation throughout Germany and internationally as an expert on sexuality, especially homosexuality, and found himself making happier courtroom appearances as an expert witness. Perhaps the most remarkable of these occasions was his testifying in 1907 on behalf of Maximilian Harden, a German-Jewish journalist who was the defendant in a libel action brought by General von Moltke, the military commandant of Berlin. Harden had published in the previous year a satirical article exposing the homosexual relationship of Moltke (known to his friends as Tütü) and Philipp Eulenberg, a prominent diplomat who was rumoured to be simultaneously conducting an affair with the Kaiser himself. In Harden's article, Eulenberg is referred to as 'Sweetie' (he was known to have a passion for chocolates, and 'sweet' was also a slang term for a homosexual) and the Kaiser as 'Darling'.

In a fascinating essay James D. Steakley has shown that this trial was one of a series of five that, together with a number of courts martial, 'rocked' Imperial Germany between 1907 and 1909. Steakley suggests that what became known as the Eulenberg trials performed a comparable function in Germany to that performed in England by the Wilde trials of 1895, for both events 'dramatically accelerated the emergence of the modern homosexual identity by stimulating and structuring public perceptions of sexual normalcy and abnormalcy'. The social shockwaves of the Eulenberg affair were, however, much more extensive, involving as it did a large number of highly placed figures in military and civilian life and even adding fuel to rumours about the Kaiser's sexual proclivities. (He was known, for instance, to be addicted to leisurely cruises in all-male company.) In a much wider context, it has also been argued that reactions to these scandals led to a shift in German policy that generated increasingly militaristic attitudes and eventually contributed to the outbreak of the Great War.

In the Moltke *v.* Harden hearings in October 1907, Hirschfeld was the last witness to be called, and his expert opinion that, whatever his conduct may have been, Moltke displayed signs of a feminine nature (for example, in his sensitivity to the arts) no doubt contributed to Harden's acquittal. Hirschfeld himself was depicted in numerous cartoons of the period and, as Steakley observes, is shown there as 'a Jewish stereotype'. Contemporary cartoons, incidentally, were often capable of startling frankness in their satirical commentary on public personalities: in November 1907, for example, a Stuttgart paper published, under the title 'Military Innovations', one that was accompanied by the following dialogue: 'Since when is an about-face order given for inspection?' 'At your service, captain – reporting that the division is being inspected by

Count Hohenau today'. Hohenau, commander of the Garde du Corps, was related to the Kaiser, and the cartoon shows a line of young soldiers, their trousers stretched tight over chubby buttocks, awaiting their commanding officer's close and critical scrutiny. Much later, Hirschfeld appeared for the defence in the less celebrated but still widely publicised trial of Adolf Koch, one of the apostles of the *Freikörperkultur* or nudist movement in the 1920s. Koch, a gymnastics instructor in a working-class area of Berlin, had been in the habit of instructing his pupils to take their classes in the nude with the worthy motive of encouraging better posture and cleanliness, and was soon charged with the corruption of minors.

In 1905 Hirschfeld addressed a Berlin audience one thousand strong on Paragraph 175 – one of numerous lectures and public meetings that over the years took him to many parts of Germany and to Britain, America, Japan and elsewhere. In August 1913 he was in London for a meeting of the International Congress of Physicians organised by the British Medical Association, and lectured (with the aid of slides from his research collection) on homosexuality, androgyny, hermaphroditism and transvestism, his message being the infinite variety of sexual instincts and behaviour, different forms of sexuality shading into one another rather than representing polarities or sharply defined categories.

The stream of books and other writings continued, the list of his publications including, among much else, *Berlin's Drittes Geschlecht* (*Berlin's Third Sex*, 1904), an account of homosexual life in the city at all social levels; *Die Transvestiten* (1910); and *Die Homosexualität des Mannes und des Weibes* (*Homosexuality in Men and Women*, 1914), this last running to over a thousand pages and being based on 10,000 case histories drawn from many countries. He also founded in 1907 the *Zeitschrift für Sexualwissenschaft*, the first journal to be devoted to the scientific study of sex.

As a compiler and classifier of data relating to subjects that had hardly received any serious scientific attention previously, Hirschfeld was the Darwin of sexology. He also engaged in laboratory work, investigating the vexed question of the physical basis of homosexuality, for instance, through the study of cells from the testes of homosexuals and heterosexuals. Other colleagues pursued their investigations in a similar direction, one, for instance, removing testes and ovaries from various mammals and substituting organs from the other sex (he apparently produced by this means, among other phenomena, a lesbian goat). The underlying conviction seems to have been that homosexuality is produced by a combination of genetic and hormonal factors, and not at all by environmental factors such as the parent–child relationship. It has recently been argued that this pioneering work had a significant influence on debates on gay identity in the 1960s and 1970s. Moreover, not only does modern sexological research owe a debt to Hirschfeld (who was acknowledged by Kinsey), but certain recent developments in genetics and endocrinology continue along lines similar to those he laid down. A distinguished German endocrinologist has been reported as paying the pithy tribute that 'Hirschfeld is my grandfather'. Hirschfeld's concept of a biologically determined third or intermediate sex, which seemed so old-fashioned as long as environmental factors were considered to be of prime importance, has in recent years taken on a new life.

Richard Plant, however, has suggested that the theories pursued so zealously by Hirschfeld may have led him in unintended directions:

> Like many turn-of-the-century psychiatrists, he wanted legal punishment to be replaced by treatment of patients who deserved to be pitied and helped rather than censured and ignored. He followed the conventions of his time when he sought the key to homosexuality by measuring the circumference of male pelvises and chests in an attempt to define a physiologically recognisable 'third sex'. Only after the Nazis had turned his lifework into ashes did he concede that, on the one hand, he had failed to prove that homosexuals were characterised by distinct and measurable biological and physiological qualities and that, on the other hand, he had unwittingly deepened popular prejudices by endowing male homosexuals with 'feminine' characteristics. This had only served to confirm the prevailing assumption that because homosexuals were 'not really men' they were therefore inferior. (pp. 33–4)

A further extension of this argument is that by trying to show that homosexuality sprang from physical origins, Hirschfeld was making his enemies a present of the argument that it was a morbid condition that could be cured by physical means. Although he has been the subject of two biographies (one in English and one, very recently, in German) it seems that Hirschfeld's contribution to the scientific study of the origins of homosexuality still awaits proper assessment.

His 'Scientific-Humanitarian Committee' moved to In den Zelten in 1912; then, in 1919, he moved to another house (number 10) in the same street, where he established his Institute for Sexual Science. Apart from being the home of Hirschfeld, his secretary and lover Karl Giese and the rest of his staff, this handsome house accommodated a research and teaching institute, a library, museum and archive, a lecture hall and a clinic for those seeking advice on sexual matters, including abortion and birth control, and treatment for venereal diseases. The rich paid through the nose, but the poor were seen for nothing, and the clinic was an instant success, with 1,800 consultations in the first year. Lectures and guided tours were open to the public and free. These were the premises that Isherwood was introduced to by Auden: Hirschfeld, Giese and their colleagues were not only the young Englishman's neighbours but his fellow members in a remarkable community.

One of the most outstanding of Hirschfeld's staff of doctors was Max Hodann, whose career was in several ways representative. A successful Berlin physician and a Communist, he worked for six years at the clinic for sexual problems in the Institute and was well known in Germany for his publications on sex education. Going into exile in England, he was sufficiently respected there for an English translation of his *History of Modern Morals* to be issued by a London publisher in 1937, and was also connected for a time with Dora Russell's progressive school at Beacon Hill.

During the 1920s the Institute became one of the sights of Berlin for visitors who had a genuine sympathy with its aims or were simply curious to see a collection ranging from photographs of transvestites to Japanese dildos. It has been said that 'it was as well known in Germany...as Erwin Piscator's theater or the Bauhaus architects'. One of the many distinguished foreign visitors was André Gide, whose haughty inspection Isherwood witnessed and later described.

In the confused and violent post-Versailles world, and with the rise of Nazism, Hirschfeld, as a Jew and a homosexual, found himself the target of verbal abuse and worse: his lectures were invaded by rowdies, and on more than one occasion he was physically attacked. In Munich in 1920 he was knocked unconscious and severely injured. Returning indomitably to the same city to give another lecture in the following year, he was, as Isherwood recounts, 'beaten up again; this time, his skull was fractured and he was left for dead'.

Apparently unstoppable, however, he had more and more ambitious plans to promulgate the ideas he believed in, and his finest hour may well have been in September 1921, when he organised the highly successful First Congress for Sexual Reform. One result of the Congress was the foundation of the World League for Sexual Reform, which in its heyday had a membership of 130,000. He carried on working, speaking and writing throughout the 1920s, though more time was spent out of Germany, with a visit to America and a world tour that included Japan, China and India. Wherever he travelled he continued indefatigably to collect data on sexual customs.

Four other international congresses were organised – successively in Copenhagen (1928), London (1929), Vienna (1930) and Brno (1932) – before the Nazis put a stop to the Institute's activities. The London congress immediately preceded Isherwood's taking up residence at the Institute, so that it must still have been a topic of eager conversation in his early days in the In den Zelten household. Hirschfeld collaborated with Dora Russell, Norman Haire and others in England, and they in turn sought to enlist the support of other liberal-minded writers and intellectuals including H. G. Wells, Arnold Bennett, the Woolfs, J. M. Keynes, Goldsworthy Lowes Dickinson and Bertrand Russell.

Hirschfeld's efforts to change the law, which had begun in the 1890s, showed no sign of flagging in the 1920s, but contemporary history was not on his side. One serious setback was the trial in 1924 of a homosexual serial murderer who had operated on an epic scale. This was the sensational Haarman case, which inflamed popular prejudice and created a climate in which reform seemed less likely. Fritz Haarman, a Hanover petty criminal and police informer, was discovered to have murdered a very large number (one figure given was 147) of destitute boys he had picked up in the city, which was notorious for prostitutes and hustlers. The case included elements of sadism, vampirism and cannibalism; the last of these practices had not been confined to the accused, since the flesh of some of the victims had reportedly been minced and sold as horsemeat for human consumption. Predictably, the case provided headline news for several months, and Hirschfeld did himself and his cause no good by appearing as an expert witness at the trial. The wave of panic and homophobia produced by the

Haarman case, and the association of homosexuality in the public mind not just with criminality but with peculiarly horrific forms of psychopathic behaviour, must have cancelled out much of what had been achieved by years of pamphleteering and speech-making. A little earlier, Hirschfeld had not only become associated with but had actually appeared in the controversial film *Anders als die Andern* (*Different from the Rest*, 1919), to be referred to later. Its producer and director, Richard Oswald, had approached him with the suggestion that he should cooperate in the making of a film on the subject of homosexuality: 'It should be a work of art, presented as a personal documentary in the framework of scientific knowledge.' Hirschfeld was enthusiastic and secured the official blessing of his Committee, and the project went ahead, his idealism not foreseeing the bitter opposition the public treatment of such a subject would arouse. It seems that Hirschfeld made an appearance in several other films, including one, *Gesetze der Liebe* (*Laws of Love*, 1927), that receives a mention in Isherwood's *Goodbye to Berlin*.

It was at the end of the same decade that Hirschfeld came closest to success in bringing about a reform in the law. In 1929 a parliamentary committee had voted in favour of putting before the Reichstag a bill to abolish Paragraph 175. The Nazi opposition to the proposal took the form of a personal attack on Hirschfeld and an outrageous distortion of his beliefs ('The Jews are forever trying to propagandize sexual relations between siblings, men and animals, and men and men'). But the timing could hardly have been less fortunate from Hirschfeld's point of view, for European repercussions to the Wall Street Crash produced an economic crisis in which social legislation had to be shelved. In the elections at the end of that year the Nazis obtained 107 seats in the Reichstag and the road to reform was closed.

By that date Isherwood had arrived in Berlin, the point at which this account of Hirschfeld began. By the time the young Englishman was shown the curious contents of the Institute, it was the beginning of the end for Hirschfeld's work in Germany. Nazi policy towards Jews and homosexuals had already become dramatically and tragically evident, and Hirschfeld had been identified as a prime target for persecution.

When the Nazis came to power they quickly took an interest in the Institute, which was searched by the Gestapo for records that might refer to party members. In February 1933, three weeks after Hitler had become Chancellor, gay rights organisations were banned, and soon afterwards Hirschfeld's chief administrator, Kurt Hiller, who was also Jewish, was sent to a concentration camp. On 6 May the Institute, which had been subjected to a barrage of abusive Nazi propaganda, was invaded by a mob of around one hundred hooligans. Isherwood rather puzzlingly refers to them as 'students', though elsewhere they have been described as Nazi stormtroopers. Whether students or stormtroopers, they smashed everything in sight and carried off Hirschfeld's lifetime collection of books and archives, which were publicly consigned to the flames a few days later – the notorious *Bücherbrennung* or burning of the books. Isherwood witnessed the conflagration and 'said "shame"; but not loudly'. Exactly one week after the destruction of the Institute, as if responding to a signal, he left Berlin.

For uncharacteristically prudential reasons, Hirschfeld himself had been spending more and more time abroad. Leaving for an extended lecture-tour at the end of 1930, very shortly after Isherwood's own departure from the In den Zelten house, he never returned to Germany and did not witness the looting of his home or the destruction of his research collections. After 1933, the physicians who worked with him, most of whom were Jewish, also left Germany. The building itself, vandalised in 1933 and later taken over by the Nazis for their own purposes, was seriously damaged by Allied bombs in 1943; a photograph taken a decade later shows it still a ruin awaiting demolition.

Dying but indomitable, the exiled Hirschfeld tried in vain to re-establish his Institute in Paris. The visitors' book has survived from his brief final residence in France and indicates that he received a stream of callers interested in his work. He died in Nice on his 67th birthday, 14 May 1935. He left money to Karl Giese to help re-establish the Institute, but the bequest was caught up in a tangle of legal problems: as an exile, Giese was unable to produce the proofs of identity demanded by French law and the money was never paid over. Giese lived for a time in extreme poverty and committed suicide in 1938. As for the famous collection, much of it must have been destroyed when the Institute was invaded and ransacked, but parts were certainly taken out of Germany and later disappeared. There are intriguing but perhaps groundless rumours that Hirschfeld's collection of pornography is in the hands of a French collector who prefers to remain anonymous.

The account of Hirschfeld and the Institute in *Christopher and his Kind* recognises the heroism while making the most of the eccentricity. Shown round the Institute's museum, with its instruments for sado-masochistic practices, its special footwear for the delectation of fetishists and its collection of photographs that ranged from famous homosexual couples (Oscar Wilde and Lord Alfred Douglas etc.) to 'the sexual organs of quasi-hermaphrodites', he finds himself giggling with embarrassment. Hirschfeld himself seemed to Isherwood to resemble (and photographs confirm his impression) a music-hall caricature of an elderly German intellectual. And yet he was not only admirable but lovable – the young Isherwood 'loved Hirschfeld . . . the silly solemn old professor with his doggy moustache, thick peering spectacles and clumsy German-Jewish boots' – and one of the 'heroic leaders of his tribe' (p. 20).

During his year's residence in In den Zelten Isherwood had many opportunities to inspect the museum and to show it to visitors, but the occasion on which he giggled with embarrassment may have been the very first day of his first visit to Berlin. For, as Auden's journal makes clear, the two of them visited 'the Hirschfeld museum' together, and a brief reference to this visit is the very first item in the record Auden made of his friend's time in Berlin: 'We waited with elderly ladies and adhesive trouser boys. Why was this so obscene? H's boy (Karl Giese) was very earnest and bourgeois yet I felt he was nice . . . .' (The boys' provocatively tight trousers would have been all the more noticeable in contrast to the prevailing fashion in England for loose trousers or 'bags'.) The priority given to this visit on Isherwood's programme suggests not only that Auden had some familiarity already with the Hirschfeld ménage, no doubt through Francis Turville-Petre, but also that he regarded it as one of the sights of the city.

Isherwood's memories, almost half a century later, of the Institute and its founder are not in a vein of high seriousness, but it is difficult to believe that, at the time, he could not also have been aware of the menace in the air and the personal anxiety of those concerned. There is, incidentally, one tiny but interesting example of unconscious autobiographical unreliability in Isherwood's references to Hirschfeld's sister Francisca as acting as housekeeper. Francisca, a talented woman who published children's books, had died in 1928 and Isherwood cannot possibly have known her, but her brother Magnus was devoted to her and must often have spoken of her – and so her name came to be substituted in Isherwood's memory for that of another sister, Teresa, who did run the house and must have come to know him well. Teresa was later deported and murdered by the Nazis.

Hirschfeld's was, in its unorthodox and sometimes eccentric way, a heroic life, the eccentricity proceeding from the single-minded pursuit of ideals not widely shared. There is an engaging solemn dottiness about some of his attempts to spread sexual enlightenment: there survives, for example, a pamphlet on the treatment of impotence that includes diagrams bearing a strong resemblance to a central heating system designed by Heath Robinson but intended to illustrate the cooperation of mind and body in the erection process. At the same time, however, his earnest confrontation with issues and human problems that most of his contemporaries preferred to leave undiscussed commands respect and admiration. In his breathlessly encyclopaedic *British Writers of the Thirties*, Valentine Cunningham performs the feat of rubbishing both Hirschfeld and Isherwood in a single sentence: 'Ordinary readers of *Mr Norris* and *Goodbye to Berlin* weren't informed, of course, that Isherwood had travelled to Berlin specifically for permissive sex with boys, nor that he had naturally fetched up in lodgings next door to Hirschfeld's notorious sex-clinic – that black museum of sado-masochistic gear, hospice for sexual freaks, mecca of homosexuals' (p. 394). I have argued earlier that Isherwood's claim, in his too eagerly confessional old age, concerning his motives for going to Berlin should not be taken literally. As for the summary judgement on Hirschfeld, the present account has perhaps suggested the extent of its intolerant failure to recognise his courage, sincerity and genuine scientific and humanitarian concerns.

As an investigator of human sexuality and a propagandist for enlightened and tolerant views, he has a place in history beside Havelock Ellis, Edward Carpenter and others. (In his biography of Havelock Ellis, Vincent Brome suggests that Ellis's work was 'derivative from Hirschfeld' in its discussion of transvestism and other topics.) In legislative terms, all his enormous labours and all his courage and initiative did not succeed in achieving a great deal during his lifetime. There were repeated set-backs that would have daunted a less energetic and single-minded man, and these came partly as a result of historical accidents and unlucky timing, but also partly perhaps as a result of his idealism, his willingness to embrace any worthy cause regardless of political expediency or simple discretion, and his inability to take into account the ruthlessness of the opposition. His long-term influence, however, though hardly measurable, must have been considerable, and Isherwood and others can hardly have failed to sense at times that they were close to a man who was likely to make an important contribution to the modification of human perceptions.

Today, it is a bronze bust of Hirschfeld that surveys the tiny crowded library of the Freunde eines Schwulen Museums in Berlin, a gay organisation situated in a less fashionable area of Berlin than In den Zelten, and one whose cramped premises, reached by a superannuated lift after crossing a scruffy courtyard, contrast strikingly with the marble halls of the Institute. How the latter was financed, so lavishly and so long, remains a bit of a mystery. Although Hirschfeld himself had bought the house (and later made it over to the Institute), and although many of his staff worked only for their keep and pocket money, the running costs must have been considerable, and it seems likely that wealthy homosexuals in Germany and elsewhere made generous but anonymous contributions.

There is, too, in present-day Berlin a Magnus Hirschfeld Gesellschaft (Research Institute) which since 1982 has made efforts, in the heroic and idealistic spirit of Hirschfeld himself, both to continue his work in sexological research and to conduct and publish historical research on Hirschfeld and his times. The plan of re-establishing an institute on the lines of his own and under the aegis of a German university has not so far succeeded, but the Society issues a newsletter twice a year and has published a series of books that includes reprints of Hirschfeld's own writings. Largely through its efforts, on 6 July 1994 – the 75th anniversary of the opening of Hirschfeld's Institute – a memorial to Hirschfeld was unveiled on a spot not far from its original site.

Sixty years after his death, therefore, Hirschfeld is something more than an eccentric or distasteful footnote to cultural history or a caricaturist's German professor in the pages of *Christopher and his Kind*. The motto he chose for his Institute was 'Per scientiam ad justitiam' ('Through science to justice'), and its nineteenth-century optimism and idealism were tragically contradicted by history and by his own last days. In many ways a nineteenth-century figure, he was gifted (or, some might feel, cursed) with an unfading vision of a world that might be very different from the fear-haunted and guilt-ridden one he knew. For all the touches of eccentricity, even absurdity – and at moments, not least in Isherwood's account, he seems to resemble a shambling figure of farce played by Walter Matthau – Hirschfeld's heroism commands our respect and he has a place in the history of the struggle against intolerance and inhumanity.

FRANCIS TURVILLE-PETRE

When Isherwood knocked on the door of that apartment in In den Zelten in November 1929, the result was dramatic. The door flew open and a figure appeared, 'tousled, furious, one hand clutching the folds of his crimson silk robe. Instantly, he started screaming in German.' The screaming over, the door was slammed in his face. This was his introduction to Francis Turville-Petre, more conveniently known in the boy-bars as Der Franni.

Francis, sleepy and hungover, had mistaken his English visitor, youthful and short of stature, for a light-fingered rent-boy who had been thrown out the previous night, but the misunderstanding was soon cleared up. He occupied a couple of rooms in the apartment, situated in the building next door to Dr Hirschfeld's Institute, and arrangements were quickly made for Isherwood to move into another of the rooms, which happened to be vacant. During the next few weeks Francis became his guide to the bars of the working-class district of Hallesches Tor. It was very much the lower end of the market to which these two upper-class Englishmen made their way, and someone who spoke German and knew his way around (as Francis certainly did) was an advantage when it came to finding the small, backstreet bars that, as Isherwood explains, depended for their business on a regular clientele rather than on catching the eye of passing tourists.

According to *Christopher and his Kind* the two of them 'got along well together', and there is a vivid passage describing their nocturnal excursions, 'like traders who had entered a jungle'. If Hirschfeld, filling notebooks with facts, was the Darwin of the Berlin sexual underworld, Isherwood and his mentor Turville-Petre were two aristocratic ivory-traders, out to exploit the natives with a handful of glass beads. Isherwood also put Francis into *Down There on a Visit*, and there was evidently something about him that made writers instinctively scent copy. (He makes other guest appearances, as we shall see shortly, in one of Olivia Manning's novels and elsewhere.) Furthermore, he was incorporated, as 'The

Fronny', into Auden and Isherwood's private mythology. As Isherwood notes, 'The name appears in several of Wystan's poems, and the Fronny character is present, though unnamed, in the published version of *The Dance of Death.*' As already mentioned, Auden's play *The Fronny* survives only in a very fragmentary state.

The period the unsaintly Francis and his disciple Christopher spent together as traders, or hunters, in the jungle of Hallesches Tor can have lasted no more than a few weeks, for quite early in 1930 both men left Berlin, though Isherwood soon returned to the apartment and, all told, spent nearly a year there. It was much longer before Francis, an incurable wanderer, was back in Berlin. But their time together must surely have constituted for Isherwood a period not quite of initiation – for the first visit to Berlin earlier in 1929 had been that – but of more exhaustive exploration of what life (especially low-life) in Berlin had to offer, and a necessary prologue to the more settled lifestyle for which he later opted. It is difficult, too, not to believe that Francis must have impressed him as something between a role-model and a solemn warning, for their backgrounds were very similar and Francis's present way of life offered Isherwood a glimpse into one of his own possible futures. Since he had more money than Isherwood, whose private income was at that time precarious, the freedom Francis enjoyed may also have made him an object of envy. He was under no necessity, as Isherwood seems to have been, to visit bourgeois households in the socially ambiguous capacity of a private tutor and to give English lessons for a few marks an hour, or to worry whether Uncle Henry's next cheque would be forthcoming.

Francis Turville-Petre was born in 1901, the son and heir of Oswald Turville-Petre of Bosworth Hall, near Lutterworth in Leicestershire. Oswald, who married in his late thirties and was nearly forty when his first-born appeared, had been born Oswald Petre, had inherited the estate at the age of 27 from his cousin, Sir Francis Fortescue-Turville, and had added the 'Turville' to his own surname. He was a country gentleman, a soldier and a devout Catholic descended from an old Catholic family. He had gone to school at Woburn Park, near Weybridge in Surrey, a short-lived educational establishment run by a relative, Monsignor Petre, who later became the 13th Baron Petre and the first Catholic priest since the Reformation to take his seat in the House of Lords. From school – unusually for a Catholic at that time – he had proceeded to Christ Church, Oxford. In due course he became Lord of the Manor of

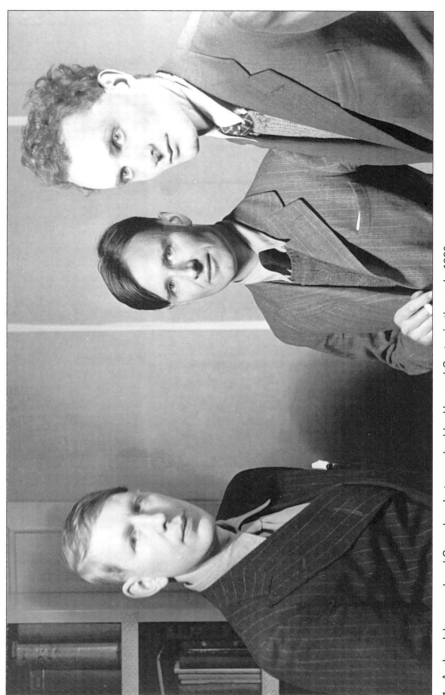

1. Auden, Isherwood and Spender photographed by Howard Coster in the early 1930s.

2. Auden and John Lavard in Germany 1929, probably at Rötehutte.

Wystan.   Stephen   Christopher.

3. Auden, Spender and Isherwood on Rügen Island in 1931; a print
   given to Gabriel Carritt and signed by all three.

4. Isherwood and Otto on Rügen Island *c.* 1931.

5. The young Francis Turville-Petre with his sisters.

6. Tauentzienstrasse, Berlin, 1930.

7. Dr Magnus Hirschfeld at his desk in the Institute *c.* 1926.

8. Part of the interior of the Hirschfeld Institute, Berlin.

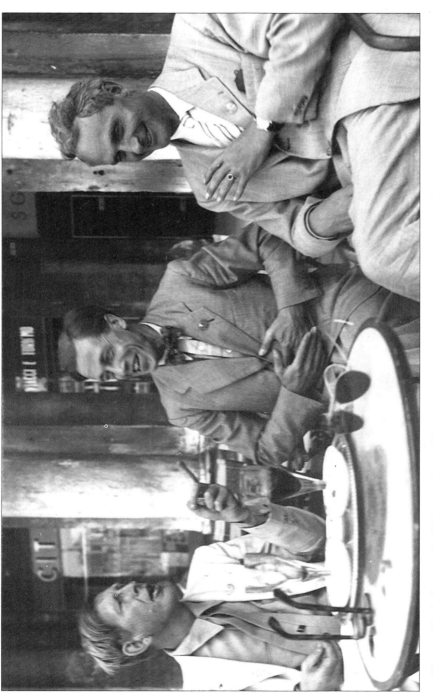

9. Wystan Hugh Auden, Cecil Day Lewis and Stephen Spender in Venice during the PEN Club Conference in 1949 (believed to be the only photograph of all three together)

10. Marlene Dietrich in *The Blue Angel*.

11. Conrad Veidt in *The Student of Prague.*

Husbands Bosworth, a Justice of the Peace and High Sheriff of Leicestershire, and served in the Great War with the Northants Yeomanry – yet another of the fathers who were away at the war during their sons' adolescence.

Oswald married Margaret Cave, 13 years younger than himself, and she bore him, in fairly rapid succession, two sons and three daughters. (The younger son, Gabriel, became a distinguished Icelandic scholar and an Oxford professor.) A drawing of Oswald shows him to have had the family face, long and narrow and tending to become deeply lined with the passing of time, that Francis also inherited.

Though he was born in London, where his family had taken a house for the winter, it was at Bosworth Hall that Francis spent much of his childhood, since the family was accustomed to pass half the year there and the other half at Whitley Abbey near Coventry, the home of his maternal grandparents. Bosworth Hall is on the edge of the village of Husbands Bosworth, through which traffic now thunders on its way to and from the M1 motorway six miles distant. In the early years of the century, though, it must have been a very tranquil spot. The park contains, a short walk from the small country house and its outbuildings, a Roman Catholic chapel, built in 1873 and still used for services and attracting a large and far-flung congregation. Pevsner informs us that the main part of the house was built in 1792, while other portions go back to the sixteenth or seventeenth century. Francis's early years were passed on the nursery floor at the top of the house, where the rapidly growing family was cared for by a nurse, a nurserymaid and in due course a governess. On reaching the age of five or six each child was allowed to pass through the door leading to the corridor at the end of which was the schoolroom, a spacious room with windows overlooking the park.

At seven he was sent to a Catholic preparatory school at Eastbourne, where he seems to have been very unhappy, and from there he proceeded in 1914 to the Oratory School, founded by Cardinal Newman in 1859 and in Francis's time still situated in the Hagley Road, Birmingham, next to the house of the Oratory Fathers. During these years, family holidays were spent at Lyme Regis, where Francis hunted enthusiastically for fossils in the cliffs. There were scientific talents in his mother's family: his uncle Charles Cave had erected a 'thunder-house' in his garden to monitor seismic disturbances. When he was about 12 Francis found a fine specimen belonging to an ichthyosaurus and was persuaded, or perhaps directed, to present it to the local museum. It was on one of these holidays that the three girls went on a picnic with an old lady who sent them to fill the tea-kettle at the brook and boiled it, or did not quite boil it, over a fire of sticks. The girls all fell ill with typhoid, and Gwenda, a year younger than Francis, was expected to die, a Home Office official actually being summoned to the house so that special permission could be granted for the burial to take place beside the private chapel. The civil servant, however, had a wasted journey, for Gwenda recovered and lived to be over 90.

Scraping and prising fossils out of the Dorset cliffs was early evidence of a passion on Francis's part for unburying the past, and at school the same passion manifested itself in a marked enthusiasm for archaeology. By a stroke of luck he was in exactly the right place for a specialised taste of this kind to receive encouragement. For the Oratory School was under the fairly new and highly charismatic headship of Father Edward Pereira (1866–1939), a brilliant talent-spotter who took pains to foster his pupils' individual interests, however unconventional. Francis was actually taught Egyptian by the science master, Daniel Arkell (who also lectured at Birmingham University); one of his contemporaries, George Bowring, who died in 1992, remembered this curious fact to the end of his life, observing justly that it was 'an unusual knowledge in a Physics and Chemistry master'. It seems likely that Francis was better served by Father Pereira and the Oratory School than if he had been sent to a more ancient and more celebrated establishment.

The historian of the school, A. J. Cornwell, has said of Father Pereira: 'I have discussed him with Oratorian nonagenarians, octogenarians and septuagenarians. Their impressions, contributed independently, leave one in no doubt that his influence was paramount, far-reaching and eternal. An interval of fifty or sixty years fails to dim the impact; the picture of him is as if they had only recently left school.'

Pereira's whole life had been closely associated with the school. He had himself been a pupil there at a time when Newman's influence was still potent, became a priest and an Oratory Father, went back to the school as a master and became head, having evidently been groomed for the succession, on the death of the incumbent in 1911. Belonging on his father's side to a wealthy

Portuguese family of tobacco importers (he eventually died of lung cancer), he was no intellectual and did not have a degree, his education having been at the Scots College in Rome, and his natural gifts displaying themselves most notably on the cricket field (he had played for Warwickshire against the Australians). More to the point, he seems to have been free from convictions, not unknown among other public school headmasters, as to the mould into which those in his care should be fitted, and Francis was the beneficiary of his wise and tactful tolerance of the educationally unorthodox.

Francis's time at the Oratory corresponded almost precisely to the years of the Great War. In the two generations before 1918 fewer than a thousand boys had passed through the school, and of those between the ages of 18 and 50 some 500 were still alive in 1914. Of that number nearly 400 served in the war; 71 were killed and 73 wounded. In a small school with a patriotic tradition and an emphasis on character-building, the war, and in particular the service given and sacrifices made by old boys, must have become during those years an inescapable part of the emotional atmosphere of daily life. For Francis, as for Christopher Isherwood, the burden of the Past must have lain heavy and the prospect of escape from it have proved irresistibly tempting.

It was a school of no more than seventy or eighty boys, and under a head less tolerant of individual tastes the atmosphere could have been stifling. Francis did well there, became a prefect, and won prizes for religious instruction, Latin prose composition and history. When he left he was awarded the Senior Norfolk Prize, the gift of the Duke of Norfolk, bestowed only on outstanding candidates, and worth £50 (a large sum in 1919) in books. His youngest sister, Alethea, remembers him at this time as a handsome boy with dark hair, and recalls the day when he came home from school with the first gramophone they had seen or heard and danced a tango with the governess.

He took a year off before going up to Oxford, probably spending at least some part of it in Palestine – for his sense of vocation, it seems, was already strong. So it was not until the Michaelmas Term of 1920 that Francis matriculated at Exeter College, Oxford, his father being described in the college records as 'landowner'. Father Pereira's encouragement of his archaeological leanings had been effective enough to make Francis disregard the family connection with Christ Church (to which his younger brother followed his father in due course) in favour of a less famous college where his specialised interests could be better catered for. One of the fellows and tutors of Exeter was Dr Robert Marett, by training a classicist but by this time University Reader in Social Anthropology and a prolific writer on primitive religion and other subjects. (There is probably no significance in the fact that, as a young man, Marett had studied philosophy at Berlin University.) E. E. Evans-Pritchard, who later became a famous and widely influential social anthropologist, came to the college from an Anglican vicarage one year after Francis.

The record of Francis's Oxford years is scanty, and neither his Catholicism nor (more predictably) his homosexuality forms part of it. The Catholic Chaplain at the time was Monsignor ('Mugger') Barnes, though he was soon to be succeeded by the more celebrated Ronald Knox. 'Sligger' Urquhart (why did university priests have names that make them sound like prizefighters?), who had become the first Catholic don at Oxford since the time of James II, was still at Balliol and used to take reading parties of Catholic undergraduates to his chalet in the Alps. But I have found no evidence that Francis moved in these circles, and it seems likely that the faith in which he had been so carefully brought up was no longer a central element in his life.

Academically, his Oxford career was remarkably undistinguished. Having done well at school, he nevertheless elected to read for a pass degree – an unusual step that was taken at that time by only about one in fifty undergraduates at the college. It meant that he was required to study a group of subjects instead of concentrating on one for honours, and his reason for taking this curious step seems clear: it enabled him to study anthropology, which was not available as an honours subject. Like A. E. Housman, whose Oxford career was even less distinguished, he seems to have been motivated by a mixture of wilfulness and intellectual passion to neglect his prescribed studies in favour of his consuming interests. In his second year he failed a Divinity examination but was successful at the second attempt, and eventually secured his BA in 1925.

He had, however, discovered his vocation, the archaeology of the Middle East, and at some stage, probably between school and Oxford, had already spent a year at the British School of Archaeology in Jerusalem as well as going to the Middle East during at least one of his summer vacations. The next stage in his chosen profession came rapidly and was dramatic, even sensational. In 1920 the study of Palestinian prehistory was, according to William Foxwell Albright's *The Archaeology of Palestine*, 'wholly undeveloped'. Francis had started surveying a site in Galilee in 1923, having probably had his attention directed to it by Marett. Two years later he 'excavated in two caves above the sea of Galilee and discovered the first stratified deposits in Palestine, in one of which he found the first remains of prehistoric man' (Albright, p. 37). The principal find was 'part of a typical Neanderthal skull'.

The skull was brought to England and examined by Sir Arthur Keith, a physical anthropologist, at the Royal College of Surgeons. Keith confirmed the general view that it was Neanderthal, but it is now believed to be much older and a significant find in relationship to one of the main issues of present-day prehistoric archaeology, the emergence of *homo sapiens*. Another historian has dated the 'systematic pursuit of prehistoric archaeology' in this area to Francis Turville-Petre's 1925 excavations: it was the first human fossil to be found in the Near East, and according to Jean Perrot, the discovery of what came to be called the Galilee Skull 'at once attracted the attention of prehistorians, and in subsequent years prehistoric studies developed on such a scale that Palestine soon became one of the principal centres of prehistoric archaeology outside Western Europe' (p. 130).

The finding of the skull aroused popular as well as professional interest, and *The Times* published reports and photographs, including one of Francis in the cave where he had discovered it. His Oxford college was not, however, much impressed by this precocious celebrity, and his record card there bears the curt and dismissive note 'Anthropologising in Palestine and journalistic fame – 1925'.

While still in his twenties, Francis had thus, at a single stroke, earned a significant and permanent place in the history of Middle Eastern archaeology. He lectured to the British Association for the Advancement of Science and published in 1927 *Researches in Prehistoric Galilee, 1925–1926*. The preface, by the Director of the British School of Archaeology in Jerusalem, states that 'the local operations were placed under the direct charge of Mr Turville-Petre, who, while still at Oxford, had made a special study of the Stone Age, and had, during a previous season (1923), made a preliminary exploration of the area.' Francis's own account, though couched in appropriately academic language, conveys something of the excitement of the brilliant hunch that paid off: 'The present writer ... decided to make the hills bordering the plains of Genesereth the centre of his researches, and to devote particular attention to caves.' He was gifted with a good eye for a site, and one he identified but never worked on was later excavated by Japanese archaeologists.

It was, then, a giant stride at the beginning of the career of a young man who had only recently left Oxford, but that career soon afterwards came mysteriously to a halt. Francis flashes across the sky of prehistoric archaeology like a rocket, and it was only a couple of years after the publication of his book that Isherwood knocked on his door in Berlin and found him a willing and expert guide to the boy-bars, devoting his full-time energies to drink and dissipation. He resumed his work briefly in 1931, when he spent three months in the Kebara Caves at Mount Carmel, seven miles south of Haifa. There he made some significant finds, and more work was later done by others on the same site, but it was his last dig. Thereafter his professional life came to an end – though this may not have been entirely by his own choice, for there is reason to believe that his scandalous reputation led to the blocking of later attempts to dig in Greece. There is a touching moment in *Christopher and his Kind* (p. 26) when Isherwood observes that Francis 'wasn't really interested in Germany.... He never felt truly at home, he said, except in the countries of the Eastern Mediterranean'. And Isherwood recalls rare moments of sobriety when Francis's conversation would reveal a profound knowledge of prehistoric Greece: 'He spoke of it often, with a quiet understated passion which Christopher found curiously moving. It was as if part of his mind dwelt continually in that world' (p. 26).

How can a career so brief, so brilliant, so bizarre in its aftermath, be accounted for? The passion for archaeology, and the choice of Palestine, are perhaps beyond explanation: it may have been (that favourite locution of the biographer at his wits' end) some lesson on the Old Testament given by Father Pereira that had ignited his interest, perhaps just the prettily coloured maps that relieve the black-and-white monotony of a schoolboy's Bible. What is obvious is that Middle Eastern archaeology took the son and heir of the strict Catholic squire away from his home, his family, his country and his religion to another land, an alien culture. He was to spend the rest of his life as an expatriate, living in Germany and Greece, and dying in Egypt.

Sex and drink obtained an early hold on him, and when he went to Berlin it was primarily to obtain treatment for syphilis at the Hirschfeld clinic. When he worked on the Kebara site in 1931, one of his colleagues was Mrs Charlotte Augusta Baines, a Catholic lady of about sixty, who is said to have cast a disapproving eye on the empty whisky bottles that were tossed out of Francis's tent and the Arab boys who crawled into it. (One story relates that he deposited a considerable cache of them – bottles, not boys – in the caves for future archaeologists to unearth and ponder on.) Reading Isherwood's account, it is easy to form a mental picture of a middle-aged man who had the confirmed habits and unmistakable lineaments produced by long years of dissipation, while references to him as 'The Fronny' seem to come from cheeky schoolboys guying one of their elders. Some biographers seem to have caught this infection, Jonathan Fryer, for instance, referring to Francis as 'much worn by years of debauchery...his aura of decay' (1993, p. 76). The truth is that when Isherwood met him Francis was only a few years out of Oxford, was still only 28, and was thus only three years older than Isherwood himself.

The period between Francis's brilliant archaeological debut and his appearance before the bemused and newly arrived Isherwood is obscure, and exactly when, in the course of his roaming life, he moved to Berlin is unknown. Early in 1928, however, and well before either Auden or Isherwood made their home in the city, the name of 'Francis Turville-Petre, London' appears on printed material issued from 10 In den Zelten by the World League for Sexual Reform. He is named there as a member of the *Gründungs-ausschuss* (foundation committee) of the League, along with Havelock Ellis, Norman Haire and others. This seems to argue that Francis was in Berlin by that time, almost two years before he opened the door to Isherwood, and was taking an active interest in Hirschfeld's campaigns. This is confirmed by another document indicating that on 28 December 1928, after Auden's arrival in the city but still nearly a year before the encounter that Isherwood described so long afterwards, he was elected to one of the committees of the Institute. He continued to participate in its affairs, for an advertisement for a lecture series on sexology given there in the spring of 1930 – that is, a few months *after* Isherwood's encounter – includes him as one of the speakers, his subject being 'sexual ethnology'. (According to *Christopher and his Kind* Francis had left Berlin early in the year, and if Isherwood's memory was reliable must have returned at this time.) This picture of the lecturer and committee member, the trained social anthropologist who has turned his attention to human sexual behaviour, does not quite fit with Isherwood's graphic portrait of a man far advanced in dissipation, and the suspicion arises that the garish colours in which Francis's behaviour is depicted may have been heightened by the novelist-autobiographer to match that crimson silk robe.

Certainly he was one of the delegates attending the League's congress held in Copenhagen in 1928, for he appears in two group photographs taken on that occasion. In one of them, taken outside the city's town hall, he can be clearly seen: erect, dapper, dark-suited, bespectacled, bow-tied, buttonholed, he seems the very model of the well turned out upper-class Englishman, and, in appearance at least, much closer to Bertie Wooster than to the raffish figure whom Isherwood encountered in the following year (or at any rate described long afterwards). Mysteriously, though, his name disappears from later lists of notabilities who lent their support to the League, such as that accompanying the invitations to the London congress issued in the spring of 1929. One can only guess at the reasons for the withdrawal of his name: some quarrel, on personal or ideological grounds, with Hirschfeld or one of his associates, perhaps.

After that first meeting, as we have seen, Francis and Christopher were together for a few weeks until Francis left Berlin 'for warmer southern lands'. His next appearance in *Christopher and his Kind* is in the spring of 1932, when he returned to Berlin full of good resolutions and urged Isherwood to share his new lifestyle. Together they went to Mohrin, where Stephen Spender joined them for a time. But Francis's resolutions were soon broken and he was going off to Berlin for long weekends.

The following year, when Isherwood decided to leave Germany, he was invited by Francis to join him on the Greek island of St Nicholas, where he was living in primitive conditions. He had bought land there and had plans to build a house and resume his archaeological work. These plans came to nothing: though his achievements are on a much less heroic scale, Francis belonged to the same tradition of the brilliant, hunch-pursuing maverick scholar as Heinrich Schliemann, and like Schliemann he incurred the disapproval of the academic establishment.

Francis met Isherwood in Athens on 20 May and accompanied him to St Nicholas; later Spender, and possibly also Auden, visited him there. The journey, and Isherwood's hot and uncomfortable sojourn on St Nicholas which lasted until 6 September, are described at length in *Christopher and his Kind*. The island remained Francis's base for some years, and he stayed there after the outbreak of war and until the Germans bombed it. He was then put, unwillingly, on the last boat for Alexandria – the previous boat had sunk with the loss of all on board – and made his way to Cairo. In her book *Cairo in the War*, Artemis Cooper has given a vivid account of the scramble to escape from Greece at this time: 'People jostled to get a passage on any ship willing to make the journey, while the Luftwaffe kept up their constant bombing on the capital's port at Piraeus...' (p. 77).

A little earlier, in February 1938, there had been a last meeting with Isherwood and Auden, when they were on their way to China, at which time Francis seems to have been in Egypt. Apparently by arrangement, he went to Port Said to greet them when they disembarked: 'He assured them that Port Said, which they had been told was the sex capital of the world, was in fact deadly dull, and he took them instead to the Pyramids, which they in turn found uninteresting, though the Sphinx impressed them with what Auden called its "huge hurt face"'. The well-known photograph of Isherwood and Auden setting off for China shows two young men smilingly eager for experience, but Francis, though belonging to their own generation, sounds old and weary, and had in fact little more than three years left to live. He died in Cairo on 16 August 1941 of peritonitis; with a final lordly refusal to do the sensible and obvious thing, he had not permitted his friends to take him to hospital as no Greek hospital was available.

He is buried in the English cemetery in Cairo, and there is a memorial window dedicated to him in the chapel at Bosworth Hall. By a curious chance he outlived his father by exactly two months and thus inherited the estate whose responsibilities he had so resolutely shunned. During his years of wandering he had kept in touch with his family and often visited his old home (the last visit was in 1939). But he seems to have made it quite clear that he was a visitor whose chosen way of life was entirely different from that of the country squirearchy into which he had been born. He would sometimes bring friends from London, where he kept a flat in Russell Square, and their camp behaviour, transferred from the West End to sedate rural surroundings, is still remembered. One of them, taken for a walk in the park, was so terrified by an encounter with a cow that he had to be gently led to a place of safety. A more sober guest at Bosworth Hall was Karl Giese, Magnus Hirschfeld's partner, who went there after the 1929 London conference. On these visits, it seems, Francis would talk 'obsessively' about his homosexuality, as if to underline his firm refusal to accept, under any circumstances, the role of Catholic English gentleman, manly, philoprogenitive and devoted to the public service, that had been assigned to him. In this firm rejection of a prescribed role, and substitution of one he knew to be startlingly unconventional, he had much in common with Isherwood.

Francis's numerous appearances in Auden's work have already been briefly mentioned. Isherwood, too, wrote about him extensively, and from a much longer perspective of time, in both *Christopher and his Kind* and *Down There on a Visit*. Francis was also put to good use by two other writers in, respectively, an autobiography and a novel. Xan Fielding, a friend of Francis, describes in *Hide and Seek* (1954) how, in late September 1939, he made his way to St Nicholas and stayed there for almost a year:

> Apart from an occasional visitor from Athens and a staff of half a dozen peasant boys, Francis was the only person I saw for the whole of the first winter of the war and for most of the following summer; and he was the last man to censure me for following my natural inclination. Certainly he had followed his. At the age of thirty, after laying the foundations of a brilliant career with his discovery of the Galilee Skull, he had abandoned anthropology because he found the profession interfered too much with his private life, and had come to retire in Greece. His pretext for settling on a deserted island was to excavate a mound on the mainland directly opposite; but it was easier to think of his premature retirement as a gesture of defiance, for the site ten years later was still untouched.

This account of Francis's desertion of his profession may be less than fair, since there is evidence that his genuine efforts to dig in Greece were frustrated by fellow scholars who disapproved of the undignified way in which earlier expeditions had been conducted. Fielding continues:

> Inevitably, I suppose, he had earned a reputation for eccentricity. His appearance was unconventional: long straight Red-Indian

hair framed a sad sallow face so lined that it was impossible to guess its owner's age; below it an emaciated body, always clothed in bright colours, stretched six feet down to an almost freakishly small pair of sandalled feet. His habits, too, were out of the ordinary; he would get up every day at sunset and sit down to a luncheon which had been ordered for three o'clock in the afternoon – a mere formality in any case, for he never ate anything at meal times but lived on brandy and dry bread supplemented by a weekly cup of Bovril. Those who did not know him well might have thought he despised the world. They would have been wrong – it was only public opinion he scorned. Any misanthropic tendency he might have had was checked by a tolerance of human foibles that was almost Armenian in its integrity. (p. 15)

Francis's entirely natural and unaffected eccentricity, like the furrowed and crumpled face, oddly anticipates the later years of Auden.

Wartime Cairo had some qualifications as an appropriate setting for Francis's last days. It has been said that 'everybody you have ever heard of was [in Cairo] at one time or another during the war', and the different elements combined to make it a hotbed (no dead metaphor in this instance) of sexual intrigue and licence. Olivia Manning, whose husband worked for the British Council, had earlier known Francis in Greece and later put him into her novel *The Battle Lost and Won* (1978), the second volume of her 'Levant Trilogy', where he makes an appearance as 'Humphrey Taupin, the archaeologist'.

[Taupin] had been a famous name around the cafés in Athens. When he was very young, on his first dig, he had come upon a stone sarcophagus that contained a death-mask of beaten gold. The mask, thought to be of a king of Corinth, was in the museum, and Harriet had seen it there. This find, that for some would have been the beginning, was for him the end. She could imagine that such an achievement at twenty might leave one wondering what to do for the next fifty years. Anyway, confounded by his own success, he had retired to the most remote of the Sporades... (pp. 151–2).

Like Francis, Taupin had escaped 'when the Germans came' and made his way to Cairo, full of British refugees and, with its wartime romances, like 'a bureau of sexual exchange'. When Harriet shakes his hand: 'She took it but not willingly. She had heard that he had been cured of syphilis, but perhaps he was not cured. Feeling his hand in hers, dry and fragile, like the skeleton of a small bird, she remembered the courteous crusader who took the hand of a leper and became a leper himself. When Taupin's hand slipped away, she felt she, too, was at risk' (p. 152). The sense of physical revulsion is striking, especially when one recalls that Francis was only forty when he died.

Both Fielding and Manning touch on the mystery of Francis's tragically aborted career, but Manning's diagnosis of him as one 'confounded by his own success' does not quite carry conviction. The rebellion and refusal to conform affected every area of his life, including his dress and his eating habits, and it would surely have been even more extraordinary if he had followed up his early success by pursuing an academic career and returning to Oxford in the fullness of time as Professor of Archaeology. Ultimately there seems to have been, beneath the surface of aristocratic indifference to the opinions of others, something wilful and even self-destructive in his nature. Early fame was quickly followed by withdrawal from the world, and in his later years on St Nicholas he seems to have been for much of the time virtually a recluse.

His background – the country house, the military father away at the war, the education at a minor public school and an ancient university – was so close to Isherwood's that the latter must very early in their acquaintance have sensed that the slightly older man's chosen way of life offered a fearful temptation, to yield to which would be ultimately fatal for one who wanted to be a writer. In the event Francis provided him with admirable copy but proved a negative role-model. As already noted, in *Christopher and his Kind* Isherwood makes a point of insisting that, while Francis remained half the night in the bars, haggling with prospective bedfellows as he had once haggled with camel-drivers, he himself went home early in order to be fresh 'to get on with his novel' the next morning.

As for Francis, the haggling with hustlers became almost an end in itself, an occupation as well as a hobby, and perhaps the most revealing sentences in all that Isherwood wrote about him are the following:

Actually, Francis didn't care who he finished up with: he wasn't much interested in making love. What did fascinate him – and what began, more and more, to fascinate Christopher, looking at it through Francis's eyes, was the boys' world, their slang, their quarrels, their jokes, their outrageous unserious demands, their girls, their thefts, their encounters with the police.   (pp. 28–9)

In his latter days, tall and cadaverous and looking twice his age, bored with love, with sex, with travel, with friendship, even with food, Francis is like a figure in a morality play, a dreadful warning against the perils of hedonism. Only, almost automatically, the reconnoitring eye and the interrogating voice continued to function.

On Isherwood's part, fascination with 'the boys' world', though real enough, did not bear much fruit in his published writings: the Berlin stories are too discreet, too evasive, too readily disposed to encode and displace, to make much use of what must have been wonderfully colourful material, both comic and sad. It was a world that must surely have been extensively and minutely depicted in his lost diaries and might have received attention in his ambitious, abandoned fictional project, *The Lost*. In Francis's case, it looks as though his eye for a promising site, his curiosity about (and intellectual satisfaction in uncovering) the ways of an alien people, had been transferred from the dusty hills of Palestine to the gritty streets of Berlin, and he was finding an outlet for his exceptional and neglected gifts as the anthropologist of the rent-bars.

JOHN LAYARD

Layard's name appears on the first page of Isherwood's *Christopher and his Kind*, and, much earlier, and thinly disguised, as 'Barnard', he had made an appearance in the autobiography *Lions and Shadows*. In the latter Isherwood had claimed that the desire to meet Layard was his principal motive for going to Berlin, but the candour of riper years compelled him to admit that in making this claim he was 'avoiding the truth'. He had, however, received enthusiastic reports from Auden about this strange Englishman, resident in Berlin, and there is no doubt that Layard was a charismatic personality who over a period of several months had a close relationship with Auden and whose ideas had a permanent influence on his thinking.

Isherwood too became friends with Layard and later admitted that he had learned a great deal from him. In *Christopher and his*

Kind (p. 13) he recalls his first impressions of Layard when they met in Berlin – his 'X-ray eyes, his mocking amusement, his stunning frankness....' This impression was reinforced when Layard practised on him some of his white magic. Isherwood had on his left shoulder-blade a patch of hair, growing on an old acne scar, of which he was irrationally ashamed. Layard explained that this was a manifestation of instinct in contrast to the control and repression represented by the hairless right shoulder-blade. In other words, the hair was not a flaw but a good thing, and to clinch his argument he kissed the part in question. Either the explanation or the kiss was efficacious in curing Isherwood of his embarrassment. Later he introduced Layard to his mother in England, and even she seems to have been impressed, referring to him in her diary as 'very striking and unusual'.

Born in 1891, Layard had gone to Bedales, the famous and at that time very unconventional co-educational boarding school in Hampshire, and then to King's College, Cambridge, where he had read French and German. Graduating in 1913, he had travelled in the following year to Melanesia as an assistant to the well-known Cambridge anthropologist and psychologist William Rivers, but on returning home he suffered a nervous breakdown so severe as to produce acute physical symptoms that made him unable to walk. (The official college record of the time, which gives for him a fashionable London address, notes that since his return from the Pacific he had 'suffered from ill-health'.) He became a patient of the American psychotherapist Homer Lane, who was living and working in England, and not only recovered the use of his legs but became a passionate convert to Lane's unorthodox doctrines, which were duly transmitted to Auden and, through Auden, to Isherwood.

Lane had been born in 1876, the son of a railway worker and a strict Baptist mother, and had run away from home at 14. He did a variety of jobs for short periods, married young and discovered that the advent of his first child made him keenly interested in education. After a teacher training course in Boston he taught for a time in a prison, then taught manual work in a school in Detroit, where he also established a club for delinquent boys and ran 'summer playgrounds' to keep working-class children off the streets during school holidays. His next job was as superintendent of a boys' home, a task he accepted on condition that the home was moved into the country, where the boys could be employed on farm work.

He was obviously a man of exceptional energy and vision, and one who quickly became the subject of anecdote if not legend. When the farmhouse burned down, he broke a wrist in rescuing one of the boys but

> spent the night finding sleeping accommodation for the boys and driving them to neighbouring farmhouses, paying no attention to his broken wrist until the afternoon of the next day. The doctor who at last set it told him that he would now never have the proper use of it again. As a fact, it healed completely in record time. Again and again Lane overcame physical disability by the constructive power with which he set himself to any creative work on hand.   (*Talks to Parents and Teachers*, p. 7)

The exercise of healing power sets the pattern for much of Lane's later work as a therapist, while the defiance of orthodox opinion contains the seeds of his later clashes with authority and his eventual downfall.

The rebuilt home was named the Ford Republic and run on democratic lines, and Lane's work there brought him considerable celebrity and made him much in demand as a lecturer. He paid more than one visit to England and in 1912 settled there as superintendent of the Little Commonwealth, a self-governing reformatory school in Dorset that was soon closed after a scandal and a Home Office inquiry. The details are obscure, but it seems likely that Lane's unconventional methods made him the victim of official suspicion, intolerance and persecution. He remained in England, however, giving lectures on education and working as a consulting psychologist in London – the capacity in which he treated Layard. Again, however, his indifference to conventional standards led to disaster. He had, perhaps innocently but certainly unwisely, accepted a substantial loan from a rich woman patient, and when her family complained to the police his office was raided and such suspicious items as pornographic pictures and contraceptives were allegedly discovered there. He was arrested on a technicality under the Aliens Act (he had not notified a change of address) and was sent to Brixton prison, tried and deported. Settling in France, he quickly died of typhoid and pneumonia in 1925. The temptation to diagnose also a broken heart is strong.

It was a remarkable career, both heroic and quixotic, and its end is little short of tragic: the spectacle of the British establishment ganging up on the unqualified foreign crank, and the readiness with which unorthodox (though evidently effective) styles of therapy were associated with sexual irregularities, is unedifying. But Lane's influence did not cease with his death, and his little book *Talks to Parents and Teachers*, constructed by his disciples from his lectures and notes and published posthumously in 1928, became a bestseller. Layard, whose treatment was still under way at the time of Lane's downfall and death, was seriously disturbed by those events and regarded the healer's disappearance as an act of personal betrayal. He had, however, thoroughly absorbed Lane's ideas, and when, after leaving England and seeking psychiatric help in Vienna, he moved to Berlin with the same purpose, he was ready to pass on the good news to willing converts.

He had settled in Berlin in 1926 and, soon after Auden's arrival in the autumn of 1928, telephoned him at the suggestion of a mutual friend, David Ayerst. Auden visited Layard and at that first meeting they spent several hours talking – so many hours, indeed, that it was too late for Auden to return home to his lodgings with the Muthesius family in a distant suburb, and he spent the night in Layard's flat. What happened that night is far from clear. Layard was bisexual and was immediately and strongly attracted to Auden, falling for him (as he later said in his fragmentary autobiography) 'like a ninepin'. Some considerable time afterwards Auden wrote in his journal that at their early meetings Layard had made a great impression on him and 'his exposition of Lane has made a difference to me.... Going to bed with him at first though was a mistake which lasts. I feel guilty about it.'

Auden did not begin to keep the journal until the following spring, and in common with many of his journal entries, the wording of this one is rather obscure at a crucial point: does 'at first' mean 'at our first meeting' or 'at an early stage of our friendship' (e.g. at their second or third meeting), or simply 'too soon'? Layard's own account states quite unambiguously that Auden rejected his sexual advances on that first occasion, remarking by way of explanation and excuse that he had ' "a boy named Pieps" '. Layard may, of course, have had his own reasons for autobiographical reticence.

The long conversations about Lane, however, had more far-reaching effects than what happened, or did not happen, in bed, and Humphrey Carpenter's conclusion that the older man made a 'tremendous impression' on Auden seems fully justified. Layard's own beliefs had by this time developed well beyond those of his healer and master, and seem to blend ideas derived from Rousseau, Blake, Wordsworth, Froebel, Freud, Lawrence, Groddeck and no doubt others. The conviction expressed in Blake's epigram 'Sooner murder an infant in its cradle than nurse unacted desires' was developed into a full-blown theory of the evil effects of repression, especially in relation to the psychosomatic origins of disease. Physical illness was the result of psychic or moral disorder, and by a neat stroke each malady was appropriate to its cause, so that (as one of Auden's poems declares) the liar suffers from quinsy and (as another demonstrates at greater length) the sexually unfulfilled woman develops cancer. The great attraction of this doctrine, of course, was that it authorised and indeed enjoined as a solemn duty the kind of acting out of desires in defiance of society and its conventions that Auden was in any case drawn to. Not to behave according to one's inner nature – the God, or good, within one – was to ask for trouble. It is obvious that Auden found these ideas intellectually exciting as well as personally convenient; they were not quickly cast off and have a prominent place in his early writings. Speaking of the development of his ideas in his *Letter to Lord Byron*, he remarks that 'Part came from Lane, and part from D. H. Lawrence;/ Gide, though I didn't know it then, gave part...', but makes no reference to Layard as the pimp or midwife of his intellectual love-affair with Lane.

During the months following their first meeting, Auden and Layard saw a good deal of each other, but the sexual and emotional elements quickly faded from their relationship – though perhaps more rapidly on Auden's side than on Layard's. Not only was Layard, now in his late thirties, an elder-brother- and almost a father-figure, but he must have been too much of Auden's own nation and class to be sexually stimulating at a period when Auden's sexual tastes seem to have run to brawny working-class foreigners. As time passed, moreover, the older man's charisma wore thin, perhaps because his own serious instability became more apparent. There are hints of discord in Auden's journal entries at this time: 'When J[ohn] disagrees with me he says "You're so young." But if I suggest to him that he is old, he is hurt.' There is evidence, too, that Layard, a man of private means and without career, vocation or occupation, was jealous of Auden's creative powers ('he hates my writing').

One of the earliest entries in Auden's journal catches the flavour of their relationship in the spring of 1929. Though still close, it did not prevent Auden from readily becoming bored and irritated by Layard's depressive state:

> Rather intimate with John. "I kept hoping you'd come and see me during the last two days" "O dear I was just longing to come" "But I never said anything to put you off coming?" "Yes you did. You said you wanted to work in the morning." Presently. "You've just got to get well. You're much too good a person to be like this." I was vilely insincere, because I don't care a hoot. I am ashamed of my laziness and so tell everyone how hard I work, and dislike them if they are lazy....

'Rather intimate' has been substituted for the deleted phrase 'I kissed'. By this stage, while fully recognising the contribution Layard has made to his own development, Auden is ready to admit, if only to his journal, that he no longer has any feelings for the older man. Layard was still, however, a sufficiently interesting figure for Isherwood to be taken to see him very soon after his arrival, an occasion on which, inevitably, Layard talked about Lane. The visit does not seem to have been repeated during Isherwood's time in Berlin.

Layard's mental health, meanwhile, was going from bad to worse. Both grieved and aggrieved by Lane's death, he had transferred his devotion to one of Lane's other patients, a young Italian woman, Etta da Viti, who was now living in Paris. Though he declared his love for her, however, she gave him no encouragement. A woman friend of Layard's from England, Margaret Gardiner, concerned at the news of his state, visited him in Berlin at Eastertime and, confronted with his suicide threats, heroically set off for Paris to find Etta in the hope of persuading her to come to Berlin. The Italian girl could not be found, however, and Margaret had to return to England.

With Auden's help, Margaret had moved Layard from his sordid lodgings into a hotel, but this did little or nothing for his state of mind, which was greatly worsened by the news of Margaret's failure. Nor was the situation helped by Layard's inability to rise to the occasion when Auden lent him his new boyfriend, Gerhart, for the night – though here again the two accounts differ (Gerhart, regrettably, does not seem to have kept a journal or written an autobiography). Auden's journal entry for 2 April, as already described, shows that he talked enthusiastically to Layard about Gerhart in the strong conviction that Layard would want to share him. Layard's retrospective account, on the other hand, says that he 'made up my mind to do the dirty on Wystan.... I knew this was a complete betrayal...' In other words Auden laid claim to a generous gesture that might help to cheer up his friend, while Layard claims he took the initiative and seduced the boy behind his friend's back. In this instance one is perhaps more inclined to believe Auden's account, in any case much nearer the event, than the self-dramatising later one.

Auden had all along taken the strictly logical view that if Layard wanted to kill himself he should be allowed to get on with it: to do so would, after all, be no more than to act in the spirit of his belief in the essential rightness of one's inner impulses. What was to be done if the inner impulses of a friend urged a rescue operation was not quite clear. But soon Auden was to be forced into action when the situation took a genuinely dramatic turn. The day after his abortive attempt to enjoy Gerhart, Layard stuck a revolver in his mouth and pulled the trigger. A little earlier in the day, perhaps only a very short time before this deed was done, Auden had been with him, had found him entertaining thoughts of suicide, and had encouraged him to proceed. Auden had found himself quite unresponsive alike to Layard's kiss and to his tears, and soon left him alone and returned to his lodgings.

The method of self-destruction selected by Layard is not, it would seem, one that can be confidently counted on to fail, but it did: the revolver must have been pointed upwards, phallus-like, when it was fired, for the bullet made its way through the nasal passages and found a home in Layard's skull without doing serious damage to the brain. The wonders were not over, however, for on regaining consciousness Layard decided to call on Auden and ask him to finish the job he had so badly bungled. He crawled into a taxi, drove to his friend's lodgings, and climbed several flights of stairs, meeting on the way a couple of boys who seem also to have been heading for Auden's room. One of them helped him to Auden's door while the other went ahead to announce his arrival.

Layard's autobiography states that he had every confidence that Auden would comply with his wishes 'out of friendship', but

Auden declined and instead bundled him into another taxi and took him, through a snow-storm, to a hospital. In Auden's journal the events of this extraordinary day are recounted, with ostentatious brevity and detachment, in a few lines; his strongest feelings on being confronted with the injured man seem to have been of physical revulsion, and it was on the next day that he made the lightning decision to go to Hamburg with Gerhart.

Yet again there is a disparity between the versions given by the two principal actors in this drama. Layard's reproduction of the dialogue that allegedly took place when he appeared in Auden's room – ' "Wystan, I've done it.... But it hasn't killed me. Please finish me off – here's the pistol and ammunition" .... "I'm terribly sorry, I know you want this, but I can't do it, because I might be hanged if I did ...." ' – need be taken no more seriously than any other conversations reproduced after an interval of many years. But he also states quite unequivocally that he had 'never talked' to Auden about suicide, and this is clearly contradicted by Auden's journal, which there is no reason to disbelieve on this point.

An odd footnote to Layard's suicide attempt is provided by an anecdote recounted in Jonathan Fryer's 1992 biography of Isherwood. It seems that in 1926 and well before his Berlin period, Isherwood in a fit of depression also contemplated suicide, bought a pistol, and sought the advice of a friend as to the most efficacious method: 'He recommended sticking the gun into his mouth, and pointing it upwards towards the brain to inflict maximum damage' (p. 59). The unanswerable questions fairly leap at one: whether, if it actually happened, Auden knew of this and passed on to Layard the advice given by Isherwood's friend; whether Isherwood mentioned it to anyone before Layard's attempt, and, if not, whether the truth is that he incorporated Layard's experience as a heroic episode in the story of his own life, just as he incorporated a fictionalised version of it into *The Memorial*.

Layard's suicide attempt had taken place on 3 April, and when Auden returned to Berlin from Hamburg on the 6th he found that Layard's mother had arrived and they went to the hospital together. A few days later Mrs Layard called on him to discuss her son's future: her notion was that all would be well if he could contrive to fall in love with a nice girl, and Auden judged this a shrewd view of the situation. She also talked about Layard's childhood, and Auden recorded some of her remarks in his journal: ' "John was a model little boy until he was five. Almost too good.

Devoted to me. Too devoted according to these modern psychological ideas."' To this no doubt accurate diagnosis Auden adds: 'John tells me that when he was at school there was love (girls) and holy love (mother).' It was, of course, a subject in which Auden, another mother's boy, had a strong personal interest.

Later Auden took Gerhart to see Layard in hospital. On this occasion Auden's principal emotion was anxiety lest Gerhart should let slip the fact that they had gone off to Hamburg the day after Layard shot himself, while Gerhart's was distaste for the sight of physical weakness. The young sailor was convinced that Layard would die and, in an unusual flight of eloquence, declared that he would not sleep with him for a hundred marks. He could hardly have made his point more strongly. Gerhart's indifference seems to have acted as a reproach to Auden, who was fully aware of his own lack of response, and indeed his conduct throughout this whole sorry affair is not easy to account for. As a doctor's son he might well have become accustomed to the idea of physical suffering in others, but he seems, on the evidence of the journal, to have taken pains to stress his total lack of horror or even concern. Layard's friendship had by now become something of a burden to him, and Layard's withdrawal from the arena of his life in Berlin would not have been unwelcome, but this hardly seems enough to explain his behaviour. Perhaps the solution is to be found in his all-consuming infatuation with Gerhart, then at its apogee.

Contrary to Gerhart's prediction, Layard made an excellent and surprisingly rapid recovery, and by 23 April was fit enough not only to accompany Auden to the Cosy Corner but to celebrate Shakespeare's birthday by going off, at Auden's suggestion, with one of the boys. Once again, however, his evening was not a great success, and the next morning he called on Auden to recount how he had got drunk and had collapsed in the lavatory so that, embarrassingly enough, the landlady had had to be summoned to show the boy out. He joined Auden and Isherwood in the Harz Mountains for a few days in July. Soon afterwards, like Auden, Layard left Berlin and returned to England. They remained friends, and Layard eventually married and found a career as a Jungian analyst. During the war he flourished briefly as an author, producing a long-delayed account of his anthropological work (*Stone Men of Malekula: Vao*, 1942) as well as *The Lady of the Hare: Being a Study in the Healing Power of Dreams* in 1944.

Despite the turbulent emotions it involved, mainly on Layard's side, the real importance of their relationship is intellectual. Auden did not hesitate to communicate his enthusiasm for the doctrines expounded by Layard to others – notably to Isherwood, who must have heard about them during Auden's Christmas visit to England in 1928 and who met Layard when he went to Berlin in the spring of 1930. The revolver was fired only six days after Isherwood's departure, and it is conceivable that sexual jealousy experienced when Layard saw the two younger men together may have conspired with his sexual failure with Gerhart to precipitate his happily incompetent attempt to act – quite consistently with his own beliefs – upon his self-destructive impulse.

GERALD HAMILTON

Like Francis Turville-Petre, Gerald Frank Hamilton Souter, better known as Gerald Hamilton, seems to have offered himself almost importunately as literary copy; unlike Francis, however, he was always ready to take up the offer himself. Part of his special appeal for Isherwood may have been his knack of fictionalising his own life and rewriting his own past – colourful enough, it might have been thought, without further embellishment – in the terms of a romantic novelist (which, among much else, he was). Charlatan and trickster though he must be judged to have been, his conversational and literary escapades on the frontiers of autobiography and fiction must have formed a source of fascination to a writer who had made that border-territory his own special field of operations. In due course Hamilton not only provided the central figure in *Mr Norris Changes Trains* and some vivid pages in *Christopher and his Kind* but himself wrote of his life in Berlin and his relationship with Isherwood and others in a couple of autobiographical volumes. The first of these, *Mr Norris and I*, contains a brief but very interesting prologue by Isherwood.

Born in Shanghai of Irish parentage in 1889, he was 15 years older than Isherwood. His career, which had taken him to many parts of the world, was that of con man and fixer: as Isherwood says in *Christopher and his Kind*,

> If you wanted to sell a stolen painting to a collector who didn't mind enjoying it in private, to smuggle arms into a foreign

country, to steal a contract away from a rival firm, to be decorated with a medal of honour which you had done nothing to deserve, to get your criminal dossier extracted from the archives, then Gerald was delighted to try to help you, and he quite often succeeded.   (p. 63)

His method was bribery, and for his pains he not only took a 'commission' but was also apt to run up a hefty expenses account. For his tastes were extravagant, and as a result he was chronically short of funds.

Over the years, Hamilton had served several prison sentences: two in England (one for gross indecency with a male person, the other for unpatriotic activities during the Great War), others on the Continent (there had been some unpleasantness in Italy over a pearl necklace). He had also published, pseudonymously, a homosexual novel titled *Desert Dreamers* (1914). But when Isherwood met him in the winter of 1930–1 Hamilton was passing through a rare period of respectable employment. Living in Frankfurt for a time, where an obliging contact found him work as a broadcaster, he had noticed that it was not easy to buy *The Times* in that major German city. He drew this fact to the attention of the London headquarters of the newspaper, and the outcome was his appointment as sales representative of *The Times* for Germany. His discharge of these duties obviously gave satisfaction, since a year later he was asked to open an office in Berlin, where he made his home in the Derfflingerstrasse.

Hamilton's later reflections on his appointment are of interest. His curriculum vitae, if he ever had one, must have been colourful rather than confidence-inspiring if it was not entirely a work of fiction, but his dignified employers in Printing House Square seemed entirely uninterested in his past, and as he remarks blandly in *Mr Norris and I*, 'This serves to show with what ease anybody can to-day obtain a responsible position, no matter what his past life may have been'. He adds, more severely, that getting such a job so easily 'is only another illustration of the vast scale of hypocrisy upon which the standards of our civilisation really depend' (p. 122). His subsequent friendship with Guy Burgess provided him with a more sensational example of the phenomenon that provoked these moral reflections, and there cannot be much doubt that Hamilton's family connections, accent and social manner opened doors to him that his criminal record might have encouraged people to leave carefully locked.

Page 140

Later *The Times* sacked him, the reason he himself gave being his involvement with the Communists in Germany. But before this time, in the winter of 1930–1, he had met Isherwood, who seems instantly to have spotted his fictional potential. Referring to the description of Mr Norris in the opening lines of *Mr Norris Changes Trains*, Isherwood later said that Hamilton and Norris were 'identical'. That description is strikingly detailed and vivid:

> My first impression was that the stranger's eyes were of an unusually light blue.... Startled and innocently naughty, they...were the eyes of a schoolboy surprised in the act of breaking one of the rules....
> His smile had great charm....
> His hands were white, small and beautifully manicured....
> He had a large blunt fleshy nose and a chin which seemed to have slipped sideways. It was like a broken concertina.... Above his ripe red cheeks, his forehead was sculpturally white, like marble. A queerly cut fringe of dark grey hair lay across it, compact, thick and heavy. After a moment's examination, I realized, with extreme interest, that he was wearing a wig.

(I give the description here as quoted, very selectively and with incomplete indications of omissions, in *Christopher and his Kind*.) If the 'extreme interest' was also Isherwood's reaction to his actual scrutiny of Hamilton, he may have had an intuition that the wig furnished a ready-made symbol for a basically dishonest personality.

In the course of time Isherwood introduced Hamilton to Auden, Spender and other friends, including E. M. Forster and Benjamin Britten. There was a notable gathering in 1935 when Isherwood and Heinz, Forster and his policeman-lover Bob Buckingham, Spender, Brian Howard, Klaus Mann and Hamilton all found themselves in Amsterdam at the same time. Hamilton himself was not short of friends, sometimes of a distinctly grander variety, and his memoirs are punctuated by frequent name-dropping. We can safely assume that his conversation was not dissimilar, and if the name in question had a scandalous or lurid reputation that was no deterrent. In the autobiographical *The Way It Was With Me*, published near the end of his life and repeating much material that had appeared earlier, he states that he first met Isherwood 'under the auspices of Alesteir [sic] Crowley' and thereafter saw him 'almost daily'

(p. 44). Whatever 'auspices' may mean, this seems to imply that
Crowley effected the introduction, though Brian Finney's account
is that Hamilton 'introduced Isherwood and Spender . . . to Aleister
Crowley' (p. 86). Finney's version is presumably based upon an
anecdote in Hamilton's earlier *Mr Norris and I*, which recounts a
visit to Crowley 'with an English friend, Christopher Isherwood,
whom I was seeing very often in Berlin at that time' (p. 126).
Probably it does not much matter who introduced whom, but the
discrepancy and the confusion are revealing: Hamilton is a most
unreliable autobiographer and, after giving so many accounts of
his own past to different people on different occasions, quite likely
did not himself know what had really happened.

If the name to be dropped was royal or aristocratic, so much the
better, and the following is, though sounding close to self-parody,
representative: 'The late Tsar Ferdinand of Bulgaria, whose guest I
was twice at Sofia when he was on the throne, and a third time at
Coburg for the so-called Coburg wedding in October 1932, had been
good enough to confer several decorations on me . . .' (*Mr Norris and
I*, p. 39). The beauty of such claims, which seem to belong to the pre-
1914 world of Saki's short stories, was that no one was likely to be in
a position either to verify or contradict them. Probably, however, no
one cared about doing so, for Hamilton's forte was that of the
brilliantly entertaining dinner-guest, the Oscar Wilde of his time
and place (for Isherwood and his friends he was 'enchantingly
"period" '), and his outstanding charm and urbanity do not seem
to have been in question. He would (the Wildean touch again) dress
up to the nines even for some commonplace social occasion, and, as
Isherwood says, would 'make you feel you were at a banquet' if the
only fare available was scrambled eggs and *vin ordinaire*. Something
of his camp stylishness and wit comes over in his writings, which,
though diffuse and repetitive, can also be witty and self-mocking.
Recounting (more than once) an anecdote about calling one day at
the Nollendorfstrasse *pension* and being invited by Jean Ross to
come and talk to her while she took her bath, he remarks: 'I have
often maintained that I am the last of the Puritans, but have never
found anybody yet to believe me' (*Mr Norris and I*, p. 44). In the
same straight-faced spirit he can correct the rumour that he made 'a
bid for peace' during the Second World War through the medium of
the Papal Nuncio – it was, he insists, actually through 'the late Duke
of Bedford' (conveniently late, one suspects) – and anyway, he adds
primly, there is no Papal Nuncio in England, only an Apostolic

Delegate. The technique of mendacity is not often displayed with such brilliance. He adds that his plan to escape to Ireland disguised as a nun was frustrated by his arrest 'before I had even got my coif in place' (pp. 38–9).

Given Isherwood's habit of drawing heavily on his real-life 'originals' while retaining the freedom to depart from them when he chose, we are bound to wonder about the nature of Hamilton's relationship to the character who was in some sense 'based' on him. Both he and Isherwood have in fact made explicit comments on this point, though well-advised scepticism towards the teller of a tale ought in this case to be extended to his model. Introducing *Mr Norris and I*, Isherwood began by saying that when he was asked whether Mr Norris was 'based on' Hamilton, 'Sometimes I answer "No" to this question, sometimes "Yes" – according to my mood and the suspected motives of the questioner. Neither answer is more than partially true'. He goes on to stress the fact that the fictional character and the 'old friend' who has written the book he is introducing differ in a number of respects:

> Just imagine poor Gerald trying to participate in the impossibly melodramatic plots of Mr. Norris and his fellow-conspirators! His prudent and fastidious nature would shrink in horror from such irresponsible antics. Just imagine Mr. Norris daring to substitute himself as host at one of Gerald's inimitable lunches! His attempts at conversation would expose him instantly as a puppet who had lost his ventriloquist.

This may well have been true, and truly meant, but one has a sense that, for entirely understandable and honourable reasons, Isherwood was concerned to play down the resemblance during Hamilton's lifetime. Certainly the account of Hamilton's personality given in *Christopher and his Kind*, written after Hamilton's death, is markedly different in tone:

> Good old, bad old Gerald! . . .
> Gerald didn't look evil, but, beneath his amiable surface, he was an icy cynic. He took it for ganted that everybody would grab and cheat if he dared. His cynicism made him astonishingly hostile towards people of whom he was taking some advantage; at unguarded moments, he would speak of them with brutal contempt . . . .　　　　　　　　(pp.　61, 63)

This suggests that the fictional portrait softened the hard edges of the real adventurer, making comic and endearing what was actually rather unpleasant and sinister. For Mr Norris is a terrible bungler, lacking the nerve and the *savoir-faire* that seem to have characterised Hamilton. The most important discrepancy, however, is frankly admitted in *Christopher and his Kind*: the homosexuality that was 'the most enduring bond' between them is not bestowed on Mr Norris except in innuendoes so discreet that some readers have missed them entirely. As we shall see in the later discussion of the novel, there is a radical ambiguity, evasiveness and unsatisfactoriness about the depiction of Norris's sexual nature. This had no counterpart in Hamilton's own life, as Isherwood very well knew.

Hamilton himself took kindly to the celebrity that the novel bestowed upon him, and lived up to and exploited his transformation into a picaresque hero. He even published in the *Spectator* (4 November 1955) a letter from 'Mr Norris' to his creator, in which the supposed writer refers to himself as 'your poor friend Arthur Norris'. This was, of course, no more than following Isherwood's own example in creating a fictional character called Christopher. His book *Mr Norris and I*, though it deals with a great many topics other than his friendship with Isherwood, bears a title that exploits the literary labours of the man who had, as he said near the end of his life, 'now been a friend of mine for nearly forty years'.

The latter phrase appears in his autobiographical volume of 1969, which reproduces an article he published in *Punch* on 17 November 1954 with the Wildean title 'The Importance of not being Norris'. The ostensible purpose of this was to deny the stories of him as a model for Norris:

> I do not know how the rumour got around. Christopher Isherwood always said that It was a composite character, and although many of my *obiter dicta* were put into the mouth of Mr Norris, I must once and for all decline to admit any closer resemblance, much as I admire the enchanting hero of so successful a novel. The rumour started when I lived in the same pension as Isherwood did in pre-Hitler Berlin.... (p. 37)

(Elsewhere, incidentally, Hamilton denies ever living in Fräulein Thurau's *pension* and cheekily, or perhaps innocently, attributes the incorrect report to Isherwood.) A few pages later, however, he is

'ready to admit...that there is much of me in the character of Mr
Norris (not, I hasten to say, in the sex life of that worthy), in his
manner of speech, his reluctance to face the issue, that would fit a
description of me at that very distant Berlin period' (p. 40). One can
only conclude that when it suited him Hamilton was quite prepared to admit, or claim, that 'Mr Norris, c'est moi'.

Ultimately, though, it would be foolish to look for consistency in
one who was by nature and vocation incorrigibly deceptive and
unreliable. Isherwood's final verdict on him in *Christopher and his
Kind* is clear-eyed and even-handed, but in reaching an estimation
of his 'misdeeds' and finding them after all 'tiresome rather than
amusing' he to some extent returns to his earlier non-judgemental
manner. Perhaps Hamilton offered a valuable lesson to a writer of
fiction as one whose character seemed to have no stability: just
when we think we have made up our minds about him, some piece
of evidence turns up – for instance, his substantial and perfectly
genuine efforts on behalf of various charities and campaigns for
social reform – that compels us to readjust the picture.

A Vicar of Bray on a European scale, Hamilton was variously a
Communist, a Catholic convert, and whatever else it suited him for
the time being to be. Forster wrote to Isherwood on 28 February
1944 saying that he had declined to see Hamilton again after hearing that he was 'violently anti-Semite', but added: 'I ought to
examine his depths for myself, since I got amusement out of his
shallows in the continental days. Occasionally, when I have been
where perhaps I shouldn't, I have been conscious of him through
the reek'. Hamilton's depths might have turned out to be terrible to
contemplate, but his shallows undoubtedly added to the gaiety of
nations, and in portraying Mr Norris Isherwood remained cau-
tiously close to the surface.

Two details from the post-Berlin years show Hamilton as a
continuing source of innocent merriment. In 1937 Isherwood, who
should have known better but was obviously at his wits' end over
the safety of his lover, paid him a thousand pounds to arrange for a
Mexican passport to be supplied to Heinz, who would be con-
scripted if he returned to Germany and for whom Isherwood was
anxious to secure some suitable citizenship. The money was
accepted but the passport never materialised. And it was a nice
touch that, according to Jonathan Fryer (1992, p. 82), Hamilton's
'ultimate coup was to sit as a model for part of a memorial statue to
Winston Churchill, who was of similar bulk'. Joe Orton, one feels,

might have made something out of this, just as Waugh or Firbank might have made something of Hamilton's life and adventures. But then it seemed to be Isherwood's fate, or instinct, to be drawn to characters well qualified to sit as life models.

4

The Other Camera – Aspects of Weimar Cinema

Though Auden's involvement with the cinema was less intense and sustained than Isherwood's, his journal makes it clear that he was in the habit of frequently dropping into a 'kino' during his residence in Germany. Almost the first entry in the journal records that he went with John Layard to the cinema (where both, for unexplained reasons, were sick). As we have seen already, he took Gerhart there during the visit to Hamburg, an occasion on which Gerhart's girl friend completed an uneasy threesome, and it had been his failure to gain admission to the house that was showing May's *Asphalt* that had led to his first meeting with Gerhart. Humphrey Carpenter has noted that Auden 'greatly admired contemporary German cinema', and like Isherwood he was later to be professionally associated with the medium.

As for Isherwood, he seems to have had a lifelong love affair with the cinema. 'I had always been fascinated by films,' he confesses in his early autobiography, *Lions and Shadows*, and he admitted to an interviewer in the 1970s that he had 'an enormous passion for film'. In Berlin he was in the right place, at the right time, to witness some of the most exciting contemporary developments in that medium. He would have had access there to a cinematic art both more experimental and more outspoken than its British or American counterparts, and it would have been strange if his profound interest in a non-literary narrative medium had not had some influence on his writing.

By his own account he saw his first film at the age of 12 – that would have been in 1916 – and by the time he was an undergraduate was already a confirmed film fan. According to his biographer Brian Finney, at one stage he was going to the cinema several times a week as well as reading at least three film magazines weekly. *Lions and Shadows*, in its account of the manifold distractions from serious study, contains a vivid sentence evoking the atmosphere of a film show in the 1920s: 'There were the flicks

146

with the films which were, even in those days, not silent, because the audience supplied the popping of champagne corks, the puffing of trains, the sound of horses' hooves and the kisses' (p. 64). At Cambridge he joined the recently established Film Club, and according to Jonathan Fryer, when Edward Upward laughed at his 'indiscriminate love of the movies', Isherwood explained it in terms of 'a fascination for the outward appearance of people'. It was a remark that could subsequently have formed an article of his creed as a writer, and is confirmed by another passage in *Lions and Shadows*:

> I was, and still am, endlessly interested in the outward appearance of people – their facial expressions, their gestures, their walk, their nervous tricks, their infinitely various ways of eating a sausage, opening a paper parcel, lighting a cigarette. The cinema puts people under a microscope: you can stare at them, you can examine them as though they were insects. True, the behaviour you see on the screen isn't natural behaviour; it is acting, and often very bad acting, too. But the acting has always a certain relation to ordinary life; and, after a short while, to an *habitué* like myself, it is as little of an annoyance as Elizabethan handwriting is to the expert in old documents. Viewed from this standpoint, the stupidest film may be full of astonishing revelations about the tempo and dynamics of everyday life: you see how actions look in relation to each other; how much space they occupy and how much time. Just as it is easier to remember a face if you imagine its two-dimensional reflection in a mirror; so, if you are a novelist and want to watch your scene taking place visibly before you, it is simplest to project it on to an imaginary screen. A practised cinema-goer will be able to do this quite easily.
> (pp. 85–6)

This acknowledged fascination with the visible details of the 'everyday', like the voyeuristic stance, applies as much to the novelist as to the cinema-goer. It is not surprising, therefore, that photographic and cinematic terms offer themselves naturally when Isherwood's writing is being discussed – a tendency encouraged by Isherwood himself. In *Lions and Shadows* he compares the episodic structure of some of his fiction to 'an album of snapshots', though (as Finney observes) he might equally well have made the comparison with cinematic 'takes'.

During his Cambridge period he not only watched films but had aspirations, never to be realised, to direct them. He was also, briefly and unmemorably, a film actor. At the Film Club he heard a talk by George Pearson (1875–1973), one of the leading British producers and directors of the period, took up Pearson's invitation to visit his studios in London, and spent a day, 'dressed up as a midshipman', as a paid extra on the set, though when the film was shown he was not to be seen. After quitting Cambridge with panache and ignominy, he applied, unsuccessfully, for jobs in two British film studios. Not long afterwards he conceived a long-distance passion for the child star, Jackie Coogan (born 1914), who had become famous as a result of his appearance in Chaplin's *The Kid* (1920). Isherwood claimed to have seen him in *Oliver Twist* (1922) seven times. His ironic self-awareness, already well established at this early date, is revealed in a letter to Upward written early in 1923, in which, admitting his addiction to the infant Coogan, he comments that 'I think paederastia is the lowest state of the human soul and the Film Industry the nadir of Commercial Prostitution'.

In Berlin he continued to indulge his enthusiasm for what the generation would have called the silver screen, and in his Californian old age would recall with pleasure the films, stars and directors he had long ago admired, many of whom – Fritz Lang, G. W. Pabst, Louise Brooks, Werner Krauss, Conrad Veidt, Peter Lorre and others – had by then taken their place in the histories of cinema. During the Berlin years, references to cinema visits in the company of Auden and Spender are on record. In Spender's *The Temple*, the character (William) based on Isherwood applauds the cinematic riches on offer in the city: ' "There are terrific Russian movies by the producers of films like *Ten Days That Shook the World*, *Potemkin*, *Earth*, *Mother*, *Menschenarsenal*, *Turkish*. There are also marvellous German movies by directors such as Pabst. *M* is hairraising and *Kameradschaft* stupendous" ' (p. 192).

It was in fact with Spender that Isherwood saw Pabst's now classic *Kameradschaft* when it appeared in 1931. As he relates in *Christopher and his Kind*, 'when the tunnel caved in and the miners were trapped, he had thought: "That makes Virginia Woolf look pretty silly." ' With his boyfriend Bubi, as he recounts in the same volume, he saw Pudovkin's *Storm over Asia* and Wedekind's *Pandora's Box*, and at some stage he saw the 1926 silent version of Henrik Galeen's *Der Student von Prag* (*The Student of Prague*), starring Conrad Veidt and Werner Krauss. The last of these became a particular favourite. One of Isherwood's early viewings of *Der Student von Prag* was in Auden's company, and when they came to collaborate on a play, *The Enemies of a Bishop*, one of the characters was based, according to Isherwood, on a figure in the film.

In the Berlin stories, some of his characters are cinema-goers: ' "Let's go to the cinema," ' says Christopher to Sally Bowles, and in the 'Landauers' section of *Goodbye to Berlin* Natalia asks Christopher whether he has seen René Clair's 1930 film *Sous les toits de Paris*. After he had left Germany, Isherwood was to write a novel, *Prater Violet* (1946), about the making of a film, to work in the Hollywood film industry and to win international fame through the screen versions of his Berlin stories. In an interview published in 1961 he stated that he 'had my first training in writing movies before I even wrote *The Last of Mr Norris* (the American title of *Mr Norris Changes Trains*)', and that 'what the movies taught me was visualisation'.

The camera with which the narrator of one of those stories famously identifies himself could thus even more appropriately have been a movie camera, and both Isherwood and Auden seem to have embraced what has since become an accepted part of the cultural world of young intellectuals: in a generation in which a traditional literary or 'high' culture was still dominant, they were representatives of a broadening of tastes and sympathies to include popular culture and the mass media. Possibly, though, they were not all that exceptional in their time, for a contemporary of Auden's is on record as having referred starchily to 'the gramophonic, cinematographic life of the Oxford set'.

This made it as natural for them to refer to a cinematic as to a literary text in their everyday discourse, and probably they were the first generation to do so. Thus, writing to Naomi Mitchison in 1932 and describing Ottershaw College, where he wished (in vain) to find employment, Auden described it as 'the buggers dream; a cross between Mädchen in Uniform and The Castle' – Leontine Sagan's lesbian film of the previous year coming as readily to mind as Kafka's novel published six years earlier. In a similar way, it occurs naturally to Isherwood, recalling the youthful Stephen Spender in his autobiography, to say that he 'illuminated you like an expressionist producer, with the crudest and most eccentric of spot-lights'. Yet again, in analysing his own youthful behaviour in *Christopher and his Kind* (p. 48), he suggests that he possessed 'a remarkable power of dramatising his predicament at any given moment, so that you experienced it *as though you were watching a film* in which you yourself had a part' (italics added). On the same page he refers to his own characteristic youthful habit of holding the hands 'extended, slightly apart from the body' as 'unconsciously copied ... from the pose of a fighter in a western movie who is just about to draw his guns'.

Isherwood's first experience of working for the film industry (if we set aside his brief inglorious undergraduate acting career mentioned above) came after he had left Berlin but before the writing of his Berlin novels. In October 1933, through the not quite disinterested agency of Jean Ross, he was hired by Gaumont-British Studios to work on a film called *Little Friend*, directed by Berthold Viertel. Viertel, an Austrian Jew, had moved from Vienna to Hollywood but had been invited to England to make three films for Gaumont-British. He was sufficiently impressed by what he read of *The Memorial*, and perhaps also by Isherwood's command of German, to offer him a job that kept him intensively occupied during that winter. Viertel was a friend of Greta Garbo, as Isherwood himself in later years became, and this contact, at one remove, with the magic world of Hollywood must have been exhilarating.

Later Viertel appeared as Friedrich Bergmann in Isherwood's short novel *Prater Violet*, a work for which its author had a high regard. (He told Denis Hart in 1961 that he considered it superior to his other early novels: 'I think it penetrated the character more', whereas 'I feel a certain coldness, an aloofness, in my attitude to the other characters.') But a more immediate by-product of the several months Isherwood spent working on the writing and shooting of *Little Friend* was a radical change in his conception of literary style and technique. As he told a lecture audience in 1975, working in a film studio 'You have suddenly the most tremendous sense of immediacy, from being a kind of introvert, shut up in this room, you're terrifically extroverted.... I think this had a lasting effect on me, starting with *Mr Norris*.... I took to hearing much more clearly what the speeches would sound like that people said' (quoted by Finney, p. 105). It is probably no exaggeration to claim, as Finney does, that this experience 'permanently affected his writing'. Certainly there is a marked and lasting shift in style and technique as one turns from the first two published novels, in which the hand (or Woolf's paw) of Modernism lies heavy, to the books that followed.

Isherwood's time in Berlin came near the end of the finest period in the history of the German cinema. It is a period that has recently received a considerable amount of attention, and Patrice Petro's feminist account of Weimar culture with special reference to the evidence of its films opens with the declaration that 'It would be difficult to name any other period or nation in film history that has sustained such elaborate and sophisticated analysis as the Weimar cinema'. The eruption of creative energy (much of it drained away in the latter half of the period through emigration), in the context of a society that fluctuated between permissiveness and censorship in a rapidly changing social and economic climate, has indeed proved seductive to cultural historians, and for 'elaborate and sophisticated' one must sometimes regretfully substitute 'self-indulgent and silly'. It is true, nevertheless, that many of the films of the period that are still remembered seem to dramatise one aspect or another of a society in crisis – and this whether they are overtly didactic and propagandist (as many are) or not.

At the same time it is as well to remember that the films discussed by historians of the cinema constitute only a tiny proportion of what was a very large output, and even the dedicated cinemagoer of the period would have been much less aware than we are of the emphases and tendencies that any present-day account is likely to delineate. As Lotte H. Eisner points out in *The Haunted Screen*, 'the films nowadays denoted as German classics were in their day exceptional, and swamped by the spate of commercial films' (p. 309).

Thus, in the period that immediately followed the Armistice, there was an overwhelming and entirely understandable appetite for escapist cinema in the form of costume dramas such as Ernst Lubitsch's *Carmen* (1917) and *Madame Dubarry* (1919). Simultaneously, however, with the brief lifting of film censorship in 1918 came a vogue for a very different kind of film: one that undertook the exploration of the social implications of sexual 'problems' such as prostitution or homosexuality. Ostensibly educational, these productions could also provide an acceptable variety of soft pornography. The brief postwar vogue for what came to be known as *Aufklärungs Filme* (instructive or enlightening films) was not entirely without precedent in Germany, for in 1917 Richard Oswald's *Es Werde Licht* (*Let There Be Light*) had dealt with the subject of syphilis, while 1919 saw the release of the same director's *Prostitution* as well as the most celebrated example of this genre, *Anders Als die Andern* (*Different from the Others*), which is usually cited as the first film to deal extensively with homosexuality.

It tells the story of a famous violinist who is blackmailed, ruined and driven to suicide following a homosexual encounter, and is based on a real-life tragedy, that of the violinst Paul Körner. Its moral (to which Vito Rosso devotes an interesting page in his study of homosexuality in the cinema, *The Celluloid Closet*) is that similar tragedies will occur unless the law criminalising homosexual behaviour is changed. Magnus Hirschfeld's appearance in the film has already been mentioned. Although, inevitably in its period, the acting and direction now seem to be afflicted by a painful slow-motion hamminess, the film still possesses a certain crude power. But the church, the press and the conservative public were outraged at the sympathetic and even romantic treatment of such a distasteful and politically explosive theme, bitter controversy ensued, and despite Hirschfeld's best efforts the film was banned in August 1920. When it was re-released in the more tolerant climate of seven years later, it was in an expurgated form in which Hirschfeld's part had disappeared.

The leading role in *Anders Als die Andern* is played by Conrad Veidt, whose career, both curious and paradigmatic, deserves the passing tribute of summary mention. He is now more readily remembered for his association with several other widely discussed films of the silent German cinema, and especially his haunting and spidery portrayal of the wide-eyed somnambulist, clad in skin-tight black, stalking the rooftops in high-wire, high camp style in *Das Cabinett des Dr Caligari* (also 1919). And it is his early career in Germany rather than his subsequent years in Hollywood that has now made him something of a gay icon. At any rate he has in recent years received a good deal of attention, including an impressive exhibition at a Berlin gay museum in 1993 to commemorate the centenary of his birth.

Isherwood spotted Veidt's iconic quality at a Christmas all-male costume ball he attended a few weeks after arriving in Berlin: at least it emerges in his much later account in *Christopher and his Kind*, where he describes Veidt's 'dazzling' presence among the drag queens and other exotics (Isherwood himself went dressed, very convincingly and not unrevealingly, as a working-class hustler): 'The great film star sat apart at his own table, impeccable in evening tails. He watched the dancing benevolently through his

monocle as he sipped champagne and smoked a cigarette in a long
holder. He seemed a supernatural figure, the guardian god of these
festivities, who was graciously manifesting himself to his devotees.'

Trained in the Max Reinhardt Theatre School, Veidt had begun
as a stage actor but turned to the films in 1916 and made unfor-
gettable appearances in *Caligari* and *Der Student von Prag* (1926);
less memorably, he also starred in some of the popular costume
dramas of the epoch, playing Nelson in *Lady Hamilton* (1921) as
well as Cesare Borgia, Paganini and Rasputin in subsequent productions. Quitting Germany in the early 1930s, he spent some years
in England, appearing in Alexander Korda's *The Thief of Baghdad* as
well as in *Rome Express* and *Jew Süss* (this latter based on Feuch-
wanger's 1925 novel), and playing opposite Vivien Leigh in *Dark
Journey*. Veidt became a British citizen in 1939 but in the following
year emigrated a second time, to Hollywood, where he specialised
in playing Nazi officers until a heart attack killed him on a California golf-course in 1943. It was a long journey, from the anxiety-
ridden homosexual of *Anders Als die Andern* to the suave German
officer of *Casablanca*, and a reminder of how far the cinema had
come, and what it had foregone, in a quarter of a century.

The problem with films like *Anders Als die Andern* is that the
motives behind them could be, and have been, readily and even
wilfully misunderstood. A curiously hostile account of this chapter
in the history of the postwar German cinema is given in Siegfried
Kracauer's standard work *From Caligari to Hitler: A Psychological
History of the German Film*. Kracauer writes:

> When, immediately after the war, the Council of People's
> Representatives abolished censorship – a measure revealing that
> government's confused ideas about revolutionary exigencies –
> the effect was not a transformation of the screen into a political
> platform, but a sudden increase of films which pretended to be
> concerned with sexual enlightenment. Now that they had nothing
> to fear from official supervision, they all indulged in a copious
> depiction of sexual debaucheries. Refreshed by the atmosphere of
> freedom, Richard Oswald felt in so creative a mood that he ...
> made a film called PROSTITUTION. Scores of similar products
> swarmed out under such alluring titles as VON RANDE
> DES SUMPFES (FROM THE VERGE OF THE SWAMP),
> FRAUEN, DIE DER ABGRUND VERSCHLINGT (WOMEN

ENGULFED BY THE ABYSS), VERLORENE TÖCHTE (LOST
DAUGHTERS), HYÄNEN DER LUST (HYENAS OF LUST),
and so forth. One of them, GELÜBDE DER KEUCHHEIT
(VOW OF CHASTITY) intermingled pictures detailing the love
affairs of a Catholic priest with shots of devotees reciting the
rosary for the sake of the priest's soul. Two other films, significantly entitled AUS EINES MANNES MÄDCHENJAHREN (A
MAN'S GIRLHOOD) and ANDERS ALS DIE ANDERN
(DIFFERENT FROM THE OTHERS), dwelt upon homosexual
propensities; they capitalised on the noisy resonance of
Dr. Magnus Hirschfeld's campaign against Paragraph 175 of the
penal code which exacted punishment for certain abnormal sex
practices.

This indiscrimate lumping together, in a respected scholarly work,
of high motives and commercial opportunism is, to say the least,
unedifying and unworthy.

In any case their period of flowering in the immediate postwar
years was very brief. David Shipman has said that such films
'would have been unthinkable in any other national cinema at the
time', and they soon became officially unthinkable in Germany, for
the censorship was reintroduced in 1920 and the harsh realism of
social propaganda yielded to entirely different styles. *Caligari*
belongs to the opening phase of a period of Expressionism in the
German cinema that lasted until Murnau's *Der Letzte Mann* (literally *The Last Man*, but usually known as *The Last Laugh*) in 1924.
According to Roger Manvell and Heinrich Fraenkel's history of the
German cinema, *Caligari* was anticipated by Martin's *Von Morgens
bis Mitternacht* (*From Morning to Midnight*) earlier in the same year.
(Isherwood was surely recalling *Caligari* when, years later in Hollywood, he was working on the script of a film based on James
Hilton's novel *Rage of Heaven* and suggested the addition of a
prologue in which a doctor explained that the protagonist had
spent a period in a lunatic asylum.)

'Expressionism' is not a very precise term in this context – as
Manvell and Fraenkel observe, it 'became a generic term for many
different forms of experiment and protest against convention' – but
the significant point is that such films engaged in an exploration of
psychological rather than social and legal problems. It has been
said of the early 1920s in Germany that 'no films of the time
attempted to come to terms with postwar social reality', and this

is the one factor shared by the Expressionist classics and the forgotten romantic or nationalistic costume dramas.

Perhaps we should not be surprised that, in an era of crisis, when traumatic defeat and revolution were followed by political and economic instability and mass unemployment, the last thing cinema-goers demanded was films holding up a mirror to current issues. Lotte Eisner, however, has detected darker forces than consumer demand at work, and has suggested that post-Versailles Germany 'seemed impregnated by an overwhelming sense of fatalism which was transformed into a violent art'. Certainly a film such as *Caligari* can still move and shock not only by its physical violence and its lurid images but by its invocation of a world in which ordinary values and even the sense of everyday reality are called into question.

The stabilisation of the German currency at the end of 1924 encouraged American companies to buy cinemas in Germany and to show therein a large proportion of Hollywood films, a policy that soon led to the introduction of a quota system that required every imported film shown to be matched by a German production. This, combined with the rapidly growing prosperity of the second half of the decade, produced a general expansion of the cinema industry. In 1927 Germany produced 241 feature films, compared with America's 743, France's 74, and Britain's 44. By 1929 there were 5,078 cinemas in Germany, compared with 3,731 in 1920, and German film-making continued on a larger scale than that of any other European country.

Almost as soon as recovery was perceived, the cinema began to confront the issues it had eschewed during the period of crisis. Thus a film such as Pabst's *Die Freudlose Gasse* (*Joyless Streets*, 1925) depicts in painfully harsh terms the sufferings of a time that had only just begun to pass away. This remarkable film set a fashion for social-problem cinema that came to be known as the *Neue Sachlichkeit* (New Objectivity) and has its counterpart in contemporary painting – though again it is as well to stress that any map we now draw of the cinema of the period might look very strange to a surviving cinema-goer with a good memory, for the available menu was large and varied.

Die Freudlose Gasse is interesting in a number of ways, including the fact that it is Greta Garbo's only German film. It belongs to a minor tradition of 'street' films and was preceded by Karl Grune's *Die Strasse* (*The Street*) of 1923. Such productions, according to

Eisner, epitomise 'the Germanic visions of the street and the obsession with dimly lit staircases and corridors'. Literary precedents and analogues for such stories of the lives of the denizens of a poverty-stricken neighbourhood are not difficult to find and go back a long way: in English one thinks, for instance, of the mainly London-based slum fiction of the turn of the century such as Arthur Morrison's *Tales of Mean Streets* (1894), Somerset Maugham's unexpected first novel *Liza of Lambeth* (1897) and Jack London's powerful *The People of the Abyss* (1903). Without being firmly situated within this literary-cinematic genre, Isherwood's *Goodbye to Berlin* shares some of its characteristics, though in a form that is sanitised and somewhat sentimentalised, at once more ironic and less committed.

That such films present, as Eisner points out, a specifically *Germanic* vision becomes clear by comparison with Anglo-American productions of the interwar period. *Die Freudlose Gasse* belongs to the same year as *The Gold Rush*, but the tramps, waifs and blind girls of Chaplin's great period seem cosily sentimentalised beside the brutal realism of the German production. Chaplin knew about poverty from firsthand experience, as the early portion of his autobiography makes clear. Therein, perhaps, lies a clue, for the account, from the standpoint of great wealth and fame, of a childhood that at times approached the edge of destitution has some Dickensian touches, and the Dickens tradition of viewing the poor as endearing or funny (when they are not squalid or criminal) dies very hard and is in fact still very much alive in, for example, a good deal of television enjoyed by middle-class audiences today.

A little later, a British film such as that based on Walter Greenwood's stark novel *Love on the Dole* displays a similar sanitising, even more grossly apparent in the marketing during the Depression of the Lancashire mill-girl Gracie Fields. It may be revealing that one of her most popular films, *Sing As We Go* (1934), was scripted by J. B. Priestley, a middle-brow novelist of the Dickensian tradition. Priestley also knew about poverty, at least as a conscientious observer, for his *English Journey*, which appeared in the same year as *Sing As We Go*, offers a still graphic account of unemployment and hardship in the north of England during these terrible years; the book owes something to Cobbett and in turn influenced Orwell's *The Road to Wigan Pier*. One of 'Our Gracie's' best-known songs (one has difficulty in thinking of the heroine of *Die Freudlose Gasse* as 'Our Greta') celebrated the solidarity and warmth of working-class life: '...don't ever wander / Away from the alley and me.' It is a very different vision of the mean streets of a slum neighbourhood from that given by Pabst's film, and perhaps this is saying no more than that the best German cinema did not readily capitulate, as Anglo-American productions usually did, to the commercial pressures of audience demand for escapism and comforting illusion.

Though set in Vienna, *Die Freudlose Gasse* clearly reflects very recent German experience. It depicts the gradual ruin of middle-class families by runaway inflation: dearly held values and even common decencies are abandoned in the face of the daily struggle to survive on the most primitive level of satisfying hunger, and the daughter (a leading role played by the 20-year-old Garbo) is driven to prostitution. Its stars included Werner Krauss, Asta Neilsen and the popular cabaret artist Valeska Gent (who plays the madame of a brothel), but its uncompromising realism led to its being banned in England and being shown only in heavily expurgated versions in France, Italy and elsewhere.

Near the beginning of the film there occurs an extraordinary scene in a butcher's shop – an almost inevitable locale, for in a starving world the butcher (played by Krauss) is the all-powerful tyrant. For hours women have been queuing in the freezing streets to await his pleasure and thankfully receive whatever he may condescend to sell them. When the virginal middle-class girl (played by Garbo) enters, there is a highly charged atmosphere of sexuality: Beauty and the Beast in a grimly contemporary, post-Freudian setting. The butcher is physically gross and obviously brutal as well as lustful; he smokes the largest cigar anyone has ever seen, and though there are times when a cigar is just a cigar this is not one of them. He is also accompanied by a fierce dog that competes with the intimidated customers for the offerings of raw flesh. At one point the butcher slices a piece of meat off a carcase and thrusts it, unwrapped, at the young girl; when she shrinks away from taking the piece of flesh into her hand – and for a startling moment one is aware that it is not just butcher's meat that she is being invited to grasp – he tosses it at the dog. As Paul Coates says of *Der Blaue Engel* five years later, it is all blatantly Freudian; it also underlines the dependence of the silent cinema, at least when it was trying to say anything significant, on a symbolism that could not easily avoid paying the price of heavy-handedness for its undeniably telling effects.

Pabst's subsequent films include *Die Büchse von Pandora* (*Pandora's Box*, also known as *Lulu*, 1928), in which the American actress Louise Brooks plays the prostitute. This was first shown in Berlin in February 1929, while Auden was living in the city. Apparently Pabst had plans to turn his attention next to the Heinrich Mann novel that became in other hands the basis of *Der Blaue Engel*, and Coates has speculated that the 'male masochism of these films is that of a self-consciously disadvantaged Germany'. Perhaps so, though I shall argue when we turn to *Der Blaue Engel* that other readings are possible. First, however, it will be as well to outline other developments in German cinema in the second half of the 1920s.

It was, in the cinema as well as in other respects, a decade of contrasts and dislocations. As already noted, the immediate post-war period witnessed both romantic and escapist costume dramas and treatments of social problems unmatched for candour anywhere in the world at that time, while the next few years saw the brief vogue of Expressionism succeeded by the social-problem cinema of the *Neue Sachlichkeit*. Dreyer's *Michael* (1924), for instance, had continued the minor tradition of films dealing with homosexuality, a theme again in evidence in Wilhelm Dieterle's *Geschlecht in Fessen* (1928). Dieterle went to Hollywood in 1929 and directed some classic 'biopics' or biographical films. One of these, *Dr Ehrlich's Magic Bullet* (1940), is notable for contriving, within the commercial and censorial context of Hollywood, to handle the story of the search by a German-Jewish scientist (played by Edward G. Robinson) for a cure for syphilis. The opening scene, in which a young patient commits suicide after his condition is diagnosed, has in its melodrama, its lighting and its solemn didacticism a strong flavour of the German cinema of the 1920s.

Some of the preoccupations of *Die Freudlose Gasse* recur in the 1929 film *Mutter Krauses Fahrt ins Gluck* (*Mother Kraus's Journey to Happiness*), directed by Phil Jutzi. Set in the slums of Berlin, it portrays the downfall of a respectable family under the pressure of circumstances as the daughter is seduced, the son arrested for debt and the mother finds 'happiness' in suicide. Such treatments of the life of the poor, including the new poor, contrast jarringly with the apolitical nonchalance of Auden's bourgeois boast about 'going to live in a slum' and Isherwood's brief spell with the family of 'Otto', whose living conditions are presented without indignation or even concern in 'The Nowaks'. Washing in the kitchen sink

and peeing in a bucket may have charms provided they are under-
taken voluntarily and for a strictly limited period.

By this point – the year of Jutzi's film being also one in which
both Auden and Isherwood were in Berlin – the brief boom had
been succeeded by the depression following the collapse of the
world's stock markets. It was natural, therefore, that concern with
contemporary issues should carry over into early sound films such
as Pabst's *Die Dreigroschenoper* (*The Threepenny Opera*, based on
Brecht and Weill's theatrical success of 1929), Leontine Sagan's
Mädchen in Uniform (*Girls in Uniform*), Fritz Lang's *M* and Pabst's
Kameradschaft (*Comradeship*), all belonging to 1931.

Before the end of the 1920s, however, restrictions on the freedom
of the cinema were becoming more acute. From about 1927 the
Nazi influence was being felt both positively and negatively,
through greater emphasis on propaganda films and also through
organised demonstrations against those films deemed to be ideo-
logically unsound. Attempts to prevent the showing of Pabst's
powerful anti-war film *Westfront 1918* (1930), based on Remarque's
novel, were not successful, but its American counterpart of the
same year, Milestone's *All Quiet on the Western Front*, was banned
after an organised riot outside the cinema. The foundation in 1929
of the Deutsche Liga für Unabhängigen Filme (German League for
Independent Films) was an attempt to counteract these increasing
pressures, but Hitler's rise to power and the Nazi victory in
the 1933 elections were closely followed by the establishment
of the Reichsfilmkammer as a branch of the Kulturkammer
(Ministry of Propaganda) responsible for controlling the film
industry and exploiting its propaganda potential. Goebbels had
long been interested in the medium of cinema and had grasped
the simple but not always obvious truth that propaganda disguised
as entertainment may be more effective than straight propaganda.
The subsequent work of Leni Riefenstahl in particular was to
demonstrate that it was possible for political and aesthetic concerns
to coexist.

Before 1933, the left-wing resistance to National Socialist pressures had resulted in a number of films intended to counteract the
cinematic glorification of nationalism, militarism and war. Pabst,
Piscator and others had set up the Volksverbund für Filmkunst
(People's Alliance for Cinematic Art) with this end in view. Slatan
Dudow's *Kühle Wampe* (1932; shown in America as *Whither Germany?*), for instance, had financial support from the Communists

and was subjected to drastic censorship at home and abroad – so much so that no unmutilated copy appears to survive.

Before the end of the 1920s, the large-scale emigration of some of the German cinema's best talents had begun. Indeed, Lubitsch had made his first Hollywood film as early as 1923. Soon the seepage turned to a flood as directors like Leni and Murnau and stars like Emil Jannings and Pola Negri, as well as Conrad Veidt and Marlene Dietrich, headed west. With an impressively professional sense of timing, Dietrich actually left Germany on the evening of the first showing of her first great success, *Der Blaue Engel*, in Berlin on 1 April 1930, going straight from the cinema to catch the night train. This film, and this star's appearance in it, have become so firmly established as icons of late Weimar culture that it and she demand, or will at any rate receive, more extended discussion. It was by no means, as is sometimes supposed, Dietrich's first film but her nineteenth, the list starting with *Der Kleine Napoleon* (*The Little Napoleon*) in 1922; she had in fact appeared in the first German feature film to use sound, *Ich küsse ihre Hand, Madame* (*I kiss your hand, Madame*) in 1929.

She had been performing in Berlin theatres from 1921, and contemporary recordings of some of her vocal performances in otherwise forgotten revues of the 1920s reveal a voice that took some time to settle down: at first conventionally light, it only later assumed the husky and sexually ambiguous depth that was to become one of her trademarks. To listen to some of these songs is to observe her androgynous image in the process of creating itself, and it was perhaps in *Der Blaue Engel* that that image and voice first defined and proclaimed their identity. Certainly in the 1928 revue *Es liegt in der Luft* the voice, while instantly recognisable, is still relatively light and feminine, but in some of the songs in the film of less than two years later there is a marked contrast, even competition, between two identities. To take the most familiar example, in both the English and the German versions of 'Falling in Love Again' the middle section is sung in a deeper, more masculine and aggressive voice – that of a seductress who intends to remain firmly in control – than the opening section, so that one has the curious impression of Dietrich singing a duet with herself. (The text of the German version, 'Ich bin von Kopf bis Fuss auf Liebe eingestellt', incidentally, conveys an almost obsessive quality of infatuation that is weakened in the more traditionally romantic English translation.)

Der Blaue Engel is not superficially of its time and place, though certainly so at a deeper level. It is based on Heinrich Mann's novel of 1905, *Professor Unrath*, which attacks bourgeois hypocrisy, but the action of the film, set in some unspecified seaport such as Hamburg or Lübeck, is quite explicitly moved to the second half of the 1920s. Its director, Josef von Sternberg, had been born plain Sternberg in Vienna and had been a painter and student of art before he turned to films. As a teenager he emigrated to America and in Hollywood had risen to be a director, making his first sound film (*Thunderbolt*) there, and returning briefly to Europe in order to direct *Der Blaue Engel*. Later he was to say, in an interview for BBC Television in 1966, that the influences upon his work as director, 'if there are any', were not from other film-makers but 'from literature and painting and other arts which I then incorporate into a film'.

Filming began on 4 November 1929 and was completed on 22 January 1930, each scene being shot twice, with German and English dialogue. Dietrich had problems with English pronunciation: in the lines 'Men cluster to me / Like moths around a flame', it seems that the word 'moths', difficult for a German speaker, kept coming out as 'moss'. (There may be some exaggeration in the story that it took her two days to get it right.) Emil Jannings, the famous star apparently upstaged by the virtual newcomer (though his performance is in the event a brilliant one), made himself extraordinarily difficult, and von Sternberg later declared that he 'would not do another film with him were he the last remaining actor on earth'. Dietrich tells us in her autobiography that Jannings 'hated the whole world, himself included. . . . this psychopathic star performer. . . . von Sternberg even whipped him when Jannings asked him to'. Even without a whip, von Sternberg was a tyrannical director who regarded himself as virtual and exclusive 'author' of the films he made, and his own autobiographical musings include the comment on Dietrich (also implicitly a comment on himself) that 'Despite her melancholy, she was well dressed and believed herself to be beautiful, though until this was radically altered by me she had been photographed to look like a female impersonator'.

There was, then, no shortage of drama and temperament on and off the set of this film of sadism, humiliation and human disintegration, and already some of its curious features have become apparent: a German classic shot also in an English version, with a non-German director and two stars about to leave Germany. It is indeed a film that seems compounded of ambiguities and equivocations, many of them belonging to Dietrich herself, the woman of legendary beauty whom at least one unsympathetic observer could claim to mistake for a female impersonator.

Von Sternberg's snide and self-serving observations apart, the history and legend of Dietrich have always been beset by ambiguity and paradox. It is, of all the possible choices, her face and no other that looks out from the frontispiece of the first volume of Paul Roen's *High Camp: A Gay Guide to Camp and Cult Films*. More, however, than any other of the group of international female stars who (for reasons not always entirely obvious) have been adopted as gay icons – Marilyn Monroe, Judy Garland, Maria Callas and the rest – Dietrich's public personality has always been unstable, one image dissolving Orlando-fashion into its antithesis. Appearing often as the incarnation of a voluptuous and exaggerated femininity, with her high cheek-boned, flawless-complexioned beauty and her timelessly slim figure sheathed in satin or swaddled in furs, she at other times discarded all this in favour of male attire. According to her autobiography she made a conscious choice of 'top hats and worker's caps' as part of her costume. One photographic record of her career shows on adjacent pages a goddess almost buried beneath a heap of white furs that must have sent wildlife statistics tumbling, and a woman who could easily be mistaken for a lesbian novelist in a man's suit, collar and tie, and who, without actually doing so, conveys a strong impression of having an Eton crop and smoking a pipe. It is said that when she arrived in Paris in 1933 wearing a man's polo coat, pearl-grey suit and beret, she was warned by the police that this outfit rendered her liable to arrest and prosecution; the advice was ignored. Her sartorial image in the 1930s was largely the creation of the gay designer Travis Banton, with whom she had a complex relationship. And it was an image that did not quickly fade: a whole generation after the end of the Weimar Republic, she was still appearing in top hat and trousers for a Las Vegas engagement.

But perhaps the most famous of all the innumerable Dietrich images is one of the earliest: that of Lola Lola (spiritual mother, one guesses, of the Lolita or young Lola created by another ex-Berliner), in black stockings and top hat, a mythological creature, half Circe, half ringmaster. For her role in *Der Blaue Engel* precisely utilises the wiles of the seductress to attain the kind of power traditionally regarded as masculine if not patriarchal. In creating for herself this persona she was drawing on a German, and specifically a Weimar, social and sexual tradition in which transvestism was a recognised mode of behaviour. It is no doubt significant that the comparable cultural phenomenon in Britain has almost always operated within a comic, even farcical context of stage or screen illusion, from the cross-dressed heroine of Shakespearean comedy to *Charley's Aunt*, the pantomime dame and her contemporary successors, the mass-audience female impersonator and the drag queen of the commercialised gay scene.

In her study of lesbianism in the cinema, *Vampires and Violets*, Andrea Weiss has shown that the early cinema's use of cross-dressing and gender-reversal for comic purposes was significantly modified in the late 1920s (the period of the controversy in England over *The Well of Loneliness*), when lesbianism began to be depicted in a more serious and sympathetic light. *Der Blaue Engel*, as it happens, falls exactly between two of the key texts that Weiss invokes to support this thesis, *The Wild Party*, a Hollywood film of 1929, and *Mädchen in Uniform*, made in Germany in 1931, both of which contain key scenes involving cross-dressing. In *Mädchen in Uniform*, for instance, set in a girls' boarding school, Manuela is still wearing the male costume she has adopted for the school play when she makes her declaration of lesbian love. Both films, according to Weiss, were 'informed by their directors' direct association with lesbian communities (in Berlin and Hollywood, respectively)'.

Even earlier, Pabst's 1928 film *Die Büchse der Pandora* presented a heroine (Lulu) who has been described as 'the aggressive suitor of other women, the ruthless, perverted competitor of the male suitor'. While Lola Lola, unlike the Lulu whose name so closely resembles her own, is not depicted as the 'suitor of other women', there is no doubt about her unfeminine aggression and ruthlessness and love of power. As Weiss relates, the making of Pabst's film was not without its problems:

According to Louise Brooks's memoirs, Belgian actress Alice Roberts as Countess Geschwitz 'was prepared to go no further than repression in mannish suits'. When she arrived on the set and was instructed to dance a seductive tango with Lulu, she responded with outrage. Pabst averted an emotional explosion by convincing her that she would be seducing him, not Louise Brooks: 'Both in two-shots and in her close-ups photographed over my shoulder, she cheated her look past me to Mr. Pabst,

who was making love to her off camera. Out of the funny complexity of this design Mr. Pabst extracted his tense portrait of
sterile lesbian passion.' (p. 22)

The unintended result of this stratagem was that in the finished
film the Countess appears to be intent on seducing the female
spectator. In Britain and America, however, this hazard was
avoided by the censors' deletion of the entire scene.

Characteristic though it was of Weimar Berlin in general and the
late Weimar cinema in particular, Dietrich's sexual evasiveness
persisted long after she had quitted her homeland and Weimar
had passed into history. In broader terms, her subsequent life
perpetuated the pattern of ambiguity and paradox. Refusing to
return to Germany, she made Paris her last home but insisted on
being buried in Berlin. In contrast to many European émigrés who
found their way to Hollywood, the unmistakable foreignness of her
English accent, an essential part of her stock-in-trade, made her
German origins seem never very far away. Her well-publicised
private life embraced a series of lovers of both sexes, though
throughout her career in divorce-happy Hollywood she remained
(as *The Times* obituarist put it in a phrase of lapidary tact) 'distantly
married' to her husband.

As Andrea Weiss shrewdly observes, while the Hollywood
image-makers 'went to great lengths to keep the star's image
open to erotic contemplation by both men and women', a hint of
lesbianism could be titillating and therefore permissible (as a comparable hint of gay identity presumably could not) – though tar-
geted less at lesbian audiences than at male voyeurism. The
Paramount publicity machine's description of the Dietrich-von
Sternberg film *Morocco* (1930) as presenting 'the woman all
women want to see' seems, though, to offer a carefully phrased
hint that 'normal' women might be excited by the carryings-on of a
less conventional member of their sex. At the same time the invitation is extended without any real threat to the sanctity of the
American home, for to see is not to be.

And in any case *Morocco*, quite unlike *Der Blaue Engel*, only flirts
with unconventionality on the road to a thoroughly orthodox and
undisturbing conclusion. For a modern viewer the film's most
memorable moment occurs in an early scene, when Dietrich, in
male evening dress from head to foot, having finished singing a
song ('What am I bid for my apples?') rich in sexual innuendo,

climbs over a barrier and leans forward to kiss a female member of her audience on the mouth. This momentary but startling reversion to European manners – Hollywood's unthinkable being Berlin's commonplace – appears to have been improvised by the star and tolerated by the director. Even earlier, the entertainer Amy Jolly, played by Dietrich, has shown herself to be a thoroughly independent woman when she tears up the visiting card given her by a rich male admirer who has gallantly offered her help. So far, so like that only very slightly earlier entertainer, Lola Lola. Even after she has come under the spell of the handsome, square-jawed legionnaire (played by Gary Cooper), Amy can still speak out for her sex, murmuring breathily that '"There is a Foreign Legion of women..."'. Eventually, though, love conquers all, including Amy's refusal to conform to conventional expectations of feminine roles, and in a final image that contrives to be both haunting and ludicrous she discards her high-heeled shoes to stumble across the desert sand with the other camp-followers in the wake of the marching soldiers, tugging a reluctant goat that she has borrowed for purely symbolic purposes.

Such a chicken-heartedly compromised ending is all very different from the ruthless, even contemptuous survivalism, the woman's victory in the struggle for power, at the end of *Der Blaue Engel*. We cannot help reflecting that Lola Lola would not have kicked off her high heels for such a purpose – would not have capitulated to the implied reproach when Amy, seeing the camp-followers for the first time, is told that they are the women who care for their men. From the Berlin of 1929 to the Hollywood of 1930 turned out to be a giant stride in the direction of conformity to an industry whose moral code, especially where the position of women was concerned, had hardly developed beyond the nineteenth century.

Sartorially, the heroine of *Morocco* moves in the direction of renouncing an aggressively male for a winningly female attire. Von Sternberg's direction again makes interesting use of unobtrusive but symbolic patterns of visual detail, tiny echoes and cross-references, and an essay could be written (perhaps has been written) on the use of headgear in this film. Amy's early gestures with her top hat, for instance, are later appropriated by the legionnaire, Tom, in respect of his own picturesque head-dress. Another nice touch is Amy's treatment of two texts: the stranger's card is torn to pieces, but the message scrawled by Tom on her mirror preserved.

J. C. Suares's recent *Hollywood Drag* documents a remarkable sweep of male and female impersonation in the American cinema and includes not only the predictables (Brooks and Garbo among them, as well as Dietrich) but a few surprises, including Rod Steiger and Boris Karloff. It comes as no surprise, however, that whereas the female impersonators are almost exclusively in a context of farce (Stan Laurel, Lou Costello, Harpo and Chico Marx, Jerry Lewis) or sophisticated comedy (Cary Grant, Jack Lemmon, Tony Curtis), male impersonation does not rule out seriousness. Garbo's Queen Christina, which Suares calls 'the most famous role reversal ever committed to film', is neither unique nor the earliest example. Very shortly before playing Lulu for Pabst, Louise Brooks had appeared in a Hollywood film, William Wellman's *Beggars of Life* (1928), which concerns a girl who murders her father after he has tried to rape her and then disguises herself as a male in order to find refuge among a group of down-and-outs. This was not, however, to be Dietrich's kind of role, and Suares suggests that her male impersonation in *Morocco* was innovative in two ways: not only did she reject the Brooks/Garbo vein of soulful and suffering woman-as-man, substituting for it a provocative and relished exploitation of the idea of cross-dressing, but she carried it over into her off-screen life. To relate this behaviour pattern to the life-styles of Weimar Berlin in which she had begun her career makes no excessive demands on imagination or credulity.

Historically speaking, the emergence of a distinctive lesbian identity in the western world around the turn of the century corresponds closely to the increased demand by women for political power and social freedom, and the central action of *Der Blaue Engel* – the assumption of power by the female and the consequent reduction of the male to ignominious helplessness – has obvious political as well as psychoanalytical implications. In general terms Petro has identified 'three different types of male figures in the Weimar cinema that exhibit an unstable masculine identity': the 'impotent, self-punishing and frequently sadistic male who projects his sense of powerlessness onto a female figure with whom he comes to identify', the 'passive and homosexual male', and the 'passive and eroticized male who elicits the desiring gaze of a textually inscribed female spectator' (pp. 155–8). *Der Blaue Engel* belongs to the first of these categories, as *Anders als die Andern* and *Die Büchse von Pandora* belong respectively to the other two. Jannings plays the bachelor schoolmaster, the tyrant of the classroom, who (for palpably if unconsciously mixed motives) pursues his boys into the local bars after school in his zeal for their moral welfare. The plot is one of tragic, or tragicomic, *peripeteia*, whereby the situation is reversed and the tyrant becomes helpless in the hands of a woman.

In a brilliant analysis of the *mise-en-scène* of this film, Carole Zucker has shown how its first half is 'divided mainly between two sets', Professor Rath's classroom and the Blue Angel cabaret, representing two morally and physically contrasting worlds. The classroom is bare and orderly to the point of rigidity: the straight lines of small desks that accommodate, far from comfortably, the sexually mature young men who are Rath's students, and the much larger desk behind which Rath sits, imply a hierarchical power system mirroring that of an entire society. Hierarchy, and the respect automatically accorded to status and title (especially by women towards men), are indeed evident from the outset, for the first words spoken in the film are the landlady's summoning of Rath to breakfast with the formal title 'Herr Professor'. It is characteristic of the film's subtle cross-references that the phrase is later repeated, no longer respectfuly but ironically and mockingly, by Lola when she announces breakfast after their first night together.

The order of the classroom, overthrown when the students riot and Rath quits the school, reflects the tyrannical conventions of an outmoded authoritarian society clinging to power and, on an individual level, the repression of natural sexual drives. In contrast the riotous life of the cabaret, on both sides of the footlights, and behind the scenes no less than on stage, draws sustenance from a much wider range of human instincts and emotions. A familiar parallel from a much earlier generation is in the schoolroom/circus antithesis of Dickens's *Hard Times*, where the opposite of a ramshackle, hand-to-mouth disorder is a stultifying and repressive power system. Ultimately, though, Dickens's horror of *moral* disorder, as well as the strict limits of contemporary tolerance, makes his circus a much tamer place, more sentimentally conceived, than the Blue Angel cabaret.

Rath himself is, visually and dramatically, a survivor from an imperial past that has faded into history – though new regimes, of course, have a habit of retaining such survivors in positions of power. His costume of cape, top hat and walking stick is that of the nineteenth century; his ritualistic nose-blowing before beginning the lesson (the straight lines of the handkerchief he holds up

reproducing those of the blackboard behind him), and his fastidious, even obsessive habits of arranging the objects on his desk
and making entries in his notebook, reveal a mind initially imprisoned in unvarying custom.

Earlier, breakfasting in his lodgings, he has observed the corpse
of a songbird lying at the bottom of its cage: one of the film's
blatant symbols, this prefigures his replacement of the dead creature by another songbird who refuses to remain in a cage and who
in due course reverses the roles and turns him into a grotesque
bird, crowing hideously and laying eggs for the entertainment of a
noisy audience that includes his former colleagues and students. At
the beginning, though, he can afford a moment of sentimentality
over the tiny corpse, immediately dispelled when the landlady
briskly consigns it to the stove. For this is a harsh world, indifferent
to the sufferings of others, as Rath will discover; and in any case
feeling is not his strong suit: teaching his class *Hamlet* (the story of
another scholar reduced to antic behaviour), he puts the main
emphasis on the correct pronunciation of the English definite article.

The transformation of the pedant into the clown comes about
through his excursion from the classroom into the alien world of
the Blue Angel, where, as Zucker has shown, 'the order of the
classroom is inverted'. In the cabaret, disorder rules, and the
straight lines and rigid hierarchies are replaced by a turbulent,
swirling world: the scenes in which Dietrich appears are crowded
with diversely costumed figures, doors are constantly opened and
closed, snatches of music and of the noise of an unruly, ribald
audience are heard.

It is also a world disturbingly indifferent to status, and Lola soon
has the professor scrabbling under the table for something she has
dropped – a casual but deft reversal of their roles (for he belongs to
an older generation as well as being her superior in gender and
status), and a foreshadowing of the way she will use her sexuality
to bring about his abasement. In the subsequent scene in which he
bemusedly watches her mounting the stairs, she is again consciously placing him literally and symbolically at her feet, and
this in fact becomes one of the recurrent motifs of the film. Later,
for instance, he picks up from the floor the pictures of her that he
will try to sell to the audience; he kneels to help her put on
her stockings; and when she insists, near the end, that he go on
stage as a clown, she is again standing on the stairs above him. In

the all-male classroom he has firmly closed the window to exclude the noises of the outside world in the form of a schoolgirls' singing lesson, but that world, including its sexuality and its music, invades and dominates his life until, having entered it as an outsider still asserting his status, he finds himself a despised and powerless part of it.

The film, still compelling after nearly seventy years, clearly has something to say about both sexuality and society, and about the relationship between the two. Rath represents a discredited pre-1914 *Kultur* that is clinging to power in the new Germany but whose days are numbered; the unrepressed (or only temporarily repressed) sexuality of his students, who escape to the Blue Angel after school, belongs to a younger generation unwilling to accept the values of its elders; and Lola embodies a powerful and morally nihilistic sexuality that wholly rejects the conventions and repressions of the past, just as so much in Weimar culture, from architecture and theatre to popular songs and satirical cartoons, defined itself along new lines.

As already suggested, though, Lola is not simply a vamp or *femme fatale* but an androgynous figure who usurps male power by calling into question hard-and-fast distinctions between the sexes. In Kenneth Tynan's phrase, revived by at least one of Dietrich's obituarists, Lola, like Dietrich herself, represents 'sex without gender'. Even after her migration to the very different and less tolerant social and cinematic world of Hollywood, the star's androgyny remained: brought there as a rival to Garbo, she seems to have set herself to outbid the strong flavour of sexual ambiguity in Garbo's screen persona – most evident in *Queen Christina*, where the Queen kisses her lady-in-waiting on the mouth even more unmistakably than Dietrich had done three years earlier in *Morocco*.

In a *Guardian* obituary (7 May 1992), Clancy Sigal wrote that Dietrich's art was not only 'blazingly erotic' but 'sexually ambiguous', and pointed out that – apparently paradoxically – this image solidified after she reached Hollywood:

The six American pictures she did for Sternberg set once and for all the faintly transvestite stereotype that drag queens henceforth loved to imitate: the smirking wide mouth, veiled eyes, angular cheekbones lighted to accentuate her dramatic gauntness. Above all, the deliberate suggestion emphasised by the tailored suits

and slacks of mannishness, lesbianism and shocking sexual inde-
terminacy.

What seems worth adding is that this 'sexual baroque', though to
some extent motivated by the wish to shock the timid public
morality of Hollywood, was a natural development from the first
collaboration of director and star on *Der Blaue Engel*. When they
travelled across the Atlantic, the power struggles, sexual indeterm-
inacy and sado-masochism of that great film were carried in their
luggage. The later Dietrich, even after she turned from cinema to
theatre and cabaret, retained the Sternberg legacy of which the
foundations had been laid in Berlin, and Sigal rightly adds that 'it
is no insult to [Dietrich's] memory to recall that she never willingly
departed from the perverse, sado-masochistic femme fatale that he
had made out of her'.

In *Morocco*, as we have seen, Dietrich appears in male evening
dress and top hat, and even the seductive Destry insists on having
the same as the boys in the back room and is at least the equal of
any man. (The latter role has some interesting points of similarity
to that of Lola; Hollywood in the 1930s was not, however, capable
of the uncompromising ending of the German film, resorting
instead to the nineteenth-century convention of having the fallen
woman square her account with respectable society by making a
good death.) It was a period in which Hollywood films at their
most popular were likely to depict gender without sex in the cause
of family entertainment: Fred Astaire and Ginger Rogers, like their
less talented but immensely popular contemporaries Jeanette Mac-
donald and Nelson Eddy, pursue their romantic love affairs while
irretrievably encased in faultless costumes that at times completely
cover the body save for the face.

In the Astaire-Rogers vehicle *Top Hat* (1935), though there is,
interestingly, some outrageously camp behaviour on the part of
the lesser characters (notably Edward Everett Horton), a single kiss
from the hero generates panic in the heroine; that the smooth-
cheeked Astaire, singing with such joyful excitement of putting
on his top hat, white tie and tails, should ever doff them to climb
into bed lies beyond our powers of imagining. But Dietrich
remained – in a context that became ever more censorious after
the 1934 Motion Picture Code forbade any reference to homosexuality in the cinema – a dissenter and a vigorously surviving representative of the Weimar tradition of sexual ambiguity.

In her *In the Realm of Pleasure*, Gaylyn Studlar has written of Dietrich that she 'is frequently mentioned as an actress whose screen presence raises questions about women's representation in Hollywood cinema. She has also acquired her own cult following of male and female, straight and gay admirers.' Studlar concludes that 'The diverse nature of this group suggests that many possible paths of pleasure can be charted across Dietrich as a signifying star image, and across von Sternberg's films as star vehicles.' This multiplicity of 'paths of pleasure' is a concept transplanted from Weimar Germany, and one that stubbornly took root in an environment that for long proved hostile or at best half-hearted.

Dietrich's post-Weimar career and personality, then, challenged convention in ways that were far from alien to the Berlin she had left behind and that found many other outlets, from Grosz's satirical drawings to Isherwood's fiction. And if *Die Blaue Engel* itself has a moral, it is that the power of human sexuality can find unexpected and disturbing modes of expressing itself: a truth to which so much in Weimar life and art lent support. The film thus becomes not just an individual masterpiece but an icon of its time and place – though, as often happens with icons, what it came to stand for was rather different from what it actually is.

Francis Bacon said of his own adolescent sojourn in the city that 'by way of education I found myself in the atmosphere of the Blue Angel', yet this kind of shorthand allusion serves somewhat to misrepresent a film that seems to teach that the wages of lust is folly, humiliation, disgrace and death. Compared with what could be readily seen in the bars and cabarets and even on the streets of Berlin at this time, it is even a rather decorous film: after seducing him, Lola makes an honest man of the Professor by marrying him (economic considerations, needless to say, entering into her decision), and even when she is at her most professionally titillating, the patrons of the Blue Angel are permitted to see no more than a few inches of bare flesh. Ultimately the film is ironic rather than pornographic, offering warning rather than stimulation: when, after the Professor's death, it concludes with Lola singing 'Falling in love again', the message is that, whatever love may be, it is something far removed from what was celebrated under that label by the Romantic poets. This scepticism, involving a rejection of the past, is very much in the Weimar spirit. At the same time, a more immediate past is recognised and suffers retribution, and in the extraordinary scene in which Rath, the victim of crowd-sadism, is subjected to cruel physical humiliation, he is the representative of an entire generation, the one that had taken Germany into war and defeat.

5

Writing about Berlin

Isherwood is a co-dedicatee of Auden's *Collected Poems*, a fact that may justify a brief digression on dedications. The sense of a group – living together or in close contact, sharing ideas and journeys and books and even beds and lovers, and collaborating on literary enterprises, much in the manner of the English Romantic poets (some of whom also headed for Germany): all this is powerfully reinforced by photographic images. It is significant that two of the most important general studies of the 1930s, those by Valentine Cunningham and Samuel Hynes, both carry on their covers portraits of the Auden-Isherwood-Spender trio. But their habit of mutual dedication equally exemplifies the sense and solidarity of the group. Auden's 1930 *Poems* was dedicated to Isherwood, the collected edition of Isherwood's Berlin stories to Auden, the original version of Spender's *The Temple* to both of them. Just a little outside this small circle are such figures as Cecil Day-Lewis (dedicatee of Auden's *Paid on Both Sides*) and Benjamin Britten (dedicatee of *On the Frontier*).

The first poem in the *Collected Poems* is dated December 1927, less than a year before Auden went to Berlin. Very recently, however, Katharine Bucknell's magnificent edition (1994) of Auden's juvenilia has made it strikingly clear that this was far from being a beginning: Auden, who had decided at the age of 15 that he wanted to be a poet instead of a mining engineer, had been writing with extraordinary talent, energy and dedication as a schoolboy and undergraduate, and over two hundred poems survive from the period preceding his departure for Germany.

He took with him to Berlin, as we have seen, an unfinished play and resumed work on it soon after his arrival. But his time there was also fertile in short poems, and although his early poetic style characteristically involves a high level of abstraction, generalisation and myth-making, occasional traces of Berlin scenes, characters and ideas may also be found in his work at this period, including poems not written, or not completed, until after he had left the city. A good example here is the fine poem in four sections titled '1929' and written between April and October of that year. German friends (Kurt Groote and Gerhart Meyer) are mentioned by name, other friends (John Layard perhaps among them) less precisely referred to, and the tense atmosphere of the times is evoked in a few urgent phrases ('anxiety at nights', 'proletariat against police'). Though not free from the inflated rhetoric and sophomoric attitudinising that mar some of Auden's earlier work – and a portentous line like 'It is time for the destruction of error' challenges the reader to devise a disrespectful retort – it is, taken overall, both a remarkably accomplished technical performance and a poem showing control, insight and even wisdom.

Some of the other poems of this period may loosely be described as political, including one, 'Let History Be My Judge', written when Auden had been in Berlin for only a few weeks. Implied in this laconic and sardonic dramatic monologue is the story of a failed *coup d'état*, and the atmosphere seems to be compounded of turbulent Central European politics in the postwar period and a schoolboy or undergraduate fantasy world of adventure that owes something to the fictional school of John Buchan and is a recurring feature of Auden's early work, both poetic and dramatic.

A poem written towards the end of the Berlin period, 'Sentries against inner and outer', on the other hand, begins with the vocabulary of military aggression ('sentries', 'enemy', 'raid') but turns out to be a love poem, and it seems likely that Auden's romantic experiences during this year, and in a broader sense his heightened awareness of love and sexuality in himself and others, provided the impetus for a number of love poems. If so, it was a development that had far-reaching consequences, for he is surely one of the great love poets in English. Though perhaps a truth not yet universally acknowledged, this claim received a sudden and unexpected boost in 1994 when the reading aloud of one of his poems in the film *Four Weddings and a Funeral* had the extraordinary effect of placing prominently on bookstore counters piles of hastily produced pamphlets of his love poems.

One of the poems in this category, 'This Loved One', is about Isherwood's feelings for Bubi, and since it was apparently written in March 1929 must register Auden's response to a very early stage of that infatuation. Coolly enigmatic in the manner of much of the verse Auden wrote at this time, it resorts at one point to the favourite metaphor of the frontier, the challenge to decisive action in contrast to hedonism and emotionalism:

Before this last one
Was much to be done,
Frontiers to cross. . . .

One of the best-known of Auden's 1929 poems, 'Sir, no man's
enemy', was written in October, after he had left Berlin, but bears
the impress, in its prayer for 'power and light', of a mind liberated
by its period of absence from England as well as, more specifically,
expressing his enthusiasm for the doctrines of Layard. In the ex-
uberant 'Which of you, waking early', written in the same month,
are lines that, though placed in an English setting, could have been
based on observations made in Berlin:

As a boy lately come up from country to town
Returns for the day to his village in expensive shoes,
Standing scornful in a ring of old companions
Amazes them with new expressions, with strange hints . . . .

Such boys, and such reactions to temporary affluence, must have
been a familiar sight in the Berlin bars.

Auden's brief return to Berlin in the summer of 1930 produced
an unexpected result in the shape of six poems written in German,
apparently soon after his return, and sent to Isherwood. Linguistic-
ally they are not above reproach: according to David Constantine,
there are 'at least half a dozen major grammatical errors . . . in every
poem'. Auden evidently spoke and wrote German as Wilde's
Algernon played the piano, not accurately but with great feeling.
These verses are, however, of great interest as an exile's view of
the Paradise of which he has too briefly been permitted to
call himself an inhabitant. Five of the six are sonnets, and not
far behind them are those of Shakespeare, a copy of which
Auden had carried with him on at least one occasion on his
German travels. As Constantine clearly shows, the 'financial and
commercial imagery' of Shakespeare's love poems finds a modern
equivalent in Auden's 'sense of love as a commodity'. 'Lacrimae
Rerum', for instance, contains the line 'Weil ich kein Geld hab',
komm ich nicht im Frage' ('Since I've no money you'll not want
to bother with me'); another declares '. . . wenn ein olle Herr
hat Dich gekusst / Geh mit; ich habe nichts hezahlt . . .'('That
gentleman who is kissing you, go with him; I have paid for nothing'). The fifth in the series agonises 'Weiss aber nicht was jezt dein

Körper macht' ('Don't know, though, what your body is up to just now').

The sombre mood of these five poems is unexpected and may of course have been unrepresentative of Auden's life in general at this time, though it is not inconsistent with his earlier statement that he was 'homesick' for Berlin after his year there had come to an end. Away from the city, David Constantine suggests, Auden 'remembers Berlin life without illusion. He wants to get back there for the sex, but he knows very well what these remembered relationships are like: mercenary'. It is surely, however, a very personal melancholy and disillusion: his anatomising of the commercial sex of the rent-bars is not, even (or especially) in his Scottish exile, a matter of moral disgust or indignation but an expression of loneliness and frustration and, ultimately perhaps, a craving for love at any price. At the same time his unillusioned sense of the commercial basis of the Berlin sexual scene is perfectly consistent with his deep and unsatisfied longing for a stable relationship based on mutual affection and respect. There may, too, have been some grain of consolation in the Shakespearean precedent: to be creatively unhappy in such distinguished company must almost have made the whole wretched business worthwhile.

The exception to the sad rule in this group of poems in bad German is the sixth, 'Chorale'. This is a jaunty, Brechtian lyric that has none of the self-pity and sense of deprivation of its companions. It celebrates, instead, the joys of the flesh and obscenely enumerates the physical attributes of the boy who awaits him in Berlin and the activities they have shared: 'Der ist ein schöne Junge / Er wohnt jezt in Berlin....' ('There is a handsome boy, he lives in Berlin right now....'). To this boy (unidentifiable, if he ever existed as a single individual) he hopes to return in four months' time. The specified period would have brought him to the Christmas holidays and temporary release from bondage at Larchfield Academy; but the plan, if it was a plan, came to nothing. A cheeky note suggests that the poem should be sung 'To the Passion Chorale tune'; it could certainly have been a witty cabaret song, a form that Auden later practised with success.

Auden's enthusiasm for the popular brand of educational and self-help psychology purveyed by Homer Lane and John Layard, and especially for the attractive but facile connections it made between psychic and bodily ills, is reflected in many of his early poems, though its fullest expression has to wait until 1937 and the grim ballad 'Miss Gee'. He wrote a large number of what John Whitehead characterises as 'comic epigrams, some of them bawdy': two-, three- or four-line squibs that in their laconic, dogmatic, uncompromising specificity owe something to Blake's prose 'proverbs'. For instance,

> If a whore shocks you
> Then she will pox you

and

> Love your cock
> Stand a shock.
> Hate your cock
> Soon a crock.

Some of these (though neither of those quoted above) found a place in a bouquet of a dozen titled 'Shorts' and included in *Collected Shorter Poems*.

Auden's short verse-and-prose 'charade', *Paid on Both Sides*, occupied him during the summer after he left Oxford, and the first draft accompanied him to Berlin that autumn. He worked at a second version, conflating old and new material, during November and December, and on the last day of 1928 sent the finished work to T. S. Eliot, editor of the London magazine *Criterion*. Eliot judged it 'quite a brilliant piece of work', published it in his magazine, and took modest pride in talent-spotting the young author.

Among other changes, the pre-Berlin version seems to have been modified by giving German names to some of the characters and also reflects Auden's absorption of the Lane-Layard doctrines. As Humphrey Carpenter has shown (p. 93), Auden himself described the piece as 'A parable of English Middle Class (professional) family life, 1907–29', these being the dates of his own birth and the charade's completion. As an attempt to exorcise his own background, it inevitably brings to mind Isherwood's first two published novels.

Another 'charade', *The Enemies of a Bishop*, was the joint work of Auden and Isherwood, though its origins lay in an idea of Auden's for a play titled *The Reformatory*. Auden seems to have begun to think about it in April 1929, very soon after Isherwood's visit, and the two of them worked on it together during the early part of the summer and finished it when they were together in London in the autumn. Its full title was *The Enemies of a Bishop, or Die When I Say When: A Morality in Four Acts*, but its original title had been *Where is Fronny?* – the reference being, of course, to Francis Turville-Petre. This rejected title is only one of a number of personal and private allusions in a work that, for all its claim to belong to the public world of the theatre, has a very strong flavour of the in-group.

The surname of the hero, Robert Bicknell, is that of Auden's mother before her marriage, while Robert's brother Augustus has one of the names of Auden's father. The two boys who escape from a reformatory and enter a middle-class world, one of them disguised as a girl, surely owe something to the ethos of the Cosy Corner and its denizens. One of the other characters is a pederast, another is based on a character in the film *Der Student von Prag*, and the Bishop himself is based on Homer Lane. Auden introduced one of his favourite lead mines, and Isherwood contributed characters who owed much to the fantasy world he and Upward had created together. It is, in other words, a gallimaufry of references, often obscure or coded, to the authors' private lives, and it comes as something of a surprise to learn that they had it professionally typed, presumably in the hope of getting it produced.

The play is dedicated to Bubi and Otto: memories of the weeks spent at Rötehutte must have been still fresh when it was written, and Otto, as it turned out, was actually an escapee from a reformatory. Isherwood's admission that the play is 'full of private jokes' is not one that need be quarrelled with, and Humphrey Carpenter's summing-up of it as 'a hotpotch of fine verse and schoolboy foolery' (p. 106) seems fair. In its introduction of extravagant characters and incidents into conventional settings such as a grand hotel, it looks forward to the anarchic world of Joe Orton, though Orton's pace, economy and wit are sadly lacking. What it does offer is strong confirmation of the closeness of Auden and Isherwood's relationship at this time and their shared exhilaration at what they had found in Berlin.

Of Auden's more private writings during this period, few letters survive. The so-called Berlin journal remains unpublished, though plans are afoot for its eventual appearance in full. What Auden would have thought of its publication can only be surmised: in one of his verse aphorisms he declares himself willing to forgive gossip columnists but expresses his scorn for literary biographers who try to justify their pryings by claiming 'it's for scholarship's sake'. On the other hand, unlike Isherwood, he carefully preserved this early diary, evidently reread it from time to time, and must have realised that it might outlive him and pass into the public domain. There may, moreover, be a sense in which almost any diarist ultimately desires a reader, whether an intimate or a stranger. Virginia Woolf's short story 'The Legacy', about a woman who achieves 'publication' by bequeathing her private diaries to her husband, perhaps dramatises an impulse that Woolf was not the only one to feel.

The worn and fragile manuscript designated as Auden's Berlin journal is in fact a number of different things: a commonplace book (he copied down with approval, for instance, a phrase from D. H. Lawrence's 'Mother and Daughter', 'The silky puppy-like sexuality of the English'), a poetical notebook (with many Lane-and-Layard-inspired squibs), and a record of notes and aphorisms mainly on psychological topics, as well as a kind of diary for the spring and summer of 1929. It is easier to say what kind of diary it is not than what it is. For the most part it certainly does not appear to be a daily record of events written within hours of their occurrence. As suggested in Chapter 1, there is clear evidence that much of it was written retrospectively, and after 26 May there is not even the pretence of regular entries, a long section headed with the date 12 June summarising what has happened in the previous two and a half weeks.

There is considerable stylistic unevenness, some of the writing being laconic or telegraphic to the point of obscurity, other parts blossoming into fully developed narratives, descriptions or arguments that at times achieve real eloquence. A phrase like 'adhesive trouser boys' (used of some of those in the waiting-room at Hirschfeld's Institute), for instance, has the flavour of a private allusion, an aid to memory rather than an attempt to communicate an idea to a reader, whereas the description of Gerhart's 'electrical' power or the analysis of the difference between Auden and his brother show a more consciously literary shaping. There is much use of dialogue, as if to catch the distinctive tone of a particular moment, and even more self-analysis: at one point Auden describes himself actually inspecting his own body in the mirror, but in a sense he is engaged in a continuous inspection of his own mind and heart.

One of the most curious features of the 'journal' is the use of headings strongly reminiscent of the captions used in the silent cinema. What seems to be an account of Isherwood's first full day in Berlin is headed 'Saturday getting tight', and later come 'Intervening period of Margaret and sex expectation', 'Meeting Gerhart and John's attempted suicide', 'The Dutchman and the Tour'. Again, the implication is of a writer less concerned with recording daily happenings than with discerning the phases into which his life has fallen, the shape and pattern of recent experience. This is consistent with what seems, after all, to have been the main purpose of this brief and almost unique spell of diarising: to reach a fuller and truer understanding of himself. Repeatedly some trivial incident or conversation is followed by an analysis, sometimes quite lengthy, of the underlying issue – infatuation, or jealousy, or infidelity, or falling out of love. For all the close and detailed observation of his friends and lovers and of certain aspects of life in Berlin, one's strongest sense is of a young man intent on watching himself, trying to understand his own emotions and to come to terms with his own nature.

In August 1930, a year after he had ceased to be a resident of Berlin but only a short time after his two-week holiday there, Auden told his brother that he was 'writing another play'. A couple of months later, with the play nearly finished, he assured Naomi Mitchison that it represented 'the best I can do just now'. Before the end of the year he had sent it to T. S. Eliot at Faber & Faber, but it never achieved publication and the manuscript subsequently disappeared. This play was *The Fronny* – again named after Francis Turville-Petre, who may well have been a subject of conversation between Auden and Isherwood during that June visit.

The medium is, again, a mixture of verse and prose, and the action seems to have concerned the quest for The Fronny after he had quitted England. After moving through scenes depicting different aspects of contemporary society, it concludes with The Fronny making his will and dying. His list of bequests in particular seems to have been full of private jokes, and as a drama for the stage it seems unlikely that *The Fronny* represented much of an advance on *The Enemies of a Bishop*. But the continuing fascination with Turville-Petre, and his incorporation into a myth by both Auden and Isherwood, is striking.

Auden's three major dramatic collaborations with Isherwood – *The Dog Beneath the Skin* (1935), *The Ascent of F6* (1936), *On the Frontier* (1928) – belong to a post-Berlin phase of their relationship, but a couple of general points are worth making. The preoccupation with frontiers, most obvious in the title of the second of these plays, is pervasive: the challenging mountain F6, for instance, stands 'exactly on the frontier line', and in *On the Frontier* itself Dr Thorvald reflects that 'Perhaps "country" and "frontier" are old-fashioned words that don't mean anything now'. A frontier is both a barrier, a restraint on freedom of movement, and an invitation or challenge to step across into a new world, and it seems likely that residence in Germany, where the frontiers drawn by the Versailles Treaty were still of passionate concern, added contemporary force to what may have originated as a more personal metaphor. In *The Ascent of F6*, the excitement of crossing frontiers and confronting the unknown is combined with an outsider's view of England and its decline to a second-class power, and again these kinds of awareness may owe something to the time spent in Berlin.

At the same time the preoccupation with frontiers links these works of the second half of the decade with Auden's poems of a few years earlier. Samuel Hynes has suggested, though, that the concept had in the meantime undergone a significant shift: in the earlier poems, 'the frontier was always a place up ahead, beyond which was a New Country. But now, in 1938, he was *on* the frontier...' (*The Auden Generation*, p. 308).

Isherwood's first published novel, *All the Conspirators*, had appeared in 1928, the year before he moved to Berlin. When he arrived there towards the end of 1929 he had with him the third draft of its successor, *The Memorial*, which he was to characterise in *Lions and Shadows* as 'an epic disguised as a drawing-room comedy' and to describe there as 'about war: not the War itself but the effect of the idea of "War" on my generation' (pp. 297, 296). He continued to work at this novel during 1930, but though it was finished by the end of that year it suffered multiple rejections and did not appear until 17 February 1932. Though pre-Berlin in its origins, therefore, *The Memorial* is a Berlin novel in the sense that it was largely composed there in the form in which we have it. With limited exceptions, however, it is not a novel that makes use of very recent experience: Isherwood, who had devoted *All the Conspirators* to the demolition of the Edwardian family, was still occupied in getting the past out of his system rather than exploiting the present. As it turned out, he was not to put the present to literary use until it had become the past. Later, with not much exaggeration, he was to describe himself as a historical novelist; as he told W. J. Weatherby in 1960, his writing 'always has to be about a few years ago with a gap between my subject and the present'.

So far as *The Memorial* is concerned, the main exceptions to this rule are to be found in the opening section, in Chapter 5 of which the hero, Edward Blake, finds himself in Berlin in 1928. With the Tiergarten behind him and the bright lights of the Sieges Allee stretching before him, he is placed in a specific spot in the city that Isherwood had come to know while the book was still in progress. Later in the same chapter Edward attempts suicide in a manner that closely resembles the attempt made by John Layard. This event had of course taken place before Isherwood's arrival, but Auden's account of it had evidently been sufficiently graphic for him to scent copy. He uses the incident again in *Lions and Shadows* (p. 196), this time applied ironically and self-mockingly to the narrator, and Spender uses it in *The Temple* (pp. 20–1), putting the story into the mouth of the Isherwood character, who is (of all things) thinking of using it in a novel. Layard was certainly in no position to complain that his sensational performance had gone unnoticed.

The final pages of *The Memorial* show the protagonist again in Berlin, his room 'overlooking the trees and the black canal and the trams clanging round the great cold fountain in the Lützowplatz'. There he receives a visit from a hustler, Franz (the name, with a slight variation of spelling, of one of the boys frequently mentioned in Auden's Berlin diary), and they talk of his suicide attempt and of the war. Franz too now has a scar, caused by a stray machine-gun bullet fired by the police through the windows of his sister's house, though his response to the question whether he is a Communist is a scornful negative. The two men remain suspended between the past and the future, their own relationship incomplete and perhaps impossible, in a manner that may owe something to the ending of Forster's *A Passage to India*.

Soon after the appearance of *The Memorial* in February 1932, Isherwood wrote to John Lehmann outlining his programme of literary projects. He was, he told Lehmann, already at work on 'an autobiographical book...about my education' (that is, an early draft of *Lions and Shadows*), and would soon be starting 'a book about Berlin, which will probably be a novel in diary form and semi-political' (quoted by Fryer, 1993, p. 86). After that he would write another autobiographical work, and perhaps a travel book. Later in life he was to write both, but nothing came of these latter plans, or ideas, for a very long time. The 'book about Berlin', however, was *The Lost*, never completed but in a sense the ancestor or Ur-text of the published Berlin novels.

Isherwood's Berlin experiences are extensively exploited in *Mr Norris Changes Trains* (1935) and *Goodbye to Berlin* (1939). (The 'Sally Bowles' section of the latter had been published separately in 1937.) The second of these in particular is historical fiction in that, published six years after Isherwood's departure from the city, it deals with a world that must at the time of publication already have seemed remote. An odd feature of these two works is that, whereas one might have expected the later one to have begun where *Mr Norris* left off and to have continued Isherwood's Berlin chronicle into a further phase of contemporary history, the two books actually traverse roughly the same period of time. Dependent as he was, however, upon firsthand experience recorded in his diaries rather than upon research or invention, he really had no choice. In *Mr Norris* the account of public events had already been taken almost up to the point at which he himself had left Berlin, and there was nothing left but to go back to the beginning and start again with a largely different group of characters and a different structuring principle.

The action of *Mr Norris Changes Trains* (retitled for American publication as *The Last of Mr Norris*) opens towards the end of 1929, very close to the date at which Isherwood had arrived in Berlin – and opens with the Isherwood-like figure of the narrator, William Bradshaw (Isherwood's own second and third Christian names), arriving in Berlin by train. (The same journey is described on the closing pages of the autobiographical *Lions and Shadows*, published three years later, so that in a curious and paradoxical way the earlier book starts where the later one was to leave off.) The narrative of *Mr Norris* thereafter is straightforwardly chronological: at the beginning of Chapter 3 it is 'a few days after Christmas', Bradshaw then meets Norris to celebrate New Year's Eve, and most of the subsequent chapters begin with some reference to time.

For this is a novel constructed with close attention to an unfolding public history as well as to a plausible framework of fictional events. In Chapter 5 it is 'towards the end of April [1930]', and three chapters later it is 'the beginning of March [1932]', with specific allusions to the campaign for the presidential elections held on 13 March. In Chapter 9 the narrator returns to England for an extended period, spending four months in the country after being in London, so that it is 'the beginning of October' before he is back in Berlin. Isherwood himself had been in England during the same summer, though for a shorter period, from early August to the end of September, and one senses that Bradshaw's absence is a convenient device for absolving his creator from depicting events in Germany during that period. Chapter 11 begins in 'the first week in November' and continues 'early in December'. By the final chapter (16), it is 'early in March [1933], after the elections...', these being the Reichstag elections on the 5th of the month that gave the Nazis a large majority.

In the closing pages, events follow each other quickly, mirroring both the rapidity of change after the Nazis came to power and the hugger-mugger quality of Isherwood's own last weeks in Berlin. It was perhaps for this reason that he described his novel, not altogether justly, as 'a sort of glorified shocker', and compared it to the work of Graham Greene. Bradshaw's young friend Otto reappears with the news that he has been hunted down and has narrowly escaped arrest by the Nazis 'two days after the Reichstag fire' – that is, on 1 March; he has then been on the run for a fortnight, so that it is now mid-March. 'Three weeks later' – that is, fictionally speaking, in early April – Bradshaw returns to England. Isherwood had gone there on 5 April, but his brief return to Berlin in May before finally leaving for Greece has no counterpart in the fiction and would have served no useful purpose there. Now immovably established in England, Bradshaw receives news during May that Norris is in Mexico City, and later messages come in rapid succession from California, Costa Rica and Peru. But by now both the novel and the reality on which it is so closely based have left Berlin behind.

In both of the Berlin novels private lives are invaded and transformed by public events, in accordance with standard practice in the historical novel – a generalisation equally true, for instance, of a nineteenth-century classic such as Dickens's *A Tale of Two Cities*. But Isherwood's is a tale of one city, with virtually no attempt to set events in Germany against the background of a quieter, less obviously threatened life elsewhere. And whereas Dickens makes an event such as the storming of the Bastille or the lynching of an enemy of the people the occasion for a rhetorical and emotional set-piece, Isherwood plays down the drama of contemporary happenings: the landmarks of history are scaled down so that, subjectively perceived, they take their place with the banalities of everyday life. The influence of Forster may again be detected here, and specifically what Isherwood admiringly referred to as his 'tea-tabling', the technique of conveying through domestic fiction a sense of momentous issues. Although Isherwood had by now left Modernism behind, there is perhaps also a trace of the Woolfian subduing of events of all kinds to the vagaries of an individual consciousness indifferent to accepted hierarchies of significance.

Chapter 16 of *Mr Norris*, for instance, opens with a reference to the weather, 'suddenly mild and warm', in early March 1933:

> 'Hitler's weather,' said the porter's wife; and her son remarked jokingly that we ought to be grateful to van der Lubbe, because the burning of the Reichstag had melted the snow. 'Such a nice-looking boy,' observed Frl. Schroeder, with a sigh. 'However could he go and do a dreadful thing like that?' The porter's wife snorted.

The mediation of sinister and momentous happenings through the gossip of the politically ignorant and innocent reduces everything to the same level – a strategy belonging to diaries rather than history books – and the outrageous Nazi plot becomes material for a boy's joke and a sentimental woman's pity for the scapegoat. These reductions, however, belong to the world of the novel's action, not that of the narrator or the reader, who are privy to the ironic and tragicomic discrepancies.

In the paragraph that follows, Isherwood's prose artfully juxtaposes the national and the local: in the Nollendorfplatz 'people were sitting out of doors before the café in their overcoats, reading about the coup d'état in Bavaria'; 'An ice-cream shop was open. Uniformed Nazis strode hither and thither, with serious, set faces, as though on weighty errands' – and the past tense of the distanced narrator is briefly nullified as we share the experience of living through a moment of history in which the ice-cream is for some as important as the Nazis. Hynes has argued that one of the themes of *Mr Norris* is the disappearance of the private life under tyranny:

> Bradshaw knows no public figures, and has no public existence, being only a poor foreigner; but that private world is gradually invaded by the public world.... As public violence increases, the private life recedes, and the private man is drawn

out of his closed world, into the streets.... [By the end of the
novel] the public drama of Germany has been acted out to a
tragic conclusion: in Berlin there is no private life left to be lived.
                                        (*The Auden Generation*, p. 178)

The passage from the novel's final chapter cited above, however,
suggests that private lives can absorb and digest a version of public
events (not necessarily, of course, an authentic one), reducing
public figures and their actions to the level of their own limited
experience. In the Berlin novels it is Fräulein Schroeder, with her
endless curiosity about the private lives of others, who is a unifying
figure, and in his introduction to the 1975 reissue of the novels
Isherwood praises her as a survivor and as 'the most genuine
Berliner of them all':

> Only Frl. Schroeder could boast that she had lived in the same
> flat on the same street since the pre-war days of Wilhelm II,
> through the war and the defeat and the Republic and the infla-
> tion. Only she was fated to remain there throughout the Third
> Reich, to witness its fiery end and the arrival of the Russians....

Another kind of levelling process can be found in Chapter 8,
where Olga, a 'woman of numerous occupations', is described: 'she
was a procuress, a cocaine-seller and a receiver of stolen goods; she
also let lodgings, took in washing and, when in the mood, did
exquisite fancy needle-work'. In the social and moral chaos of
'those bankrupt days', it is clear, needlework and cocaine, laundry
and prostitution, no longer belong to different worlds.

The novel's central character, Arthur Norris, though an outsider
and a kind of picaresque anti-hero, embodies this confusion. He
has been seen by Brian Finney as a representative figure in more
ways than one:

> His self-centred hedonism in fact parallels the attitudes of the
> Berlin population at large during the final years of the Weimar
> Republic. His sexual masochism is like their political self-
> abasement. His distortion of language to conceal the truth from
> Bradshaw and everyone else is paralleled by the debasement of
> linguistic meaning by the politicians and the press as the political
> confrontation between the right and the left heightens. And like
> them he is made to pay for his abandonment of responsibility by

the escalating intrusion of public affairs into his private life.
(pp. 115–16)

Persuasive though this view of Norris is, it presents two problems. It leaves out of account the fact that Norris is a comic figure: even at the end, his 'paying for' his shortcomings takes the form of a farcical scamper from one uncongenial hiding-place to another. And in its emphasis on representativeness it does not do justice to the individuation, even the wild eccentricity, of a character whom we know to have been based on a real-life original.

Whatever it may have been intended to express about Weimar society at large, the ambiguity of Norris's sexual orientation parallels his political and financial deviousness while at the same time handily insuring Isherwood against the personal and professional risk of being suspected of creating a homosexual protagonist. A passage in Chapter 4 summarising Norris's early life indicates that he came of age in the 1890s, so that he may be supposed to be in his fifties, perhaps sixty, when Bradshaw meets him. This makes him considerably senior to his prototype Gerald Hamilton, born in 1889, and much closer to Isherwood's father's generation. In the postwar world Norris remains a Nineties Decadent: one who has in his youth ' "learnt the meaning of the word 'luxury' " ', who has an interest in the Wilde circle and passes off a Wilde epigram as his own, who boasts of his library of erotica and his Swinburnian collection of whips, and who in the age of Eliot and Pound admires the work of the poetaster William Watson – still alive in the early 1930s, but, like Norris, a relic of the 1890s, when his most popular volumes appeared. His espousing of 1890s aestheticism, moreover, places Norris conveniently above or beyond morality, and his criteria for commercial or political action are less a matter of truth and justice than of self-gratification and self-serving.

With his wig, his cosmetics, his camp locutions (' "my dear boy" ') and his high-pitched giggling and tittering, he seems at moments like an unmistakable portrait of an ageing but still effervescent 'queen', and Isherwood from time to time comes close to allowing himself to say as much unambiguously: sitting at his dressing-table in a 'delicate mauve wrap', Norris invites Bradshaw to ' "Come and talk to me while I powder my nose," ' and even the guileless Fräulein Schroeder is moved to comment on his silk underwear (' "More like a lady than a gentleman" '). Yet Isherwood deliberately blurs this portrait or caricature by occasional references to more socially acceptable forms of dissipation: Norris's inheritance has 'disappeared with magic speed into the mouths of horses and the stockings of ballet girls', and his only current form of sexual activity seems to consist of masochistic sessions at the hands of Fräulein Anni (he even makes it plain that ' "some equally charming young lady" ' would be quite acceptable).

On the subject of Norris's sexual ambiguity, then, Isherwood is himself ambiguous. There was nothing ambiguous about the homosexuality of his model, Gerald Hamilton, but Finney's reference to 'Hamilton's fictive heterosexual counterpart' (p. 85) seems to bypass a real problem. Nor can Isherwood's stance quite be accounted for by talking about androgyny or bisexuality, though the title metaphor of changing trains may conceivably be, among other things, a discreet gesture in this direction. Muddying the waters was an effective way of preventing publishers, reviewers and readers from looking into the depths and being startled by what they saw there, and this prudence – which might less charitably, and perhaps unfairly, be called failure of nerve – is characteristic and pervasive in Isherwood's early work. It is evident, for instance, in a curious non sequitur in the closing pages of *Goodbye to Berlin*, where the desperate plight of civilians during the closing stages of the Great War is recalled: 'Everybody sold what they had to sell – themselves included. A boy of fourteen... peddled cocaine between school hours, in the street'. What is interesting here is that the candour promised by 'themselves included' simply evaporates between the two short sentences. Isherwood knew more than most about boys who sold themselves, but was unprepared to come clean.

In the end, though, Norris is not just a louche expatriate who might have been equally at home on Norman Douglas's Capri: like Bradshaw, he is drawn out of his 'closed world' (in Hynes's phrase) by the force of public events. Until nearly halfway through the book, these events impinge only marginally on the action of the novel. In Chapter 7, a quarrel between two young Germans over a girl is the occasion for a minor coup by the rapidly developing Nazi propaganda machine: the men are enemies, 'both political and private', and the occasion of the quarrel is Anni's appearance with Otto's rival 'in a Nazi *Lokal* [pub] on the Kreuzberg'. In the Nazi newspapers, Otto's drunken attempt to fight his rival appears as ' "an unprovoked and cowardly attack on a National-Socialist *Lokal* by ten armed communists..." '. It is the lives of these three minor characters that are foregrounded, the satirical reference to Nazi propaganda and the Nazis' invasion of social life being still held at a distance – which is no doubt, after all, how most residents of Berlin would have treated such a matter at this time.

By the next chapter, however, the restrictions on personal freedom ('Each week there were new emergency decrees...') and the outbreaks of violence have suddenly moved into the foreground:

> Berlin was in a state of civil war. Hate exploded suddenly, without warning, out of nowhere.... In the middle of a crowded street a young man would be attacked, stripped, thrashed and left bleeding on the pavement; in fifteen seconds it was all over and the assailants had disappeared. Otto got a gash over the eye with a razor in a battle on a fair-ground near the Cöpernicker-strasse....

The sudden specificity of the last sentence quoted brings us back to the immediate world of Bradshaw's daily experience, but it is now the generalisation that is given precedence, and the paragraph that follows is a miniature essay, somewhat in the manner of George Orwell, on the corruption of language and mass culture (popular songs and cinema) under a tyranny. At the beginning of Chapter 9, when Bradshaw returns from England and goes by taxi from the station to his lodgings, the presence of uniformed Nazis in the streets is unmistakable: the new regime has now invaded the small stage of Isherwood's fiction.

And yet Bradshaw remains, as Isherwood himself had been, an outsider, conscious of the menace in the air of the city he has made his home but free, after all, to quit it at a moment's notice whenever he chooses. Towards Germans and his own compatriots alike, Bradshaw's feelings are always more or less detached: he is never shown forming the kind of passionate attachment that Isherwood felt for certain German youths, and again this may have originated in a necessary or at least an irresistible prudence. Isherwood is an autobiographical novelist, but only up to a point: the confessional impulse is always under firm control. In the penultimate chapter it is made quite explicit that, despite the interest Bradshaw finds in Norris's personality and behaviour, he has no intention of ever crossing the frontier that separates an acquaintance from an intimate friend: 'Here we were, as so often before, at the edge of that delicate, almost invisible line which divided our two worlds. We should never cross it now.'

The age difference partly accounts for this, and Norris may be seen as an alternative father, as disreputable and unreliable as 'real' English fathers of the Edwardian middle class (like Isherwood's own) were conventional and dependable. Though the passage appears to lay the blame at Norris's door, however, the real reason for the failure to develop a closer relationship is surely Bradshaw's refusal to become involved. It is the same trait that makes him partially withdraw his spontaneous reaction of horror and pity to the news of the homosexual Kuno's death – '"Poor devil"' – by adding 'apologetically' that he '"knew him slightly"'. (Kuno's name, incidentally, may have been intended to recall that of one of the highly placed figures in the notorious Eulenberg affair, General Kuno Count von Moltke, the military commandant of Berlin.) Standing up to be counted was not the strong point of Bradshaw or, at this stage, his creator. And the bantering tone in which the novel ends – a tone curiously at odds with the picture of Norris fleeing, not altogether successfully, for his life – seems to affirm once and for all the refusal to be involved in the life or destiny of other people. A sense of his own failure to speak out or come clean may have been one of the reasons why, in later life, Isherwood tended to disparage his Berlin stories.

Isherwood's narrative technique mirrors this detachment, or caginess, by eschewing psychological analysis in favour of a largely dramatic mode of presentation replete with the equivalent of stage directions. Characters blush, frown, shrug their shoulders, sweat with embarrassment, sink heavily into chairs, look away or up ('like a spaniel that is going to be whipped') or at their finger-nails ('with dismay'): the fictional text is often very close to a play script or (more pertinently) a film script. *Goodbye to Berlin* has on its first page (though not, as is often supposed, in its first sentence) the only phrase of Isherwood's that everyone knows and the only prose quotation of his to find its way into the *Oxford Dictionary of Quotations*: 'I am a camera'. The words that follow make it clear that it is not a movie camera that is in question, though this might have made the analogy closer.

Yet a close analogy it can never be, and the famous dictum turns out to be a confidence trick that would not have disgraced Mr Norris himself. For the famous 'camera' is not quite the tightly fitting symbol of sharply accurate but wholly detached observation that it has often been taken to be. Even if, as Isherwood stipulates, it has its 'shutter open, quite passive, recording, not thinking', somebody has had to point the camera in one direction or another, and the words that immediately follow – 'Recording the man shaving at the window opposite and the woman in the kimono washing her hair' – imply a rigorous selection of details, and details of details, from the vast unsorted mass or mess of visual stimuli in the surrounding world. Language, after all, can never simply 'record', and any pretence to this effect is naive or duplicitous. As for the final sentence of the paragraph, 'Some day, all this will have to be developed, carefully printed, fixed', the reference is presumably to the processing by which memory becomes art, but there is scope here too for a selectivity and distortion, even for a wholesale reordering of the past, just as the developing of a negative involves decisions and judgements that affect the end product. As Gore Vidal has pointed out, though Isherwood 'became famous' with this four-word statement, he is not really a naturalistic writer, a 'recorder of surfaces'. He must be judged in this instance to have been as evasive about the nature of his art as he is about Norris's or Bradshaw's sexuality.

Understandably, writers tend to become impatient with such of their own dicta as are turned into clichés, and in two interviews he gave in the 1970s, Isherwood discouraged emphasis on this familiar phrase and also on his own identification with the fictional character or characters who bear his name. Insisting in 1972 that far too much prominence had been given to 'I am a camera', he explained that what he was trying to do was to 'describe my mood at that particular moment. Obviously the description does not fit Christopher Isherwood in many of the other sections [of *Goodbye to Berlin*]'. There is perhaps scope for misunderstanding here as to which Christopher Isherwood is being referred to.

Another statement five years later is less ambiguous:

'You see, "Christopher Isherwood" in the early books wasn't *me* at all. He was a device used to tell the story in the first person. If he had been a person, and he had announced that he was homosexual, he would have upstaged everyone else. The reader would be constantly wondering what he would do next. So he had to shut up, push the other characters into dialogue, and so on.

But 'wasn't *me* at all' is hard to swallow, and this statement is obviously intended to get Isherwood off a double hook: the reader is discouraged from taking the stories as autobiographical (though they are certainly that to a significant extent), and what we may feel like regarding as evasiveness is given an aesthetic justification. The problem with the second of these points is that the evasiveness over matters of sexual orientation or conduct is by no means limited to the narrator. And in any case it is surely disingenuous of Isherwood to insist that the Christopher figure is not himself 'at all' when he has made that character a young upper-class Englishman, with a public school and Cambridge education, who is teaching English in Berlin and has published a book called *All the Conspirators*. Similarly unconvincing is the implication that only technical considerations inhibited him from making the character's homosexuality explicit. It is as well to be prepared, therefore, for some degree of evasiveness, even of inconsistency, in the handling of this protagonist-narrator who is also, if only up to a point, a portrait of the artist.

Disingenuity and evasiveness apart, it has of course often been argued (by, for instance, Jeffrey Meyers in his *Homosexuality in Literature 1890–1930*) that reticence, suppression and ambiguity, whether or not they are morally reprehensible, may be a source of artistic strength. Certainly the marked inferiority of, say, Forster's *Maurice* to his less explicit fiction implies that speaking out, whatever marks for moral courage it may earn, can result in a diminution of literary power and a thinness of literary texture. There is, indeed, a very striking contrast between the force and richness of some of the masterpieces of suppression that Meyers discusses (by, among others, Mann, Proust, Conrad and Lawrence) and the depressing banality of much contemporary gay fiction, which seems unable to steer a course between the hard rock of crude pornography and the softer one of maudlin sentimentality. The act of throwing off one's chains does not, as some have supposed, automatically provide a valid literary objective. Isherwood's fiction, even as late as *A Single Man* (1964), which many regard as his best novel, remains doggedly reticent, though by the 1960s greater explicitness would surely not have involved very serious risks, commercial or personal. His fiction includes no *Maurice*, and certainly nothing like the self-indulgent stories that appear in Forster's posthumous volume *The Life to Come*: perhaps he had learned from *Maurice* (despite his early enthusiasm for it) that reticence pays. The eleventh-hour outspokenness of *Christopher and his Kind* looks like an attempt to atone for a lifetime of watching his step.

Possibly, however, the real justification for the virtual exclusion of sexual politics from the Berlin stories is that they are concerned with a wider and more tragic politics, that of a Germany reeling from one war to the next. Isherwood himself made this point, even if rather elliptically, when he was interviewed by Arthur Bell for a gay magazine in 1972 after the publication of *Kathleen and Frank.* Asked, in the context of a discussion of his role in gay liberation activities, whether the Berlin books were 'political stories', he replied: 'Yes. They certainly have strong political overtones; that's true. But not of that kind [i.e. sexual politics] because that wasn't the current concern.'

The time-scheme of *Goodbye to Berlin* begins in the autumn of 1930, almost exactly the point at which William Plomer went to the city and found there (as he wrote 45 years later) a 'feverish atmosphere' in which

> Acute political and economic uncertainty and tension were not concealed by the flashy up-to-dateness of life in the centre of the city. Naked ambition and naked despair were both conspicuous. Two strong currents, often intermingling in a puzzling way, especially puzzling to someone unfamiliar with the German character, were earnestness and cynicism. And resentment was visibly gaining over disillusionment.
>
> (*The Autobiography of William Plomer*, pp. 273–4)

Translating these abstractions into the daily experience of ordinary people, Isherwood takes something like this account as the agenda for his book, though he is in no rush to bring political and economic issues to the surface. In the opening section, Fräulein Schroeder, her home and her lodgers are introduced: one lodger is a barman, another a prostitute, and it is clear that both derive their living from the city's considerable influx of foreign visitors, whether tourists or business men, for his bar is visited by Dutchmen and one of her best regular customers is a Japanese. Fräulein Schroeder herself is a representative figure of her generation, a bourgeoise whose independent income has been annihilated by postwar inflation and whose standard of living has dramatically dropped.

Covering as it does the same historical ground as *Mr Norris*, *Goodbye to Berlin* adopts an entirely different, episodic technique, its six sections dealing with separate individuals or groups of characters in a variety of socially and topographically contrasting settings in and outside Berlin. The introductory note to the first edition describes the book as a 'short loosely-connected sequence of diaries and sketches' and recalls that its origins lay in the 'huge episodic novel of pre-Hitler Berlin' that was to have been titled *The Lost*. The 'Berlin Diary' that provides the first and last sections (dated a little more than two years apart) serves as a frame for what amounts to a sequence of linked stories, the three longest ('Sally Bowles', 'The Nowaks' and 'The Landauers') being almost of novella length. The opening and closing passages, and many that lie between, are written in the present tense, the traditional mode of lyric poetry and dramatic soliloquy rather than prose fiction, and the effect is not so much that of a diary as of a running commentary on a scene that lies before the narrator's eyes.

The book makes extensive use of autobiographical material, but, as usual, what is more interesting is the divergences between the fiction and the knowable facts. Some of these divergences follow naturally from the reordering to which real experience, so often untidy, repetitive and long-winded, must be subjected in the process of being turned into narrative, but as in *Mr Norris*, the author's self-censorship also involves him in strategies of concealment and displacement. In 'Sally Bowles' – the most familiar, though in itself one of the least interesting parts of the book – Christopher's relationship to Sally is never clearly defined. It is instructive, too, to see how subsequent theatrical transmogrifications of this story, seizing on this vagueness, move in the direction of making Christopher unblushingly heterosexual, the musical stage in particular being less tolerant of ambiguity, or nonconformity, than fiction. Little wonder that Isherwood told an interviewer, Denis Hart, in 1961 that he had become 'fairly tired of the Berlin material by now'. A production one would like to have seen is a musical based on the Berlin stories in which Isherwood collaborated with Auden and Kallman, and Marilyn Monroe played Sally Bowles; nothing, however, came of this intriguing idea.

'"I'm glad you're not in love with me, because, somehow, I couldn't possibly be in love with you,"' Sally tells Christopher, and the reader inclined to do so is left to ponder the significance of that 'somehow'. In *Christopher and his Kind* (p. 53) Isherwood comments that it 'may be taken to suggest that Sally knows instinctively that Christopher is homosexual – or it may not', the different responses presumably reflecting the sexual sensibilities of the reader. This is confirmed by Isherwood's reply to an interviewer, Tony Russo, in 1977, when asked whether he felt there was 'a certain gay sensibility' in his early work; he considered that 'anybody who really had any sensibility of that kind could tell at a single glance', not only in the Berlin stories but in the two novels that precede them.

It is clear, though, that other characters in 'Sally Bowles' see them as potential lovers, and Fräulein Schroeder is 'rather shocked' at Christopher's easy acceptance of Sally's affair with another man. Near the end Christopher wonders 'whether I hadn't, all this time, in my own peculiar way, been in love with Sally myself', but the reflection is not pursued and there is a thinly coded saving clause in the reference to his 'own peculiar way'. They are together constantly, but the relationship remains not only chaste but curiously distant and even indifferent, so that Sally's abrupt disappearance at the end of the story causes no pangs for either narrator or reader. That disappearance, complete and unredeemed, departs from the biographical facts of the case, since Isherwood and Jean Ross remained friends until the time of her death.

Sally owes something to the nineteenth-century tradition of the *femme fatale* that remained alive and kicking in Weimar popular culture, but as a sister of Lulu or Lola Lola she seems strikingly vulnerable and almost insipid, her outrageousness willed rather than springing from deep within her nature. But then Christopher, though sharing the same profession, is no Professor Rath. Rejecting the society and the morality that have produced and shaped him, he nevertheless hesitates to commit himself to an alternative. Had Isherwood possessed the courage or foolhardiness to write it, a section of *Goodbye to Berlin* that depicted the Cosy Corner as a rival establishment to the Blue Angel would have been worth having. But then no English publisher, in the decade that began with the furore over James Hanley's realistic but totally non-pornographic *Boy* (1931), would have touched such material.

Like Isherwood himself, Sally has come to Berlin to escape the constraints of a conventional family, and to some extent she acts as a reflector of late Weimar social and sexual mores. In this moral fable of the limitations of hedonism, politics are marginalised: one or two contemporary events, such as the failure of a bank, are briefly mentioned, but they remain peripheral and domesticated (' "The milkman says we'll have civil war in a fortnight!" '). In the most serious passage of the story, though, the detachment of these expatriates is suddenly perceived as soul-destroying: 'Perhaps in the Middle Ages people felt like this, when they believed themselves to have sold their souls to the Devil.... Yes, I said to myself, I've done it, now. I am lost' – the last word recalling the origins of this book in the unwritten panoramic novel thus named.

In 'On Ruegen Island', dated 'Summer 1931', the manipulation of the autobiographical basis is more palpable. This story utilises memories of the experiences of the two summers Isherwood spent in the Baltic resort, especially of the summer of 1931, when Auden and Spender as well as the youth referred to as 'Otto' were his companions. Isherwood had met the real Otto in Berlin and had known him for more than a year before taking him to Ruegen, but the fictional 'Christopher' meets 'Otto' by chance on the island and only subsequently sees him in Berlin. Auden and Spender have no counterparts in the fiction, but a character named Peter is introduced who has much in common with Isherwood, so that the latter's actual characteristics may be seen as being divided between the innocuous Christopher (more readily identified, of course, with the author) and the weaker, more problematic Peter. (Hugh David's suggestion that Peter is based on Spender does not carry conviction and is explicitly denied by Isherwood in *Christopher and his Kind* (p. 40).)

There is something a little perfunctory about the disguise bestowed on Peter, who was at Oxford (instead of Cambridge) and has lost his mother (instead of his father) but who comes from a social background resembling Isherwood's own and whose feelings for the youth are similarly compounded of lust, sentimental affection, and anger and jealousy at his cupidity, disloyalty and heterosexual philandering. Peter is unconvincing as a character, and the expository section that summarises his early life is clumsily done, reading like a synopsis for a *Bildungsroman*, but he enables 'Christopher' to be presented as coolly in control of the situation and fully detached from Peter's humiliating entanglement. 'Very much taken up' with the novel he is writing, he spends a lot of time alone, taking long walks and observing the other man's turbulent emotions with mild and noncommittal interest.

Since Isherwood's feelings for the real Otto have been tactfully displaced onto Peter, it was open to the author not only to identify but to analyse the nature of Peter's feelings for the youth. That would perhaps be expecting too much, however, from a writer who hoped to be published and sold, and it would certainly be expecting too much from Isherwood at this stage. Although it is clear that Peter and Otto share a room, and that Peter waits up late for him, gives him money and is tormented by jealousy, their relationship is never made clear, and the reader is left with the sense of something missing. (Much later Auden was to complain, not unjustly, to Isherwood about a similar hiatus in his novel *The World in the Evening*: ' "We have to know who was fucking whom. And you never make that clear in the book". ') The riskiest statement in the whole story is the narrator's observation that 'It is quite natural for Peter often to feel bored with Otto – they have scarcely a single interest in common – but Peter, *for sentimental reasons*, will never admit that this is so' (italics added). Isherwood no doubt knew a good deal at firsthand about both the boredom and the sentimentality that such a relationship could entail, but any further discussion of this emotional dilemma is blocked, promising though such an exploration might in literary terms have been.

In the next section of *Goodbye to Berlin*, 'The Nowaks', he moves a little, though only a little, closer to candour and confession. Back in Berlin, and with Peter returned to England, Christopher now develops a relationship with Otto and moves as a lodger into his home in a slum tenement. Isherwood had, as we have seen, done the same, quite briefly, in October 1930 – but that was before, not after, the first summer at Ruegen. In *Christopher and his Kind* (pp. 44–5) he describes this postdating of the fictional event by about one year as a 'falsification' but gives two reasons for it. One is technical – that it was important to introduce the major characters associated with Fräulein Schroeder's establishment before the relatively unimportant Nowaks – but the second is more interesting: 'since "Isherwood" is not overtly homosexual, he has to be given another reason for knowing Otto and another motive for going to live with his family'. He adds that the decline in the value of sterling following the British government's abandoning of the gold standard in September 1931 provides his fictional protagonist with 'a respectable motive for going to live with the Nowaks: he becomes their lodger because he is poor, not because he wants to share a bedroom with Otto'. This again demands a fictional ordering of events that is chronologically different from their autobiographical counterparts. Isherwood, furthermore, had quitted the tenement in Simeonstrasse after a month or so, whereas the fiction involves a longer stay, the story moving from 'clammy autumn weather' to a period 'after Christmas'.

In 'The Nowaks', then, Christopher is shown as sleeping with Otto because sharing beds is a normal way of life in the slums, but not as 'sleeping with' him in the euphemistic sense which usually denotes the opposite. The real Isherwood had never been so hard up that he had to live in such conditions, nor was he driven into the leaky tenement by any Orwellian urge to discover how the poor lived. He was there because he had yielded to Otto's persuasions, and even in the story there are hints that the more sophisticated or more cynical reader might respond to: for instance, Otto receives money from a Dutchman for unspecified services. (Was Isherwood perhaps recalling Auden's Dutch friend Dan, about whom he must have heard?)

The narrative ice gets even thinner when Isherwood describes the Alexander Casino, identified as 'a cellar *lokal*' at the end of the street. This is clearly, though not explicitly, a rent-bar and quite possibly based on the Cosy Corner. The narrator is taken there by Otto but recalls visiting it a year earlier during Saturday night tours of the city dives (just as Isherwood, almost a year before moving in with Otto's family, had been introduced to the boy-bars by Francis Turville-Petre). Boys are sitting around waiting, some in 'sweaters and leather jackets', one in shorts and an open-necked shirt (sartorial details paralleled in the description of the Cosy Corner in *Christopher and his Kind*); an elderly bourgeois is sitting in earnest conversation with a boy who from time to time lays his hand on the man's knee; at weekends foreign visitors invade the place, the Englishmen talking 'in loud, high, excited voices'. There cannot be much doubt as to the nature of the business transacted in this establishment, but the text contains nothing explicit. When the police raid the place they are looking for 'wanted criminals or escaped reformatory boys' (the latter phrase perhaps forming a discreet memorial to Auden's Otto Küsel). Christopher becomes a regular but seems to content himself with sitting and observing the scene. Perhaps, though, he is not always just an observer, for later, for obscure reasons, he worries about 'an unpleasant and mysterious rash' that 'might be due to Frau Nowak's cooking, or worse'.

One is reminded a little of the scenes in certain Victorian novels that, daring by the standards of their day, are yet worded with sufficient evasiveness not to bring a blush to the cheek of virgins of either sex or any age. In 'The Nowaks' sexuality remains a subtext until very near the end. There is then, however, a curious epilogue that seems almost irrelevant until it becomes clear that the narrator's homoeroticism has been displaced onto the dying women in the sanatorium who crave sexual satisfaction as an assurance that, for just a little longer, they are still alive. The real Otto's mother had actually been sent to a sanatorium, and this had evidently prompted Isherwood's departure from the crowded Simeonstrasse tenement, but the scrap of actuality is transformed and elaborated in the fiction – a nice instance of Isherwood's waste not, want not policy towards actual experience.

The sanatorium scene has a quality of brutality at odds with the normally relaxed tone of the book. One patient recalls with relish how her husband ('"such a great strong man"') used to thrash her; another describes salaciously how Erika, '"such an innocent girl until she came here"', has now been sexually initiated by the other women and takes a doll ('"a little mannikin"') to bed every night '"because she says she must have a man in her bed!"' The sexuality displaced onto these women is of a violent and morbid kind, suggesting the extent of the repression that the main part of the story has involved.

That repression comes close to failure once or twice, notably in the descriptions of Otto. With limited intellectual equipment, and viewed entirely from the outside, the youth can only be presented as a healthy animal with a strong instinct for self-preservation: when first glimpsed by Peter in 'On Ruegen Island' he is turning somersaults on the beach, and then exploits the stranger's interest by the time-honoured gambit of asking for a light. Thereafter, like a very model of contemporary *Naktkultur*, he expresses himself by physical, especially athletic, feats as much as by speech. (Compare the behaviour of the hustler in the final scene of *The Memorial*, whose form of greeting is to perform 'three rapid handsprings on the back of the sofa'.) There is in particular a scene in 'The Nowaks' describing Otto's habit of remaining in the room and stripping after bringing Christopher breakfast in bed, to 'do exercises, shadow-box or stand on his head'. He is, as the for once not-so-detached narrator observes, 'so animally alive, his naked brown body so sleek with health'. The frequent emphasis on Otto's taste for running after girls is not an entirely adequate counter-weight to such revelatory moments.

In the Nowaks' Berlin slum, and even on Ruegen Island, politics invades private lives. Otto's brother Lothar joins the National

Socialists and even Otto expresses a preference for ' "a communist revolution" ', while their mother longs for a return to ' "the good old times" ' of the Kaiser. On the beaches of Ruegen, sandcastles fly the swastika. But it is in 'The Landauers', which immediately follows 'The Nowaks', that politics moves closer to the foreground, and in a more menacing shape than flags on sandcastles and young men dressing up in uniform.

The two central characters in this episode (not counting the Christopher-narrator) are both Jewish and both based quite closely on real-life prototypes. The model for Natalia Landauer, the daughter of the wealthy and cultured owner of a large Berlin department store, was Gisa Soloweitschik, a Jewish girl whom Spender had met on a skiing holiday in Switzerland when he was at Oxford and she was 17. Later they met again in Berlin, whither Spender had come to join her, and he introduced her to Isherwood. The two Englishmen would go often to Sunday lunch with Gisa's family at their Wilmersdorf flat; in the story the Landauers also live in Wilmersdorf, and Christopher goes there for lunch, but there is no figure in the story corresponding to Spender. Gisa was a student of art history who left Berlin in 1933 for France and there married a nephew of André Gide; Natalia too goes to Paris to study art and eventually settles there.

There are several other points of correspondence between Isherwood's story and the account of Gisa given in Spender's *World within World*. Gisa's family, according to Spender, 'called Christopher Shakespeare and me Byron', and the conversation at the Landauers' turns to Byron as well as (more riskily) Oscar Wilde; both girls, in the autobiography and the fiction, speak breathlessly of their enthusiasm for art and music; Gisa had 'an Oriental sense of untouchability' and 'could not drink from a glass if anyone else had drunk from it', while Natalia is fastidiously unwillingly to share a coffee-spoon with Christopher. What one cannot be sure of, naturally, is how far Spender's portrait of Gisa, some twenty years after the event, may have been derived from his friend's story rather than his own uncorrupted memories, though the chances are that Isherwood's version bears in any case a close resemblance to actuality.

Natalia's cousin, the young businessman Bernhard, is more loosely based on another of Isherwood's friends from the Jewish community of Berlin, Wilfrid Israel. Wilfrid, like Bernhard, worked for a department store owned by his family. Five years older than

Isherwood, he had an English mother (Bernhard speaks 'beautiful English') and was actually a British subject, born in England. After fleeing from Nazi persecution he lived in England and helped with the resettlement of refugees, but in June 1943 was killed when a civil aircraft flying from Lisbon to London was shot down by German fighters over the Bay of Biscay. (One of the other victims of the crash was the film star Leslie Howard.) At the end of Isherwood's story Bernhard dies mysteriously, presumably murdered by the Nazis, but at a date more than ten years earlier than Wilfrid, and Isherwood later admitted that this dating, demanded by the timeframe of the book and its 1933 terminus, was 'unconvincing' (*Christopher and his Kind*, p. 60).

Bernhard's sexuality is the subject of hints and implications: he lives in 'a quiet street not far from the Tiergarten' (as Isherwood had done when he first came to Berlin), quite alone; he is wearing 'a beautifully embroidered kimono' when Christopher visits him, and has a habit of resting his hand on the other man's shoulder. He also owns a luxurious villa 'on the shores of the Wannsee' somewhat resembling the Muthesius home where Auden had lived and which he may well have described to Isherwood. Near the end of the story, as the atmosphere in Berlin grows more tense, an oddly equivocal little conversation follows Christopher's announcement to Bernhard that he is going to England. Bernhard proposes that they should go to China together, leaving Berlin that very evening: Christopher treats it as a joke, but enters for the moment into the spirit of this fantasy, only adding with narratorial hindsight:

> Perhaps I am slow at jokes. At any rate, it took me nearly eighteen months to see the point of this one – to recognize it as Bernhard's last, most daring and most cynical experiment upon us both. For now I am certain – absolutely convinced – that his offer was perfectly serious.

The arresting word here is 'daring', which seems to mean that Christopher was being invited to 'come out' to his friend and to enter into a romantic relationship with Bernhard.

If so, it was a test that he failed, though a homoerotic subtext gives a meaning to the friendship between the two men that otherwise seems curiously lacking. In *Christopher and his Kind* (p. 59) Isherwood states: 'I believe Christopher suspected that Wilfrid was a severely repressed homosexual', and he adds that the novel

seemed to imply that Bernhard was concealing 'a romantic attachment to "Isherwood"'. These hints he found, with hindsight,
'offensive', and he was uncomfortable to reflect that Wilfrid had
read the book. He also notes (p. 56) that Spender's account of
Wilfrid in *World within World* differs radically in some respects
from his own.

'The Landauers' picks up a detail mentioned in the opening
section of the book – that one of Christopher's pupils is a Jewish
girl, Hippi Bernstein – and makes the increasingly hazardous situation of the prosperous Jewish business community the central issue
of the story. In that earlier passage, the Nazi threat still seems
'quite unreal': 'Hippi never worries about the future. Like everyone
else in Berlin, she refers continually to the political situation, but
only briefly, with a conventional melancholy, as when one speaks
of religion.' Even her father is dismissive towards the signs of the
times:

> 'You can go in the tram,' said Herr Bernstein. 'I will not have
> them throwing stones at my beautiful car.'
> 'And suppose they throw stones at me?' asked Frau Bernstein
> goodhumouredly.
> 'Ach, what does that matter? If they throw stones at you, I will
> buy you a sticking-plaster for your head. It will cost me only five
> groschen. But if they throw stones at my car, it will cost me
> perhaps five hundred marks.'

By a later stage in *Goodbye to Berlin* daily life has been invaded by
political events that cannot be turned aside with a jest, and 'The
Landauers', unlike any of the preceding stories, opens in an atmosphere of contemporary violence: 'One night in October 1930, about
a month after the Elections, there was a big row on the Leipziger-
strasse. Gangs of Nazi roughs turned out to demonstrate against
the Jews . . . .' It is still, however, only 1930, and after this opening
politics recedes until the last dozen pages. Nevertheless, the essential keynote has been struck.

Towards the end of the story, there is a sudden access of political
awareness: at a party given by Bernhard at his Wannsee villa,
many of the guests are 'talking politics in low, serious voices', for
it is the night of the August 1931 referendum and there is a sense
that this may be 'the last night of an epoch'. Time passes quickly
during these final pages of the story, and after an interval of eight

months the overthrow of the government seems even more imminent: as Christopher says to Bernhard, ' "And what do you think
will happen in Germany now? . . . Is there going to be a Nazi putsch
or a communist revolution?" ' A few pages later there are references to events in the early months of 1933: to Hitler becoming
Chancellor (30 January), the Reichstag fire (27 February), the boycott of Jewish businesses (1 April), and the narrator's departure 'for
the last time' – closely coinciding, as in *Mr Norris*, with Isherwood's
own.

The concluding section of *Goodbye to Berlin* offers not sequential
narrative but a series of vignettes drawn from Isherwood's last
winter in Berlin, and here he comes closer than ever before –
though still not very close – to candour concerning his own sexuality and lifestyle. With a friend he goes on a tour of what are
noncommittally referred to as 'the dives' but which are plainly gay,
lesbian and transvestite bars:

> It was to be in the nature of a farewell visit, for the Police have
> begun to take a great interest in these places. They are frequently
> raided, and the names of their clients are written down. There is
> even talk of a general Berlin clean-up.

There is an unusually vivid snapshot of the grotesque glitz of
contemporary Berlin nightlife ('a young man in a spangled crino-
line and jewelled breast-caps' painfully does the splits), its outrageousness magnified through the eyes of an American tourist:

> 'Say,' he asked Fritz, 'what's on here?'
> 'Men dressed as women,' Fritz grinned.
> The little American simply couldn't believe it. 'Men dressed as
> *women*? As *women* hey? Do you mean they're *queer*?'
> 'Eventually we're all queer,' drawled Fritz solemnly . . . .
> 'You *queer*, too, hey?' demanded the little American, turning
> suddenly on me.
> 'Yes,' I said, 'very queer indeed.'

The moment of confession, or proclamation, passes – or is, rather,
brushed aside with an ironic and ambiguous jest – but it has been a
close shave, and there is another nasty moment for Christopher a
few pages later when, on a visit to a reformatory, he is suddenly
overcome by guilt and shame at the sight of the boys: 'I seemed, at

that moment, to have become the sole representative of their gaolers, of Capitalist Society. I wondered if any of them had actually been arrested in the Alexander Casino, and, if so, whether they recognised me.'

Again, there is a hidden logic beneath the non sequitur: having been the exploiter of these boys (or boys like them), whose sexual services he was rich enough to purchase, he is now alarmed by the possibility of betrayal and exposure. But the alarm must be Isherwood's, not that of his fictional namesake who has apparently done nothing more than sit and watch the proceedings at the Alexander Casino. Again, as so often in the early writings, we have a sense of a 'wobbling' between invention and confession – of an indiscreet subtext speaking almost, though not quite, loudly enough to be heard. The appearance of these passages very near the end of the Berlin stories (the word 'queer' appears for the first time on page 562 of the omnibus edition) suggests a last-minute, barely repressed confessional impulse that, as it turned out, had to wait almost another forty years before it was fully articulated in *Christopher and his Kind*.

The guilt-feeling evident in the closing pages of *Goodbye to Berlin*, most obviously in the somewhat implausible visit to the reformatory, is interestingly glossed in the introduction Isherwood wrote for Gerald Hamilton's *Mr Norris and I* (the essay was later included in the volume titled *Exhumations*). He writes there that

> What repels me now about *Mr Norris* is its heartlessness. It is a heartless fairy story about a real city in which human beings were suffering the miseries of political violence and near-starvation. The 'wickedness' of Berlin's night-life was of a most pitiful kind: the kisses and embraces, as always, had price-tags attached to them, but here the prices were drastically reduced in the cut-throat competition of an overcrowded market.... The only genuine monster was the young foreigner who passed gaily through these scenes of desolation, misinterpreting them to suit his childish fantasy. This I later began to understand – which is why my second book about Berlin is at least somewhat better than my first.

That the comparative judgement is exclusively moral rather than aesthetic is a natural corollary of the intensely personal nature of these works.

Almost thirty years after he left Berlin, Isherwood put one of his Berlin acquaintances to fictional use in *Down There on a Visit* (1962), the 'Ambrose' section of which has as its protagonist a character closely modelled on Francis Turville-Petre. This story thus serves as a kind of pendant to the Berlin novels. Or perhaps a postscript: for 'Ambrose' opens in May 1933 with the narrator leaving Berlin, and the main action derives from Isherwood's far from blissful period of residence on Francis's Greek island. It was, however, to be another 15 years before Francis's Berlin days received their fullest and frankest commemoration in *Christopher and his Kind*.

At first glance this latter book appears to be the long-delayed second instalment of an unfinished autobiographical work, though on closer examination it turns out to be something rather different. *Lions and Shadows* (1938) had been subtitled 'An Education in the Twenties', had begun with the narrator's schooldays and had ended with him leaving London for Berlin on 14 March 1929, exactly as Isherwood had done. But the preface contains a warning that the work is 'not, in the ordinary journalistic sense of the word, an autobiography;...it is not even entirely "true"', and the reader is urged to 'Read it as a novel'. Though figures readily recognisable as Auden, Upward and others make an appearance, most of the names are fictitious and 'a novelist's licence' has been used in recounting incidents. Its subject, Isherwood claims, is 'the education of a novelist': what is in question is representativeness rather than uniqueness. Hence there is no special virtue in truth-telling, and this is a convenient arrangement in more ways than one. As Sir Philip Sidney said of the poet, Isherwood cannot be blamed for falsifying because he is entering into no contract to tell things as they were, and this also grants him a licence for evasiveness. Published between *Mr Norris* and *Goodbye to Berlin*, *Lions and Shadows* shares their reluctance to come clean, and in fact the gap in Isherwood's practice between fiction and autobiography is so nearly invisible that the validity of these traditional generic labels is called into question by the one as much as by the other.

Characteristically evasive is the account of the sexuality of the young Auden (Weston in *Lions and Shadows*):

Weston's own attitude to sex, in its simplicity and utter lack of inhibition, fairly took my breath away. He was no Don Juan: he didn't run round hunting for his pleasures. But he took what came to him with a matter-of-factness and an appetite as hearty

as that which he showed when sitting down to dinner. I don't
think that, even in those days, he exaggerated much: certainly,
his manner of describing these adventures bore all the marks of
truth. I found his shameless prosaic anecdotes only too hard to
forget, as I lay restlessly awake at night, listening to the waves,
alone in my single bed.   (p. 195)

Little or nothing here, perhaps, is untrue (though 'no Don Juan'
may have been intended to point the reader in the wrong direction): what is missing is the central fact of Auden's homosexuality
and his influence on Isherwood as lover, mentor, trailblazer and
role-model.

Almost forty years later, *Christopher and his Kind* (1977) opens
with the words 'There is a book called *Lions and Shadows....*' The
warnings and recommendations of that earlier book's preface are
recalled: that work of his youth is 'not truly autobiographical' and
'should be read as if it were a novel' (an injunction that is, in
practice, not easy to obey). The new book, however, will be quite
different, 'as frank and factual as I can make it, especially as far as I
myself am concerned'. Given this resolve, it was obviously an
option for Isherwood to rewrite his earlier book in a spirit of
new-found candour. What he does, however, is to begin where
Lions and Shadows leaves off, with his first visit to Berlin. The earlier
book had covered the years 1921 to 1929; the second covers 1929 to
1939, and about two-fifths of it are devoted to the Berlin years. It
was, of course, a phase of his life that provided plenty to be frank
and factual about.

Christopher and his Kind is not subtitled 'An Education in the
Thirties' but, superficially at least, the heavy hand of the *Bildungsroman* tradition lies upon it. Adrift in Berlin, the hero encounters
colourful figures like Layard and Turville-Petre, explores the city's
day-life and night-life, and finds himself pulled between two sexual worlds: that of Hirschfeld's Institute, where homosexuality is
treated with sympathy and scientific tolerance and daily life is
decorous and respectable, and that of the Cosy Corner and the
other boy-bars, raffish, intensely exciting, exploitative and at least
semi-criminal. Karl Giese, representing the former, and Francis
Turville-Petre, his guide to the latter, offer him two contrasting
models of homosexual lifestyles, the domestic and the cruising,
and the urgent, though largely unspoken, question is which
one (if either) can both grant personal fulfilment and sustain his

vocation as a novelist. In the event he effects a compromise: the bars give him material to write about, but the disciplined world of the Institute defines the conditions in which the writing can be done.

None of this is very far away from the kind of nineteenth-century autobiography that describes the narrator's struggles with religious doubt or some other burning contemporary issue. What Christian faith or its rejection were to Newman or Gosse, homosexuality was to Isherwood. But as we turn over the pages of *Christopher and his Kind* it becomes clear that there is another theme to which this narrative of early experiences is subservient: the book becomes an inquiry into the nature of memory, the processes by which experience is turned into art, and the very possibility of autobiographical writing as conventionally understood. And inevitably these concerns raise doubts about the initial promise that the book will be 'frank and factual' and about the attainability of this objective. For if it turns out that the truth about the past is irrecoverable, what is such a promise worth?

On one level the book exposes, ridicules and repudiates the author's own earlier attempts to mythologise the past. A self-confessed myth-maker, Isherwood now presents himself as coming clean about his earlier autobiographical statements in the same spirit as that in which he has recently come out as a homosexual. A good example of this is in connection with the destruction of the diary he kept in Berlin:

> Christopher's declared reason for burning his Berlin diary was unconvincing. He used to tell his friends that he had destroyed his real Past because he preferred the simplified, more creditable, more exciting fictitious Past which he had created to take its place. This fictitious Past, he said, was the Past he wanted to 'remember'. Now that I am writing about Christopher's real Past, I sadly miss the lost diary and have no patience with this arty talk.
> (p. 37)

There is no reason, however, why we should find the new stance more credible than the old one: myth-making may be habit-forming, and if there were formerly motives for falsifying the past, there may be different motives for doing so again. In any case, recovering the past is more easily said than done: however firm the resolve, the task may be simply impossible, and

Isherwood is surely naive or disingenuous in claiming that the existence of the diary would enable him to tell the truth. For the diary itself can only have been a version of the truth, selective, sometimes unconsciously or wilfully distorted, as artful a compound of lights (or lions) and shadows as an Expressionist film. He is more honest when he admits that he cannot really remember Jean Ross because the original image has been obscured by too many actresses playing Sally Bowles.

The detached, ironic, sometimes cynical tone of *Christopher and his Kind* nourishes the illusion of truth-telling, as does the careful nomenclatorial distinction between his past and present selves (respectively 'Christopher' and 'I'). Among the self-created myths that undergo an apparently scrupulous process of dismantling is that of his first Berlin lover, 'Bubi', as The German Boy (see p. 42 above). But if there was self-delusion in the past, there may now be an overstating or oversimplifying of the case for the sake of literary effect, and neither account may succeed in conveying the genuine flavour of a relationship that was clearly of considerable intensity and duration. There is perhaps something suspicious in Isherwood's deft exchanging of one simple version of events for another, and more honesty in the young Auden's recognition, in his scribbled journal, of the complexity and contradictoriness of his feelings for Gerhart.

It is true that Isherwood is ready enough to admit that the Berlin stories misrepresented actuality for aesthetic or other reasons. As already noted, he was never so poor that he was compelled to live in a slum, and he spent a month with Otto's family for sexual rather than economic reasons, though he found it tactful in the story based on this episode of his life to adduce the more respectable motive. The description of Otto, he acknowledges, is inaccurate in its reference to his 'spindly, immature legs': there was nothing wrong with the real Otto's limbs, far from it, but the homoeroticism of the passage was nearing danger point and a little dust needed to be thrown in the reader's eyes. Even in a much later book, *Down There on a Visit*, there is some misrepresentation in the portrait of Francis Turville-Petre as 'Ambrose', though Isherwood himself maintained that all he says is true except for three sentences. Despite this reassurance, among so many confessions and corrections of the record one is bound to wonder how much has gone consciously or unconsciously unconfessed. True confessions, excellent in principle, may be next to impossible in practice.

In an earlier chapter I have questioned the belatedly acknowledged 'genuine' reason given for going to live in Berlin ('Berlin meant Boys'), which perhaps does little more than replace one myth, handy enough in its generation, by another more appropriate to an age of tolerance, enlightenment or authorised exhibitionism. But in the most significant passage in this connection, and one of the most striking in the whole book, Isherwood comes close to recognising that his homosexuality may itself be part of his personal myth. Asserting his right to 'live according to my nature', he nevertheless admits that even if his nature were different he would still have to fight those he saw as his enemies (the Others of his undergraduate myth-making, shared with Upward) and would adopt sexual nonconformity as a mode of protest: 'If boys didn't exist, I should have to invent them' (p. 17). He turned to homosexuality, that is, as some others of his class and generation turned to Roman Catholicism or left-wing politics, as a mode of protest. His rebuttal of the charge of 'repressed heterosexuality' amounts to no more than a reminder that his sexual inclinations have not changed with the passing of time – a point at which one recalls that myths can be of sufficient power and permanence to be indistinguishable in their effects from the truth.

The promised 'frank and factual' book – the book that could not have been written, and certainly could not have been published, forty years earlier – does not quite materialise in *Christopher and his Kind* for the very good reason that such a promise embodies an impossible ideal. Franker and more factual as well as funnier and more graphic than *Lions and Shadows* it certainly is, though it has the advantage of dealing with a more colourful phase of the author's life, and a book about late Weimar Berlin that was as pussy-footed as *Lions and Shadows* is difficult to imagine.

Ultimately, however, it does not matter a great deal whether the promise is fulfilled or not: the biographers can be relied on sooner or later to fill in the gaps and correct the false impressions. What is significant in the pages that follow that opening statement is the deep interest in the relationship between autobiography and fiction, and the concessions and compromises to which both are subject. It is an interest that ensures a continuity between Isherwood's practice of these two genres, much closer together in his case than is customary: so much so, indeed, that a new taxonomy of genres, more subtle and flexible than the existing one, seems called for.

Epilogue:

After the war a publisher invited Isherwood to spend six months in the city and to write a book about it. He refused the invitation, partly because he was too busy with other projects, partly because such an idea seemed 'terribly willed'. One suspects, though, that, as with Kipling declining to revisit India, some deeper motive was involved: the ruins of the city he had known in its heyday might have turned out to be an irresistible metaphor for the loss of his own youth. Two postwar visits to Europe failed to include Germany in their itinerary, but at last in 1952 he spent a short time in Berlin and revisited the now famous house in Nollendorfstrasse. His old landlady, Fräulein Thurau, cognisant of her own literary celebrity, greeted him rapturously, and in later years Isherwood would mimic for the benefit of his friends her exclamations of joy at their unexpected reunion. Once she had calmed down, she gave him news of Otto, who was prospering in the postwar world of shortages and black markets, and he called on Heinz, now married with a child.

In his own later years, Auden was back in Berlin on several occasions for short periods and did not entirely escape reminders of the personal as well as the public past. On one occasion he was startled by the vision of a former boyfriend who had turned into the fattest man he had ever seen ('he should have been in a circus'), and was made wistful by the reflection that 'the city of my youth has now gone'. In 1945 he was (somewhat improbably) sent to Berlin by the Morale Division of the United States Strategic Bombing Survey with the rank equivalent to major, the team of which he was a member being charged with investigating the effects of bombing on the German population. Twenty years further on, in 1964–5, he spent six months there as a Ford Foundation writer-in-residence. This latter visit was not a success: after thirty years, both he and Berlin had changed too much. It was during this stay that he kept a diary, the only one he is known to have kept apart from that which belongs to his period of residence in 1929. Re-reading the earlier diary at that time, as he is known to have done, must have induced an overpowering sense of then and now.

For both of these writers, Berlin had constituted a short but crucial chapter in their experience. It must be said, though, that to link their names, as this book has constantly done, is to risk giving a misleading impression of long-term personal intimacy and literary parity. Their gifts and achievements were after all of a very different order: beside the creative energy, the formidable intellect and the profound originality of Auden, Isherwood's talent, though distinctive, seems narrow and low-pulsed. There is a case for regarding Auden as the greatest British poet of the mid-century, while Isherwood remains a minor novelist and autobiographer who was shrewd enough to recognise his own strengths and limitations at a fairly early stage. It is the difference between a stream and a geyser, or between a great waterfall and a backyard swimming pool – which is not necessarily to say a word against streams or swimming pools. It must also be said that they were unequal in the direct use they made of their Berlin experiences. Almost inevitably, the novelist and autobiographer exploited them more fully and obviously than the poet.

Still, the significance of the time the young Auden spent in Berlin ought not to be undervalued. Without the experience, at a particular stage, of that extraordinary place, so much in the future lives and work of both Auden and Isherwood might have been different. Auden spent a relatively short time there but did so when he was, in more ways than one, standing at the crossroads. He came to recognise his own sexual identity, rejecting the notion he had brought with him of his homosexuality as a passing phase, an entertaining sidetrip from the well-marked route to heterosexual love and marriage. Perhaps more importantly for his work, he also had there his first experiences of intense sexual passion and his first yearnings for a stable and mutual relationship. His Berlin journal offers compelling and moving evidence of his intellectual and emotional strivings to understand himself and others: in the words of one of his own poems, the appeal he made to Berlin was to tell him the truth about love. It was in Berlin, too, that he first became seriously aware of politics. Though he initially, for reasons beyond his control, returned to England, Berlin seems also to have given him a taste for the life of the exile that was to be satisfied by his later residence in America, Austria and elsewhere. Without the nine or ten months spent there, the rest of his life might have been very different – and might have beens, though fruitless for the subject, may be profitable for the student of biography.

Isherwood told W. J. Weatherby in a 1960 interview, ' "I write fundamentally about foreigners, about exiles, about oddballs, the excluded and so forth . . . " '. His own lifestyle was to remain that of the permanent voluntary exile, but he was to continue over many years, and almost to the end of his days, to draw on his Berlin experiences for literary copy. At the same time the transmogrifica-tions of his work into stage and screen entertainments, like the books by or about Mr Norris and Sally Bowles in which he had no hand, gave those experiences and writings an autonomous life, so that *Goodbye to Berlin* has become, like *Hamlet* or *Frankenstein*, not only a work of literature but the starting point for a metaliterature or mythology.

Bibliography

WORKS BY AUDEN AND ISHERWOOD

W. H. Auden

Juvenilia: Poems 1922–28, ed. Katherine Bucknell, London, 1994
Collected Poems, ed. Edward Mendelson, London, 1976
Berlin Journal (unpublished: Berg Collection, New York Public Library)

Christopher Isherwood

The Memorial (1932)
Mr Norris Changes Trains (1935)
Lions and Shadows (1938)
Goodbye to Berlin (1939)
Prater Violet (1945)
The Condor and the Cows (1949)
Down There on a Visit (1962)
Exhumations (1966)
Kathleen and Frank (1971)
Christopher and his Kind 1929–1939 (1977)

W. H. Auden and Christopher Isherwood

The Dog Beneath the Skin (1935)
The Ascent of F6 (1936)
On the Frontier (1938)

OTHER WORKS

Albright, William Foxwell, *The Archaeology of Palestine*, Harmondsworth, 1963.
Alexander, Peter F., *William Plomer: A Biography*, Oxford, 1989.
Bell, Arthur, 'An Interview with Christopher Isherwood', *Fag Rag*, Summer 1973.
Bell, Arthur, 'Christopher Isherwood: No Parades', *New York Times Book Review*, 25 March 1973, pp. 10, 12.
Boyd, Brian, *Vladimir Nabokov: The Russian Years*, London, 1990.
Brome, Vincent, *Havelock Ellis, Philosopher of Sex: A Biography*, London, 1979.

213

Bullock, Alan, *Hitler: A Study in Tyranny*, London, 1964.

Carpenter, Humphrey, *W. H. Auden: A Biography*, London, 1981.

Coates, Paul, *The Gorgon's Gaze: German Cinema, Expressionism, and the Image of Horror*, Cambridge, 1990.

Constantine, David, 'The German Auden: Six Early Poems', in W. H. Auden *'The Map of All My Youth': Early Works Friends and Influences* (Auden Studies I) ed. Katherine Bucknell and Nicholas Jenkins, Oxford, 1990, pp. 1–15.

Cooper, Artemis, *Cairo in the War*, London, 1989.

Cunningham, Valentine, *British Writers of the Thirties*, Oxford, 1989.

David, Hugh, *Stephen Spender: A Portrait with Background*, London, 1992.

Douglas, Don, 'Christopher Isherwood Speaks Out', *Gay Scene*, V, 9, February 1975.

Eisner, Lotte H., *The Haunted Screen*, London, 1969.

Farnan, Dorothy J., *Auden in Love*, London, 1984.

Farson, Daniel, *The Gilded Gutter: The Life of Francis Bacon*, London, 1993.

Fielding, Xan, *Hide and Seek*, London, 1954.

Finney, Brian, *Christopher Isherwood*, London, 1979.

Forster, E. M., *Selected Letters: Volume 2, 1921–1970*, eds Mary Lago and P.N. Furbank, London, 1985.

Fowler, Marian, *The Way She Looks Tonight: Five Women of Style*, New York, 1996. (Includes a section on Marlene Dietrich.)

Friedrich, Thomas, *Berlin: A Photographic Portrait of the Weimar Years 1918–1933*, London, 1991.

Fryer, Jonathan, *Eye of the Camera: A Life of Christopher Isherwood*, London, 1993.

Fryer, Jonathan, *Isherwood*, New York, 1978.

Gardiner, Margaret, 'Auden: A Memoir', *New Review*, 3 (July 1976), pp. 9–19.

Gay, Peter, *Weimar Culture: The Outsider as Insider*, London, 1968.

Geherin, David J., 'An Interview with Christopher Isherwood', *Journal of Narrative Technique*, 2 (September 1972), pp. 143–58.

Green, Henry, *Pack My Bag: A Self-Portrait*, Oxford, 1986.

Green, Martin, *Children of the Sun: A Narrative of 'Decadence' in England after 1918*, London, 1977.

Hamilton, Gerald, *Mr Norris and I: An Autobiographical Sketch*, London, 1956.

Hamilton, Gerald, *The Way It Was With Me*, London, 1969.

Hart, Denis, 'Here on a Visit' (interview with Isherwood), *The Guardian*, 22 September 1961.

Heilbrun, Carolyn G., 'Christopher Isherwood: An Interview', *Twentieth Century Literature*, 22 (October 1976), pp. 253–63.

Hillier, Bevis, *Young Betjeman*, London, 1988.

Hollis, Christopher, *In the Twenties*, London, 1976.

Hynes, Samuel, *The Auden Generation: Literature and Politics in the 1930s*, London, 1976.

Kane, Martin, *Weimar Germany and the Limits of Political Art*, London, 1987.

Kracauer, Siegfried, *From Caligari to Hitler: A Psychological History of the German Film*, Princeton, NJ, 1947.

Lane, Homer, *Talks to Parents and Teachers*, London, 1928.

Lehmann, John, *Christopher Isherwood: A Personal Memoir*, London, 1987.

Lehmann, John, *In the Purely Pagan Sense*, London, 1985.

Lehmann, John, *The Whispering Gallery*, London, 1955.

McAlmon, Robert, *Being Geniuses Together 1920–1930*, New York, 1968; rev. edn, 1984.

McAlmon, Robert, *Distinguished Air: Grim Fairy Tales*, Paris, 1925.

Mackay, John Henry, *The Hustler (Der Puppenjunge)*, trans. Hubert Kennedy, Boston, Mass., 1985.

Mann, Klaus, *The Pious Dance (Der Fromme Tanz)*, trans. Laurence Senelick, London, 1988.

Mann, Klaus, *The Turning-Point: Thirty-Five Years in this Century*, New York, 1984 (originally published 1942).

Manning, Olivia, *The Battle Lost and Won*, London, 1978.

Manvell, Roger and Heinrich Fraenkel, *The German Cinema*, London, 1971.

Meyers, Jeffrey, *Homosexuality and Literature 1890–1930*, London, 1987.

Mitchison, Naomi, *You May Well Ask: A Memoir 1920–1940*, London, 1979.

Osborne, Charles, 'Berlin in the Twenties: Conversations with Otto Klemperer and Lotte Lenya', *London Magazine*, 1 (May 1961), p. 49.

Osborne, Charles, *W. H. Auden: The Life of a Poet*, London, 1980.

Perrot, Jean, *Syria-Palestine I: From the Origins to the Bronze Age* (Archaelogia Mundi series), Geneva, 1979.

Petro, Patrice, *Joyless Streets: Women and Melodramatic Representation in Weimar Germany*, Princeton, NJ, 1989.

Plant, Richard, *The Pink Triangle: The Nazi War against Homosexuals*, New York, 1986.

Plomer, William, *Autobiography*, 1975.

Read, Anthony and David Fisher, *Berlin: The Biography of a City*, 1994.

Riley, Thomas A., *John Henry Mackay*, New York, 1972.

Roberts, Susan, *The Magician of the Golden Dawn: The Story of Aleister Crowley*, Chicago, 1978.

Russo, Tony, 'Christopher Isherwood' (interview), *Christopher Street*, I, 9, March 1977.

Sawyer-Laucanno, Christopher, *An Invisible Spectator: A Biography of Paul Bowles*, London, 1989.

Scobie, W. I., 'Christopher Isherwood Interview', *The Advocate* (Los Angeles), No. 179 (17 December 1975), pp. 6–8.

Scobie, W. I., 'The Youth that was "I": A Conversation in Santa Monica with Christopher Isherwood', *London Magazine*, 17 (April–May 1977), pp. 23–32.

Shipman, David, *The Story of Cinema*, Vol. I, London, 1982.

Shirer, William, *The Rise and Fall of the Third Reich*, London, 1960.

Sinclair, Andrew, *Francis Bacon: His Life and Violent Times*, London, 1993.

Spender, Stephen, *Journals 1939–1983*, ed. John Goldsmith, London, 1985.

Spender, Stephen, *Letters to Christopher*, ed. Lee Bartlett, Santa Barbara, Calif., 1980.

Spender, Stephen, *The Temple*, London, 1988.

Spender, Stephen, *World within World*, London, 1951.

Steakley, James D., 'Iconography of a Scandal: Political Cartoons and the Eulenberg Affair in Wilhelmine Germany', in Martin Duberman et al. (eds), *Hidden from History: Reclaiming the Gay and Lesbian Past*, London, 1989.

Steakley, J. D., *The Homosexual Emancipation Movement in Germany*, New York, 1975.

Sternberg, Josef von, *Fun in a Chinese Laundry*, New York, 1965.

Suares, J. C., *Hollywood Drag*, Charlottesville, Va., 1994.

Upward, Edward, 'Remembering the earlier Auden', *Adam International Review* (1973–4), pp. 17–22.

Vidal, Gore, 'Christopher Isherwood's Kind', *Pink Triangle and Yellow Star*, London, 1982.

Vogel, Bruno, *Alf*, trans. Samuel B. Johnson, London, 1992.

Völker, Klaus, *Brecht: A Biography*, trans. John Nowell, London, 1979.

Von Eckardt, Wolf and Sander L. Gilman, *Bertolt Brecht's Berlin: A Scrapbook of the Twenties*, New York, 1975.

Weatherby, W. I., 'Christopher Isherwood', *The Guardian*, 17 November 1960.

Weiss, Andrea, *Vampires and Violets: Lesbians in the Cinema*, London, 1992.

Whitehead, John, 'Auden: An Early Poetical Notebook', *London Magazine*, 5 (May 1965), pp. 85–93.

Willett, John, *The New Sobriety 1917–1933: Art and Politics in the Weimar Period*, London, 1978.

Willett, John, *The Theatre of the Weimar Republic*, New York, 1988.

Willett, John, *The Weimar Years: A Culture Cut Short*, London, 1984.

Wolff, Charlotte, *Magnus Hirschfeld: A Portrait of a Pioneer in Sexology*, London, 1986.

Zucker, Carole, *The Idea of the Image: Josef von Sternberg's Dietrich Films*, London and Toronto, 1988.

Index

We Kissed

What Does It Mean to Be Married to Someone with Dementia

ELTON NELSON

NEWMAN SPRINGS PUBLISHING
320 Broad Street
Red Bank, NJ 07701

First originally published by Newman Springs Publishing 2022

ISBN 978-1-63881-618-8 (Paperback)
ISBN 978-1-63881-619-5 (Hardcover)
ISBN 978-1-63881-620-1 (Digital)

Printed in the United States of America

Contents

Preface

In the early spring of 1975, I was part of a singles Christian group at Monte Vista Chapel Church in Turlock, California. A young lady, Jan Larson, was living in Turlock and attending Monte Vista Chapel. I was living in Patterson, attending Patterson Covenant Church. She was a group leader; I showed up when there wasn't anything more exciting to do. She mailed out a flyer saying there would be a coffee hour on a particular Saturday night, at another group member's apartment. That sounded like an exciting way to spend a Saturday night. So I went over to the apartment. It turned out that Jan had put the wrong date on the flyer. Most of the others in the singles group went to the Monte Vista Church and got the word of the wrong date. But I didn't.

The following flyer she sent out announcing an event had the correct date on it, and I went. She had heard about my going the last time. When she saw me, she came to me, noted her mistake, and thoroughly apologized. Of course, being a gentleman, I graciously accepted her apology. We had some pleasant conversation for a time after that. I then invited her to a game of bumper pool. Another guy coached her, and she won.

Pondering this set of events, I realized that this was an attractive young lady, pleasant to be with, and someone who will admit a mistake and apologize. I decided to check her out. I consulted an ancient form of literature known as a telephone book. I found that in Turlock, there was a whole page of Larsons and looked for her name in vain. But the Lord preserved for me that last flyer from Jan (well, actually, I just hadn't bothered to throw it away), and it had her phone number on it. I used the telephone (an ancient form of long-distance communication used before the cell phone invention) to ask her for a date. She must have had a case of temporary insanity because she said yes.

When I beheld her on that first date, she was definitely pleasing to my eyes, and she soon became a treasure to my heart. That date went well, but sometime later, she said she saw a banana peel in my car that night and didn't find it at all appealing. I acknowledged that I had slipped there, and our relationship continued (that's enough puns, at least for now).

After about a year and a half of dating, we were married. We had a good marriage and raised three children, a boy and two girls. About thirty years into our marriage, I began seeing changes in Jan. Increasingly she was not acting the way I had always known her. I later came to learn that she had acquired dementia. I did not recognize what was happening for about four years, even though my mother had dementia for several years before she died. Jan's disease profoundly changed how I could relate to her. It changed me and altered my entire life.

I often shared my experiences in caring for Jan, on Facebook. I received responses suggesting that I could, and even should, write a book on what I found to be happening. In my relationship with Jan, I was confronted with the reality of her impending death. I knew I would want to address the entire process leading up to her death and its effect on me afterward. For some time after her death, I was not ready to start on a book. I also became involved in various volunteer activities, and the thought of writing a book, while not forgotten, was put on the back burner. Then came the COVID-

19 era, and everything changed. Much of what I had been doing was no longer possible. A close friend suggested that this could be a good time for me to write that book. That made sense to me, and I proceeded.

In rough form, I had already written much of the material for this book. As I became aware of Jan's condition, I began writing in a journal. I did not try to write something every day, but only when I had something that seemed meaningful. On the other hand, sometimes I would write something two or three times in one day. My dad used to say, "If you don't have anything to say, don't say it." I applied the same principle to writing in my journal.

Nevertheless, I wrote over 250 pages, plus other articles. I found it helpful to express my thoughts in writing. I often enjoyed and profited from looking back to what I had written months and years earlier. Using the word-search function on my laptop was very helpful. I recommend at least trying this practice and seeing how it might work for you.

I do not claim to be an authority about dementia or how to care for and relate to someone with dementia. I wrote this book from the perspective of my experience, convictions, and beliefs. I am hopeful that what I have written will be helpful to others. Each person is, of course, free to decide their course of action.

I have not tried to write a chronological autobiography. There are several books written in that format. I have attempted to organize this material to give a more meaningful sense of what I experienced, hoping that it might be more beneficial to you, the reader.

In college, I majored in math, with an informal minor in philosophy. Then I went to seminary and engaged in a three-year systematic study of the Bible, theology, and church history. So I like to get things, especially my thoughts, organized. But life is messy. And the life of a caregiver can feel incredibly messy, confusing, and disturbing as one tries to handle his circumstances and emotions (incidentally since I happen to be male, I ask you to permit me to use the masculine pronouns instead of using he/she, his/her, etc.). The table of contents gives how I organized this book. While I suggest reading from the beginning to the end, you are, of course, free to jump to what most catches your interest.

During this decade, I was very involved with what was happening in my relationship with Jan and how that affected me. At the same time, I was as much or more concerned with my relationship with God and how that affected me. I dedicated my life to God in Christ at the age of eight. I have pondered many questions and had my share of struggles with doubt. And then I have raised questions about and had doubts about my doubts. I will mention that I attended college at the University of California at Berkeley in the early '60s. So I know something of what it is to raise questions.

Incidentally, you will notice that I use capitals in pronouns referring to God or Jesus Christ. Not all writings do this, including many Bible translations. It's simply a matter of my personal preference. Speaking of translations, on several occasions, I have written a direct quotation from the Bible. All these quotes are from the English Standard Version of the Bible (ESV).

In reading this book, you will see many descriptions of what I did and felt. Each person with dementia is a unique person, and each person who has a loved one with this disease is also an individual. It is often said, "If you meet one person with dementia, you have met one person with dementia." My descriptions of Jan will not be the same as how other people with this condition would be described. If you have someone in this condition, you will go through times that

I went through, but you will also have your particular relationship and activities with your loved one and your grasp of what that meant to you.

But even as we may have different experiences, we still have much in common. We have a loved one in a most special condition. It makes for much heartache, stress, and loss. But traveling the caregiver road can be a very precious and heartfelt time that can give great gain.

If you are not a caregiver, have not been one, and never become one, I believe you can still find reading this book profitable. I invite you to ponder what I have written about the life journey of changes, suffering, and loss, death, etc. I do not want to set myself up as the example of how to go through this experience of being a caregiver, much less of how to go through life. I do not, and will not, claim such expertise. But I have put in the time and effort to write this book, trusting that it can help you and others.

If you are married or considering marriage, I am convinced that much of what I wrote applies not only to a marriage where there is dementia but to any marriage. This book could perhaps have a second subtitle of *What Does It Mean to Be Married?*

Finally, this book can also be viewed as a picture of what it means to be on a spiritual journey. It speaks, in particular, of the journey of being married to a wife with dementia. One might use this book to reflect on the spiritual journey of living through the pandemic era. We can speak of any period of history as an era. The people of that era had an opportunity to be on a spiritual journey for that time. An era may be the Depression era, the War years, the '50s, the Vietnam era, etc. Or one could reflect on being through any particular period of one's life—the childhood years, the high school years, the college years, the years one lived in a specific location or was in a particular vocation, or the retirement era. And so as you read this book and afterward, I invite you to ponder what period of your life you are now living or ages you have lived. Then reflect on the spiritual journey you have lived or are living now. If you are anticipating a new phase of your life, now could be the time to reflect on the journey you might have when that time comes.

I wrote this book with my family very much on my mind. My children, and most of my grandchildren, had many opportunities to see me go through the caregiver experience. There were also many friends and casual acquaintances who saw what I was doing, at least on occasion. Now I have an opportunity to share with others, both those who know me best, to those I have never met and never will personally meet, as deeply as possible, what that decade with Jan meant to me. If it at all inspires you, a reader, on your spiritual journey, I will be deeply gratified.

There is a classic Spanish saying, "*Vaya con Diós.*" It means "Go with God." As you read this book, I pray that God will go with you.

Life Is Changing

Early Signs of Change

For at least thirty years, I admired all the positive qualities of Jan. She was a very spiritual person, having dedicated her life, since she was a young child, to serving God. She was very much an extrovert who met people with no difficulty. She came from a large extended family and could always do an excellent job telling how extended family members were related. I was much more reserved and came from much smaller family ties. Jan worked, for many years, as an elementary-school teacher. For five years, she taught children at a Wycliffe Bible Translators training setting in the jungle area of southern Mexico. Her organizational skills were excellent. She liked nice things, but she was not a big spender. My wife was an intelligent charming woman, very much a lady. I often considered her to be more mature than I was.

About ten years before her passing, three early signs of her changing developed that I did not recognize until years later. They were not initially overt, but I later wondered why I didn't recognize them sooner. My mother had dementia during the last years of her life. So I had some acquaintance with the disease. But then, the manifestations of the disease in her were different than those that came out in Jan. Nonetheless, facing that a loved one has this condition is very

11

difficult, as I shall be discussing later. So I would not deny that I was experiencing at least some denial.

As one becomes familiar with this disease and its various symptoms, it is easy to get the impression that someone has it when they do not. This impression is especially true when observing older people. Everyone is forgetful at times, is often no longer able to do certain things as well as they once could, and goes through at least some changes over time in handling various circumstances. Any diagnosis of dementia should only be made by someone with the proper medical qualifications.

This first change typically occurred after dinner, either at home or at a restaurant. I had decided that I needed to share more of my thoughts and feelings with Jan. I figured that she would appreciate it, and it would be good for me to express myself more. Even without her suggestions, I would seek to share things with her that were quite personal. I expected that she would focus her attention entirely on me as I engaged myself in this endeavor.

However, as I continued to do this, I noticed a change in her. She increasingly did not focus her attention on me when I was sharing. At times, she even randomly changed the subject. I found that to be very frustrating, at times, even becoming angry. When I pointed out to her what she was doing, I received no response, increasing my frustration.

Some years later, I realized that her lack of focus resulted from her brain's deteriorating state. A disease had damaged her brain to the extent that she could not focus on anything for very long. She was like so many school children diagnosed with ADD (attention deficit disorder). It saddened me to realize that she was no longer able to listen attentively. Of course, it was not the first time I had misunderstood her; after all, I was her husband, and that is something husbands can do with excellent proficiency.

The second change was what I came to see as a personality change. Jan had always been an energetic person, very engaging, and very interested in life. I saw her coming to what I referred to as a retirement rocking chair mentality. She had always been interested in and pursued a life of service to God. She began talking about how she had done that and increasingly backed off of things she was doing. For example, she had been quite involved in a children's program at church, keeping records of attendance and the children's achievements. She always enjoyed this kind of record-keeping and was good at it. But now, it no longer was of interest to her.

I came to see my wife as developing a whole new identity. She came to see herself as old, with lost capabilities and life increasingly difficult. She seemed to have a sense of entitlement, not needing to be the responsible person she once was, just wanting to take life easy and only doing what she wanted to do. Her emotions changed. She lacked joy and enjoyment. The illnesses, incapacities, and deaths of others deeply moved her. There seemed to be a change in her spiritually as she was not so concerned with what God would have for her. At times she expressed anger at God for the life of obedience she understood Him to have called her to live.

As happened so often, I didn't realize, until much later, that all this was part of the developing disease in her brain and affecting her entire being.

The third change started even earlier and continued for three or more years. She seemed particularly interested in getting the house in good shape. She noted that she was getting things done that would be harder for us to do in the future as we became older and less capable. That seemed sensible at the time. She arranged for the house to be painted outside and in. Purple became her favorite color.

I thought she was decorating with an excessive amount of the color purple. However, I just brushed that off as being her favorite color. So I didn't give more than a glance when some entire walls were the color purple. She arranged for us to get a new roof, had some overdue repairs done, and did some clearing out of things that no longer had any value for either of us.

What she was doing was certainly beneficial, and I raised no objections. But with these projects, I felt I saw in her a premature and somewhat negative focus on our impending deaths. I later came to wonder if she had a premonition of what was in our future. I made some weak and futile attempts to discuss this with her. I now wish I had tried harder. At any rate, I am thankful that as the result of her efforts during those years, I did not have as many concerns later on with home repairs and upkeep, in addition to everything else that I had to address.

As time went on, I discovered more and more changes in her. Each of these was a matter of her being able to be increasingly less responsible. As a result, I progressively had to take on more responsibilities. Each of these significantly affected my life and our relationship.

I mentioned that Jan had always been a very social person. She was very definitely an extrovert. One evening, we went for a walk in the neighborhood. There was a couple, about our age, doing yardwork in their front yard. They struck up a conversation with us and then invited us to go in and have coffee with them. Jan declined, saying something about our needing to get home. In the past, she would have been the one to invite them over for coffee. In this kind of situation, Jan would have told me that we should get to know them. I asked her why she declined.

She replied, "I don't know those people."

It was apparent that not only had she become less social, but she was also more uncomfortable around people she didn't know.

I later went over to their home. They were very friendly and understanding. I developed a good friendship with them.

In the area of finances, Jan's father had a successful insurance business. He also made several profitable financial investments. Jan inherited her father's business sense and ability to handle finances well. So it was a big adjustment for me when I found her making mistakes in our checking account. Usually, any errors were my fault. She couldn't understand why I made such mistakes since I majored in math in college. I tried to explain that mathematics wasn't really about numbers, but that is another subject. I would get after her for making these mistakes. She would simply say she would try to do better.

Jan did an excellent job of keeping financial records due to her abilities and enjoyed doing it. For years, she did most of the work in gathering the information for our income tax obligations. In 2012, I was a little nervous about her taking care of this, but everything seemed to be in order. In 2013, she was clearly incapable of doing this. Fortunately, I had records on my Quicken software and saw that her records were very incomplete. She was unable to realize the state of her records. By the grace of God, this did not result in any conflict between us. From then on, she was not involved in getting our taxes done. While that was extra work for me, it was also a relief.

When Jan's parents passed from this earth, she and one of her sisters became the estate's executors. It became apparent to her siblings and me that she had become incapable of carrying out these responsibilities. We agreed that one of her siblings needed to take over this responsibility. Jan initially resisted this, feeling she could still carry out this responsibility. She was unwilling, or perhaps unable, to consider the time coming when she could no longer do this.

I did not realize at the time that as her condition was changing, her capacity to look ahead was declining. She lived very much in the present. While she had some recognition of the changes in her abilities, it was increasingly difficult for her to see that they would continue to lessen. She became increasingly even more unable to see the implications of that development.

Some people with dementia live in the past. They may think they are much younger than they are. They may say they want to go home. By "home," they are referring to some place they used to live, perhaps several decades ago. One man thought his wife had left him, and there was an older woman now living in the same house with him. He was thinking of his wife as she was, perhaps, twenty years ago. That "older woman" was his very-present wife. Fortunately, I did not have that situation with Jan.

We decided not to make an issue of Jan's decreasing ability to carry out the responsibilities of an executor. As time passed, she became more willing to do what I asked of her. On one occasion, I needed her to sign some paperwork on this matter and have it notarized. I took her to a notary who, it was apparent, wondered if Jan understood what she would be signing. Fortunately, the notary seemed to also understand and be in sympathy with my situation. So she asked Jan to raise her right hand and affirm that she understood what she was signing. Jan obediently raised her hand and said, "Yes."

Her ability to sign her name declined. Fortunately, we were able to complete the paperwork to have another sibling replace her as an estate executor before this happened.

Jan had always had fine smooth penmanship. She maintained this quality as her writing ability declined. In time, the only writing she could do was her name. It is common as people get older that their writing becomes shaky. But even when all she could do were scribbles, they were smooth scribbles. It was interesting to observe what abilities she lost and what she retained.

A common problem with someone with dementia is the matter of driving. It is often a challenge for loved ones of a dementia patient who should not be driving. An incident, one evening, demonstrated to me that this was another area of change for Jan. I was working at a Teen Challenge drug/alcohol rehabilitation program. One night there was a fundraiser dinner for this program. I went to it early, as part of my duties with the program. Jan went later, and we had dinner together. As we had gone in different vehicles, we drove home separately. I followed her home. We were approaching a left turn to the street where we lived. Before getting to our street, Jan made a left turn onto a driveway. I was in my vehicle behind her. There was nothing I could do but panic and say a quick, "Oh, my God" prayer. Fortunately, she did not hit the garage door. She backed out of the driveway, and we made it home safely.

After this, I kept all the keys to both vehicles out of her sight. Jan did not give me problems about driving after this but still wanted to keep her license. DMV sent her a notice that she would have to pass a driver's test to maintain her license after her birthday. Jan said she wanted to show she could still pass the test. She said she also wanted to drive legally if there was an emergency. I preferred for her license to end, thus finishing any issues about her driving. I suspected she could not pass the test. I obtained for her the pamphlet that has the material one needs to know to pass the test. I told her to let me know when she was ready for the test. I would then go online and make an appointment for her to take the test. I didn't say anything more about this to her. I noticed that she was not reading the booklet. Her birthday came and went without her taking the test. The driving issue was over. Thank God!

Jan had always done an excellent job of housecleaning. For the record, when she worked in elementary education, I also did housecleaning chores. As she retired from being gainfully employed, she took over nearly all the housework, and the house was always clean. But I began noticing house cleaning that wasn't done. I tried to work out a plan with her to clean just one or two rooms a day. She would seem to go along with this, but it didn't happen. I asked her if I should take over at least some, probably most, of the housework. She didn't like that idea. I then suggested that I hire someone to do housework. That too was unacceptable for her. I noted that she needed to do the housework herself, or I would do it or hire someone to do it. She didn't like any of these alternatives.

My problem was that I was not yet able to understand two realities. First, one does not reason with someone with dementia (which I had not yet grasped that Jan had). Second, the state of her brain made her unable to process this situation. My solution was to go ahead, apart from her, and hire housecleaning help. She did not raise a fuss about this, and it worked out fine.

Jan had always been an excellent cook. I learned that even before we married. I can't affirm the adage about the way to a man's heart is through his stomach, but it didn't hurt. I noticed that the meals she prepared were increasingly simple but still adequate. One night, she served a meal of bananas and leftover rice. She said that that was all we had for her to prepare. I knew that wasn't true. I also told her that I was upset that she had not planned better. I realized and reflected that there were many people worldwide, including in this country and in the community where we lived, for whom this would be a better-than-average meal. Nevertheless, I did not think this meal was acceptable.

My immediate response was to take her to the grocery store each week and have her get what we needed for food for the next week. I would have her decide what we would have. I also became increasingly involved in cooking meals. In time, I took over it entirely. Once, someone noted to Jan that I was doing the cooking for us. Her response was, "Nah, he just warms up stuff in the microwave." I must acknowledge the truth in her description. Incidentally, I bought a second microwave to make my cooking more efficient. However, for the record, I did make good use of the stove, oven, pots, and pans.

When Jan was still doing nearly all the cooking, the kitchen was very much her kitchen. So it was vital, whenever I put things away in the kitchen, that I put everything exactly where they belonged. So when I took over the cooking, I was now free to put things in the kitchen where I wanted them to be.

However, in time, I had two women helping me in the care of Jan. Now both of them, and the woman who did housework for me would, on occasion, put at least some things away in the kitchen. Needless to say, they each had their own ideas on where things should go. That was not a problem for any of them, or of course, for Jan, but it certainly was for me. They often had good ideas of where things should go, and I did adopt a number of them. But I also had numerous incidents of having to look for something that had previously been easily accessible.

All this to say that I had three women coming into my home and, in particular, into *my* kitchen to manage, plus Jan. These three women were a tremendous help for me. I was very grateful for them, and I dearly loved Jan. But having these four women in my home did have its challenges, and here I am, only speaking of the kitchen.

My conclusion from this experience is that any man who thinks he likes the idea of having more than one woman in his life, much less four, has got to be crazy.

Incidentally, you might wonder about the expense of hiring these women. Yes, I certainly did pay them. I mentioned before that until this disease set in, Jan had a good sense of finances. It was suggested to us that we get long-term care insurance. I was hesitant because of the cost. But Jan noted that it could be beneficial if one of us someday needed help caring for the other. It could also be helpful if one of us had to place the other in a care facility. So we took out a long-term care policy on each of us. Given what happened later, I was exceedingly glad for Jan's financial wisdom. This policy was the best financial decision I ever made. There is a moral from this experience. There is definitely wisdom to be gained by listening to one's wife.

Unfortunately, it is becoming more difficult and more costly to get long-term care insurance. It is the result of more people getting older and needing care. So the word to the wise is to take out a policy when one is still young enough and healthy enough to get a policy.

Perhaps the change that was the real clincher had to do with the laundry. Jan always picked nice clothes to wear and took good care of them, certainly keeping them well cleaned. And having much better taste than me, the all-too-typical male, she always made sure that I was well dressed and that my clothes were clean.

One day, I saw her open my underwear drawer, take out a pair of my underwear shorts, and put them on herself. I asked her why she was doing that. She replied, in a simple matter-of-fact way, that she was out of clean underwear for herself. In her mind, since she didn't have any clean underwear, and I did, it made perfect sense for her to wear mine.

My logical mind immediately kicked into gear, causing me to ponder the implications of what she had just done and said. It occurred to me that by her logic, if I ran out of clean underwear, and she still had clean underwear, then I was to—I quickly decided that *no*, that was not going to happen. I determined right then and there that I would take over all the laundry duties. And I made sure that both of us always had clean underwear.

One of the common recommendations to hold off the symptoms of dementia is exercise. Even mild exercise is helpful. Working out was not of interest to her. I could get her to go walking, at least if I went walking with her. A benefit of this, as her disease developed, was that I did not have to be concerned about her leaving the house, wandering around, and getting lost.

Her ability to speak gradually declined. With that, her ability to understand what was said to her also decreased. Often I would have to rephrase what I said for her to respond. For example, I asked her to let go of an object she picked up. She didn't respond. So I asked her to open her left hand. Then she understood.

It is commonly noted that as a person declines, they do understand a lot more than what it might appear. I think Jan had an active intuitive understanding, perhaps much like that of many animals, especially those often involved with humans, such as dogs, cats, and horses. For example, Jan might understand that a person is praying, might have

21

a sense of the spirit of the prayer, but not likely, or at least necessarily, understand the prayer's content.

When I would hold her and weep over her condition, she increasingly lacked any response; it didn't seem to bother her. I sensed that she did pick up my love for her, but not my grief. At a very early stage of her dementia, she could feel and express appreciation for my care for her. At what could be noted as the next stage of her dementia, she seemed to be losing emotion, except anger. Her voice was typically flat. However, her feelings probably remained all along, but her capacity to express them steadily declined. And it was harder to read her emotions because her understanding of her environment steadily became less. But as her whole condition deteriorated, the profundity of what she sensed became simpler and, at the same time, more profound.

I think it is safe to assert that Jan always knew more than she was able to express. All of us have many things that we know, and even understand, but cannot, at least in any adequate sense, put into words. This gap only increases with dementia. So for example, she knew she couldn't get the laundry done but was unable to say something like, "Elton, I can't do the laundry like I used to do."

I fully admit that I can't prove what I just wrote. If you are caring for a loved one, you will draw your own conclusions, at least some of which are unique to you. And you are entitled to those conclusions. From a practical standpoint, I continued to talk to and express myself to her, and for me, how much she intellectually understood didn't matter. There was a connection between her heart and mine, and that is what beautifully mattered.

After thirty years of marriage, we were used to making decisions together. That clearly became increasingly less possible. Decisions came to be entirely in my hands. This was most notable concerning financial matters. The hard part was emotional. While I could make decisions on my own, I missed making them with her. It was one of many losses that I experienced over the years. I had a financial manager handling our investment portfolio. He was very helpful.

I was able to discuss this with Jan. This included facing situations where I found that I had to make decisions that she might not like. One of the effects of dementia is a literal shrinking of the brain. That obviously affects mental functioning. There is a principle shared among caregivers that it is essential to remember who has the bigger brain. Jan came to acknowledge that we had reached the point where her judgment was not as good as mine. It came out that what made her angry was that she was no longer significantly involved in decisions. There was truth in her observation that I would consult with our very adult children more than her. She could feel that it was like she had been on the first string and now was second or third string, and even benched. So it was apparent that her anger was not at me but at her diminished capacities.

As I have noted, this was a time of my increasingly taking over all our household duties. I felt I was able to manage this satisfactorily, with minimal stress. It did seem like I continually had to figure out how to handle new situations. I did a lot of problem-solving. I suppose my math studies background, with all the assigned math problems, was helpful.

I'll give a couple of simple examples. Jan was having trouble getting out of the car. I realized that the bucket seats made it difficult for her to maneuver. So I put a pillow in her seat, and she was able to do much better. Second, she was needing my assistance to get out of the bathtub. I would get in front of her and pull her up with my arms under hers. I found it was much more effective if I got in the back of her.

23

I realized that things were not the way they used to be, they were not ever going to be as they were, and in the future, life will be even more difficult. It typically felt that before I could fully adjust to one change, another was developing. It wasn't really that these changes happened in such rapid succession. The rate of changes in dementia patients varies widely among different patients and over different periods in the same patient. Jan's was comparatively slow and relatively close to the same rate.

The most profound change was seeing her appearing to become another person. It was as though I had come to be married to two different Jans. The first Jan, I married on November 27, 1976. The formal proclamation of our state of being married occurred at about 8:00 p.m. The marriage to the second Jan did not happen at a specific time but was a process over several years. The proclamation of the second marriage was explicit. It occurred in April 2011, when a doctor gave us his diagnosis of her having dementia.

Of course, I was married to the same Jan from our wedding in 1976, until she died in 2017. But the deteriorating state of her brain made it seem like I had two different Jans. It was tough to realize, fully accept, and make all the adjustments to Jan not being the person she used to be. Much less was my ability to open up to the reality of the Jan she was increasingly becoming.

When I read something about how dementia advances, or when I would see someone in a more advanced stage of dementia, I would formulate thoughts of what the future held for Jan and me. These thoughts could become overwhelming. It helped to realize that my life had already had many changes, and with God's grace, I had adjusted well to each of them. I had adjusted to new schools, living in different places, different kinds of work, and two marriages. I was confident that the God who got me through those and other challenging changes would somehow get me through this change as well. Reflecting on my life, it seems that whenever I think that life has settled down, a significant change, or set of changes, would disrupt it. I don't think there is any need to comment on the year 2020.

I find that God, in His grace, spares us from knowing too much. I have been impressed by Psalm 131 that states, "I do not occupy myself with things too great and too marvelous for me. I have calmed and quieted my soul." As I think back, there are numerous occasions when, had I known what was going to happen, I might well have become too anxious to be able to function. God, at times, gives me a gift of denial. It is like when a dentist injects Novocain into his patient. If there were not this initial numbing, the patient would be too overwhelmed with pain for the dentist to do his work. Afterward, the Novocain wears off, the patient does feel pain but in a measure that he can handle. "I will speak more on denial later."

That so much of the future is unknown does not omit the need for planning. It does not leave out the necessity of considering the consequences of one's actions. Exercising good judgment is essential. However, the unknown places limitations on our plans.

Human beings will fail to recognize that all change does involve a loss. The advent of something new means there is something old that is no longer available. Even an excellent change carries a loss with it. All change involves some difficulty. There is that within us that resists change, even when we want it. It is part of human nature to desire stability. In any change, there is at least some disruption of equilibrium. There is, in every change, a venture into the unknown. This maxim is true even when the new thing appears to be quite familiar. The unknown always creates at least an element of anxiety. Uncertainty means there is the possibility of something terrible happening. So it is natural to desire certainty and stability.

Decades ago, there was a TV program called *The Millionaire*. In it, someone fabulously wealthy anonymously gave someone a million dollars, tax-free. The person receiving this gift was always initially quite uncomfortable. In this pandemic age, there is widespread insecurity that we will not get back to normal. A significant component of marriage is that it is designed to assure stability. In marriage, I know that someone is committed to being with me "as long as we both shall live." And I have, likewise, settled to be with her. It is not unusual for someone with a very uncomfortable life to prefer that to a better but unfamiliar life. If an inmate who has spent much of his life in jail is released, he may commit a crime so that he can get back to the familiar setting of his cell.

None of this is to imply that change is something negative. It can be very positive. It can be vitally necessary. As people who desire stability, we also are easily bored. There is also, in us, a strong desire for change. We like to see, hear, experience new things. We are in a state of both wanting stability and desiring change. It is one of many perplexities of the human condition.

The changes that were occurring in Jan were typical for someone in her condition. But for me, life with her had become anything but ordinary. I had never seen these kinds of changes in Jan. Before I realized it was a matter of dementia, I didn't understand what was happening to her. I couldn't stop these shifts. And I learned that I couldn't control it. At best, I might slow down the process. What happened in Jan, I would not wish on anyone. I sincerely feel for anyone who has to go through what I experienced. Yet that last decade with Jan was the most precious time I had with her in our forty years of marriage.

It was beneficial to have an established strong belief in God, who is unchanging. As Scripture says, He is "the same yesterday and today and forever" (Hebrews 13:8). Yet He is the most creative God, from the very beginning and on into eternity. He forever makes all things new.

I sometimes try taking a hand at writing poetry. I hardly consider myself a poet. Here is something I composed, giving some of my thoughts on change.

Change

Change brings opportunity—
to sow ending and reap beginning,
sow loss and reap gain,
to sow death and reap life,
sow tears and reap joy.

Change brings choice—
to cling or let go,
to grow or decay,
live or die.

In hell there is no change—
no faith, no hope, no love.
In heaven faith and hope unite
into love eternally new

Becoming Childlike

As Jan's abilities declined, there was a significant change in her conduct and personality. She came increasingly to think and act like a child. The decrease in her abilities made her more dependent, as a child is, for things she couldn't do for herself.

I might describe it as a rephrasing of the Apostle Paul's words in 1 Corinthians 13:11. The paraphrase would be, "When she was an adult, she spoke like an adult, she thought like an adult, she reasoned like an adult. As she became a child, she gave up adult ways."

I have long played with a fantasy where everyone came to earth at some stage of life. Some were quite old, some middle age or younger, and even some as children. Then everyone kept getting younger and younger. Finally, as infants, they would enter a mother's womb for the last months of their life. It did seem like that happened to Jan, except that her body didn't get younger.

There is an amount of reversion to childhood that almost everyone experiences if he lives long enough. Physical declines make us dependent on others for what we can no longer do. Our minds may be fine but not as sharp as they used to be. They do not, as readily, adapt to new situations, methodologies, and technologies. We need someone to guide us through these changes. As my parents moved into a retirement center, I became very involved in their care. I became very aware of my having a parent-to-child relationship with them.

Her decline in various abilities was a sign to me of her approaching death. This decline in her maturity had the same effect. I knew where this decline was going. As in my fantasy, after she became as dependent as an infant, she entered another world.

I had always considered Jan as very mature. That attracted me to her. We usually related adult to adult. As in any good marriage, we had our times when one of us needed parental support from the other. And there were times when we could be like kids together and related child to child. But usually, we acted mutually as adults. After thirty years of marriage, this childlike nature was a significant and challenging change.

The question became, how do I relate to my wife now? At the same time, I was her husband, her parental caregiver, and widowed from the Jan I once knew. These roles made for more than a set of contradictory emotions. They produced a complex relationship. In this situation, the parental-caregiver role is always front and center. It is easy to place one's focus there. It takes effort to balance that role with the marriage relationship and with the ever-present loss and grief. I will share my experiences of loss and grief and about our marital relationship during these days. But first, let me share more about this parent-child relationship.

There was a teenage stage for Jan. This is the stage where she sometimes could be very adult and, at other times, could be very childish. She could think she could do things she couldn't do or shouldn't do. While acting immature, she would want to be treated as an adult, and I wanted to treat her that way.

For a time, with a typical adolescent perspective, she both wanted adult freedom but not to be responsible. My best solution was to talk with her as an adult while setting limits with her, as one would a teenager. That's not easily done, but it's what every parent of a teenager must do.

About a year after Jan was diagnosed with dementia, she was due for a dental exam. The dental office was just around the block from our home. I was still working full-time. Jan was no longer driving. I could take her there and then go on to work. I was going to arrange for someone else to bring her home. Jan asserted that she could walk home. I wanted to let her. I had some concerns. It did involve her crossing a street, although she could use a stoplight. I stipulated that she was to call me as soon as she got home. She did, and everything was fine.

It struck me that what I did with her was exactly what any parent might do with their child, i.e., have her call to let me know she was safely home. I wouldn't say I liked having to do that.

I noticed that Jan came to relate more easily to children than to adults. If she saw a mother with a small child, she would engage the child and ignore the mother. This behavior seems to be natural for people with dementia and makes sense. Being more childlike herself, she could more easily interact with a child than with an adult.

She became more unsure of herself. She would check with me to see if she had done something right. This insecurity included checking if she had gotten dressed okay or if she had written a check correctly. She used to take attendance at a Sunday morning Bible class we attended. She would have me check to see that she did it accurately.

We began praying together more. Jan initiated it more than me. I could easily detect in her prayers indications of her insecurity. It was good that we prayed together more. More of it should have come from me.

She would blurt out what she thought without any consideration of how it might come across to others. When she saw me after a gym workout, instead of suggesting I shower, she would say, "You stink." If she saw an overweight woman at a restaurant, she would tell me, "She sure is fat." I was very thankful that she didn't speak loud enough for others to hear.

There were household chores that she could do fine if I were with her. If I left her to do them without me, they didn't get done or not done correctly or done incompletely.

With all this and more, there was the constant parenting role of guiding her, setting limits, and making decisions she didn't like. I was always on duty for her care. Wherever I went, I had my phone with me. It could become wearisome. As a typical parent, my most common time for relaxation was in the evening, after I had Jan bedded down for the night.

Most of my time and physical energy for Jan was in being a single parent of her. Most of my emotional energy for Jan was in being widowed from her. What was left of my time, physical energy, and emotional energy, went into being married to her. Yet from a strength beyond myself, I was able to be profoundly aware of the special relationship I had with Jan and of the spiritual and psychological impact that was having on me.

I was very aware that Jan's death would be the final loss of my wife. But for years, I took care of an increasingly young child. As a de facto single parent, I had bonded with her as my wife and as my child. Her death would also be the loss of my child. That is often considered the most difficult kind of death of a loved one to endure.

I frequently felt that I should do a better job, both in caring for Jan and how I was handling my emotions. As a Christian, shouldn't I be doing better? I finally came to realize that I needed to heed the advice I often counseled to others, "Don't be so hard on yourself. Christians turn to the Lord. He does give strength and endurance, but Christians are still human."

I think Jan's childlikeness had a maturing effect on me. Our children were all grown and out of the nest. My parents had departed from this earth. I would naturally think that my parenting days were over. Jan's condition gave me a parenting experience at a whole other level.

Diagnosis

Other people also saw changes in Jan. In July 2010, my daughter Lisa and I took a day to go to Yosemite National Park and hiked up to Half Dome. She can be very straightforward and was that day, as she asked, "What's going on with Mom?"

I didn't have satisfactory answers, but it did take much of the denial and aversion to that question out of me.

It still took some time for me to face Lisa's question. I gradually came to recognize that I had to find out what was going on with her. I finally wrote a letter to a doctor who had been administering some prescriptions for her. In the letter, I described much the same symptoms that I described in the previous chapter.

The doctor examined her and did some testing, including a computerized test. He then called us into his office. He informed us, "Jan showed symptoms of early onset of dementia." My reaction was immediate. I knew that she wasn't just showing signs of anything. She had dementia. And my first thought came from the most gripping characteristic of that disease. She was going to die, and not just in the sense that all of us will die someday. My wife, Jan, is going to die.

Jan's reaction was much different. She did express some frustration, and even anger, over not being able to do things she had been very capable of doing. But in particular, her reaction to having a terminal disease was much different from mine. Notably, I never sensed her grieving over her losses. As she faced her death, she had a classic saying when people asked her how she felt about this disease causing her to die. She would say, "Bad things happen to good people as well as to bad, to Christians as well as to non-Christians. I'm going to die. And I'm going to heaven, and it will be great."

I agreed with her statement, but I couldn't fully embrace her sentiment. She would give this statement in a very matter-of-fact vocal tone. But anyone hearing her knew that she meant what she said. I could say and mean that statement about her, but not with the same degree of acceptance. I felt that I could learn from her. She couldn't explain/teach her perspective. I learned from her by being with her.

We would sometimes give Jan a pen and a piece of paper to see what she would do with it. One day, she wrote "new life" and "go home." It was evident that heaven was very much on her mind.

As part of Jan's medical treatment, I took her to see a neurologist. She gave her a diagnosis of a form of Parkinson's disease. Jan had a slight tremor in her left hand and foot. The doctor prescribed some medications for her. There wasn't a lot that could be done for this condition, as some of the prescriptions for Parkinson's would exacerbate the symptoms of dementia. Oh, the complications of modern medical technology!

To explore all treatment avenues, the neurologist referred us to a Stanford Medical Center specialist. There Jan was diagnosed with a rare form of Parkinson's disease—corticobasal degeneration. Research on this dementia has been complex. A firm diagnosis is only possible with an autopsy. That, of course, is only possible after the patient is deceased. The result of such autopsies is that in many cases, it was a misdiagnosis.

The implication of the bottom line from this diagnosis was obvious. It was just another confirmation of Jan's terminal condition. I was not surprised. But hearing it from a medical specialist made the reality hit and hit hard. I broke down in front of Jan. Her response was a matter of factual, "We'll survive," she said. As can happen so frequently with a wife, she was right again!

Incidentally, there are many different types of dementia. Jan's form was associated with Parkinson's disease. Alzheimer's is just another type of dementia. It is generally considered to be the most common type.

The Stanford specialist had no recommendations for treatment other than for her to see Jan every six months to monitor her progression. I saw no point in doing that. I, as a layman, was quite capable of observing that her disease was progressing. So the only result of this endeavor was a further confirmation that Jan was going to die.

Someone suggested that when Jan passed, her brain could be donated for scientific research. I was certainly in favor of research into this disease. I have also given permission that my body's organs may be used for organ transplant purposes at the time of my death. However, Jan had told me, sometime earlier, that she wanted her body buried without any such procedures performed. I intended to comply with her preferences fully. I did not feel any need to have an autopsy to determine the exact cause of her death.

The question naturally arises as to how Jan contracted this disease. Medical science has several theories but no established proof of what causes dementia. It is known that the symptoms, and very possibly the condition itself, are exacerbated by sedation. Jan had colon cancer surgery in 2008, and her symptoms did seem to increase after the surgery. She subsequently had a colonoscopy. Her oncologist later advised that there was no point in her having any further colonoscopies. Her body had declined enough that she would not have been able to withstand surgery or any other cancer treatment. He, therefore, discharged her as a patient.

Very simply, dementia is a gradual deterioration of the brain. Brain cells are destroyed. Cavities develop in the brain. The brain shrinks. When the patient dies, the brain is typically about one-third of its standard size. This deterioration typically starts years before any symptoms are apparent. Eventually, a vital part of the brain is damaged enough, or the brain's overall condition is damaged enough, to cause the patient to die.

Learning what physically happens to the brain with this disease was a distressing experience. I could not help but imagine that that was Jan's brain. Thinking of what her brain was looking like and was going to look like gave me a sick feeling. It did help me realize and understand that she could not help her condition. And on the other hand, I had to marvel at how well she was able to function with the damage done to her brain. During her last days, I was impressed that her brain was even able to keep her alive.

There is no cure for this disease. Some medications will temporarily slow down the development of the symptoms. There can be spaces of time when the patient seems to be in a stable state. No new symptoms occur. There is no apparent deterioration of her functioning. However, brain deterioration continues. In time, the brain deteriorates to the extent that these medications are of no effect. I read in the Scriptures and hear cases of God miraculously healing many different diseases. I have never read of God ever curing dementia. Even the televangelist faith healers do not claim healings of this sort.

There is also no way to prevent this disease. There is no vaccine or medication to stop its development. There are ways to lessen the probability of the disease or at least to slow down its growth. There is a saying that what is good for the heart is also good for the brain. There are measures one can take to help protect both the heart and the brain. These include regular healthy physical exercise, a nutritious diet, good sleeping habits, avoiding smoking and excessive alcohol, avoid undue stress, and, interestingly, an active social life. Mental stimulation such as reading, writing, and learning new skills appear to help. It is my personal conviction that a healthy spiritual life also helps. None of these practices, nor any combination of them, guarantee that one will not get dementia. Jan did practice all of them, except she wasn't interested in physical exercise.

It is well established that with age comes an increased probability of having this disease. If a couple lives long enough, at least one of them will probably have a case of dementia.

Considering this certainty, I often thought of a prayer that I commonly heard at the Teen Challenge Center, where I worked for many years. This is a Christian faith-based substance abuse rehabilitation program. The prayer was, "Thank you, Lord, for another day not promised to us." And so I endeavored to regard each day as a day with Jan that was not promised. So in the days ahead, no matter how difficult they could be, this prayer made each day a precious gift.

Resolutions

Having now understood Jan's condition, there were four resolutions that I vowed to keep. They profoundly affected how I cared for her. It was not a matter of sitting down and coming up with these four. They came naturally over some time. I certainly prayed about the care I would give her. I am convinced that the Lord did reveal them to me. But the revelation was over a period of time. It was more a matter of gradually discovering that I had established these four resolves.

First Resolution: Keep Jan at Home

Jan and I were in complete agreement on this. If it were at all possible, she would continue to stay at home. I would not place her in a nursing home or other care facility. Our place was where she would die.

This resolution did not completely rule out the possibility of placing her. Sometimes it is necessary. Some studies show that sometimes the stress of being a caregiver for one's spouse can result in the caregiver dying before his spouse. I met a man whose health was steadily declining as he tried to care for his wife. One night, he woke up from a sound sleep when he heard the front door slam shut. He got up and discovered his wife with advanced dementia, out in the middle of the street. Fortunately, he was able to get her safely back inside. That convinced him that he needed to place her. After he did, his health and spirit greatly improved. In this case, he realized that he could not continue caring for her himself. He had to abide by the principle that sometimes, placing one's spouse is the most loving thing a man might do for her.

I discussed the possibility of placement with my adult children. They said they would support whatever I decided. They made it clear that they did not want to have my caring for their mother at home affect my physical health or cause me a lot of emotional stress.

Sometimes the hassles and stresses of caring for Jan made the prospect of placement tempting, although not attractive. Cleaning her after her soiling was stressful, especially during the middle of the night. We were still sleeping on the same bed. Sometimes, even though I had a pad under her, I would still have to change both her and the bedsheets.

Nevertheless, when I seriously considered the prospect of placing Jan, I got a sick feeling, and I also got feelings of guilt. The idea of increasing the caregiver help also gave me a sense of guilt.

I'm not saying, for a moment, that this was rational. It was simply the way I felt. I did consider that placement would relieve me of the stresses I now felt in caring for Jan. Considering everything, I questioned whether a placement would be a relief for me. I felt caught in a bind. I felt discomfort both in considering placing her and keeping her at home.

There was no simple solution. So I fell back on this first resolution and continued to keep Jan at home. I realized and endeavored to accept that whatever I did would be emotionally challenging. There would always be questions of whether I was doing the right thing, no matter what I decided. Increasing the amount of caregiver help I had did make things better. I looked for divine guidance and came to trust that God was enabling me to make good decisions.

Second Resolution: To Not Try to Be Present When She Died

People sometimes obsess with wanting to be present when a loved one dies. The problem comes with not knowing exactly when that might happen. She could die at night while sleeping. A person might step out to get something to eat or go to the bathroom, and she could die during that moment. So that desire can create a lot of stress. It can also generate a lot of disappointment if it doesn't happen.

I decided that if I was present when she died, I would certainly like that. But I would not make it a matter of concern. I made sure that I had said my goodbyes to her well ahead of time and in several ways.

Third Resolution: To Help Her Live as Fully as Possible for as Long as Possible

To better understand this resolution, think of a coach who knows that his team has no potential to place better than last in the league. They will do well to win one or two games and never get creamed. But his job is to keep their spirits up, to keep them practicing and playing to the best of their ability, and to make better athletes and better human beings of them. I would do all I could, knowing the result will still be the same, but the accomplishments will be much different.

What will be the accomplishments?

a) I will have given Jan as full a life during these days as possible.
b) I will have become more the man of God that God created me to be.

c) I will have had an impact on others for the king-
dom of God.

d) I will have been obedient to God.

As part of this endeavor, I arranged for Jan to have
speech, physical, and occupational therapy. Physical therapy
addresses the lower part of the body, the legs. Occupational
therapy addresses the upper part of the body, the arms. These
therapies were made possible through a referral from her
neurologist. They produced a minimal amount of improvement. No doubt, they did slow down the deterioration of the
functioning of her arms, legs, and speech.

We noticed that her left hand appeared to be closing
and less functional. We took three measures to attempt to
correct this. The first was to put a device on her hand to keep
it open as much as possible. This measure had very little success, primarily because she kept taking it off. Second, the doctor prescribed muscle-relaxing medications and increased the
medicine given to Jan to address her Parkinson's. Drowsiness
was a known side effect. In Jan's case, it made her so tired that
we took her off this medication regimen.

The heel of her left foot kept rising. It was as though
the foot was in a stiletto shoe when she was barefoot. This
condition made her already-very-limited walking much more
limited. The medications that were not effective on her hand
were also not effective on her foot.

The second attempt was to use Botox injections. The
rationale was that her hand closing was the result of muscle
tightening. However, no one locally did the kind of Botox
shot that Jan needed. Cosmetic surgeons do work on the face
to reduce wrinkling. They were not adept at using Botox on
the hand or foot.

We made several trips to the Stanford Medical Center for Botox treatments. Each time there was little or no effect on her hand or foot. So the dosage was increased for the subsequent treatment. It was finally determined that the problem was not in her muscle or nerve tissue. Instead, the tendons involved in moving her hand and her foot had become shorter. There was no known way to lengthen these tendons.

By this time, Jan had essentially lost her ability to walk anyway. So it was decided not to do anything with her foot. However, her hand being closed made it impossible to keep the palm of her hand clean. To pry her fingers open would cause her a lot of pain. There was concern that an infection could develop in the palm of her hand. So it was decided to cut the tendons that were keeping her hand closed. The attempt to improve her quality of life transitioned to addressing a health issue. The surgery on her hand was relatively simple. As anticipated, the cutting of the tendons to her hand did open up her hand enough to keep the palm of that hand clean and free of infection.

With a disease like dementia, it is sometimes necessary to do something that ordinarily would be wrong. But having a loved one with dementia is not an ordinary situation.

The benefits of exercise to living a full life are well established. For dementia, it has become apparent that the simple act of walking can have a positive effect on the brain, thus slowing down its deterioration. We had always taken occasional walks together. I tried to have her take daily walks, usually with me. Jan was not one for exercise. She wasn't interested in taking walks on any scheduled basis, certainly not daily. After a while, my encouraging her to walk was causing stress in our relationship. I soon decided that our relationship was more important than Jan walking. So I backed off.

Sometime later, she did agree that the walks were good for her. There were challenges. We live in a quiet neighborhood. When a car went by, she would stop to look at it. So it was hard to get her to walk enough to get an exercise benefit. Once in a while, for any number of reasons, she would refuse to take a walk.

Her walking kept getting slower, and the distance she would travel kept getting shorter. I couldn't help thinking of Jan any longer being even minimally mobile. It made me uneasy. I sometimes contracted a queasy feeling in my stomach that I can easily get when I'm anxious. However, when that time came, I found ways to handle it. It is interesting how the future can seem to be so foreboding. Yet when the impending becomes the present, it turns out to be manageable. I could avoid a lot of stress by remembering this principle.

I found a little trick to get her to walk a little farther. As we approached our house, I would have us walk on the opposite side of the street with myself between her and our home. Thus she wouldn't see that we were walking past the house. Later she would ask if we had walked past the house. I would then comment something like, "Oh, looks like we did." I would then head us back home. It was a case of not being fully honest with her to do something for her benefit.

I obtained a wheelchair. Jan did not like the idea of being in one. Sometimes that motivated her to try harder to walk and for longer distances. However, in our daily walks, I had to use good judgment. If I had her walk too far, she would not make it back to our house. On at least two occasions, I had to run home and get the wheelchair. Fortunately, we were no farther away than the other side of the neighbor's house. I soon ended all attempts to take her on walks outside.

I tried getting her to use a cane. She would take a few steps with it and then discard it. Fortunately, if her legs gave out before getting to her destination, she would not get hurt, and I could get her up again. The best way to lift her was to get behind her, put my arms under hers, and pull her up on her feet.

Getting from a sitting to a standing position became increasingly difficult for her. I helped her with this by putting pillows on any chair where she might sit. After a while, she could no longer stand up by herself. By that time, she had lost all walking mobility. So I would put a wheelchair nearby. Then I had her put her arms around my shoulders. I then put one arm around her lower back and the other under her hips. After getting her up to a standing position, I would pivot her around and sit her on the wheelchair. I also used this procedure to get her to and from the wheelchair to the car. A nice bonus to all this was getting a good hug from her. I also used this procedure to get her to and from a commode. That had the additional challenge of getting her pants down and up.

We felt it was good to get her outdoors whenever the weather allowed this. So I, or a caregiver I had for Jan, would take her out for a stroll in a wheelchair.

The next challenge came as Jan's legs could no longer support her in a standing position. And her arms around my shoulders were not strong enough to hold her up. My solution was to simply pick her up with one arm under her legs and the other across her back. For years, I have worked out at the gym. I am not a weight lifter, but Jan was light enough that I could do this.

These techniques worked fine in getting her from one sitting position to another. However, there was the exception of getting her in the car. That involved leaning forward with her, at best a challenge for my arms. Someone suggested that I put a towel on the passenger seat. I picked her up right-handed, with my right hand on her back and left hand as far up on the back of her legs as possible (note: I am left-handed). This process made it easier than the other way to get her seated on the passenger seat.

That worked well. It wasn't too hard to get Jan onto the towel on the outer edge of the seat. Then I would get into the car from the driver's side, pull on the towel, thus moving her into the car. Finally going back to the passenger side, I could bring her legs in so she was sitting comfortably in the car.

I received numerous warnings about how I could injure my back with all this lifting. I understood and appreciated their concerns. I received multiple aches and pains from my workouts. However, God, in His grace, always had my back. Their well-intentioned concerns were in vain.

Her mobility increasingly declined. One might wonder about all this effort to keep her as mobile as possible. If we live long enough, all of us will experience declines in many— if not most—of our abilities. All of us are given some limited amount of time that we are to redeem (Ephesians 5:16). So as each of us experience our declines, we are still to live our lives as fully as possible. And as we are able and have the opportunity to help others do the same.

One might well ask if this was just a postponing of the inevitable, as her mind also declined. There was certainly a strong case that it was. In time, she reached the stage where she lost all ability to talk or even make a sound.

However, our body and our mind exist because the divine Creator created them. They were given to us to use to live as complete a life as possible. They do not belong to us. They are gifts to us from God. Scripture describes our body as a "temple of the Holy Spirit" (1 Corinthians 3:16,17; 6:19). God gives us a responsibility to take the best care we can of what belongs to him. We are to use what He gives us in service to Him for as long and thoroughly as possible.

This responsibility does not end with the onset of dementia. God calls us to encourage each other (1 Thessalonians 5:11). We are to help others live as fully as possible. The is certainly no less accurate for the caregiver of someone with dementia. It is even more true if a caregiver is caring for his spouse.

Fourth Resolution: No Excessive Measures to "Heal Her" or to Find a Cure

Instead, I would put my time, energy, and prayers into care for Jan and relating to her as closely as possible in the present circumstances.

As I was developing this personal resolution, I had contact with a friend whose wife also had dementia. He had been researching various treatments to, if not cure, at least improve her condition. I saw that as one approach to caring for a loved one with dementia. The course I found was to give your loved one good care but accept that she will die. After her diagnosis, I decided that I wouldn't chase after cures—medical, nutritional, spiritual, etc. I did administer established medications to Jan that could temporarily slow down the development of her symptoms. But I would not put in any significant time or energy pursuing new medicine.

Carrying out this resolve included having Jan eat nutritionally but let her have treats that she enjoyed. Have her exercise as much as she could handle well. Take her places to keep her socially active and to stimulate her brain. Then see that she gets good rest and sleep. I would make sure she got good physical and medical care. I would constantly try to connect with her, have the best marriage with her possible in her condition, explore new ways of connection as the old ways are taken away. Finally I would go on the spiritual journey that God has been using Jan to have me take. I sometimes departed from the trail but was always in sight of it and knew how to get back on it, and did.

People might expect I would be earnestly praying for Jan to be healed. That never happened.

I once listened to a talk by Joni Erickson Tada. She is a quadriplegic resulting from a tragic accident in her late teens. She had been married to the same man for over thirty years. She noted that many people had told her that they are praying for her physical healing. She would thank them for doing that. Then she would ask them to pray to heal her negative attitudes that can creep into their lives. They have a deep faith in God. But Joni is honest about times each of them can become impatient, angry, or depressed. So she asks people praying for her to pray that the Lord will give them the strength to face the challenges of each day.

Christian writers on suffering and loss will advise, focus on the Lord and what He is doing, not on your pain and what it is doing. Scripture gives an account of the disciple Peter walking on water and taking his eyes off Jesus. Instead, he focused on the storm. (Matthew 14:23–33) This incident is often the biblical basis given for this attitude. It sounds like ignore the pain by focusing on something else. I find that to be unrealistic. I have come to look at this another way. I used to run road races of distances up to the marathon distance of just over twenty-six miles. In each race, there was the challenge of the last mile. I would be very aware of all the pain of many aching muscles and the discomfort of oxygen debt. But my focus was on the finish line.

I would sometimes wonder how I would feel if God told me that she was to be healed. I had grown accustomed to facing her dying. I had been thinking, even planning, for her death for a considerable time. I had oriented my thinking to being devoted to Jan until she died. Then the Lord would have something new for me; perhaps a new ministry that was developing even then and a new relationship with someone else. Perhaps a difficulty was that I had been with Jan so long and so closely in her dementia/Parkinson state that I had lost some of the memory of how she used to be.

This resolution could be challenging. A doctor who was related to Jan offered several treatments, at least, to improve her condition. I was skeptical of essentially all of them but did go along with them to a basic extent since he was a relative. One was to test for sleep apnea. This treatment involved having her wear a device to measure her breathing and pulse. It proved impractical as I couldn't get her to keep the device on during the night. He recommended various medications to help reduce her restlessness. They resulted in her vomiting as a side effect. I quickly took her off those pills.

The most challenging was an oxygen enhancement treatment that he offered. This procedure consisted of a series of treatments in his office in which Jan received a heavy dosage of oxygen. The hope was that it would stimulate her brain functioning. The results were minimal at best.

Her neurologist tried various medications. One was designed to help her Parkinson's condition but would exacerbate her dementia symptoms, and was discontinued. She tried variations of the dosage and variations of their frequency. She even gave me some liberty to vary the dosage and frequency of some of the medications. It began to feel hit and miss. Again any positive results were minimal. After a while, it was apparent that she had run out of options to recommend.

I became very tired of all these endless attempts to try some new medication, dosage changes, or schedule changes. I became skeptical of the various treatments and therapies that were available. I would wonder if trying all these different measures could end up being more for the benefit of a caregiver who is having difficulty facing reality. It is hard to face the truth that the caregiver's deep and devoted love in whom he is putting so much time and energy will die.

I found myself in a dilemma as I tried to carry out both the third and fourth resolutions. How do I work to enable Jan to live as fully as possible without getting bogged down chasing endless cures or, at least, prospects for improvement? Sometimes I thought that if I didn't do all I could and didn't at least explore whatever anyone, especially a doctor, suggested to me, then I wasn't doing all I could for her. I had to ask myself a question for which the answer is a matter of judgment. Will the potential benefits of a particular measure offset the drain that it can be on the caregiver? If not, it could reduce the quality of care provided by the caregiver.

I found a sense of resolution with this issue in resolving the possibility of Jan someday having a feeding tube. If she were to have some difficulties with swallowing, a feeding tube might be an option.

I took Jan to her doctor for a discussion on this issue. The doctor did comment that there can be complications with this procedure. For example, food inserted into the stomach through a tube can sometimes travel up the esophagus. The best usage of a feeding tube is a temporary measure as part of a process moving toward a cure. That would not be the case with Jan. It would appear to be simply an extensive measure for keeping her alive longer. It would be hard to argue that it would help her live life more fully.

The doctor asked Jan if she would want one. Jan unmistakably shook her head no (by this time, Jan had no verbal ability). Both the doctor and I felt Jan knew what she was saying. That settled the issue for me. It was a relief in that

I now knew that I would not be facing that decision. But it was also tough. It brought the reality of her impending death a step closer.

I had a meeting with one of my daughters and her husband to discuss what is known as end-of-life directives. These directives were to establish an understanding of what measures should be taken when Jan might be in end-of-life status. They would be on a form called the POLST form, POLST standing for physician orders for life-sustaining treatment. It is an agreement between a patient and her physician. It provides several options, from taking all means possible to keep the patient alive to taking no measures to keep her alive. There are options between these two. Most physicians have copies of this form, or people can download it off the Internet. Placing it in a home in a readily seen place such as the refrigerator would give EMTs directions if they should be called to a home. A copy of it can be kept at a local hospital.

At this meeting, I asked Jan to give us her thoughts. She still had some ability to articulate. Her response was, "If I'm dead, let me stay dead." I'm sure we will never forget that response. We agreed that she was clear and knew what she was saying. There were to be no extensive measures taken just for the sake of keeping her alive.

During those days, I also took several steps to have financial matters covered after her passing. With the assistance of an attorney, I had all our accounts placed in trust so that when she passed, they were all available to me. As part of this process, I had a will drawn up that included the basics for burial provisions.

Carrying out these resolutions was unquestionably a challenge. In time, I came to see and embrace "a more excellent way" (1 Corinthians 12:31) to do this.

The Greatest Resolve

I finally realized the best that I could do for her. It would not be in the search for better pills, therapies, and treatments to make her body and mind better, or at least to get worse less quickly. Instead, it would be to give myself completely to love her and serve her to the best of my ability. For me, this naturally raised the question of what it meant to be married to someone with dementia. One afternoon, I sat down and wrote the following paper. I invite you to read it slowly, thoughtfully, and prayerfully.

What Does It Mean to be Married to Someone with Dementia

1 Corinthians 13

1 Co 13:1 If I speak in the tongues of men and of angels, but have not love, I am a noisy gong or a clanging cymbal.

1 Co 13:2 And if I have prophetic powers, and understand all mysteries and all knowledge, and if I have all faith, so as to remove mountains, but have not love, I am nothing.

1 Co 13:3 If I give away all I have, and if I deliver up my body to be burned, but have not love, I gain nothing.

1 Co 13:4 Love is patient and kind; love does not envy or boast; it is not arrogant

1 Co 13:5 or rude. It does not insist on its own way; it is not irritable or resentful;

1 Co 13:6 it does not rejoice at wrongdoing, but rejoices with the truth.

1 Co 13:7 Love bears all things, believes all things, hopes all things, endures all things.

1 Co 13:8 Love never ends. As for prophecies, they will pass away; as for tongues, they will cease; as for knowledge, it will pass away.

1 Co 13:9 For we know in part and we prophesy in part,

1 Co 13:10 but when the perfect comes, the partial will pass away.

1 Co 13:11 When I was a child, I spoke like a child, I thought like a child, I reasoned like a child. When I became a man, I gave up childish ways.

1 Co 13:12 For now we see in a mirror dimly, but then face to face. Now I know in part; then I shall know fully, even as I have been fully known.

1 Co 13:13 So now faith, hope, and love abide, these three; but the greatest of these is love.

It means everything stated in 1 Corinthians 13

Perhaps more than any other marriage, it means marriage is not 50-50 but is 100% no matter whether or not anything comes back in return.

It means going through a lot of grief over and over and over…again and again and then doing it over again some more.

It means having to do things for and to my spouse that she doesn't want me to do.

It means being misunderstood by my wife and not infrequently by others.

It means treasuring moments, however brief, of connection with, appreciation from, and perhaps even a smidgen of love from my wife.

It means longing for the intimate sharing that I once had that is only possible with a wife.

It means being completely responsible for someone who is completely irresponsible.
It means making decisions myself that in the past I could make with my wife.

It means humbly accepting help and not feeling irresponsible in the process.

It means being on the edge of being defined and defining myself as the spouse of someone with dementia but constantly fighting that definition.

It means accepting what is totally unfair.

It means having a lot of guilt over whether I am doing enough or doing the right things or even doing too much.
It means constantly seeking God's mercy and Grace.

It means a type of total aloneness because even other caregivers of a spouse do not have exactly the same situation.

It means facing death constantly as I experience my wife dying bit by bit by bit…

It means being widowed but married, and at the same time being married, but widowed.

It means having the responsibilities of marriage without its rewards.

It means having the loneliness of being single without the freedom of being single.

It means being a single parent to my wife, who now has the mind of a small child.

It means being married, widowed, and a single parent to the same person all at the same time.

It means having a sense of Divine Purpose in my situation with the condition of my wife but not being able to define it.

It means having hope for a new day and a new life.

1 Corinthians 13 paraphrased for a caregiver of his wife—

Though I provide my wife with the best personal daily care, no matter how menial, provide her the finest medical care with the most skilled medical personnel and the most effective medications available, and provide her the fullest experiences and enjoyments she can grasp and enable her to live as fully as possible for as long as possible, but have not love for her, then in my caregiving for her I am just doing a job.

And if gain expert knowledge of all that is known about all the different forms of dementia and if I closely follow all the latest research in the field of memory care and if I have great optimism that a cure will be found for this disease, but have not love for my wife I am just an intellectual snob.

If I donate all my assets to research for a cure for dementia, and if I wear out my own health through involvement in dementia awareness causes but have not love for my wife, I am just a do-gooder.

Care and love for my wife requires extreme patience and kindness. It is very humbling. It is nothing to brag about.

It means giving up what I want to do without becoming irritable or resentful.

There is no pleasure in treating her the way she treats me. There is joy in the victory of being able to treat her well in spite of her behavior toward me.

Being a loving caregiver to my wife often means bearing what feels unbearable, believing what seems unbelievable, hoping for what seems hopeless, and enduring what feels unendurable.

It never ends, but somehow neither does love. Other diseases and injuries are either cured or come to a decent ending. Dementia just keeps continuing its slow but steady downward path.

I know; I don't have the whole picture. And I can't even express much of what I do know.

But I do know we'll understand it better by and by.

When I married Jan, I said I would love her "for better or for worse," and I meant it with all my mature understanding of what those words are really all about.

I realize that at this time, I only have a myopic picture of what all this really means. But when I see Him someday face to face, I will rejoice and be glad for the reason why for all of this and more.

So now I cling to faith and hope for a better day. And someday, I will not need faith or hope. All I will need is agape Love, and I will have it and give it with great abundance.

Writing this paper was an unusual experience. I had been thinking about what it meant to be married to Jan in her condition for some time. At some point, it seemed natural to look at the classic love chapter in Scripture, 1 Corinthians 13. I heard a professor say this chapter was the best description of love he had ever seen. Incidentally, this professor gave no indication that he had anything of a Christian faith.

One afternoon, I read 1 Corinthians 13 again and then began to write. The thoughts, words, sentences seemed to flow out effortlessly. I found it coming from deep within me, yet it was not from me. I experienced it coming from outside me and flowing through me. Yet it was so entirely of me. I have done a lot of writing, sometimes struggling with what I want to say, and sometimes it does come easily. But it had never come like this. Yes, I can say I wrote this. But the truth is, it was a gift from God.

In Jan's condition, I had a sense that God was doing an uncommon work in me and giving me a calling. But I don't want to claim too much in saying this. We might call it God's difficult grace. I decided I had three reasons for writing this article: (1) I wanted people to see what it is like to be married to someone with dementia. (2) I hoped it would be a ministry to people married as I was. (3) I discovered it was an expression of me that helped me handle my situation in a healthy way.

A couple Scripture passages were significant to me in connection with this writing. In Luke 14:12–14, Jesus gives some advice. If someone wants to put on a dinner, he should invite people who did not have the financial means or the capability to return the favor. Obviously in my loving and caring for Jan, she would not be able to repay what I had given her. Yet as the text suggests, I found that I received far more than I had given. The second passage was Matthew 25:31–46. Here it is communicated that as one does the simple things of providing food, drink, clothing to those needing these things, or simply being present with someone needing presence, he serves God. He does ministry. Jesus spoke of doing such things to "one of the least of these." *Least* would not mean lesser value or least essential acts of service. Instead, it speaks of the least capable people and often people of minor social status. In the eyes of God, such actions are of great importance.

I read this dissertation to several groups, including the caregiver support group and the local ministerial association. I shared it with some of my family and close friends. I posted it on Facebook. It seemed to strike a response in people. The caregivers were the most responsive. They could quickly identify with it. I gave out several copies.

I practiced reading it out loud before reading it to others. It was very personal and emotional.

I wanted to have self-control as I read yet be able to present it from my heart.

I came across a couple of sayings that impressed me. I don't have the author's name. The first was, "A lot of what is love is persevering." Over the years of caring for Jan, I learned how true that was. The second was, "The love of a young man for a young lady is nothing compared to the love of an old man for an old lady." I think this saying was implying that the old couple had been together for several decades. I don't see this saying to be putting down young love, but it speaks to the profundity of love that has traveled over many trails.

What was the greatest lesson I learned through Jan's degenerating health? It was to love without receiving in return. More accurately, to love without receiving *what I would like to receive* in return. I wanted from her companionship, connection, and intimacy. I received a closeness to Jan that only comes by giving without conditions. In loving this way, I came to realize that I did receive from Jan in her condition much that I could not have received if Jan had been well.

It is the nature of human beings to expect something in return for whatever they do. In college, I once argued with a roommate who maintained that there was no such thing as a person doing an unselfish act. As I later thought about this discussion, I acknowledged that he was more correct than I was. I will admit that I never let him know of this change in my thinking.

I later read some of the work of Erik Erikson, where he noted that a newborn baby is completely selfish, not even being aware of the existence of anything but himself. As he becomes aware of the other, especially other people, he assumes that everyone exists for his benefit. It was shocking for me to realize that a baby's cute supposedly loving hugs were very self-centered. The entire parenting task must teach their children to consider others in their actions, not just themselves. It is most probably accurate to say that the biggest tragedy of drug addiction is that it makes the person self-centered.

This human nature puts me in a quandary. I am to be like Christ, who came not to be served but to serve. Paul asks me to imitate him, who describes himself as a servant (actually a slave). As a song says, I am sent by Him to "labor unrewarded." Like so many commands in Scripture (e.g., essentially every phrase of the Sermon on the Mount), I am commanded to do what I will never wholly do, perhaps not even minimally.

But what I can do is realize, at least as much as the Lord enables me to accept, that I have no right to expect anything of a positive nature for anything I do. As a result of my sinfulness, I am only entitled to negative consequences for my actions. Anything positive I do receive is by the grace of God.

Does that mean I must be a doormat for every wrong and unfair thing that happens to me and that I cannot set any boundaries? Sometimes the most loving and unselfish act is the setting of limits. It is entirely possible that not setting some boundaries is making a person worse than he was before. It could be enabling him to go further and deeper into his negative behavior.

Loving 100 percent has many applications. Not only when one's spouse has dementia, being married means giving 100 percent, even if she returns nothing. At work, I am to do my best possible job as long as I have that position, even if I am mistreated. In any personal relationship, I am to treat the other person as well as possible, even if I end up being badly hurt by that person. In giving, wherever I choose to donate, they could misuse the funds I give. No matter how spiritually healthy a church I join might appear to be, it could have severe conflicts and other problems. As for my physical health, no matter how well I take care of myself, I could end up with a terminal disease. And regardless of who I vote for in an election, if that person is elected, he/she could end up quite different than I expected. So living a life of love, giving, and not necessarily getting anything in return can get very old, wearying, and depressing.

This perspective could leave me feeling extremely vulnerable, unable to trust anyone or anything. The problem is that there is no way for me to know the future. But coming to this perspective puts me in an excellent position. It makes me realize, to a great degree, what Friedrich Schleiermacher meant when he described the religious experience as "the feeling of absolute dependency." We are indeed totally dependent on God. And God has no problem with expectations. Knowing the future as He knows the present and past, for Him, expectations do not exist. Therefore, God can and does act without expectation. That is to say, He and He alone can and does act unselfishly. The Lord calls me to perfection and holds me accountable for my imperfection but does so without expectation. And it is accurate to say that He does this with perfect love. His love is perfect because He is love. So is an unselfish act possible? The answer is *yes*. But that act is an act of God.

Loss and Grief Before Death

Being a caregiver of someone with dementia means experiencing loss. That is reality. It is very tempting to try not to think about it. To a limited extent, and for a brief period, one might have some success in doing that. However, reality is a powerful force and ignoring it always has unpleasant consequences. At worst, it can result in much misery and, finally, in death.

The reality of experiencing loss means one is experiencing grief. Grief is an unpleasant emotion. It is very natural to want to avoid this emotion. We can easily assume that if we shove it back far enough into the recesses of our mind, we can not only ignore it but can live as though it doesn't exist. However, when there is loss, it still exists.

In my involvement with hospice, I learned the following analogy: Suppose you were to take a beach ball and wade into a body of water, about chest-high. There you try to keep it underwater while moving around and engaging in other activities. Sooner or later, that ball will get loose, rise, and smack you in the face.

The good news is that with God's grace, facing reality and finding release from grief is possible. But it is a process, and it will take time. We begin by gaining an understanding of three types or categories of grief that are common for caregivers. I think we will find that grief is far more involved and complex, especially among caregivers, than people generally think. It can feel overwhelming. But the Lord does get us through times that seem too much to handle.

Three categories of grief for caregivers:

1. *Anticipatory grief* (she's going to die)
    Anticipatory grief is grief coming from dwelling on the impending death of the caregiver's loved one. It is also common for caregivers of a loved one with cancer where the loved one has a possibility of living. But here, we are speaking of grief over the certainty of the death of a loved one. This certainty is far different than the certainty that all of us will eventually die. To even think of saying that is to insult such a caregiver. This grief experience can be as intense as experiencing the grief of the actual death of a loved one.

2. *Loss grief* (she can no longer do what she once did well)
    Loss grief is grief coming from the losses in capabilities of the loved one. She becomes increasingly less able to go places, do things, converse with, be intimate with, and even argue with you. These losses make it harder, perhaps almost impossible, to connect and bond with his loved one as had always been possible before. These losses create a longing for the connections of the past. Sadly it can result in an affair, hoping to get a bond back by using another person. However, it can also result in the caregiver seeking new, or, at least in the past, ignore or having paid little attention to, forms of connection and bonding with his loved one. It may lead to a relationship that is beyond words. The healthy

course of action for the caregiver in this category of grief is to do the following:

a) Engage in healthy grieving over the lost capacities and aspects of his loved one.

b) Pursue the kinds of connection that might be even more available, now that the former kinds of connection have dissipated or are even totally gone. Those more apparent forms of connection may have gotten in the way of the less-obvious forms.

3. *Alive grief* (how long does this have to go on?)
This category of grief can be said to be grieving that the loved one continues to live in her present state. For some caregivers, this state of their loved one is so painful that they put their loved one in placement and seldom, perhaps even never, go to see her.

This category of grief essentially, if not actually, carries with it a desire for the loved one to die. I have not ever heard any discussion of or seen any writing on this category of grief. It is generally socially acceptable for a caregiver to say of his loved one, "I don't want her to have to continue living this way." It can be socially acceptable for the loved one to say, "I want to die." The Apostle Paul said and wrote, "For me to die is gain" (Philippians 1:21). He was stating that he wanted to die.

Perhaps the problem is that there are cases where a caregiver has carried out the death of his loved one. I suspect a high percentage of caregivers of a loved one with a long-term terminal illness who have this category of grief and are afraid to share this emotion with anyone else or acknowledge it to

God or even to himself. So he lives with a highly charged but deeply suppressed emotion. The fact that it is probably legally possible in California and other states for such a caregiver to end the life of his loved one makes this matter even more difficult. Personally the thought of doing such a thing to my loved one is too distasteful to imagine even a moment.

The even more profound problem is that it is, at best, difficult, if not impossible, to experience this category of grief without guilt. The truth that this is an emotion of shame rather than guilt over any misdeed or sinful thought does not make it less difficult to resolve. Perhaps it makes it even more difficult.

When such a loved one has died, it is generally not difficult for people to say such things as, "It is a blessing that she passed away," generally adding something like, "now she doesn't have to suffer anymore. She is in a better place," etc. True, I can tactfully express alive grief to people in ways they can handle and be affirmative of my sentiments. I did it in a poem I wrote and then read at my mother's funeral. It was very well received. But people hearing me speak in this manner do not hear and are probably generally not able to grasp the depth of emotion this category of grief entails.

Perhaps this grief category is generally recognized more than I have been aware. Or maybe it can come to be identified, researched, and approaches developed to help people who struggle or try to avoid grappling with this grief category.

What All This Was Like for Me

Category 1: The reality she is dying—Before Jesus was crucified, He went to the Garden of Gethsemane and prayed. He prayed with astonishing intensity. His prayer was so intense that blood dripped out of his forehead. He pleaded not to have to die and especially not to die an excruciating death. He finally came to accept that this was the way it was going to be.

I think I can accurately assert that His Gethsemane experience was more difficult for Him than His crucifixion experience. On numerous occasions, Jesus spoke of His impending crucifixion. He had been grappling with this reality for a considerable time. Then at Gethsemane, it hit excruciatingly hard. But once He fully faced and fully accepted the cross was not going away, He was ready to be crucified. It was of utmost importance that He come to this fact. Otherwise He could not and would not have gone through with the crucifixion. Even letting Himself be nailed on the cross, He could have jumped down from it.

When I heard the diagnosis of Jan's dementia, I had my own Gethsemane to experience. I cannot say there was a specific point when I fully accepted the reality that Jan would die. Both Jesus and I, and most people who have a Gethsemane to go through, experience it over an extended period. Often there is not a specific climactic Gethsemane-resolution moment. But one knows it after it has happened.

I often wondered how I would react when Jan died. I initially thought that I would mourn her death just the same as if she had never had this dementia condition. I based that on my experience of mourning Mom's death, even though I knew for years that it was coming and even wondered why God didn't take her sooner.

But then I thought that after anticipating her death for years, I might be mourned out and at peace when she did die. People might wonder why I was not mourning, and I could only note that I had been grieving for years. I might feel relief that the trials of daily seeing another deterioration, another loss, were finally over.

I sometimes wondered if I might have the opportunity to see Jan leave. It would be different than seeing her die. I would not even have to be with her geographically when her body died (it would be good if I was but okay if I wasn't). How would that be? I wouldn't necessarily see her go up but go out to heaven. But going up might be the best description. Beyond that, I probably would not be able to describe in human speech what I saw. Reading 2 Kings 2, Elisha was edgy before Elijah left (verses 2 and 5). But there is no indication that he felt any grief after Elijah went. Instead, he immediately started doing the ministry God called and gifted him to do.

I would not necessarily see her leave at the time—in the human sense of the word *time*—she left. As the Lord and the next life is beyond time, I might see her go well after, or even at some point, before her body dies. That wouldn't matter. It would be accurate to say I saw her leave. It would not be some fantasy. But it could be a dream. That might even be the best way because it would be easier for others to accept what I might share that I saw.

Yes, this might spare me of the grief of only seeing her die. It would be a further confirmation that she hadn't just died. She had left and, indeed, for a "better place." These thoughts can be comforting, but they do not take away the reality that death is a profound loss for those of us who remain behind.

Category 2: The losing of her abilities to do what she once did well—Each time I saw a deterioration of ability in Jan, it felt like something of her had died. I created an image of this in which I compared her death to the removal of a bandage. Someone might take a bandage off with one quick rip. It's painful. It can be a shock. Another way is to take the bandage off about a quarter-inch at a time. Each small partial removal is agonizing, especially if one's skin has a lot of hair.

Corrie Ten Boom was known for saying that people need to hold everything in their *hands* lightly, or it would hurt when God pried their *fingers* open. I applied this personally in this way. God gave me a wife to have and to hold and to release back to Him. So it's not just that she is dying bit by bit; I was somehow destined to let go of her bit by bit. And in that process, to still take care of the Jan who is here.

As a person is dying, everything is stripped from him. The time over which this happens varies widely. With Jan, the stripping away of what she could do was a process over at least a decade. This stripping away was, at the same time, a what and who I had for a wife. God was taking all this away to bring me to a new life with Jan. In this stripping away, we learn who we really are. A person with advanced dementia knows who he really is because everything else he considered him is taken away. Thus dying people are the most authentic people. And they can be the most real to others because they only have who they are. Having nothing but themselves, they can only be who they are. They have nothing that isn't real to hang onto. In all they do, they have nothing left to lose.

Do we conclude that all there is to life is losing what one has to get to his true self? Not at all! Life is full of transitions: from childhood to adult, from one profession to another, changes in marital status and other relationships, etc. Each change is a loss, even when it results in very desirable gains. Each transition is entering into a new life. It is an opportunity to grow and be who you are.

One needs to be careful about drawing conclusions or making judgments about a person with dementia, especially in this last stage of life. The disease damages the brain. That can, and often does, bring about significant personality changes. My mother, for example, was not a nice lady in her last days. She did not care about anyone coming to see her, including her immediate family. She made that very clear whenever she had company.

Was that a manifestation of who she was? I don't think so. There was no question in my mind, from the many decades that I knew her, that she was a person with a genuine relationship to God in Christ. Reflecting on those days, I have come to understand her behavior in a different way. She had lost most of her brain and mind function. That did not mean she had lost her relationship with God. Stripped of so much, she was free to have a more vital interaction with God than ever before. So it was not surprising that she was not interested in the physical world around her.

It would have been nice if she had explained this. Instead, she would make it clear in harsh terms that she wasn't interested in seeing her husband or me. But with the state of her brain, this was the best she could do.

When we went to her, she would say, "What do you want?"

We would respond, "We came to see you."

Then she replied, "Well, you've seen me." Then she would shut her eyes and be unresponsive. Yes, our hearing her this way hurt. But this understanding of where she was at in life and understanding her limited communication capabilities is very comforting.

No, I cannot prove this was what happened. You, the readers, are under no obligation to agree with me. But let me make some observations. When someone is going on to and looking forward to a new life stage, he commonly loses interest in his current life. For example, as a college senior, especially the last semester, I was looking forward to seminary. I lost much of my focus on studies, grades, and campus events. I have often observed that when someone is moving on to a new job, he doesn't take as much interest in his work during the last days in his present position. In 2 Kings 2:1–14, Elijah is aware that he will soon pass from his life on earth. Elisha, and numerous other prophets, tried to be with and talk with him. Wanting to be alone, he wasn't interested. His life and work were over. He was ready to move on.

And so I don't think it is unreasonable to understand that when a person is aware that he is moving on from this life, he doesn't have much interest in this life. That can include people he has known and loved for many decades. So if you find a loved one in this condition, regardless of whether or not they have dementia, be understanding.

I mentioned that we saw an indication of Jan's thinking one day when Debbie, a caregiver I had to help with Jan, gave her a pencil and piece of paper. Jan wrote "new life" and "go home." It would be hard not to conclude that both statements were a reference to heaven.

Category 3: How long, oh Lord!—I sometimes contemplated which was more stressful and which I most dreaded and feared. Was it Jan's actual death, or was it the long slow process of her dying? Both are hard. I concluded that it was the latter. I think this was because I couldn't sense what her death would be like. I was familiar with her dying. Somehow my mind couldn't grasp her death. I'm sure some denial dynamics were involved. On the other hand, I soon experienced and became very aware of her long journey toward death. I often wondered how long this would go on, both dreading how long it might be and dreading its end.

Interestingly Jan would say that she did not fear death but was uncomfortable with the prospect of dying. She had always said, for years, that she did not want to live too long. I came to understand that in her mind, that meant a long lingering dying process where she would be in a nursing-home level of care for a significant time. Ironically this was precisely what was to happen. And the Lord gave her and me the grace to live through all those days.

On the other hand, she was confident that she would be going to heaven when she died. She looked forward to that. In that sense, she looked forward to her death. Her only desire with how long she lived came as we were caring for our children. She wanted to be sure to live long enough to bring them up to adulthood.

As for Jan's days, the Lord had them numbered. I knew it would likely not seem like the right time from a human standpoint, whenever it would be. And her death would be harsh, whenever it was. Sometimes I felt caught between feeling selfish to want her with me because I knew that to die for her was gain (Philippians 1:21), but I also felt selfish as I wondered how long this would go on and keep getting more difficult for me. As I could see it, my only solution—and I found it to be very biblical—was that the Lord knew the right time for Him to take her, and I was content to submit to that.

I anticipated that when Jan died, it would feel like at a very inopportune time. Yet I acknowledged the validity of C. S. Lewis' contention that when the Lord brings something to its proper perfection, it is time for that thing to end so we can and will move on to the next thing He has for us.

There was, in me, a dread for when she would die. There was also, in me, a dread of her condition dragging on and on and on—the latter trepidation could feel like I might want her to die. I knew in my head that what I was wanting was for this state of things to end. While I couldn't accept wanting her to die, I could accept wanting this state of things to end. I was reasonably sure that when she did die, I would grieve. But I would also feel relief. I gradually came to understand that that was okay too. I was convinced that my longing for comfort was not just wishful thinking. Instead, I based it on a biblical hope for a better day.

Many have lost their spouses quite differently. For many, the death was sudden, perhaps through an accident. There is no time to prepare and no time to say goodbye. Sometimes there is a brief time in which to prepare and to say goodbye. I will comment that no matter how long that time was, it will feel like there was not enough time to prepare and say goodbye. Or one might think that he did not adequately take advantage of the time available. Or it can be both.

Others lose their spouse through divorce. I have lost two marriages. The first was through a divorce, and the second was through death. In my experience, divorce was the more difficult. Divorce is a death, the death of a marriage. It has immense grief. Even with today's high divorce rate, there is still an acceptability of being widowed over being divorced. The finality of death is lacking in death. One's wife, ex-wife, is still alive. Divorce is the result of a long period of conflict. Death is the end of a love relationship. There is a closure to death that is not available in divorce. Yet with both, one no longer has the person he once had.

I have had contact with several people where there was a very likely prospect of death of their spouse and also a hope for a cure and continuation of life. Such people have to contend with the very apparent chance of death. They have the Gethsemane place of accepting the possibility of death. At the same time, they cling to hope for life. But hope brings

71

the anxiety of doubt. They can easily go through a myriad of complex emotions.

I concluded that certainty, even if undesirable, is less difficult to handle than uncertainty, even if there is a possible positive outcome. Although these people had a hope that I did not have, I never experienced a desire to trade places with them. I did not feel any envy that they had it better than me. Instead, I found myself sympathizing with them. I could even be thankful that my situation was not theirs.

People often say that the worst death of a loved one is the loss of one's child. We presume that our children will bury us. We don't even consider that we might have to bury our child. We hope to have all our children and be in close contact with them for the rest of our lives.

However, when we look at parenting, it is a process of separating. Birth is a separation from the child in the womb of its mother. Children have an instinctual desire to grow up, i.e., they want to be increasingly independent. This desire often creates challenges for parents. Yet much of good parenting consists of helping a child take increasing responsibilities in care for himself. While parents hope that children will keep a close relationship with them, the goal of good parenting is for the child to be able to leave the nest.

The goal of a marriage is the opposite of that of parenting. While married people need to be mature adults, they also, in a healthy marriage, develop an increasing dependence on each other. They each have their separate friendships, goals, interests, and approaches to life. At the same time, every aspect of their lives together—physical, emotional, intellectual, financial, vocational, recreational, and spiritual—contributes to greater closeness, love, and intimacy. There is to be no leaving the nest. Their marriage is "until death do us part."

What can make the death of a child tragic is that it goes so much against our expectations that we would die well before any of our children. However, the closer one has been to someone who dies, the more difficult it is to experience that person's death. Marriage is the most intimate relationship possible between two human beings. That is what can make the death of a spouse harder than the death of a child.

The bottom line is that the death of anyone we care about is hard. The cause of the death doesn't matter. Even where death brings relief from intense suffering, it is still hard. It has a finality that is not present in any other event. No matter how certain one is of a better life after death for that person, there is still the end of this life.

However, while death has unsurpassed finality, the grief that goes with the loss of a loved one does not. While we cannot do anything about the fact that a loved one has died, we can do, and need to do, much with our resulting grief. That is what makes the next chapter so vital as we consider the grief process.

The Grief Process

It is certainly understandable to say that we do not like being in pain. Physical pain is hard, but emotional pain is much worse. The grief that comes with a loss of a loved one has its particular difficulty. Loss of money, possessions, a job, or a game each has the possibility of restoration. When a loved one dies, he will not be restored. Death may be the avenue for new opportunities, a new job, a new relationship, or something not even considered. But the current pain is still prominent.

We often try to find ways to forget the loss and thus remove that painful grief. A major cause of chemical addiction is taking alcohol or other drugs to deaden the pain of death. The person may feel fine while on his high. Then at some point, the high is over, he comes back down to reality, and the pain has not changed, except to be even worse.

Others try to fill, as much as possible, their life focusing on some activity. They fully engage in a profession, a hobby, a new relationship, travel, or watching TV. They might do anything not to think about the loss. They hope that one of these activities would lead them to forget the loss or its pain.

I thought of the possibility of a partial lobotomy. Couldn't there be some form of laser surgery to delete the part of the brain where those sad memories are stored? Of course, the rest of the brain should be kept intact. With any of these ventures, I would certainly want to retain the positive fond memories of the person I lost. Unfortunately, there is no way to have it both ways.

In my involvement with hospice, I learned some things about what happens when one tries to suppress emotions. They talk about a STUG reaction. One can appear to be doing fine and feeling good. He is not feeling grief and can even express good memories. Then something triggers a reaction, or it could come out of nowhere. One has a sudden temporary upsurge of grief, i.e., a STUG reaction.

I previously mentioned how Hospice pointed out the following imagery of trying to suppress emotions. It is like wading into a pool of water with a beach ball that you hold under the water. You move around as you might generally like to do in the pool. At some point, you are caught off guard and let go of the ball. The water forces it up, and it smacks you in the face.

In the classic movie *It's a Wonderful Life*, George Bailey is having a rough time and is under a lot of tension. He comes home full of anxiety. He tries to act like everything is fine, but soon he is yelling at his daughter, arguing with his wife, and creating havoc for the whole family. His beach ball had smacked him and was out of control.

There is another problem with trying to suppress emotions. We cannot simply select which feelings we want to hide and which ones we want to enjoy. In suppressing negative emotions, we end up suppressing positive emotions. We end up cold, without feeling, stoic. It's a life without enjoyment, love, or expression. It can be a hard lonely life.

There is a better way. We do not have to grieve "as others do who have no hope" (1 Thessalonians 4:13). A first step is to accept that all of one's emotions, negative and positive, need expression. They were made to be expressed, not suppressed. They are like steam in a tea kettle. They need to be released. Of course, one needs to use good judgment about when, where, and how they are expressed.

A second step is to understand that every person is unique. Every person has his way of expressing himself, thoughts, aspirations, disappointments, grief, and many other emotions. As I share some things that worked for me in working through my sorrow, I am not saying this is what you should do. What works for me may or may not work for you and vice versa. I hope and pray that sharing what was helpful for me will help others discover what works best for them.

Also each person has his own flow of grief recovery. With some, when a loved one dies, they instantly pour out their grief, even if the death was not at all unexpected. With others, grief comes after the funeral is over or at some other time. With some, grief comes out gradually and in small doses.

Also there is no set time after which someone should be "over it." With some, it may be a matter of a few weeks or less. This shorter time is common if one has been anticipating his loved one's death for some time, especially if he has been sorrowing over the loss to come. Other people may need months or even years. If it is that long, one can be experiencing grief yet still have much enjoyment in life. Whatever the time that is needed, that person needs it.

In general, as one addresses and goes through his grief, things will get better in time. There can be good days and tough days. Note I didn't say bad days. A day during which one experiences much grief can be one of the most profitable days in grief recovery. Grief recovery is often like the stock market that may be doing well but has many downtimes.

There is an old saying that "time heals all wounds." That saying is not true. Time itself doesn't do anything. The only thing we can say time does is to say that time does pass.

However, healing and grief recovery do take time. One needs to take the time for it.

My living room was my grief room. It is closed off from the rest of the house. It became the place where I could release my deepest emotions and contemplate my deepest thoughts. As Jan declined, and for some time after her death, I would periodically feel this sensation of grief come over me. Sometimes it came on rather rapidly, and sometimes I was aware of it gradually developing.

At such times, I would go to the living room alone. With just God and me there, I would feel completely uninhibited. I would tell God exactly what I was thinking and feeling. My prayers could become extreme. There were times I would yell, "God, this is too much!" I would say whatever I wanted to say and however I felt like saying it (Jan was the only other person in the house at these times. If she heard me, it didn't seem to faze her). These sessions were usually about ten to, at most, fifteen minutes. Afterward I would feel much better. But I knew that after a week or so, I would need another such session.

I had confidence in God that He could handle it. I took my cue from the book of Psalms. A random cursory reading of the various chapters of this book will find many with surprising content. The writers wonder why God allows so much evil, injustice, and suffering. He lets God know how he feels and what he wants to happen to those who do evil and seem to get away with it. And still, he continues to believe in and trust God.

I would take whatever time I felt I needed. Usually it wasn't more than about ten to fifteen minutes. I would feel much better afterward, ready to continue with life. I understood that this state of being wouldn't last. Like eating, sleeping, tooth-brushing, etc., it would need to be done again and again, and I chose to accept that, just as I had, in some way, chosen to accept those other functions for my well-being.

Sometimes I felt that I was experiencing grief but not able to fully let it be released. I sensed there was something inside me that wouldn't let go. I felt a need for full release. For that to happen, I needed to face what I was feeling.

I decided to attack grief head-on. I found several triggers that would bring up the grief that was inside me. One day I went to the funeral of a friend's wife. They had been married for sixty-five years. I never knew her, but the service brought me to tears. I personalized his grief. For about a year and a half, starting well before Jan passed, I attended a funeral almost every month or two. Toward the end, I found myself feeling for the deceased's loved ones but not overcome with emotion.

I thought of looking at picture albums that had pictures of Jan. I found myself reluctant to do that. I took that as a good reason to look at them. I finally did. It was not as difficult as I thought it might be.

After Jan died, I visited her gravesite several times. On occasion, I read the poem "This Year I'll Spend Christmas with Jesus" (you can google it for yourself) and imagined Jan saying this message to me. The first time I took Communion without Jan was very hard.

I knew these and other triggers would deeply stir my emotions. And that is precisely why I brought myself to them. I did not avoid but instead directly faced what will stir up the grief that is in me. These triggers helped me to be able to heal and recover. It has been said, "Grieve well to heal well." Another way to say this is, "You need to feel it to heal it." Or as Jesus said, "Blessed are those who mourn, for they shall be comforted" (Matthew 5:4). And the negative of this might be expressed, "Woe to those who do not mourn, for they shall be tormenting themselves with unresolved grief."

Some may say that this just sounds like torture, like asking for punishment. I do advise, don't take on more than you can handle. There is a recourse with a negative connotation, but does have a place in the grief recovery process, called denial. It is common when one first hears of the death of a loved one to call out the one word *no*! The person doing this is saying that this news is more than he can handle. Initially he denies what has happened.

We can compare this to what often happens in the dental office. The dentist gives his patient a shot of Novocain. The injection enables the patient not to have any feeling of pain. We might say that the patient is in denial that the dentist is inflicting pain on him. Later the Novocain gradually wears off. Then the patient feels pain but at a dosage that he can handle.

Likewise, denial enables the grieving one not to feel the pain of loss that he is initially unable to handle. In due time, he can let the reality of loss come to him. He can then experience and release grief. Later he will take in triggers that will bring out and release more profound levels of sorrow.

There are many ways to release grief. Each person needs to explore and use those methods that work best for him. It is good to have understanding friends with whom one can openly express thoughts and feelings. If possible, it is good to get together with one or more other people going through a similar loss. Meeting this way allows discovering that your experiences are not unusual or strange. They are just new to you. At the same time, you will find your unique journey and that it is okay to grieve your way.

A year before Jan died, I became involved, through hospice, in leading support groups for men who had lost their wives. Most of these men had been married for forty to sixty or more years. It is often said that men don't express their emotions as well as women. Indeed, many more women than men would sign up to participate in a grief recovery support group. These men's groups were never more than four or five men. But the men who did come did very well.

Even though Jan was still alive, I found that I had gone through enough loss with Jan and grieved enough over those losses that I could identify very well with them and their grief. I felt this was a verification that anticipatory grief is real. The dynamics of what one may go through before a person dies are very much the same as after a person dies. This is especially true if one has come to accept the certainty of the impending death of one's loved one.

I found that pastors and counselors were less inclined than others to participate in a support group. Their stated reasoning was that with their training and experience counseling others going through loss, they didn't feel the need for such a group. I would compare this thinking to what a medical doctor might think if he was sick or injured. Regardless of his training and experience, he needs medical care. He is just as ill as anyone else. And a pastor who loses a loved one is just as needful for support as anyone else. We can also note the classic saying that "the lawyer who represents himself in a legal case has a fool for an attorney." This is true no matter how well trained, experienced, and skilled he might be.

One of the ways grief is sometimes misunderstood happens when it is expressed as anger. A man once told me that when his wife died, it felt like she had left him. In his rational state, he was fully aware that she had not decided to leave him by dying. However, his emotions sometimes led him to think that way.

Death feels very unfair. It doesn't seem right that someone we dearly love should die. When Jan would say, "Bad things happen to good people as well as to bad, to Christians as well as to non-Christians," she was giving full recognition to the truth that life is unfair. Remarkably she fully accepted that reality.

Someone can easily have a sense of unfairness alongside the feeling of loss. The result is grief expressed as anger. People can easily misinterpret someone going through this set of emotions.

For example, in such a situation, a person can easily experience anger toward God. After all, it is God who "numbers our days" (Psalm 139:16).

During these days of Jan's decline, I didn't think that I had any anger issues. Searching to see if this was true, I reflected on my fondness for racquetball. I had several racquetball buddies. I didn't feel anger when I played, including when I lost, which was not unusual. But I found that I especially liked to get on the racquetball court alone. I enjoyed taking hard swings at that ball with minimal concern about how well I was doing. I found that playing this way was a great release.

During these days, I often turned to God for comfort and strength. It gave me a very positive perspective about God. It is hard to be angry at someone while, at the same time, looking to him for support. I could see and accept that God was testing me through hardship experiences. That made those experiences much more palatable.

I found journaling to be very helpful. I like to write, so this became a natural outlet for me. It had value simply in doing something I enjoy. It had the added benefit of helping me collect my thoughts and gain perspective. It enabled me to look at my circumstances in fresh ways that were much more insightful than my initial impressions. Most important, it was a great way to release my emotions.

Besides the support groups that I was involved in, I found it helpful to share with close friends I could trust. Some of them were going through similar experiences. I felt a connection with such people. Being aware that there were others in my situation helped take away feelings of unfairness.

Sometimes the deceased person with some unhealthy practices in their lifestyle did contribute to their death. It is natural in such circumstances to resent and have feelings of anger for that person for their choices. It is natural to feel guilty for one's anger at someone you loved dearly yet are grieving deeply for their death.

I have noted that Jan lived a healthy lifestyle, except that she was not inclined to engage in any regular physical exercise. I would encourage her to go for a daily walk and go walking with her. After a while, she resented my efforts, regardless of my good intentions. As this began to stress our relationship, I backed off from this effort. After a passage of time, she did agree that it was good for her. We then continued to have daily walks that shortened in length until she could no longer walk.

Indeed, she might well have lived longer and delayed her symptoms of dementia if she had exercised more. Of course, the result would have been the same.

For anyone experiencing anger at their deceased loved one, there is the need to forgive. Forgiving does not mean that one is to decide that the person's behavior was good. The departed person may indeed have made some bad choices. There is a classic saying that not forgiving is like drinking poison and hoping it will hurt someone else. The point is that not forgiving, especially in not forgiving someone who has died, is only to harm oneself. Forgiveness here means to no longer hold any resentment against that person.

We are all very aware that to genuinely forgive is not easy. It can be challenging. If one is a person of faith, there is a simple practice that can be very helpful. It is to consider that God has forgiven that person and holds no resentment for what that person may have done. Therefore, ponder the following thought. If God has forgiven that person, would it not be well for me to forgive him? So imagine you are talking to that person. Then say to your loved one, "God has forgiven you, so I forgive you." You might want and need to do this several times.

Jan helped me with any subtle anger issues I might have. Recall her phrase, "Bad things happen to good people as well as to bad and to Christians as well as to non-Christians." So reflecting on her saying this, I would have to conclude that obviously, I was not exempt.

It is not unusual to hear caregivers of a loved one express a lot of frustration. I participated in a caregiver support group for people caring for a loved one with dementia. There is certainly a lot to be frustrated about in caregiving. People with dementia are often difficult. They are not always appreciative of the care they receive. As I heard other's frustrations, it informed me that such exasperations are natural and should not be denied or suppressed. There can be a fine line between frustration and anger.

Both frustration and anger can be another way of expressing grief. These expressions have the drawback of being easily misunderstood. The person with grief may not realize that the more profound emotion he is experiencing is grief. As with any emotion, it is wise to discern what more profound emotion may be behind the surface emotion.

In another chapter, I will discuss the concept of being on a spiritual journey. As part of this journey, I have compared God to a demanding but loving athletic coach. I also sometimes think of Him as a teacher who gives challenging assignments. These analogies give me a more positive perspective on the hard times I experience. I come to see such times much differently than only my receiving unfair treatment.

Finally I had to acknowledge that while these years were tough, I also had much for which to be thankful. For just a few examples, I had two great caregivers to help me with Jan, an excellent long-term care insurance policy to finance their work, supportive people to talk to, many people praying for us, good health, etc. I could even feel guilt over having it so good.

It is always essential to take good care of oneself. That is not self-centered behavior. God created our body and a mind to use it. He expects us to take good care of both. Someone experiencing grief often feels tired. Going through grief takes up a lot of energy. Frequently it is more of a drain than we realize. It is vital to get a lot of rest.

Naps are very appropriate. It is also common to have trouble sleeping at night. That can soon result in more time taking naps during the day. I knew a man who said he reached the point of sleeping most of the day and not sleeping at night. It can be helpful to resist, at least sometimes, the urge to take a nap and instead go for a walk or some other enjoyable form of exercise.

The third step is to recognize and accept that one never wholly ends the grieving process for a loved one. The memory of that loss remains as long as one is alive. There is no getting over it.

However, this is not the negative reality that one might reasonably suppose. One can reach the point of being ready to go on with life. He can enjoy life. He can have fond memories of his now-gone loved one. All this takes time. And it takes the releasing, usually many times, of the emotions of grief. Releasing means accepting the times of missing one's loved one, of feeling loss, of feeling grief. Don't forget, "Feel it to heal it."

About the first day of kindergarten, I met a boy, Johnny, my best friend from then on through grammar school and high school. In the spring of our sophomore year, he suddenly died of encephalitis. I lost my best friend as a teenager. When we got the news, I went to my room and cried profusely. I remember Mom putting her arm on me and saying, "I know you lost your best friend." No one else expressed any empathy for me. Our pastor paid a pastoral visit to our family. At one point, someone mentioned something about Johnny. I went to my room and cried. Mom told the pastor that I was very upset about Johnny dying. The pastor never came to me.

In those days, I concluded that it was best to keep my emotions to myself. I got a clear but unspoken message that this was not safe to discuss with anyone. In my adult life, I have occasionally happened to meet up with a high school classmate. If I even quite casually mentioned Johnny and his death, my classmate would change the subject. So often, death, especially the death of someone we knew well, is not a subject for polite company.

Now about that pastor who came to our family for a pastoral visit. He visited with us, he read some scripture, and he prayed. He said nothing about Johnny. But please do not misunderstand. I always thought highly of him. He just wasn't prepared to minister to a grieving teenager. Yet he did. In keeping my emotions to myself, I kept them from myself for many long years. The day he came to our home, I needed to let out a lot more grief. His presence resulted in my doing just that. So simply by being with us, he did minister to me.

When Jan died, many people came and expressed their condolences. Some gave me a hug. People often remark that they don't know what to say to someone who has lost a loved one. Just say, "I'm so sorry about your loss." It will mean so much! Those going through loss may not know how to respond. "Thank you" is very adequate.

There are several things a grieving person does not need to hear. He is not ready to hear someone say, "I understand." Since each person's grief experience is unique, you don't understand, even if you have experienced a similar loss. Unless he asks if anything good can come of this, he is not ready to hear that good will come of this. Even if he is a person of deep biblical faith, be very careful about quoting Romans 8:28. "And we know that for those who love God all things work together for good, for those who are called according to his purpose." Unless he asked if other people do work through grief, he is not ready to hear someone else's success in working through grief. That can easily make him feel that there is something wrong with him. Be careful in asking, "How are you," unless you sincerely want to know and are ready to take the time to listen. Respect his right to share only as much as he feels prepared to share.

One young pastor, in his straightforward manner, came to me and said, "It sucks." Yes, he was so right. It does suck. It sucks down deep into one's guts. Oh, yes. I believe deeply and wholly that Jan is in heaven and is still and will forever continue discovering how great it is. I will mention here that I have remarried. I love my wife, Linda. Yes, and I enjoy her, and life is good, even through 2020. But still, death sucks. In this life, it always will. That young pastor told it like it is.

Doing this writing naturally brings back many memories. So far, they have not stirred up a lot of emotions. But these last few paragraphs did and for several minutes. That was okay. The key to handling grief and working through grief is to accept grief. In the future, there will be incidents that, again, trigger moments of grief. That too will be okay. I will be able to handle it and then go on.

It may seem strange that talking about Johnny's death stirred up more emotions in me than talking about Jan's. Jan was not only my close friend; she was my wife. And her death was much more recent. And so, a fourth step is to realize that emotions are often not rational, at least as far as we can discern. We don't always have to explain them in verbal terms.

Initially triggers will produce great emotions. Over time, these feelings still come up, sometimes more frequently than others, sometimes more substantial than others. But overall, if one does the needed healthy grieving, the grief responses will be less frequent and less intense. One may wonder when that will be. The prayer may be "How long, Oh Lord?" The answer is different for each person as each one has his own emotional makeup.

The good news is that the time does come when one can enjoy life again, enjoy old activities, develop new ones, and move forward. Life will be different, yet it will be good.

During this grief recovery time, it is not wrong to be selfish. One will have times when he wants and needs to be alone. There will also be times when he wants and needs to be with others. It's okay to decline social invitations if you need alone time. It is also good to reach out to others. Some recluse so much that it is an unhealthy attempt to escape facing life without the lost loved one. Some try to spend most of their time with people to avoid thoughts of the loved one and the grief emotions. Each one needs to find his own unique healthy balance.

It is also not difficult to use being busy to suppress the emotions of loss and grief. Some caregivers get all wrapped in the medical, physical, financial, and legal care of their loved one and do that as a way of suppressing the emotions they go through in caring for their dying loved one. After the death of the loved one, some will put all their time and energy into funeral and burial preparations and the many financial and legal matters that go with the death of a loved one.

These things are essential and need to be addressed. However, it is possible to use these matters to avoid one's emotional needs. That can have significant consequences on one's mental and emotional health. Not attending to one's personal needs can make it more challenging to pay attention to these other matters.

Personal Emotional Support

Any advice given to caregivers and anyone seeking to be of service to others will include the admonition to take good care of oneself. Anyone who fails to do this will deteriorate to the point of not being able to be of service to anyone else. The classic illustration of this is a passenger in an airplane with a baby. If the oxygen masks drop down, the caregiver needs to put the mask on himself first and then on the baby. The logic, of course, is that if the caregiver were to pass out for lack of oxygen, he would be of no help to the baby.

As human beings, no matter how introverted we might be, we are social beings. Everyone needs contact and relationship with other people. There have been many cases of someone kept in social isolation having a mental breakdown. In Genesis 2, God notes that it is not good for a man, a human being, to be alone. So for Adam, God created another human being. In chapters 1, 8, and 9 of Genesis, God commands people to "be fruitful and multiply." This command enables people to have the human contact they need.

It is easy for caregivers to get so wrapped up in their work that they lose contact with almost everyone except the person in their care. As that person's condition declines, his ability to interact can become increasingly limited. Even if that is not the case, a caregiver needs more social interaction.

I had an experience where a close friend cut off all relationships with me. The person said I had not been responsive in some of our contacts and concluded that I was unhappy with our relationship. That could not have been further from the truth. I had always considered that person a very close friend. Fortunately by God's good grace, we were able to talk things out and restored and reconciled our relationship.

As I reflected on this experience, I realized that with my thoughts and emotions about the real possibility of these being Jan's last days, with the extra care that she required and with other concerns, I could come across to, at least, some people as aloof. And I could understand that they might misunderstand that as my feeling negatively toward them. I shared this experience on Facebook and made the following appeal:

> If any of you have that impression, please know that that impression is completely wrong. If you have that impression, please don't draw any conclusions; talk to me, preferably face to face. Above all, do not turn away from me in silence. I think that the silent treatment is about the worst thing someone can do to me.

Caregiving affects one's emotions deeply, often more deeply than the caregiver realizes. That can easily affect how one interacts with others and, again, without the caregiver realizing it. If a caregiver feels that people are withdrawing from him, there is the possibility that they think that it is the caregiver who is withdrawing. These misunderstandings can add to the caregiver's burdens.

God did not design us to go through difficult times alone. He created us to need other people. We need to take care of ourselves in the way God designed us to do. Therefore,

I encourage caregivers to seek out friendships where they can receive understanding and personal support. Reflecting, it has seemed that one of the many benefits I received from my caring for Jan was a deep appreciation for the value of friendships, especially close relationships where one can share very personally and openly.

I developed a deeper appreciation for acts of kindness. Jan's condition declined so that I could no longer take her to church on Sunday mornings. So I stayed home with her and listened to the service on the radio. I even took part at home during the Communion service. I took whatever was available in the kitchen for Jan and me for the bread and wine elements.

Then someone offered to come over and watch Jan while I attended the church service. Going to the worship service meant a lot. I realized that it's just not the same hearing it on the radio. It wasn't only the opportunity to interact with other people. Being there with people around me was very pleasant. There was the relaxation of being able to worship without having to attend to Jan. After the service, I participated in a class that we had been part of for many years. I was given some time to share what was happening with Jan and my care for her.

It occurred to me that one of the benefits I received as a caregiver was a greater appreciation when I received some act of kindness. When Jan was still able to get around, a close friend of hers would occasionally take her out for a walk or root beer float, a favorite treat of Jan's. At the time, I appreciated her doing that. But as my appreciation of acts of kindness grew, I valued what Jan's friend did more than I did when she was doing it. Acts of service came to be very meaningful. Sometimes I would feel almost overwhelmed by such deeds.

I was fortunate to have numerous friends who were very supportive. There were people and groups that I met with regularly, varying from weekly to monthly. Most of them were people I had known for many years. I had active contact with several of them before Jan's dementia became apparent. I was fortunate to have the caregiver support to be able to do this. I found that I needed a lot of this contact. People are different and have different needs. Each caregiver needs to explore his needs, including how much he needs to be in touch with others.

Another resource for me over the years has been Facebook. I know that it has gone in a lot of directions with people expressing their political views. It also has a lot of trivia on it. One can easily waste a lot of time on social media. I first went on Facebook in 2008. By that time, I had been seeing changes in Jan and wondering what they were. Through the decade of having and caring for a wife with dementia, I found it helpful to make postings on Facebook. It was another opportunity to share what was happening in our lives. It gave me a platform to share my thoughts and emotions. I appreciated the responses of people who took the time to read and respond to my writings.

I experienced the value of having friendships before some personal difficulties created the need for friends for sharing. A caregiver has enough to contend with. It is nice to have some good companions already in place.

Members of our family could be quite helpful, notably in practical ways. Jan's two sisters and my daughter, all living nearby, occasionally brought over dinner for us. I was blessed to have so many good cooks in our family. They each indicated that they simply prepared some extra food when cooking for their family. Various family members, from time to time, helped with matters about the upkeep of the house.

Sometimes I was able to get some unusual help. The following e-mail that I sent to my daughters illustrates this.

> Lori, Lisa,
>
> I took Mom clothes shopping tonight and came to some conclusions. So far. I've been able to handle whatever I needed to do for her: transporting, laundry, dishes, cooking (at least plausibly), finances that she used to cover, dressing and bathing her, etc.
>
> But shopping with her for clothes is beyond my pay grade, especially at the Mall, especially on a Friday night. I was able to buy us cinnamon rolls, and that went well.
>
> So, if one or both of you could help out here: in particular, she needs some nice dress flats shoes, preferably that still give some support, and she needs some panties her size. The last ones she got were too small.
>
> Thanks for your help,
> Dad

I trust that you understand that that last clothing item was a bit much for me. One of my daughters did take care of these matters. I was very grateful.

Interesting situations could happen when grandkids came over. One day, my daughter brought over her two little boys. I began playing with them, wrestling as boys like to do. Jan had a Life Alert device around her neck in case she was to fall or otherwise need help. She decided things were getting too rowdy for her. So she pressed the button on her Life Alert device. That resulted in a voice coming from Life Alert over our land phone. The agent asked, "Mrs. Nelson, do you need help?" I had to quickly explain to the Life Alert attendant that everything was fine.

We would get together for birthdays, holidays, and other occasions. Near Jan's last birthday, before her passing, we had a family gathering to celebrate her reaching one more year. We had pizza and carrot cake, that being Jan's favorite cake. By this time, Jan was bedfast and only able to eat pureed food. So I pureed some pizza for her, and as far as I could tell, she enjoyed it. We had birthday candles on her cake. Our young grandchildren helped her blow out the candles. I also pureed some cake for her. It was the best and, undoubtedly, most meaningful birthday party I have ever known.

For one family gathering, Jan wrote a note and put it on the kitchen table. It read, "Message to my family, Keep following Jesus." She especially underlined the word *keep*. Jan had a strong spiritual influence on others, especially her family, throughout her life. I still have that note.

On a couple of occasions, I brought as much family as I could to discuss care for Jan if I should die before she did. I brought up the concern of a possibility of an illness, accident, or death, making me unable to provide any care for Jan. This could be a serious concern if it happened suddenly. My kids had discussed this. They asked me to list their mom's medications. They decided the daughter living nearby would initially care for her. Then they would decide on the need to place her. They explored the possibility of one of them caring for her for an extended time. I suggested a facility Jan and I had visited for some activities. It had the advantage that Jan had some familiarity with that place. These are not the most pleasant matters to discuss with family, but they are undoubtedly high on the list of priority issues.

Family relationships take on special meaning. Bonds did deepen over our shared concern for Jan. However, each one of us had a special family relationship with Jan. She had three siblings; I had two. Then there were grandchildren. Of course, I was the only one who had a marriage relationship with her. There was a sharing with family that could not be duplicated with anyone outside of the family. At the same time, the special relationship each one of us had with Jan made it difficult to share certain things with other family members.

Family dynamics have a lot of variations. Some families are very open and freely share their thoughts and emotions. Other families have a great love for one another but do not readily share deep personal matters. Personality characteristics run in families. Culture and family history also affect how members of families interact. What is happening in the private lives of different people affects what they can handle emotionally. All of these factors and more affect how much families share. Each member of a family must respect the feelings of other members and appreciate how much each member is comfortable in sharing with others.

I found that with family, and much more so with friends, people saw me as an example for handling a caregiver situation. Someone commented that I had shown what it is to give love. I gave this some thought. I decided that it was good to take Jan places and let people see us together. But I wanted to be sure that what they saw was real and not a display. Reflecting on this, I felt comfortable that when I took her to events, and people saw us, it was real. I decided that I could keep it genuine by simply being myself and not giving it any further thought.

Several people commented to me that they didn't think they could do what I was doing. Some added that they could not even bear the thought of having a wife in a condition like Jan's. I suppose that if circumstances were different, and I were to see someone else in my situation, I might have similar thoughts.

Perhaps the best compliment I received was from a waitress at a restaurant where Jan and I had eaten on several occasions. She shared how she and other waitresses were talking about what they had seen in my care of Jan. She said that all of them decided that they hoped they would have a husband who would be willing and able to take care of them like I was caring for Jan.

I decided to look at all this from a biblical perspective. The Apostle Paul was not reserved about setting himself up as an example for others to follow. Note Philippians 3:17; 2 Thessalonians 3:7, 9. These texts might come across as audacious, except they are in inspired Scripture. And there are plenty of passages where Paul takes a very humble view of himself. Paul was open about his weaknesses: Romans 7:14f; 2 Corinthians 12:7f; Philippians 3:10f; 1 Timothy 1:15; 1 Corinthians 15:8. In addition, he also calls on others to be an example: 1 Thessalonians 1:7; 1 Timothy 4:12; Titus 2:7.

Perhaps that is how he understood what Jesus meant when He advised us to let *our* light shine so that people will see *our* good work and give glory to our *Father* (Matthew 5:16 [emphasis mine]). If we can see our good efforts pointing people to God and not to ourselves, our exampling is not self-centered but gives us a humble thankfulness for the privilege of being used by God to lead people to Him.

According to Matthew 5:14, we are an example whether we like it or not. And we are always an example that points beyond ourselves, either to God or to Satan. And apparently, that is the case, whether we recognize it or not.

For years, I sensed this calling and humbling responsibility to be an example to others as a caregiver and in all aspects of life. I received compliments from numerous people about how I modeled in caregiving for Jan. While I appreciated these compliments, I was also often apprehensive about them. I was very aware that there is much about me and what goes on inside me, my thoughts, emotions, and desires about which these people know nothing. And so, it was hard for me not to think, *If they only knew.* I often wanted to share with them what they didn't know.

I was very aware that I could do such sharing with only a very few people. But I sincerely thanked God that there were these few people that were, in this way, safe for me. As for the rest, to share with them would be damaging, not only to me but also to them. To complicate this, it is not just a simple classification of people into two categories: those with whom I can safely share and those with whom I cannot. In between these two extremes are those with whom I can share some things but careful not to share too much. The TMI danger is always present. Yet if I can share up to the TMI boundary without crossing it, it is of significant benefit for both them and me.

I know that I cannot just say whatever I think at any time and with anyone around me. That does put me on the horns of a dilemma. If I don't share with others the Elton they don't know, am I dishonest? Am I presenting to them an Elton that is, to at least some degree, false? So am I thus being a hypocrite? Am I putting on an act? But if I am open and honest, there can be all the results of the previous paragraph.

I have been fascinated by a poem written by Dietrich Bonhoeffer while imprisoned by the Nazis and not long before his execution. This poem can easily be googled on the Internet.

Who Am I?
Dietrich Bonhoeffer

Who am I? They often tell me
I stepped from my cell's confinement
Calmly, cheerfully, firmly,
Like a Squire from his country house.

Who am I? They often tell me
I used to speak to my warders
freely and friendly and clearly,
As though it were mine to command.

Who am I? They also tell me
I bore the days of misfortune
equably, smilingly, proudly,
like one accustomed to win.

Am I then really that which other men
    tell of?
Or am I only what I myself know of
    myself?
Restless and longing and sick, like a bird
    in a cage,
Struggling for breath, as though hands
    were compressing
My throat, yearning for colors, for flow-
    ers, for the voices of birds,
thirsting for words of kindness, for
    neighborliness,

tossing in expectation of great events,
powerlessly trembling for friends at an
    infinite distance,
weary and empty at praying, at thinking,
    at making,
faint, and ready to say farewell to it all.

Who am I? This or the Other?
Am I one person today and tomorrow
    another?
Am I both at once? A hypocrite before
    others,
And before myself a contemptible woe-
    begone weakling?
Or is something within me like a beaten
    army
Fleeing in disorder from victory already
    achieved?

Who am I? They mock me, these lonely
    question of mine,
Whoever I am, Thou Knowest, O God,
    I am thine.

Like Bonhoeffer, I often wonder, struggle over who is the real me, the real Elton. I can wonder, when am I real? Thus sharing the real me can be a challenge, even with someone I could do that with, and it would be safe.

I think the most threatening difficulty I had was the feeling of being put on a pedestal. People would sometimes say that they couldn't do what I was doing. Some would say that they couldn't even bear the thought of having a wife in Jan's condition. I also seemed to get extra credit for taking on this caregiver position as a man. It is generally taken for granted that a woman would be capable of doing this, but it is more unusual for a man. As Jan's condition developed, I never considered whether my gender would affect my capacity to care for her.

I sometimes imagined that the pedestal could develop a smaller diameter at the base than at the top. The bottom would keep getting smaller, and the pedestal would keep getting higher, and even the maneuvering room at the top could get smaller. There would be nothing securing the pedestal. It just sat on the ground. Keeping balance would become increasingly difficult. The pedestal could also get bumped. At some point, I would inevitably fall. But then I considered that it wasn't any people who placed me on that pedestal. God did. He did it as a testing of me. And the Lord knew that at some point, I would fall. In His foreknowledge, He even knew when and how I would fail. And that was all part of His plan. But when I fell, it was because of my wrong choices for which I alone would be responsible and could cast no blame on anyone else or God.

Then the question is, what does a man of God do when he falls? He is to repent before God, apologize to whoever he has offended or hurt, and make amends where he can. And he is to forgive himself, this being the most challenging task. When I am back on my feet, people may, again, put me on a pedestal and of the same structure. It looks like it could happen again and again. Yet somehow, in this process, God will be making me a better and stronger person.

It has been suggested to me that I am guilty of over-thinking. There may well be truth in that analysis. I'm also told that I think differently. I like to respond to that by noting that I went to Cal Berkeley in the '60s and am left-handed. So what would you expect? It is my conviction that most people need to think more deeply than they usually do. So perhaps this is another area where in God's providence, I am, in some way, called to be an example to others.

People say I am more open than I used to be. I used to be a very private person. That was the result of my insecurity rather than a following of the Lord's leading. But to live life is to live with risk. There is risk in being private and risk in being open. James 3:1 says to me that fair or not, whenever I end up being an example/model for others, I "will be judged with greater strictness."

For the Christian, the answer is to live a life of faith. I need to be confident that when I err, either too far in the openness or the privacy direction, the Lord will protect me. He will get me through the valley of the shadow of the consequences of my errors and wrongdoing.

And so, even though I can identify with Bonhoeffer in being mocked by all these questions, I can also follow his example in concluding, "Whoever I am, thou knowest, O God, I am thine!"

I have noted being part of a support group for caregivers of a loved one with dementia. For the most part, we did not know one another except through this group. That gave an extra dimension of safety. As is standard in support groups, the rule was to keep confidentiality about what transpired in the group. So one could share personal matters without concern that it might become a matter for town gossip.

It was comforting to hear that our experiences in caregiving were not unusual. Our thoughts and emotions were familiar to other caregivers. What I was going through was normal. At the same time, we recognized that each one of us had our own unique story. There are wide variations in how dementia is manifested, even with a set of common characteristics. We often noted that when you meet one person with dementia, you have met one person with dementia. No doubt, people reading this book who are caregivers will note in their loved one characteristics similar to Jan's and some that are different.

It was good just to be with others with whom I could identify. We had something very significant in common. It could be particularly beneficial when our loved one reached her last days on earth. We often attended the funeral service when someone's loved one died. It was common for a caregiver to continue to participate in meetings for a while after their loved one died.

Besides the personal emotional support, it was a setting where we could get a lot of helpful information. One of the best resources for help in the practical matters of caring for someone is a series of videos readily available on the Internet, created by a woman named Teepa Snow. She understands dementia in a manner that is very helpful in getting a healthy perspective on the disease. Her website is www.teepasnow.com.

I observed that it was usually easier and more comfortable to share ideas on the practical matters of caregiving than to share the emotions we experienced. That is certainly understandable. The practical matters discussions could be beneficial. They also served to help us express ourselves more comfortably and to be better listeners. That could then help us in sharing the emotions we were having.

One of my three adult children suggested that I have some counseling. I decided to follow through with her suggestion. I arranged for Jan and me to see a counselor I had personally known and trusted for years. I felt it could be helpful for both of us to explore how we could better relate to each other during these days. It would help me accept the loss and grief I was experiencing. It could also help Jan better handle the limitations her condition was placing on her.

Jan was not excited about being involved in counseling sessions. While she had always been a very social person, she was also a very private person about her thoughts and feelings. She was very open with me, but there were things about her that I did not discover until after years into our marriage. I found a simple effective way to get her to go with me to counseling. After our session, I would take her to a nearby donut shop. With her dementia, she developed a sweet tooth, making this reward very effective.

As I bring up throughout this book, caregiving carries with it a myriad of emotions. They include feelings of guilt as I ponder how well I took care of Jan, feelings of loneliness, wanting all this to be over but not wanting Jan to die, etc. As I met with my counselor, I could address these emotions and many more with much more clarity.

One's emotions can vary widely from day to day and sometimes from hour to hour. Sometimes things seem to go well, and I could feel confident that I was handling things all right. Then a situation could come up that was hard to handle. My thoughts could go in different directions from hour to hour. One of the benefits of counseling was to gain enough perspective to help me avoid being on an emotional roller coaster.

To make the sessions as profitable as possible, I would give some thought to what I might want to cover in the next session. Sometimes I would go to a session thinking I didn't have anything too deep to cover. But as we delved into something, I would often discover matters that I had not considered. These things were not always comfortable.

I realized something about counseling. Those things that I was comfortable discussing were generally matters that

I didn't need to bring to a counselor. On the other hand, I might think about something and realize that I didn't want to bring it up with my counselor. Usually that was the very topic that I needed to address in a counseling session. Of course, a capable counselor is skilled at detecting such issues and bringing them to his counselee's attention.

There are three aspects of trust that are important in sharing personal matters with someone else. The first is confidentiality. That is the most common aspect of the term. The second is to be confident that the person I trust will be able to emotionally handle what I say and not be overwhelmed, shocked, or judgmental. The third is to have confidence that the person will not jump to any conclusions about me but will work hard to understand accurately what I am saying. It is difficult to say which of these is the most important.

As important and helpful as friendships and family relationships are, there is still the grief of loss, and there is still the loneliness of the loss. Personal relationships can help one through his grief journey. They do not remove loneliness and grief. I don't think I ever had such quality deep social contacts as I did during those many days and nights before and after Jan's death. Yet I don't think I ever experienced loneliness like I did when she died. I do not begin to imagine what it would have been like without these people. Thank God I did not have to find out.

If anyone could form close relationships, it was Jesus of Nazareth as he lived a very human life for about thirty-three years. He had a special relationship with each of His disciples. The night before His arrest, He came together with them to celebrate the Passover and institute what we know as the Lord's Supper, or Communion. He also wanted to share His deepest thoughts and emotions. He knew that within twenty-four hours, He would be executed. Yet as we read the accounts of that night, we see that the disciples were simply unable to connect with Jesus and what He was facing. They even went so far afield as to get into an argument over which of them was the greatest.

And on the night that He was betrayed, His disciples, His closest friends, were physically present where He was, but none were with Him. They were distant at His last meal before His death. At Gethsemane, He prayed so earnestly that blood dripped out of His forehead. They fell asleep on Him. As He hung on the cross, they completely cut out on Him.

A Spiritual Journey

Sufferings of Christ—a gift we are given.
—Philippians 1:29

A particular form of counseling that is becoming increasingly popular is known as spiritual formation. It is different than most forms of counseling. It might better be understood as a form of coaching, with the counselor referred to as a coach, a spiritual coach.

The goal in these sessions is to look at what one is doing, thinking, and feeling from the perspective of gaining insight into how God is working in one's life. It is to see God working to change and develop a person to be increasingly more of the person God would have him to be. I began to have monthly spiritual formation sessions while caring for Jan. I am still meeting with my counselor/coach as of the writing of this book. These sessions help one to understand being on a spiritual journey.

Scripture often speaks of living one's life as being on a journey. Psalm 23 describes the Lord leading one through trying times to green pastures. In Psalms 119:105, Scripture speaks of guiding us through the life journey. Both Psalms and Proverbs talk about the path of life on several occasions. Jesus tells of the way or path that leads to life and the way that leads to destruction (Matthew 7:13, 14).

To speak of one's life as a spiritual journey is to assert that he is not just living his own life. He is not just living his life in relationships with other people but also in a relationship with the God of the entire universe. He recognizes that God is involved in the direction his life is heading. He looks to see the working of God in the circumstances of his daily life. He doesn't wander. He is on a path.

As we look back on our lives, most people can recognize several phases. Each phase was a journey. And each journey can be seen as a preparation for the next. Finally how we live this life as a preparation for the next.

It has been my experience that when I think I have settled down and know where my life is going, it changes. The road makes a turn, the scene is different, and even the familiar has a whole new aspect. And the rate of change constantly seems to increase. That is not just a matter of getting older. Anyone can look back a few years and recognize how different life is now than it was.

I find that life typically swings back and forth from good times to bad and back again. I find it wise to prepare for the bad times during the good, even when we have no idea what will characterize the bad times. However, it is the nature of human beings not to learn when the going is good. It is usually, if not entirely, in the difficult times that we learn and grow. Our retirement days are also a challenging phase with its particular difficulties. The saying that "old age isn't for sissies" has profound truth.

All this is not to say that one only lives for the future. Today prepares for tomorrow, but today is to be lived. The resolve for Jan to live as fully as possible for as long as possible is an appropriate resolution for everyone. Ideally we live in the present, learning from the past, and preparing for the future.

Many, perhaps most, people do not see their life as a journey that has direction. They may see it as a road without any direction except to the grave. They may not even see themselves on a path. Instead, they are simply wandering around out in the wilderness. To see oneself as on a journey is to see one's life as having goals and purpose. One may not be able to clearly define that purpose. That doesn't matter. It is enough to realize that God has designated a direction.

It is interesting that while she was still able to do so, Jan came to regard Psalm 138 as her favorite chapter of the Bible. The last verse, verse 8, is the key verse. "The Lord will fulfill His purpose for me; Your steadfast love, O Lord, endures forever. Do not forsake the work of Your hands." The Apostle Paul expressed this thought when he wrote, "And I am sure of this that he who began a good work in you will bring it to completion at the day of Jesus Christ" (Philippians 1:6). Jan carried with her, from the Lord, a sense of purpose in her life.

My mother spent the last year of her life lying on a bed in a nursing home, being in little more than a vegetative state. I would wonder why the Lord had not taken her. Yet when she died, I had a sense that there had been a fulfilled purpose in her life. It is not necessary to speculate on the content of that purpose. It suffices to assert that God's creation of each one of us is not incidental. It is intentional. Since God does fulfill His purpose in each person, when he dies, I can know that somehow, God did carry out His purpose. That does not mean we can be arbitrary about people dying. There is a good place for pursuing medical advancement to cure disease and prolong life. However, there often is no need to take extreme measures to keep someone alive. There is a place for hospice, palliative care. War, as terrible as it is, may sometimes be necessary. Murder is wrong.

With this perspective, in particular, I cannot agree with the growing movement of euthanasia. There is a difference between allowing a person to die peacefully and as comfortably as possible rather than actively bringing about the end of a life. As much as we can speak of human involvement and each person's responsibility for how he has treated others, we are to submit to God determining when a person is to live and when he is to die.

I am wise enough not to try to state definitively any particular person's God-given life purpose. I think I can, however, point out some signs of why God kept Jan alive in a minimal state for a long time.

As Jan declined, I came to see that she was more at peace than I was. From a mental health standpoint, she was healthier than me. She was at peace with God while I was wrestling with Him.

Later, as Jan lay in an almost-vegetative state, people who came over would comment about how peaceful she was. They would also say that in the family room, where she lay on a bed, they felt peace. In a world filled with turmoil, she performed a much-needed ministry.

Jan was peaceful because the Lord had her at peace. What the Lord placed in her flowed out from her to others in our home. I sensed that I had, in my marital relationship with Jan during those days, something that few people experience in their marriage. I have difficulty describing exactly what that was. But I think it is true that few people experience the peace of God through their spouse that I could know through Jan. As she was weak, both physically and mentally, God made her strong, spiritually and in ministry.

Some may object that what I observed was merely the result of the state of her demented brain. But not everyone with dementia exhibits the peacefulness that was in Jan. It was a quality seldom seen in those whose bodies and minds are strong and healthy.

During this time, I met with a man who had lost some of his family to death, had family conflicts, property, financial difficulties, was socially isolated, and had other problems. While we had long sessions on all his stresses and losses, he also took an interest in my challenges with Jan. He gave me some good helpful advice. I followed up on his advice and appreciated his help to me.

In this situation, I saw that Jan helped this man get beyond all his problems and to look at the needs of others. So the Lord used someone who was utterly unable to provide any care for herself to minister to someone else.

On another occasion, a friend came to my house. After we had visited for a while, she asked if she could see Jan. I said certainly, and took her to our family room. She talked to Jan for a while (Jan has been unable to say anything for almost a year). While she spoke, Jan looked directly at our friend. Then she prayed for Jan. While she prayed, Jan closed her eyes and kept them closed during her entire prayer (yes, I unapologetically acknowledge that my eyes were open and fixed on Jan). When she finished praying, Jan opened her eyes and looked at her again. What happened? What was going on inside Jan? I can only comment that she touched both this woman and me.

I often thought that the Lord still had Jan on this earth because there was more for me to learn through her being here alive. Was I holding Jan back from being released to heaven? Perhaps the Lord told Jan something like, "I'm all set to bring you to your new eternal home, but that husband of yours has some things to learn first, and he can be a slow learner. So be patient."

And so when the Lord's purpose for Jan was complete, she would die. That purpose involved me and involved others as well. Death can be understood as the time when one's purpose is completed. It could be the purpose of a person or a nation, era, pandemic, etc. On this earth, all things have their ending. In ways far beyond our understanding, God brings about the completion and, therefore, the death of every earthly thing. Someday there will be the death of the earth as we know it (2 Peter 3:7,10).

It is often said that human beings cannot live with meaninglessness. Some life philosophies purport that the solution is to choose a purpose for oneself. How much better it is to have the assurance that the God of the universe has ordained His purpose for me! Going through what I did with Jan was very challenging. At times it tore me up inside. I often prayed, "How long, Oh Lord?" Having the conviction of divine purpose for those days helped tremendously to make them bearable. It was not necessary to have that purpose spelled out.

I expressed this thought in a poem I wrote for my mother's funeral and also read at Jan's funeral. It applied well for each of them. I titled it "The Reason Why."

The Reason Why

Her mind was gone for well over a year.
Why wasn't her end yet here?
But when she died, I cried tear upon tear.
Then somehow after I wept and I cried
I knew why she had not yet died.
Now I can't say in words the reason why,
But we'll understand it better by and by.

And then we'll praise God with a thou-
     sand tongues
For the reason why.

Before a man is executed for a capital offense, there is
a tradition that he receives the last meal of his choosing. He
eats it alone in his cell. I can't imagine how that must be.
Before Jesus's execution, He chose to have a last meal, the
Passover meal, with His disciples. It is even harder to imagine
what that was like for Him. Yes, He was with the company of
His choosing, but they were not with Him. They had no clue
what He was going through.

Then He took them out to the Garden of Gethsemane
and urged them to pray with Him. He prayed His heart out.
He was so intense that blood dripped from His forehead; His
clueless disciples fell asleep. His warnings about what was
about to happen sailed over their heads.

But suppose they did grasp that He was facing a tortu-
ous execution. He was the one about to die. The cross only
held one person. No one could go there with Him. He knew
and confronted that. He separated Himself a short distance
before beginning to pray.

He knew and, for a long time, had been talking about
the fact that He was going to die an excruciating death. But
then, reality hit. He did not want to die. He had been willing
to die. And then, time's up. Was He still willing? Could He
accept what His Father had called Him to do? After three
prayer sessions like no one has ever prayed before or since,
He was ready. He accepted that He was going to die.

The Romans designed crucifixion to be as torturous
as possible. And His was no ordinary crucifixion. It was a
crucifixion that took on the burden of all the wrong of all
humanity. But even more torturous for Jesus was His time

at Gethsemane. Once He fully accepted what was ahead, He was prepared. He could go forward.

I knew but had to face the truth. Jan was going to die. I do not, for a moment, compare what I experienced to that of Jesus Christ. But I do think my experience helped me get a slight grasp of His. I did discuss what was happening with other people. They could listen better than the disciples. But I too, as does anyone facing a situation like mine, had to, in the end, face it alone.

As I was with Jan and watched her decline, every day was a reminder of where she was going. While I grieved all the losses of her, I also learned to paraphrase Philippians 4:11 to say, "In whatever state my wife was in to be content." That was by no means easy, and I did it far from perfect. I would never say that I liked it, not even for a moment. I grew tired and weary of it.

I did and always did enjoy Jan. To understand that, it is necessary to make a distinction between joy and happiness. The book of Philippians has been called an epistle of joy. It is not called an epistle of happiness. The difference is that happiness is dependent on circumstances. I am happy if my team wins, if my boss and wife (two different people) don't give me any trouble, when I don't have to wear a mask, etc. If I have joy, I have it even if my team loses, I'm in trouble with my boss and wife, and I must wear a mask. In other words, joy does not depend on circumstances. Joy comes from the Lord. Happiness comes from our surroundings and our body that surrounds our being. So Paul, doing time, could talk about rejoicing. And so, I enjoyed Jan. I enjoyed being with her. I enjoyed taking her places. The last decade of her life was a precious time.

I have seen the following saying from more than one source, "Anxiety lives in the gap between what you have and what you fear. Irritation lives in the gap between what you have and what you want."

Yes, I experienced anxiety, an uneasiness about what life would be like when Jan was gone. Yes, I could get irritated with some of Jan's behavior and numerous things I had to do in my care of her. But I did manage to stop at various times to consider what I had. I realized that, through all this, the Lord was good to me. And that significantly helped shorten those gaps.

In James 1:2, we are told to, "Count it all joy, my brothers, when you meet trials of various kinds." James goes on to list the benefits of what he calls tests. He is writing to a people going through persecution for their faith. Then in James 1:14, he notes that "each person is tempted when he is lured and enticed by his own desire." Then he goes on to discuss the dynamics of temptation.

Interestingly, the word translated "trials," in verse 2, is translated "temptations" in verse 14, namely the Greek word *peirazo*. James is saying that in our journey, a given difficult situation can have two possibilities. It could be a temptation from Satan to bring us down if we give in to it. Or it could be a test from God to build us up as we accept it that way. We have a choice. We determine which it will be.

Thus I could respond to Jan's condition by giving in to the temptation to be angry, resentful, depressed, or other emotional reactions. Or I could accept it as a test from God to help me grow in my trust in Him and my relationship with Him. It is easy to vacillate between these two perspectives. In verses 5 through 8, James advises us to be wise and consistent in our decisions. I cannot say that I always kept a better perspective. But I found the Holy Spirit bringing me to face these choices. Seeing these choices as tests from God on my journey was very helpful in getting me through the most trying times.

Sometimes God's blessings are challenging to recognize. They may come as trials. Then we only recognize them as temptations or unpleasant situations. It can be profitable to see such times as God working for good.

As Jan's ability to articulate in an ordinary matter declined, I occasionally mused on the thought of the Lord giving her a temporary healing so I could, at least once again, have a normal conversation with her, as we had in days long past. That was not an unrealistic thought. When Dad died, Mom's dementia was well along, so a normal conversation with her was not possible. But when I approached her to tell her of Dad's passing, I could see, even before saying anything to her, that her mind was in a normal state. She maintained that mental state for an entire week. The staff at the nursing home where she resided corroborated that her thinking was good all through the week. She talked about Dad with them and me, and she grieved very appropriately. At the funeral, she greeted people she had not seen for years so that they could not see any dementia in her. Then the day after the funeral, her mind reverted to its former state. Soon she was in a noncommunicative and almost-vegetative state until she died a year later.

I was amazed that this happened. Knowing the state of her brain, it didn't seem possible. The staff at the nursing home said they didn't have an explanation any more than I did.

I wondered how I would have responded if Jan had a similar temporary healing. The first natural thought would be that it would be wonderful to have at least one last chance to be with the Jan I had known for three decades. Would that make it easier or harder for me when she died? With her mind essentially gone, I could rejoice that she would be in a new state in heaven. If she had a sound mind, it could be much harder to let her go. Perhaps I didn't want my wife back until the next life. Which would have been better? I'm not sure.

I have had contact with some people who had a loved one with cancer. Sometimes the cancer went into remission for a little while, only to then return. That could happen several times. It can be very stressful.

Mom's temporary normalcy was mystifying but not hard to accept when it was gone. I have wondered why. Perhaps it was because I had completed saying goodbye to Mom but wasn't ready to say goodbye to Jan. Mom was ninety when she died. Jan was seventy-seven and in the ballpark of my age. I expected Mom to die well before I did. I did not expect that of Jan.

I remember, in college, struggling with the concept of surrendering to God's will. It gave me a picture of God as being like a drill sergeant whose orders I was to obey instantly and without questioning. Now often, like in this matter, surrender to God means letting Him decide these matters that I am not qualified to decide, knowing that His "decision" (not theologizing on whether God makes decisions) is always better than mine. In matters far too complex for me, there is great comfort in the assurance that there is One who knows, can, and does carry out what is best.

As I continued developing my care for Jan, I found that the Sunday morning church worship services became more emotional for me. I often pondered this. Feelings were permeating much more of my whole life. So that itself made experiencing worship more emotional. I could also tell that having Jan with me made a difference. It was apparent that the only part of the service that Jan could connect with was the old gospel songs and classic hymns sung with the traditional melody. Worshipping with her in these moments was very meaningful and gave me precious memories. I found those times deep and stirring.

I came to find songs that expressed God's love and care for me to be very stirring, sometimes almost overwhelming. I also responded to songs about how we so totally need and can trust God. A favorite song for me was "It Is Well with My Soul." These songs meant a lot to me in other settings when Jan was not at my side. I appreciated songs about the nature of God (e.g., "How Great Is Our God," "Holy, Holy, Holy") but was not as stirred by them.

At times during the church music worship, I would become quite emotional, but it wasn't over Jan and her impending death. It was hard to define, but it did seem to have to do with the Lord's and my relationship. I had a strong sense that that is where it needed to go.

As I delved into the Scriptures, I was struck by how much emotion I saw in them. The Gospels often speak of Christ's emotions. A study of the words used reveals that His feelings were powerful. In his letters to various churches, the Apostle Paul often speaks of his deep love for the people of that church. Psalms, the hymnbook of the Hebrew people, is a book of a special kind of poetry. It is rich in imagery. Deep emotions of many types run throughout the Psalms. There are expressions of great gladness, wonder, sadness, anger, and many other emotions. Seeing this opened the Scriptures to me in a new way.

I was fortunate to have a good sense of closeness to God during these days. There was a period in my past where I was on an arduous journey and believed in God, but He seemed far away. On another journey, I sensed an assurance of His presence but did not have a good sense of His leading me forward. The future felt uncertain, uncomfortable. As difficult as these days were, I sensed God present and guiding me to what was ahead.

Never before had I so deeply poured out my heart so profusely to God in prayer. I did experience the Lord giving me just enough strength to go on. He did answer prayer. The promise in 1 Corinthians 10:13 that God will not give us more than we can take can quickly become a cliché in Christian circles. But I did find it to be true for me, although it was not unusual for me to feel that He was taking me right up to the border.

I thought of this journey as having three types of trails:

- Trail 1: I would mourn Jan's impending death. It was the last thing I wanted to happen. The thought of it brought me grief. Each new disability was a step closer to her grave.
- Trail 2: I wanted her dementia, Parkinson's, etc. to be over. But that implied that I wanted her to die as that was the only realistic way for her incurable disease to end. That brought feelings of guilt, even though wanting her illness to end didn't mean I wanted her to die. But I had to acknowledge that I got thoughts of how it would be nice to have a wife I could interact with adult to adult, and I knew that such prospects were out there.

  It was common for these two trails to merge into one trail. I walked both trails at the same time. That could make my thoughts and emotions very confusing and hard to handle.
- Trail 3: I saw this as a trial that the Lord has given me for a purpose that I cannot yet define.

But sometimes I feel like Isaiah in his call in Isaiah 6. At first, he is excited about his call, but then the Lord explains that he will not be a "successful" prophet. People are not going to change after hearing him. At that point, he asks the Lord how long he will have to do this. The Lord says to keep on doing it (I take the liberty of doing a lot of paraphrasing in this text).

Likewise, I had a sense of call to serve Jan and that in doing so, I am serving God. Thus I am rising to a challenge (trail 3). But I don't want this challenge just to drag on and on (trail 2). But in the end, she dies, and I do not have success (trail 1).

I know that success and failure need to be redefined. I know I have no right to the world's definition of success where the client is cured. I know that if I am faithful to what God has called me, I am successful. But success in being faithful is hard to embrace, much less to embrace with any sense of thanksgiving.

Sufferings of Christ

As I traveled on this journey, I came across and pondered what the Apostle Paul meant when he talked about taking part in the sufferings of Christ. I considered if what I was experiencing would constitute a participation in the sufferings of Christ. At least three times in Paul's letters, he speaks of this. We find the first one in Romans 8:16, 17, "The Spirit himself bears witness with our spirit that we are children of God, and if children, then heirs—heirs of God and fellow heirs with Christ, provided we suffer with him in order that we may also be glorified with him."

Here Paul notes that if we suffer as Christ suffered, it gives an assurance of salvation. How did Christ suffer? He didn't just endure suffering, he suffered for others. There is a difference. Which it is can be a matter of one's perspective. Being married to Jan those years, I could have just looked at what I was going through, i.e., just seeing myself as having a hard time.

But when Jesus saw people sick, hungry, or being like lost sheep, He felt for them, had compassion for them, wept for them, i.e., suffered for them. He grieved over their sin. It was hard caring for Jan because I cared for her; I loved her.

When it is painful for us to see the hardships of others, we are participating in the sufferings of Christ. When we are willing to give ourselves, to sacrifice ourselves, we suffer as Christ suffered. If we suffer for others, as Christ suffered for others, that offers an assurance that we are with Christ, i.e., an assurance of salvation.

Second, Philippians 3:10 states, "That I may know him and the power of his resurrection, and may share his sufferings, becoming like him in his death."

It was Paul's goal, and the goal of every Christian, to be the kind of person that Jesus showed Himself to be when He lived on earth. How do we become more like Christ? In particular, we do so by being a man for others as Christ was. By caring for others. By suffering for others. When we do this, we feel what Christ felt. In doing that, we come closer to Him.

Paul had been on a very long and arduous journey when he wrote the letter to the Philippians. He was in prison while writing this letter. It wasn't his first time behind bars. And he had been through many other difficult times. If there was anyone of high spirituality, it was the Apostle Paul. Yet as we continue reading in Philippians, we see that Paul considered himself to have still a long way to go to be all he hoped to be in Christ.

It's not an easy path. Jesus describes it as "taking up a cross." He advises us to "count the cost" of following Him in the direction He sets out for us (Luke 14:25–33).

On top of all the challenges and difficulties Jesus had in His earthly ministry, there is evidence that He took time to care for Mary, His mother on this earth. Even on the cross, He took time to see that there was someone to provide for her when He would no longer be doing this (John 19:25–27). By comparison, those days of my care for Jan do not seem to have been nearly so draining.

Finally, Colossians 1:24 states, "Now I rejoice in my sufferings for your sake, and in my flesh, I am filling up what is lacking in Christ's afflictions for the sake of his body, that is, the church."

Christ showed the greatest possible love by suffering and dying for us. No other penalty had to be paid for our salvation. The book of Hebrews states emphatically that no additional punishment or sacrifice had to be paid as the penalty for our sin (Hebrews 7:27, 9:12, 9:26, 10:10).

However, something was lacking in His suffering on the cross. People worldwide and through all the ages needed to see the sufferings of Christ for themselves. How can that happen today, some twenty centuries after the crucifixion? God calls the followers of Christ to live as a personal picture of the self-sacrificing love of Christ for others. In doing this, we "fill up what is lacking in Christ's afflictions." People see in us what Christ has done for them.

When they see us suffering for another, they see Christ's suffering, even if that is not what they recognize. Not realizing what they are observing, they are still impacted by what they see. So in what I went through in caring for Jan, as she was on her journey to death and the next life, people had an opportunity to see in me something of the suffering love of Christ for them. It was much more than being an example of how a husband might love and care for his wife with her dementia.

God Is a Tough Coach

As I continued on my journey, I came to see the Lord in a new way. I don't know if it is original, but I have not come across anyone else give this description of Him. The Bible has numerous pictures of God, such as Lord, Creator, King, Shepherd, etc. This image of God that I encountered is not in Scripture, but I think it fits with the picture the Bible gives of God. It is the image of a tough but loving coach. There are certainly sports references in the Scripture, particularly in the Pauline literature—e.g., 1 Corinthians 9:24; 1 Timothy 6:12; 2 Timothy 4:7; and Hebrews 12:1.

Think of a coach putting his athletes through hard workouts. Such a coach is also quick to point out mistakes his athletes make. It is not unusual for a coach to have his athletes repeat the same drill numerous times until finally, they can do it well. Some athletes will feel that the coach wants to be mean with his workouts and corrections. They may become angry at the coach and want nothing to do with him. But other players recognize that the coach does this to try to improve his athletes so that they can perform better.

With the Lord, these drills are referred to in Scripture as trials or as tests. In Scripture, sometimes the goal of these trials is spelled out, as in James 1:3, 4. In Romans 5:3–5, Paul calls trials sufferings, and the results of going through the sufferings are listed.

A. W. Tozer is often quoted saying, "It is doubtful whether God can bless a man greatly until He has hurt him deeply." It would be nice if the Lord would teach and develop us in a more pleasant manner. One concept of heaven is that we continually make new, pleasurable, and exciting discoveries in delightful settings. But we're not living in heaven. We live in a sinful fallen world. And we are such ourselves.

The Lord has pointed out to me that He would be pleased to teach and grow me in pleasant circumstances, but I don't learn in those environments. Like the athlete, I must go through rough times to learn and grow. And like the athlete, I can easily have to go through those times repeatedly. But like the athlete under the coach's discipline, I can see where his regimen produce positive results.

I can compare my life to going to the gym, getting used to lifting a certain weight, only to have the weight increased and having to adapt to the extra weight, etc. In the gym analogy, improvement happens as long as I keep lifting heavier weights. Enduring increasing hardship may result in growth, but sometimes it is not so simple. Sometimes I have to struggle to see what the Lord is doing.

These were perhaps the most difficult days of my life but also the most meaningful and fulfilling. I constantly faced temptations, unpleasant tasks, difficult decisions, a sense of guilt even when it was clear to me that I had done nothing wrong, unfair treatment, being misunderstood, mixed emotions, deep emotions of grief, loneliness even when closely connected to others, and above all, death, especially the death of someone who has had such a tremendous impact on my life. The Lord would not lead me over, under, or around the valley of the shadow of death, but only through it (Note Psalm 23:4).

He gave me a conviction that all this, and much more, was not by accident or misfortune. His hand was in all these things. And He is using all these things to change me and use me as He determined. Some of these things I am privileged to recognize and appreciate. I am unaware of other things God is doing, could not even think of, but trust that they are happening. That is what makes the otherwise unbearable "workouts" bearable and even desirable.

I composed a paraphrase of Psalm 23, using the coach imagery in place of David's shepherd imagery:

The Lord is my coach—I will not stop training. (v. 1)
He settles me down. He keeps me focused. (v. 2)
He brings me back to my first love of the game. (v. 3)
He keeps me doing the right drills.
I do them for him.
Even though his workouts are killing me, I'm not afraid that I can't do them, for you are with me; your toughness and your love comfort me. (v. 4)
You keep me calm when the other team's players look like giants.
You chose me for my position.
I will be victorious. (v. 5)
It's a done deal. I will always be a champion, and I will always be with my coach. (v. 6)

In building the muscles of our body, whether for weight lifting or aerobic exercise, such as running, cycling, or swimming, it is a continual breaking down of muscle tissue, and then it grows back bigger and stronger. God works with us using a breaking down and building-up process as well. Scripture uses the imagery of a potter breaking up the pot he appears to be creating to make it a new and better pot (Jeremiah 18).

All marriages, even the best, are a union of two broken people. We all have a defective nature that goes back to the time of the origin of humanity. Two flawed people are going to have an imperfect marriage. The marriage may be good, but it is still defective. Such was our marriage. The Lord saw to break Jan down daily with her disease. In my care for her were many breakdowns. Out of that, the Divine Potter broke down our marriage to make it something new. And so, to paraphrase Tozer, it is doubtful that God can use a marriage greatly until He has hurt (broken) it deeply.

We may also perceive God as an instructor/teacher. We are living on a school called earth, and the lessons are called life. The course of study lasts a lifetime. Death is the graduation. He doesn't just give lectures/information. He does do that through the Scriptures and the Holy Spirit. However, He also provides challenging assignments. Often the student learns more and does his deeper pondering through these assignments. A student grasps math, physics, and chemistry by solving problems. He takes in English, history, and philosophy by writing essays. One learns the skills of a trade by doing those skills over and over. In my care for Jan, I learned about emotions and handling them, relationships and relationship skills, and many other lessons.

That is not to de-emphasize the reading and study of Scripture or of preaching and teaching. It is an amplification of James 1:22–27 on being a doer of and not just a hearer/reader of the Word.

Throughout this spiritual journey of caring for Jan, experiencing God as a tough loving coach and teacher, the challenges of ordinary life continued. Someone got into my checking account. I had to close it, open a new account, and notify several businesses where I made payments by automatic withdrawal. I had a fender bender car accident. Jan was with me. Fortunately no one was hurt. However, with the way cars are today, there was enough damage to total the vehicle. I had the usual insurance hassles. There was the routine upkeep of home repairs. I also had solar panels put on the house.

By the six months before her death, I had developed several health issues. I could make a case for being as healthy as most men twenty years younger than me, but I had to address three significant issues. I was diagnosed with prostate cancer, glaucoma, and needing cataract surgery. The last two had to be addressed to prevent blindness. The cancer was still in the first stage but had to be stopped before it metastasized. Just for good measure, I was on a three-year cycle for a colonoscopy, had problems with grinding my teeth, and had a wart on my right foot.

I needed cataract surgery to pass the eye exam for my driver's license renewal. With the ophthalmologist's schedule, it wasn't clear if that would be possible before my renewal deadline. By the grace of God, it was all taken care of just days before that date.

Until about a year before Jan's passing, I had not been on any medications. I must admit that I had a certain amount of pride in that. It is good but not pleasant to be humbled. Age catches up with all of us. And when things happen to us, they don't take our circumstances into any consideration.

John Piper is known for his advice, "Don't waste your cancer." He speaks from personal experience, having had cancer treatment. With this advice, he encourages us to take whatever adversity we encounter, whatever rough road we find ourselves on, and put that adversity to good use. The good use is to understand that part of our journey as a particular time to see God working in and around us.

Perspective on Injustice

When things don't go the way a child thinks they should, he will often complain, "No fair." Very small children have an innate sense of fairness or justice. That sense stays with us throughout our entire life. Life should be fair for everyone. Our judicial system is based on that concept. It did not seem fair that my wife should get a terminal disease while other husbands have a wife who outlives them and does so in sound mind and relatively healthy body.

We commonly think of injustice as someone getting something they didn't deserve. This can be either getting a hardship or a benefit that was undeserved. Regarding the former, we consider it unfair if something bad happens to a good person. Few would deny that the crucifixion of Christ was the ultimate act of unfairness. The only truly good person who ever lived on earth suffered the cruelest execution ever invented. Regarding the latter, as Christians, we understand that we deserve utter damnation but instead are given total salvation. Every Christian has been given the most unjust benefit possible that was made possible by the greatest injustice possible.

According to Scripture, all injustice, pain, suffering, and death is the result of sin. In Genesis 2, before wrong choices and wrong actions had occurred, there was no injustice, pain, or suffering. Life was good. But then came Genesis 3, and everything changed. The first humans were presented with the opportunity to know and experience what they had never experienced before. They got their wish and got more than they bargained for.

And so, with all of us. We make choices we later wish we had not made. We come to know and experience things we wish we had never known or experienced. Whether we realize it or not, our words and deeds affect others, people who did not deserve to be part of the results of our actions. So we are all participants in the injustices that comes to people. We don't see all the consequences of our actions. We like to think what we did wasn't serious because we didn't hurt anyone. That only adds to the injustice we instigated.

Experiencing injustice, pain, and suffering can easily give us a very negative attitude. A common reaction to that experience is to act negatively to other people. This includes people who don't deserve to be treated the way we treat them. Again we contribute to the injustice present in the world.

Our perception of injustice is furthered by the fact that all of us are on a different path or life and spiritual journey. Two golfers each play on a different course. One gets a better score than the other. But the one with the better score played on a less-difficult course. Is there injustice? The golfer on the more difficult course may not score as well, but the challenges he faces may, in the long run, make him the better golfer.

The book of Job gives us the insight that there can be events happening in realms unseen by us. Were we aware of them, they would give us a different perspective on the question of injustice. Likewise, there are many influences on events around us of which we have no awareness. With all these factors and more, we are able to have a very limited access to what is just and what is unjust.

God often works through unjust circumstances to bring about His design for someone and to prepare that person for what He has designed. I often think of the story of Joseph. His father had him have oversight over his brothers (Genesis 37:2, 13–14). That gave him supervision experience. The brothers sold him to slave traders. That brought him to Egypt where God wanted him to be. He was sold to Potiphar, who placed him in charge over his farm operation and his servants. That gave him experience in farming and in running an agricultural program. Potiphar's wife framed him, and he was put in pharaoh's personal prison. The chief jailer put him in charge over those prisoners. That gave him more administrative and leadership experience and brought him to where he would be in contact with the pharaoh. Joseph had had a lot of experience with dreams and was prepared for interpreting the pharaoh's dreams. When pharaoh gave him his promotion, he would have been resented as a Hebrew for being in a position over the Egyptians. But he had been trained to handle that. He had been over his brothers. He had been a slave over other slaves. He had been an inmate over other inmates. God had used all these circumstances to get Joseph where He wanted him and also used them to prepare him for that position.

Could God have accomplished His will without putting Joseph through all this? Yes, but God shows how great He is. He can and does use evil for good (Genesis 50:20).

So the wise alternative is to recognize and accept what Jan asserted when she said that bad things happen to good people and to Christians, as well as to bad people and non-Christians.

I have mentioned that John Piper is known for his sage advice, "Don't waste your cancer." He went through a personal bout with prostate cancer. He uses the word *cancer* to represent any form of hardship, suffering, or injustice. His advice for us is to see our journey through such times as coming from God and designed by Him. God has a plan for that journey that is to our benefit. It is meant to teach us, to grow us, and to bring us more completely to where He wants us. Our failure to recognize and accept such a journey in that way is a waste of one's cancer. So don't waste your cancer.

Doubt

When the going gets rough, even those with solid faith may struggle. Questions arise about why this is happening, how it happened, how long, how much worse it might get, and where is God. Even with solid belief maintained, God may seem far away. In Scripture, John the Baptist, after proclaiming Jesus as the Lamb of God, came to wonder if that was true (Matthew 11:2, 3).

Going through Jan's condition did not lead me to doubt if I still believed, but it led me to think more deeply about it. If belief contains the quality of trust, what actually was my faith? I found that there was a choice I had to make. The struggle was to see that my most difficult struggle was not with my responsibilities for Jan. Ephesians 6:12 spells this out very clearly. My most significant and most crucial challenge was to keep in perspective that my real struggle was a spiritual one. Perspective is important. How will I see my situation, and will I maintain that perspective?

There are times when God does not seem to be present. It may be helpful to think about a farmer planting seed for a crop. Sometimes it may be several weeks before any plants come up from that seed. It looks like nothing is happening. But the farmer believes that under the top of the soil, a lot is happening (cf. Mark 4:26–29).

It does not happen that the farmer wakes up one day and sees his field covered with full-grown plants and with

131

vegetables ready to be harvested. Nor do all the plants come up at the same time. It takes time before the farmer can see that there will be a harvest. Couldn't God do it differently? Couldn't He speed things up and bring a harvest with less hassle? He heals all kinds of diseases. What's His problem with healing dementia?

Children, especially teenagers, often wonder why their parents do things the way they do. Parents try to explain, but sometimes their children are not ready to hear the explanations. And we are children of God.

When going through rough times, we choose our attitude toward God. That is especially true when we are in a situation not of our making. Jan's dementia was a prime example. Nothing she or I did or did not do caused her condition (we'll skip over whether God brought about the circumstance or if He allowed it to happen). The book of Job illustrates that there can be factors, especially in the spiritual realm, of which we have no awareness.

One choice is to be angry at God for allowing this circumstance. We can blame God because He could have prevented it. We might conclude He is not a good/loving God. Or we can decide that He is more like the pagan gods that are not good and must be appeased. Generally, in modern society, we do not try to appease an angry god. We reject Him; we might even deny He exists.

What is the result of this choice? You're on your own. Other people can be supportive; they might be able to be of some help. But what of those circumstances beyond human control, such as Jan's dementia? No one can remove the loss and grief that I had. With all the personal support that people can give and as helpful as it might be, I face much of my situation alone.

The classic question for a person with this stance is, "How is that working for you." Your circumstances have no positive value. The best that can happen is that they end. A lot of bad situations might end. Financial loss, illness, and physical injury might heal. A conflicted relationship might be restored, etc. But there is no getting over death.

So the end of this stance is to be bitter. And living a life of bitterness is a miserable life. This attitude permeates the rest of one's life. It negatively impacts our relationships, our focus on our work and other responsibilities, our ability to enjoy recreation, entertainment, or anything else.

Our other choice is to turn to God for all that He offers us. After a funeral, everyone else typically goes on with their lives. You are left alone and lonely. But the Lord is always there for you. He offers His peace—peace that is not dependent on circumstances. He provides His strength when we are too weak to go on ourselves. He gives His love when we feel lonely because even our closest friends cannot travel with us.

He gives the assurance that your circumstance is not meaningless. We can define our meaning to it as existentialists often do. But just because I make up a purpose does not give it meaning. Who am I to decide the purpose of anything? But God, who is always in control over everything, has a purpose for everything, and the objective is good if we love God (Romans 8:28). But if we are bitter because we reject God, we will see adverse circumstances as having no purpose. Believing, we can see the negative circumstance as a setting in which God develops us. We can see them as trials. God is so great that He can use even the worst situations for good.

Unfavorable circumstances are an opportunity to "let your light shine" (Matthew 5:16). They give you an excellent setting to be an example. Negative circumstances are often an opportunity for ministry, even if it is not a very glorious ministry. They may be what God uses to put us on a spiritual journey to the lifestyle, setting, and ministry of His calling. I have discussed how God used a series of adverse circumstances to take Joseph, in Genesis, to the place He had planned for him. The circumstances trained and prepared him for his great promotion. They moved him to the position God had for him.

Choosing to trust God doesn't itself prove God's existence or anything about God. Yet choosing to be bitter to God is to acknowledge His existence (how does one be bitter toward what doesn't exist?). Choosing to trust God is not just positive thinking because trusting God is to surrender the circumstances to God. As often as not, He has a different result than what I had in mind (Isaiah 55:8, 9). In trusting God, it is legitimate to make plans and accept that the Lord may change them because He has a better plan (James 4:13–17; Proverbs 5:21). All this makes trusting God interesting, it can seem frightening, but we are trusting a good God.

I realize that you can certainly raise questions about attitude being a choice. It needs to be made clear that attitudes are not the same as feelings. Feelings simply are. They are neither right nor wrong. Attitudes are a choice, even when we don't realize we are making a choice. There are good and bad attitudes. We are accountable for them.

If you have a particular attitude, modifying, much less changing it, can be a difficult challenge. I suggest that deciding to have a different perspective is the first step. It is wise to be aware of your attitudes. It is easy to have a particular mindset and not realize it. After becoming aware of your attitude in a specific matter, there is the option to ask yourself some questions. Is my attitude valid considering the circumstances? That is not just to ask if it is understandable but to ask if it is accurate. What effect is this attitude having on me and others? Do I want to have this attitude? Does my attitude please God? It will probably be uncomfortable but helpful to ask the Lord and ask others about what they see in your attitude. But it is worth doing.

It is difficult, at best, to change your attitude on your own. You will most likely need help. So call on God the Holy Spirit to bring it to your consciousness whenever you fall into that attitude. And ask other people you trust to bring it to your attention when they see you with that unhealthy attitude.

Even when we get our attitude straight, there certainly can still be questions. A prominent one is to ask why God doesn't cure someone with dementia. He is God. He certainly could. No doubt one can raise many more questions. It is not wrong to do so. The question for us is what we do with these questions. We can let them lead us back into doubt. If we honestly grapple with our questions, they will deepen our faith. They will cause us to think more deeply, and that will lead us to know God more fully. In grappling with our questions, we are dialoguing with God. Scripture calls us to love God completely, and that includes fully with our mind (Matthew 22:37). For those we love, we ask questions of them to know them more fully. We can do the same with God.

As we do this, we come to recognize that there are limits to what we can know. Acknowledging and accepting those limits helps us live life with greater contentment and, therefore, more fully. Psalm 131 expresses this thought well.

Despite everything, we may still have doubts. One of the best pieces of advice I received in college was to doubt your doubts. You most likely will find that your belief is firmer than you thought it was. At this point, I identify with the father, in Mark 9, who brought his son to Jesus, desperate for his son to be healed. When Jesus questioned his belief, he said, "I believe. Help my unbelief" (Mark 9:24). I love that prayer.

Caregiving: What It Is and Does for the Caregiver

I have heard it said that being a caregiver for someone is emotionally harder than being the one with a disease or disability. From my observations and personal experience, I would assert that this is true. There is a lot of emotional wear on a caregiver. An Internet search will turn up data showing that a significant number of caregivers die before their loved ones.

In an earlier chapter, I discussed changes I observed in Jan. In all those changes, I needed to take increasing responsibility for her. For most of our marriage, she wrote checks for our bills. Then I recorded them in Quicken. She gathered the information for our taxes. I took them to our accountant. She took care of her car and I of mine. Over time I took over all these responsibilities and much more. And over time, I took over personal care of her. I took care of her being cleaned, clothed, fed, etc.

Much harder was my having to take responsibility for decisions that we had always made together. Money management, getting a new vehicle, medical determinations, arranging home repairs, when and where we might go out, and many other matters were increasingly up to me to decide. I certainly made decisions with significant consideration of her but without any involving her.

It was not unusual that I would need to make a plan that she did not agree with or like. When it came time to get a new car, her main interest was color. I had several other things to consider, and color was not a high priority. I had to face the reality that she no longer could make sound decisions. As we would say in the support group, I had to recognize who had the bigger brain. She reached a state where it was not possible to reason with her. Sometimes I simply had to decide to do something she didn't like. I knew I was making the right decisions, but it was hard to go against her preference. Later when I had obtained some caregiver help, I told the caregiver that I trusted her judgment over Jan's. If she found that she had to contradict Jan, that was okay.

There is a lot of mundane work for any caregiver. It was reassuring to read Matthew 25:31–46. Jesus talks about feeding the hungry, giving drink to the thirsty, clothing people who had none, and caring for the sick. Caring for a loved one with the disease of dementia, we do all these things. He mentions inviting in a stranger. Our loved one may change so much that she feels, to us, like a stranger. He speaks of going to the one in prison. Our loved one is confined to the limitations of her mind and body. He asserts that we are doing them to Him when we do these things to the "least" person. By "least" He did not mean of lesser worth or value. It could well refer to someone not generally valued in human society. Tragically sometimes people with dementia are not even considered to be persons.

Jesus noted that these actions, often not highly regarded, were recognized as acts of ministry by Him. At the Last Supper, He ministered to His disciples by washing their dirty smelly feet. In Luke 10, Martha became so concerned about her cooking that she lost focus on the person for whom she was cooking. How unfortunate that she didn't realize that in her cooking, she was doing ministry.

The experience of giving care over an extended time will inevitably have a profound effect on the caregiver. It will change him. I spent some time reflecting on and listing areas where I saw the Lord using my caregiving experience to change me. I grant that this list is very subjective. I have tried to be as honest as I could. Any other caregiver might experience many of these changes but would undoubtedly have their unique list. I would encourage anyone with any profound experience to reflect on how it changed them. Do please understand that I take no pride in this list. It is merely a reflection of some of what I could sense of God working in me during those days. The list is in no particular order.

Changes

The list is as follows:

- Sinfulness—With trials and temptations, I faced a much greater sense of my weaknesses and vulnerabilities.
- Social—Since I had to interact for both of us, I had many opportunities to improve my social skills.
- Patience—People had credited me with being patient. Caregiving took patience to a whole new level.
- Endurance—It's different from patience. Endurance is an active virtue. For example, the distance runner develops endurance by patiently running daily.
- Responsibility—I had to be responsible for much more than ever before.

- Mental alertness—I had to be aware of things that I formerly could take for granted. Examples included how Jan was dressed, did she put on her lipstick, did she have her purse, making sure she didn't wander off, and figuring out ways of speaking to her that she could understand, such as telling her to open her hand rather than telling her to let go of an object.

- Emotions—They became much deeper. This was much more than emotions of grief but of all forms of emotion. Music became much more stirring. I needed to be much more aware of my feelings, realizing how much they could affect my speech and behavior.

- Support—I discovered a greater appreciation of what it means to have support from others. This appreciation increased as support became not so much something desirable but a necessity.

- Ministry—My ministerial interests shifted much more to those with dementia, to their caretakers, to geriatric ministry, and to those with grief over loss.

- Submission to God—I became increasingly willing to give up other activities and ministries for the ministry God has given me to care for Jan. I didn't know how long Jan would live. There was no reliable medical prognosis, and God didn't reveal any timetable. I didn't know if there might be some form or degree of healing and for how long. So submission to whatever God chooses to do with her took on much more importance. In my experience, I have found that He often—if not usually—does something different than what I might have expected.

- Joy—I learned about experiencing joy during a difficult sorrowful situation. As the Apostle Paul said, "Rejoice in the Lord always" (Philippians 4:4).
- Humor—I gained an appreciation of humor. It can help one handle the most difficult times.
- Love—I had many lessons on learning to love and serve without receiving in return. It was true that many gave me compliments about being a good caregiver. But I would have liked more affirmation from Jan. Luke 14:13, 14, on inviting dinner guests is applicable.
- Retirement—Caring for Jan strengthened my conviction that, barring or within the limitations of health and financial constraints, one does not ever retire from serving God. A Christian who retires is to use his retirement from the being-gainfully-employed time of his life to continue to serve God, perhaps in ways that he could not before retirement.
- Example—The Apostle Paul occasionally called on fellow Christians to follow his example, stating, "Imitate me." I sensed the Lord calling me to be an example of how I cared for Jan and how I used my retirement and overall lifestyle. It felt like an awesome responsibility. It gave me a concern that I would be vulnerable to some temptation and hurt someone who looked to me as an example of living for Crist.
- Authenticity—It helped me be more natural and genuine with others and before God. I came to be who I was, both in strengths and weaknesses.
- Appreciation of gestures of kindness from others—I learned about asking for help. I was espe-

cially appreciative when someone, totally on their initiative, offered an act of kindness.

You may go through the caregiver experience or any difficult time and not be able to identify any areas where God has used it to change or develop you. That is okay. As I write this book, I am having a more difficult time identifying how God is using this pandemic time to grow me. As we have already noted, God often works in us without our realizing it. Romans 8:28 and Jeremiah 29:11 call us to believe God is working for our good even if we don't recognize what He is doing.

In college, I majored in math. I also took several philosophy courses. I was very involved with logic. A fundamental principle of reasoning is that if a statement is true, then the opposite statement is false. For example, take the sentence, "Johnny is outside." If that statement is true, then the assertion Johnny is inside is false. That works fine for doing math. It makes for solid arguments for a particular position. What I learned and experienced was that this principle of non-contradiction does not work with emotions. One can and often has contradictory or what is often referred to as mixed emotions.

I began to be aware that I was experiencing a myriad of contradictory mixed emotions. I made a list. Most people could make their own list, regardless of their situation. My list for those days was as follows. Again, it was not in any particular order.

Mixed (contradictory) emotions:

1. I never felt so distant from Jan as during those days.
   a. I never felt so close to, and intimate with, Jan as during those days.

b. With her dementia diagnosis, I entered a process of both drawing closer to her and letting her go.

2. My biggest dread consisted of two inseparable parts:
   a. Jan's death
   b. Her prolonged life in a very debilitated state

3. I took comfort in the belief that someday, Jan would have a new body and a new mind.
   But that meant she would be dead, and I would not have her at all.

4. All in the present time, I felt that I had lost Jan, was presently losing Jan, and going to lose Jan.

5. There was both a sense of genuine connection with Jan and, at the same time, a sense of being totally alone and without her.

6. Jan's death would make for a significant change in my life.
   Jan's death would make relatively little change in my life.

7. I was married to Jan, widowed from her, and a single parent for her and, again, all at the same time.

8. I was married to Jan, but it also seemed like I was married to a different person. It was like this was another marriage. However, this was an arranged marriage. God arranged it. He also orchestrated my first marriage with Jan. In that marriage, He at least let me think I had something to do with its development.

9. God gave me great comfort, strength, a sense of purpose, and love.

He did it both directly and through other people.

Yet I would have felt the loneliness of hell if I didn't suppress at least some of my feelings of loneliness.

10. The most relaxing time of day for me was when I had Jan settled in bed for the night, and I was free to do whatever I wanted for the rest of the evening. Yet I knew that I would experience very difficult but profound loneliness when she died.

11. I didn't feel like I was doing enough for Jan.
    I felt like I was trying to do too much.

12. My life was full of difficulties.
    My life was very good at that time. I wouldn't have traded it for any other time of my life.

13. I was amazed at how fully the Lord was guiding my life and in such a marvelous manner.
    I was fearful of how much I might be going after my desires instead of the Lord's.

14. People praised me for how well I cared for and loved Jan, and I did deeply love her.
    Yet people had no idea. If they had only known.

15. The twelfth step of the twelve-step program is to help and serve others. I experienced that step as part of my grief recovery. I could also see that it could be an escape from my trials. Or it could be a respite that gave needed rest and refreshment. Which was it? Or were there elements of all three?

16. I longed for the Jan I had before the onset of her dementia. But I knew that was not going to happen, even though I strongly believed that "with God all things are possible" (Mark 9:23, 10:27).

17. While loving Jan deeply, I felt a longing for a new relationship.

18. I had anxiety about the vulnerability this could give me.

    But I was confident that God would protect me during any temptation trials.

19. I grieved all the Jan that was lost to me and also enjoyed all the Jan I had. I did not want Jan in this condition, but her condition gave me something of her that was not previously available.

20. I did not choose to be a caregiver. It was thrust— no forced—on me.

    I chose and chose daily to be a caregiver.

21. I often sensed some of the closest aspects of my relationship with Jan when I was not with her. It was a part of our connection and communication without words.

22. Seeing her the way she had become was hard. But I knew I would miss and have fond memories of her the way she was. It happened.

23. I could be fine with saying I didn't want Jan to continue living the way she was. I could be fine with saying that I looked forward to her being in the place God had prepared for her. I could accept knowing Jan's prayer was, "Lord, take me," and I would say amen to that prayer. All this would imply being okay with saying, "I want Jan to die." But I wasn't.

24. Tears over Jan were expressions and releases of grief. They were also expressions of joy over the relationship I had known and now had with her.

25. Those last days with Jan were the most meaningful days of our marriage.

During those days, I deeply missed having a marriage with her.

145

There is nothing unusual about a caregiver going through such a mix of emotions. It is enough to make one feel that he is losing his mind. He is not. He is just going through a difficult situation. He needs to keep this perspective. The word *hope* occurs some 150 times throughout the Scriptures. God is a God of hope. The Word calls us to hope. Dementia is a condition that cannot be humanly controlled. In that respect, it is very much like death. There is no hope in what cannot be managed. The uncontrollable in itself only brings despair. But there is the assurance we can avoid hopelessness. We can live with hope that comes from God, who is in control of all things. He is even in control when everything appears to the contrary. Everyone can choose the option that such a God does not exist. Such a person can then try to accept that there are elements in his life that are uncontrollable. The question for that person is, how is that working for you?

In Ecclesiastes 3, there is a writing on the season for everything (v. 1). The following verses are a list of pairs. They appear to be contradictory, with a season for each one. It is generally assumed that the time for the season for one is a separate time in which the season for the other takes place. But as an old song said, "It ain't necessarily so."

As soon as a baby is born, it is on a journey toward death. A seed dies to be a plant (1 Corinthians 15:36).

Muscle tissue grows through a constant process of breaking down and building up. As previously noted, one can simultaneously have joy and sorrow. One could be anxious about something yet be confident the Lord is going to work it out. It is in giving that we best receive (Acts 20:35).

Jesus noted several times that we find, save, and keep our life as we lose it. There is a sound of silence. A woman married to an alcoholic will love him dearly while hating him intensely. The father who said to Jesus that he believed in him also pleaded for help with his unbelief (Mark 9:24).

The Apostle Paul experienced personal contradictions. He shared how he would want to do one thing while doing its opposite (Romans 7:15f).

He expressed both having a desire to die and a desire to continue living (Philippians 1:21f).

The Nitty-Gritty of Caregiving

In the chapter on injustice, I discussed how God prepared Joseph, through a set of circumstances, for the work He later had for him. Reflecting on my life, I can identify specific stages that God used to prepare me to go through the journey of caring for Jan that last decade of her life.

I was the oldest child in my family. My sister was eleven years younger than me. Mom was a stay-at-home housewife and mother. As soon as she and my baby sister were home from the hospital, she trained me in all aspects of caring for my sister. I held her, clothed her, bathed her, changed her diapers, and fed her. It never occurred to me that it might be unusual for a boy to do all these. Mom didn't explain to me why I should do all this care. She just had me do it. She also had all of us kids do household chores. I washed dishes, cleaned bathrooms, and vacuumed and swept floors.

As a little boy, I had a little boy doll. I abandoned it as I grew older but never thought anything strange about a boy having such a thing to play with. I also had tractors, cars, an erector set, and plenty of other boy toys.

Dad had an apricot orchard. As I grew up, I worked in that orchard. I shoveled, irrigated, pruned trees, and hoed lots of weeds. I learned to drive in that orchard, both a tractor and his 1922 Dodge pickup. I also mowed lawns. I had plenty of "boy" work.

Later I worked as an orderly in a local hospital. I provided basic care primarily for adults. I fed and bathed patients. I had some quite messy cleanup jobs. I walked patients who were recovering from surgery. I did a lot of lifting of patients. But most significantly, I cared for patients who were not always in the most pleasant disposition.

In my parents' later years, my mother developed dementia. I was very involved with my parents during those years. It gave me a personal introduction to this disease. In their last few years, they lived in a retirement home facility. I lived within a mile of that setting and had a caregiver relationship with both of them.

I have mentioned that as I cared for Jan, I became aware of a series of videos on caring for someone with dementia. The narrator is a woman by the name of Teepa Snow. She gives practical advice on caregiving. She also offers a lot of insight into how a person with dementia thinks and perceives the world where she lives. I highly recommend these videos to anyone caring for someone with dementia. The website is http://teepasnow.com/resources/teepa-tips-videos. If you don't want to copy this address, go to Google and search for Teepa Snow videos.

I took in a dementia simulation. As participants, we were given some simple tasks to do. However, numerous distractions made completing even one or two of them difficult. Nevertheless, it helped me better understand Jan's difficulties with focusing on something without being easily distracted.

I found I constantly needed to reassess Jan's capabilities. It was easy to settle into a level of care for her. When I did that, I could be caught off guard with some decline in her abilities. Jan's decline was usually constant. Once she lost a capacity, it was usually gone. Some with dementia can fluctuate. What they couldn't do yesterday, they might be able to do today. Tomorrow is anyone's guess. It can sometimes give an illusion that the person with dementia is getting better. The caregiver needs to realize that overall, his loved one is, over time, going to decline.

I considered Philippians 4:11, where the Apostle Paul, while doing time in prison, states that he had learned in whatever state he was to be content. I personalized that verse by paraphrasing it to say I have learned in whatever state my wife is in to be content.

Providing meals for Jan wasn't simply a matter of cooking. Sometimes she would eat a few bites and seemed to forget to eat any more. I would remind her to eat, and she then continued to eat. With her short attention span, she sometimes got up from the table and go to wherever she wanted. I would get up and guide her back to the table. That wasn't a significant problem. It ended when she was no longer able to walk.

At restaurants, she was distracted by other people, the activity of waitresses and cars. She sometimes made comments about other customers, such as, "That lady sure is fat." Very fortunately, she did not say such things with much volume. Her eating practices made it increasingly necessary to ask for extra napkins. Waitresses were very understanding. A friend gave us a couple of bibs that were very helpful. When she could no longer walk, I moved her in a wheelchair. One restaurant where we frequently ate offered that I could park almost next to the front entry.

As she declined further, it was necessary to feed her, putting food in her mouth as one does a small child. That was an adjustment for both of us. It was emotionally demanding for me to have to care for her this way. I held off these measures as long as I could out of regard for her dignity. But in time, there wasn't a choice. It took a while for her to accept this way of eating. Still later, I had to puree all her food. In her last few months, I was advised to put a thickener in her water or other liquids to prevent choking.

As trying as providing meals for Jan could be, it was a very positive experience. Throughout history, there is a long tradition in virtually all cultures of the significance of people eating together. There is a lot about this in Scripture, especially about Jesus and occasions when He ate with others. In all my married life, I always had the majority of my meals with my wife. Being involved with feeding Jan was an act of intimacy with her. It drew us to each other. It was a special connection not involving words. It had something of the flavor of the Communion or Lord's Supper sacrament. There is something to the tradition at a wedding celebration of the bride and groom feeding each other the first bite of the wedding cake.

I saw, and Jan did acknowledge, that she was not regularly brushing her teeth. Reminding her created problems of her feeling I was treating her like a child. I did feel like I was, and that bothered me as well. My solution was to develop an Excel spreadsheet to check off when she had completed her brushing. That worked well for a while. Then she started making her checkoff note in random places on the spreadsheet. I did not find another solution until she was unable to brush her teeth.

Jan had several medications. Some were to slow down the symptoms of her dementia and some for other conditions. I discovered that she often only took part of her medications. I suggested that I put out her pills for her. At that time, she still wanted to take them on her own. Rather than have a source of conflict, I set up an Excel spreadsheet to check off the pills she had taken. For a while, that worked fine. Then as with the spreadsheet for her dental care, she became unable to use the spreadsheet accurately.

In time, she was more willing to let me supervise her medication regimen. However, sometimes she still did not want to take at least some of her pills. I sometimes found that if I switched the tablets to my other hand, she would take them. I don't know why that worked. It must have been God the Holy Spirit inspiring me to do that.

For a while, I had to mix her pills into something she would be eating to get her to take them. But she still had good taste buds and might refuse to eat food that had pills in them. Then someone told me that peanut butter drowns out the taste of anything. So I gave Jan lots of peanut butter jelly sandwiches, and that took care of getting her on a regular medication schedule.

There were times when I needed to give her a laxative. That presented some challenges. As the brain deteriorates due to a person's dementia, their body's response to a given medication can fluctuate. As a result, the prescribed laxative quantity may not be enough to be effective. At other times, it could be too effective. I had to constantly adjust the dosage and frequency of the laxative dosage I gave her. There were consequences if I didn't get it right.

As a safety precaution, I obtained a Life Alert necklace for Jan. It was worn at all times, even when bathing. It had a button that she could press at any time. When pushed, some-one from the agency that issued the Lift Alert would ask Jan if she needed help. If she were to fall and be unable to press the button, the device would automatically alert the agency, and they would contact emergency personnel.

I explained the device to Jan and why she needed to wear it all the time. My first challenge was that Jan would decide she didn't want to bother wearing it and take it off.

I solved that problem by tying it firmly enough around her neck so she couldn't do that. After that, she soon accepted wearing it.

The second challenge was that she sometimes misused it. For example, if she wanted one of the caregivers to come to her, she thought she could press the Life Alert button. We did manage to teach her that it didn't work that way.

Jan became increasingly unable to get herself dressed. So I became involved in dressing her. Being of the male gender, I was well able to figure out how to get her undressed. But dressing her presented some challenges. For example, one morning, I had a difficult time getting her blouse on. After I finally succeeded, she announced, "It buttons in the back." Now really, how was I supposed to know that?

I learned some skills about fixing up her hair. She had, for years, gone to a hairstylist to get her hair done. So with input from the stylist, my caregiver helpers, and even some from Jan, I did develop some skills in fixing her hair. I even learned what it was to tease her hair. I had always considered teasing as not a nice thing to do. But it can be nice to tease hair.

Finally I even learned some things about putting makeup on her. One morning before church, I noticed a spot on her face that didn't look good. I decided to cover it with some makeup. After applying it, I didn't think I had done a very good job, but I decided it was better than that spot showing. Later one of the caregivers pointed out to me that what I thought was makeup was actually nail polish. I do understand that there is a difference.

Sleeping at night had its challenges. We continued to sleep together until the last year of Jan's life. Jan developed a tendency to become restless. I sometimes resorted to sleeping in our guest room. Occasionally she would say something to me like, "Are you awake?" Then she tended to get up and wander into the family room. By this time, I used a wheelchair with her as she could only walk a short distance. My solution was to place the wheelchair by the bed on her side. Sometimes she would get up and sit on the wheelchair. At least then, she was safe. When I happened to wake up, I would put her back to bed. After a while, it was no longer safe for her to try to get up by herself. I went to a pharmacy that supplied medical equipment and obtained a set of hand-rails that a person could hold onto to get out of bed. I set them on the bed in such a way that it prevented her from getting up on her own.

As much as possible, I would take her places. I even took her to the gym (and they didn't charge her a member-ship). I liked to play racquetball. I would set her up in front of the court in her wheelchair. I would joke with others that she was my coach. She sometimes rested her head on her hand. She looked like she was saying to herself, *That player of mine can't even hit the ball straight.*

I even took her on a few plane trips. That had some particular challenges. When we were out anywhere, I would have to watch her closely because she tended to wander off (fortunately, she did not do that at home). That could be a challenge while checking if the plane was leaving on time, getting us and our baggage checked in, etc.

The day after Thanksgiving, we were driving to the coast to spend a couple of days in the Monterey area. Along the way, Jan asked if we could take a side trip to the Gilroy Outlets. I should have known there would be some difficul-ties when I had to park on a country road almost a mile from the outlets.

It was packed with people. Just getting from one store to another could take some time. Suddenly Jan disappeared.

I had the same emotions that a parent has when losing a small child in a crowd. As I walked around, I started thinking about how I would describe her to security, how she looked, tried to remember exactly what she was wearing, etc. After a while, she very casually walked out of a store. She had decided to check it out but didn't say anything to me. After that, I kept my hand well gripped on hers. It wasn't very romantic.

On one trip, we stayed in the second story of a motel. There was an elevator, so that wasn't a problem. One morning, Jan decided to go to the elevator while I finished turning off the lights and making sure the room was ready for the cleaning service. I figured that was fine as it was a long hallway to the elevator. When I stepped out of our room, she was standing in the elevator, and the doors were closing. I ran down the hallway and the stairs. I pressed the elevator button, the doors opened, and the elevator was empty! There were only two stories, and I didn't think Jan had gone to a twilight zone third story. I went up in the elevator to the second story, and she was walking down the hallway to our room. Once again, we had a less-than romantic time of hand-holding.

On one occasion, we were in a streetcar. We got to our destination, and I stepped out. Jan decided she didn't want to step down that far from the bus to the ground. I knew the bus was about to move on. So I grabbed her wrists and pulled her down. I wasn't about to let her stay on the bus while I chased it to the next bus stop.

As her decline continued, I did have questions about what it meant to her when I took her someplace. How much fuller did that make her life? And it wasn't easy to manage her, as I have demonstrated. I held to the principle that as a person mentally declines, they are aware and responsive to significantly more than what it appears. At the same time,

I had a strong desire to have her with me. If I took her to a play, a movie, or a concert, she might seem to be oblivious to the performance. But we were someplace together, and it felt like that was what mattered.

I have noted that Jan had an impressive acceptance of her condition. Yet there were times when she found it frustrating. I could see her frustration expressed as anger. How does anyone both accept and be angry at their situation? In counseling, I understood that the safe way for her to do that was to take that anger out on me. It was hard for her to be so dependent, and she had to depend on me.

In my routine care, I would have to accept those incidents of her being angry at me. My head understood this, but my emotions were inclined to react quite differently. When my son and daughters were children, I could, with much less difficulty, accept times when they were angry at me. I could chuck it up to their immaturity. It was difficult but necessary to remember that Jan had come to operate at the same level of immaturity.

On the one hand, I needed to be careful not to take what Jan said personally. I needed to think of what she might say as not coming from her. Instead, it was the disease speaking. That helped me not take what she might say personally, even though it sounded and looked like Jan. At the same time, Jan needed personal care. My care required touching the person, Jan, who was there. That wasn't easy, and I did it far from perfect.

In general, Jan's dementia reduced her expressions of emotions. One might think that this meant she had lost much of her ability to feel. That was not necessarily the case. Instead, it was apparent that Jan had thoughts, desires, and emotions that she wanted to express but had lost that ability. One can only try to imagine that irritation.

The one emotion that Jan could still capably express was anger. It would have been nice if dementia had taken away her anger and other negative emotions but left other positive ones. However, we live in a world that is far from ideal. According to Scripture, all of us human beings collectively carry responsibility for the way things are. Consequently many things remain that we would like to have gone, and many things go away that we would like to have stayed.

All this was taken to another level when she began slapping me, or at least tried. That was most common when I would clean the most private parts of her body. Of course, this was unpleasant for her. She had lost the ability to understand that I was doing something good for her.

One day, I asked her why she slapped my arm as I couldn't see that I had done anything displeasing to her. Her response was, "Because you were there." Whether or not she fully understood what she was saying, it was a confirmation that I was in the role of being a safe target for her frustrations.

On one occasion, Jan slapped me while I was putting her sweater on. It occurred to me—and I noted to Jan— that the reason her slaps bothered me so much was that they almost always happened when I was trying to do something for her—dressing or undressing her, moving her, etc. I had no concerns about her physically hurting me, but the emotional hurt was another matter. I realized how much it affected me when I did a word search in my journal, and some form of the word *slap* came up fifty-two times.

She raised her hand at me again one day and slapped my arm. She had done that numerous times before. This time, it got to me. I got angry and emphatically told her off. She got what I was saying, at least for the moment.

On another occasion, Jan slapped me, and I did slap her back, not hard, but it deeply bothered me. I broke down.

Jan said, "It's going to be all right." She then gave several love pats on my arm (it's easy to tell the difference between a love pat and a slap). That stirred me. Then one of my caregivers, Renee, "happened" to call. It helped to process what happened with her. These are some conclusions that I reached at that time:

a) God is working on me. Sometimes this valley of the shadow of death feels more like a Grand Canyon.

b) God is giving me the character quality to work on self-control, meaning to handle myself, my emotions, and my behavior in a healthy way.

c) I unexpectedly profited from Renee. She probably understood what I was going through in many aspects more than anyone else. She came to know Jan well and saw much of me with Jan.

I had to put up with Jan's wrath/anger in the form of slaps. Jesus had to take God's wrath. There was no comparison of the physical difference. The emotional pain Jesus endured was many, many, many times worse than mine. However, Jesus understood precisely why he was bearing the cross. I had, at best, a limited understanding of why I am on my "Delarosa."

Considering this episode, I fully realized that I had to come up with some alternative reactions. I developed several strategies. Whenever she raised her hand, I would firmly but calmly instruct her to put her hand down. She was almost always compliant. A better response was to have her slap something else. A pillow worked exceptionally well. The reaction I liked more was to say to her, "Gimme five." Some humor helped. The nice thing about this response was that it didn't matter how hard she slapped my hand. Then I discovered the best technique. When she might start to slap, I would say, "No slaps, love pats." It worked.

In John 13, Jesus begins his Last Supper with the disciples by washing their feet. In those days, all modes of transport, except walking, involved animals. Animals don't use bathrooms. All roads were dirt roads and became very messy. Everyone walked on those roads where the animals walked. The feet of most people were not well covered. Feet were dirty, nasty, and odorous. To clean someone's feet was an unpleasant task. One cleaned someone else's feet only because he was a low-level slave or had a deep love for that person. Pupils of a rabbi would wash the rabbi's feet, but not the other way around.

Consider Peter's reaction. He was as resistive as Jan was. He expressed his resistance verbally, but no doubt, he also raised his hand in protest. Jesus washed the disciples' feet as an act of service and, more profoundly, as an act of love. Peter's refusal was an act of rejecting Jesus's love. But Peter did not, at that time, understand what Jesus was doing (John 13:7). But he quickly got an understanding that he better let Jesus wash his feet (John 13:9).

In this act, Jesus set a powerful example of what it is to love without receiving in return. What He did was not appreciated; it was even resisted.

Before Jan had started to show symptoms of dementia, we had been fortunate to have a three-decade-long good marriage. We had worked through many challenges that marriage can bring and enjoyed our life together. That helped prepare me for the challenges of caring for her during her last decade.

Many couples are not so fortunate. Although they manage to stay together, they have many unresolved conflicts. They grow further apart instead of closer together. The love that brought them together seems to have gone.

I have often wondered what it must be like for them if one becomes disabled, either physically, mentally, or both. There was always never a question that Jan and I loved each other. That helped both of us through many difficult situations. I never resented all the time and energy I gave to care for her. I did all I could to continue caring for her and not have to place her in a facility.

But what about couples that had come to a very different relationship. Having had years, perhaps decades, of conflict and anger at each other, now they must work together with one taking care of the other. In their new situation, some may leave their past behind and form a new and positive relationship. For others, this is a tough time at best. I came across one situation where a couple was living together. He decided he didn't want to marry her. He wasn't making any plans to leave her, but he wasn't planning to stay with her either. Then she came down with an incurable disability and needed care. She was dependent on him. He didn't want to walk out on her, but he didn't want to care for her for the rest of his life either.

There are times when God might use a caregiver-needed situation to bring a couple together and restore their relationship. He might use it to develop someone to be able to love the unlovely. Sadly there are caregiving situations that result in abuse or worse.

If a couple lives together long enough, the probability is very high that at some point, one of them will have to provide care for the other. Therefore, it is wise for them to do all they can to develop a good, healthy, loving, highly committed relationship. Where they have hurt or at least offended each other, there needs to be complete repentance and forgiveness. The day will come when they will be glad they did.

I mentioned that I came to experience humor in a new way during those days. It was interesting how humor came to me with much more significant meaning during difficult and sorrowful days. I came to see humor as a gift of God. Proverbs 15:13 tells us that a glad heart makes a cheerful face. The Hebrew for *glad* has the idea of gleeful or merry. Proverbs 17:22 tells us that a joyful heart is good medicine.

Elton Trueblood is the author of a book titled *The Humor of Christ*. It is his thesis that Jesus used humor much more than is generally recognized. He argues that some of Jesus's sayings cannot be adequately understood unless one realizes that He is using humor.

Proverbs 14:13 states, "Even in laughter the heart may ache." Here is a scriptural affirmation that one can have not only joy but even laughter while experiencing sorrow. It is not that humor takes away grief, but it can help make heartache more bearable. It is profitable to understand good humor as a gift of God.

Jan gave me several humorous moments. Laughing about them did not mean disrespect for or making fun of Jan. Such incidents were one of the ways the Lord enabled me to enjoy Jan more during those days. Some of the humorous statements that came from Jan's lips will always be a precious memory for me.

I mentioned Jan saying, "If I'm dead, let me stay dead." It was her way, at that time, of expressing her desires. But I find myself having a little laugh every time I remember that incident.

I had, some time ago, taken over cooking duties. A friend had given us some zucchini bread (I'm not going to claim that my culinary skills reached far enough to make such a delicacy). One night I put out a piece for each of us to have with the dinner I had prepared. Jan got up and got the butter from the refrigerator. Then she came to my plate and buttered my piece. I thought that was quite thoughtful of her until she proceeded to eat it herself. I realized that I could: (a) get angry, (b) cry, or (c) laugh. I chose *c* and traded pieces of zucchini with her. She voiced no objection to my trade. I also realized that this was a fine example of her developing childlike self-centeredness.

One morning, one of my caregivers, Renee, noticed a knife in the kitchen with a curve in the blade. She asked me what that knife was for. How should I know? I was just the husband in the house. She decided to go to a better source of information. Renee showed the knife to Jan and asked, "What's this knife for?"

Jan answered, "Cutting." Ask a straightforward question, get a straightforward answer. That was still another example of her developing childlikeness. Her thinking increasingly became more simplistic and straightforward.

One Thanksgiving, we were asked to make a fruit salad for a family Thanksgiving dinner. Thanksgiving morning, "we" made the salad. Jan's part was to leave me in the kitchen, sit in the family room, and give me the directions on how to make the salad. Her detailed directive was, "Put the fruit in the bowl and mix it up." I figured I couldn't go wrong with that. So with Jan's "help" and some advice from one of my daughters who dropped by, the salad was a success.

One day, Jan was sitting on the couch. There was a glass of water on a small table in front of her. She informed me that she had put the glass as far away from her as possible. I asked her if that was to keep it from spilling. She said, "That's so you won't think I'm pregnant." Both of us at that time being well into senior citizen status, you can imagine that I was greatly relieved to hear her give me that assurance.

There was a time where Jan's walking ability would vary from day to day. Getting her ready for bed one night, she could only walk a couple of steps from the couch. I placed her on the commode while I prepared the bed for her. I turned around and saw her get up and proceed to start walking. For obvious reasons, I didn't want her walking at that point. I noted to her, "You don't walk when I want you to, yet you walk when I don't want you to." She looked at me and gave me a mischievous grin. At that time, we had been married almost thirty-seven years. I could recognize a given look on her face. I knew that she knew what I was saying. I will say that that incident was the best connection I had had with her in weeks or even longer.

Jan had, at various times, said that she didn't want to be buried at the Denair Cemetery. She would jokingly say that was because several of her relatives were buried there, and she might argue with them. One day, I told her that I would bury her at the Denair Cemetery if she didn't behave herself. Jan laughed. I felt a pleasant connection with her.

I was preparing Jan for a colonoscopy. She was to take the last preparatory solution at 3:30 a.m. While giving her that final solution, I jokingly suggested that we should call the doctor who prescribed that solution for that time. We didn't make the phone call, but we had a good laugh together.

Incidentally, I had a difficult time accepting Jan wearing Depends. I just had a hard time coming to grips with my wife wearing that kind of underwear. But as I worked with her on that colonoscopy prep, I became convinced. I made a quick trip to the pharmacy and bought a package. Renee made it sound better by calling them Victorias.

During these days, humor drew us closer together. It made me fonder of her, leading me to love her more. It made those days with her more precious. Humor was a gift from God.

Conclusion: In mathematical equations, what is on one side of the equal sign (=) must be the same as what is on the other side. If one could set up a mathematics of emotions (only someone with a math background would think of such a thing), what was on one side of the equal sign would be the opposite to what is on the other side. Every emotion needs another emotion to balance it. Joy balances sorrow, birth balances death, humor gives balance to sorrow, etc. Ecclesiastes 3 speaks to that balance.

Getting Caregiver Help

I have indicated that being a caregiver can be very stressful, tiring, and draining. Some studies have shown that it is not unusual for the caregiver to die before the one receiving care. The advice is commonly and well given to get at least some help with caregiving.

It is not a simple process. Unless there is another family member or other relative to help, there will be a financial cost. I mentioned getting long-term care insurance. That too is costly. A more significant concern is getting good, reliable, and trustworthy help. I have heard several horror stories of hired caregivers doing shoddy work, not dependable, or stealing from the home. Unless a caregiver knows someone personally, it is usually wise to get someone from an agency providing that service. Even then, results may vary.

People usually don't realize how hard it is to hire help. The above paragraph is only part of the difficulty. The greater challenge is the emotions of both the caregiver and the one receiving care. For over three decades, if one of us was sick, the other could meet her/his needs. Getting help is a change. Dementia usually comes on gradually. Likewise, does the need for assistance. It is hard to recognize when the time has come that help is needed. The well-being of both the caregiver and the one cared for need to be considered.

Having a caregiver helper come into the house means a loss of privacy. The help becomes aware of many of the aspects of life in the home. It can be a big adjustment, depending on the privacy needs of the couple. There needs to develop a trust relationship where the help may become aware of private family matters.

The biggest issue is seldom recognized by anyone. Getting help is a harbinger of the impending death of the loved one. With dementia, once support is needed, it will continue to be necessary until the loved one dies. Getting help brings one a step further into facing what lies ahead. The caregiver may not be conscious of this association, but it is there in the recesses of his mind.

I considered other alternatives. A day care center where I could take Jan for several hours, and as many days as needed, seemed like a possibility. The nearest one was some distance away and didn't seem to be practical. There was a retirement center nearby with a continuum of care, ranging from essentially independent living to nursing home care. At that time, Jan didn't need nursing home care. We could have both moved there, but I wasn't ready to live in that setting. Retirement homes are for old people, and I wasn't even seventy.

Getting help is also a big adjustment for the one receiving care. I came to the point of accepting the need for assistance well before Jan. She resisted the idea. I tried to explain why I needed help. I noted that among other tasks, this caregiver would do some laundry. Jan replied, "You do a good job with the laundry." I appreciated the compliment. However...

For at least the previous decade, Jan had retired from her elementary-school teaching career. She had done very well as a housewife. She was unable to comprehend that she could no longer do what she once did. She had even less understanding that taking over these tasks and increasingly needing to provide more personal care for her was becoming more than I could handle. I was still working full-time. I could also understand that it must have been hard for her to accept having someone else come to the home and take care of things that she used to do.

There was a couple that did some volunteer work for the Teen Challenge Center where I worked. They worked under my supervision, so I came to know them personally. The wife, Renee Cross, had a lot of caregiver work experience and also had a CNA (certified nursing assistant) certification. She expressed an interest, and I decided to have her come to our home and meet Jan. That visit went well. Renee and I agreed that she would start coming out four hours per week.

I wasn't sure how Jan had responded to Renee. After Renee left, Jan said to me, "Do you want to know what I think of her?" She said this with a clearly negative tone. That set off alarms in me. I could see how Renee could very capably establish good rapport with someone in her care. If I couldn't get Jan to accept Renee, I saw no way to get her to approve anyone else.

I held my breath, gave a quick silent prayer, and said, "Yes."

Jan replied, "She's a nice lady." I let out a big silent sigh of relief and prayer of thanks.

Initially Jan started doing some chores that I otherwise would assign to Renee. I saw this as a success in keeping Jan as active as possible. One day, she decided to wait to sew on a button until Renee came again. She needed Renee's help to thread the needle. So Jan was starting to accept and appreciate her.

About three months after we began with Renee, Jan had a medical appointment. With Renee's medical background, I decided it would be good to have her with us. I got Jan up and dressed and had her sit in the living room to wait for her. Jan became very anxious about Renee coming on time. She could see from the window when Renee arrived. Nevertheless, several times, she went to the front door and opened it, looking for Renee.

Renee came in plenty of time, and the medical visit went fine. But this was clearly a sign of Jan's full acceptance of Renee. It took Jan a while longer to accept thoroughly Renee bathing her and providing other personal care. With some patience, that worked out as well.

I gradually increased Renee's hours to full-time work. Then one day, Renee came to me and said she was having difficulty with pain in her hands, making it difficult for her to handle Jan. Renee knows I have decided that if she couldn't manage Jan, I might have to place her. Renee said Jan told her that she didn't want anyone else to come into the house to care for her in place of Renee. I decided to see if I could get someone to come mornings for one, possibly two, hours to help lift Jan to get her up, bathed, dressed, and out to the kitchen table. I contacted a local agency. I also contacted the business where I had my long-term care insurance. They did not initially even promise to reimburse for a second caregiver.

Several people in the caregiver support group had a caregiver help with their loved one. The husband of a woman in the group had recently died. I learned that she had used a caregiver to help with her husband. She helped me get in contact with that caregiver, whose name was Debbie Youngdale. I interviewed her and had her meet Jan. I brought her on for an hour each weekday morning.

Jan was unable to understand why it was necessary to add someone new. Fortunately Debbie was also an experienced caregiver and able to be patient. It took a while for Jan to accept her also. I had to come home from work a few times because Jan wouldn't cooperate with one of the caregivers.

It worked out very well. They both came to be very close and personally involved with Jan. They became personal friends. My adult children and their families got to know both of them. They essentially became part of the Nelson family.

I gradually increased the amount of time these women worked. Eventually Debbie worked full-time, and I established a part-time program with Renee. As Jan's condition declined, she needed increasing care. Hence the need to increase the number of caregiver hours.

Even with this additional help, caring for Jan, plus working full-time, increasingly wore on me. I finally came to the decision that I couldn't continue to work full-time. I was, fortunately, able to arrange with the director of Faith Home to continue on a half-time basis.

About a month before going part-time, I woke up one morning feeling faint, dizzy, and nauseous. I was almost not able to get up out of bed. I arranged for help from Jan's brother-in-law to transport me to the local hospital ER. After several tests, I was diagnosed with vertigo. It felt like the world was spinning around me. My doctor prescribed Valium. That made me sleepy. I returned home, got some rest, and felt fine. It was apparent to me that I was worn out and needed some rest.

I worked for two more years part-time and then entered full retirement. It was evident to others that I had needed to increase my caregiver help hours and to enter retirement much sooner than I did. I did have a sense of that myself. It was not an easy decision. I have noted that every new disability I saw in Jan was a clear sign of her getting closer to the grave. Likewise, arranging for more care for her and moving to retirement also felt like I was walking with her closer to her end. It was one thing to accept that Jan would die; it was another thing to take the practical steps needed to face it.

As I noted in a previous chapter, Jan and I had long agreed that I would not authorize any excessive measures to keep her alive at the end of her life. I had a concern that medical personnel might put Jan on life support without her or my consent. That happened to my father, and it caused a lot of stress for me. I didn't want to repeat that experience.

A friend noted that if Jan was on hospice, I would not need to contact 911 or the county coroner at the time of her death. There didn't have to be an official determination of the cause of death. Instead, I could contact hospice, and an on-call nurse would come out and certify her passing. I investigated and confirmed that this was the case. It was apparent that this action would make her passing much simpler. By May 2016, Jan was still home and officially on hospice. We established that a hospice nurse would see her at least once a week.

Hospice care is distinguished from standard medical care. Traditional medical care aims to cure or heal someone who is sick or injured or make the patient healthier. It is usually attempting to keep the person alive as long as possible. The goal of hospice care is to help the patient be as comfortable and free of pain as possible until the person dies. It does not try to cure or heal. Therefore, all medications and other forms of medical care come through hospice.

There are numerous hospice chapters throughout the land. They do not have geographical boundaries. There were two chapters in the area where we lived. I had some acquaintance with one of them and felt comfortable with what I knew of that chapter. I had even done some volunteer work under that chapter. So I had Jan on hospice there.

By the time I decided to have Jan on hospice, I had come far enough to accept her dying that it was not a difficult decision. By this time, I was actively making preparations for her death.

Hospice provided several services besides regular medical checkups. An on-call nurse was available 24-7. If I had any questions or concerns, I could call any time. Jan's arms and legs began to curl, putting her in a prenatal position. Hospice had a massage therapist come out and massage her arms and legs. It temporarily straightened them out. More importantly, it made Jan feel more comfortable. About a year before she died, hospice provided a hospital bed for her. The bed not only made her more comfortable, but it also made it easier to care for her. Jan even had her hair washed and done through hospice. In the last few months of her life, hospice provided the materials to give Jan oxygen to make her breathing more comfortable.

Hospice had a social worker, a chaplain, and a grief counselor. I had several sessions with each of them, especially the grief counselor. I got to know a number of the staff. It almost seemed like they had become part of our family.

It has occurred to me that life is more like hospice than like a hospital. We are all going to die. For that, there is no cure and no healing. We all need to accept that. We all need to receive the One who will guide us to live our lives as fully as possible, for as long as possible.

Respite

Caregiving work can be exhausting. It isn't just the work itself of feeding, cleaning, dressing, etc. It is work that, if done well, involves much personal, emotional energy. That can be much more draining than any physical work. Anyone physically exerting himself knows that he needs break times. A person doing work that involves a lot of mental energy is in just as much need for times of rest. Work that involves personal care is the most draining.

That makes getting caregiving help crucial. A caregiver needs time to take care of himself. He needs time to eat, sleep, relax, enjoy himself, and do something besides caregiving. If he doesn't do well caring for himself, he will do a poor job caring for a loved one.

That is why I needed caregiver help. And it needed to be good caregiver help. With Renee and Debbie, I could go to the gym and get some good exercise. I could do some volunteer activities that I enjoyed. I could read for relaxation. I could engage in spiritual practices of prayer, Scripture meditation, and worship. I could have refreshing relationships with the Lord and with other people.

Occasionally I would get away for a couple of nights. I usually either went to my sister in the Bay Area or a cabin in the mountains. The change of scenery was refreshing. My caregivers would tag off each other in being with Jan so that she was never alone.

A respite is not the same thing as an escape. An escape is getting away from an undesirable place, person(s), or activity. The goal is to stay away for as long as possible. The best result is not to have to return. While one has escaped, he tries not to think about going back. If he does, it is with a sense of dread. Some people live for their escapes.

A respite is a temporary separation from a place, person(s), or activity. The person engaged in a break is well aware that he will be returning to his former work. During his respite, he may deliberately not think about his usual duties. However, if he does, it is not with a sense of dread. Instead, he looks forward to when he will leave his respite and resume his regular activity.

The purpose of an escape is to get away. It does nothing to help handle anything better. Depending on the nature of his escape, and especially if he spends a significant amount of his escape time dreading his return, his escape may make his return even worse.

The purpose of a respite is to provide a time for a person to regroup, be refreshed, and return ready, able, and desiring for his normal activities. He hopes to be able to carry out his service ever more effectively.

Our Relationship

As I observed other couples where one was the caregiver of the other, I often thought about which of two situations was more difficult. By difficult I am speaking of which of two situations is more emotionally difficult. In one situation, the one cared for has their mind well intact, but their body is seriously handicapped. In the other situation the body of the one cared for is basically healthy, but their mind is seriously handicapped.

It might be easy to prefer the former. One can still communicate with and relate to their loved one. How does one relate to a loved one whose mind isn't fully there, and they are not the person they used to be? In my father's last days, he had a healthy mind but a deteriorating body. My mother's body was healthy until her very last days, but her mind was in a very poor state.

One of the difficulties in trying to relate to a loved one with dementia is that they have little or no capacity to respond to someone else's emotions. If I told Jan, "I love you," usually her best response was thank you. With the self-centeredness that goes with dementia, Jan had very little, if any, capacity for gratitude or appreciation.

With physical diseases, there is often the possibility of a cure. The person might be well again. In the case of a sickness of the mind, specifically dementia, there is not a hope the person will be well again. They will be in their present declin-

174

ing condition until they die. I've seen people go through the experience of getting better and then declining, only to get better for a while again. It is very stressful. Even when the person appears to be cured, there is the concern that they might get sick again.

It has been my observation and experience that it is harder to live with uncertainty than with a not-wanted certainty. That is why I decided it was wiser to accept that Jan was going to die rather than cling to a hope she might get better.

The only healthy way to handle uncertainty is a life of faith. Christians may use Romans 8:28 in ways that make it a cliché. But there is comfort in clinging to the hope that is much more than a wish or desire. It is the hope that affirms firmly that God does "work all things for good for those who love the Lord." A difficulty in affirming this promise comes as we realize that we have no idea when that good might come about. In Jeremiah 29:11, another favorite verse of Christians, God promises that he has good plans for us. But look at the context of the verse. Originally addressed to the people of Israel, those plans would not be carried out for another seventy years. Yet there is the assurance that ultimately, good will come.

I was always thankful that Jan always knew who I was. It is not uncommon for people with dementia to no longer recognize those who are closest to them, such as a spouse of many decades. She did experience the common short-term memory limitations. She might repeat the same question to me several times. Sometimes she would even say, "I know I already asked you, but..." And then she would repeat the question. My bigger struggle was with her reduced capabilities, especially relational capabilities.

Jan's diseases caused me to spend more time with her and have her in a way, and to an extent, that I would not have otherwise. This had an effect of drawing us closer together. With couples, a situation like this can result in their relationship going either direction. It is possible to let the various duties of caregiving become simply duties. They can become just elements of a job. A caregiver of a loved one can drift in either direction without realizing it. It is wise to give thought to the effect the caregiver relationship is having on the marital relationship. Making a conscious decision to draw close together will help it happen. It will be very worthwhile.

I became uncomfortable with the thought that this losing-her process caused me to love her more. Why didn't my love for her deepen without this? Actually I think it did. But there is a love that comes out of this kind of relationship that cannot develop any other way.

Could it be that God, in His wisdom and providence, wanted me to love Jan more, and this was the way He used to bring it about? Virtually every couple will have some difficulty, challenge, even a crisis that will have the potential to drive them apart or bring them together in a new special way. The choices each of them make is crucial. They need to recognize what is happening.

As the weeks wore on, it occurred to me that how Jan used to be increasingly became a blur. I suppose it was a matter of being so concentrated on how she was that I didn't think a lot about how she used to be. Perhaps it was also a matter of God's mercy. It spared me from a lot of longing for how she used to be. That helped me love her as she was.

There is nothing automatic about a couple like Jan and me coming closer to each other like I am attempting to describe. There are obvious challenges. It is a matter of choice. Each person caring for a spouse with a disability needs to ask himself, "What kind of relationship do I desire to have, and can I have, under these circumstances?" To not ask these questions, at least in some fashion, lead to a couple going increasingly distant from each other. Even when a couple naturally stay close to each other, so much more can be gained when drawing closer is a deliberate decision.

The idea of marriage as centered primarily on intense romance that is highly emotional has long been both popular and analyzed. Certainly a marriage needs romance. But anyone married for any length of time knows that that is only part of marriage. With far too many marriages, romance is the part that gets the most attention. In many cases, as the emotional romance declines, so does the marriage.

The Biblical concept of marriage is summarized in Genesis 2:24. It speaks of a unity in marriage where it is accurate to say they are one. Some translations have it that there is a sense of the two becoming one person. Much has been written about what this means. In my experience with Jan, I became impressed with the meaning of this phrase to include the concept that what happens in marriage to one has, in a real way, happened to the other. It wasn't that when Jan got dementia, I got dementia. But Jan's dementia was also my dementia. Whereas it was a significant part of her life, it was also a significant part of my life. So the same dementia came to both of us. However, since we were also distinct and different from each other, we experienced that dementia differently.

The deeper the marriage bond, the deeper is this sharing. So much so that what happens to one in a very real sense happens to the other. I enter into her experiences. Her joy is my joy, and her sorrow is my sorrow. I am aware of her difficulties, frustrations, angers, and victories as being hers, yet I also know them as part of me.

It could become easy to define Jan as a person with dementia. That would define me as a person married to someone with dementia. Some caregivers do come to center their whole life on caring for their loved one. But right up to, and including, the last day of Jan's life, there was more to her than that she was a person with dementia. She was still a wife, a mother, a grandmother, a lady, a child of God. And I was a man married to someone who was all of these and more.

In this way, her limitations did not make my life more limited. I was intimately aware of her limitations, but that was a broadening and deepening of my life. I not only lived my life, I also lived hers. And even in her mental state, she had a knowing of me and my life.

For a marriage to be as thus described takes time. It doesn't just snap into place at the wedding and the wedding night. A church we attended would put up some sayings on the screen before the service began. I didn't catch their authors. The sayings were, "The love of a young man to a young lady is superficial compared to the love of an old man to an old lady," and, "A lot of love is just persevering." It is not to say that the love of young people isn't real, nor does it displace romantic love.

It is to say that love, especially marriage love, is not based on feeling. Love is a decision. The decision is to commit oneself to the other person. The commitment lasts until the couple is separated by death. As Dietrich Bonhoeffer wrote, "It is not your love that sustains the marriage, but from now on, the marriage that sustains your love" (Dietrich Bonhoeffer, *Letters and Papers from Prison**).

A discussion about the marriage relationship needs to include the sexual relationship. It is very generally acknowledged that usually, men want sex more often than women.

---

* https://www.goodreads.com/quotes/497793-it-is-not-your-love-that-sustains-the-marriage-but.

This can be a source of conflict. And women with dementia often have even less desire for sex. As her condition worsens, her desire often also lessens. For the husband caregiver, this puts him in the position of having to give increasingly more to his wife and receiving increasingly less. And this is in all areas of their relationship, not just with sex. In fact, it is characteristic of caregiving that one is called on to give more and more while getting back less and less. And while there is great reward in unrewarded giving, it takes mature spiritual development to reap this reward.

Men can easily experience guilt, both from others and from within, over their—at least from their wife's perspective—excessive desire for sex.

Men can easily think that since they are married, and especially if their wife has extra care needs, they are entitled to frequent sex. We have noted the Biblical concept of marriage that a married person is to give 100 percent, and if he gets anything in return, that is a bonus. And the stewardship concept is that his wife belongs to God, not to him. He, as a good steward, provides for the woman who belongs to God, not to him as his wife. Nowhere does the Bible indicate that a man is entitled to sex.

As for my situation, since Jan had very limited ability to express what she wanted or didn't want, and since all decisions involving her were carried out by me, I could have sex with her any time I wanted. However, while she would give me some limited gestures of affection, that was about as far as it went. Sex had no apparent significance for her. That took away the biggest portion of its appeal for me. Having sex with someone who isn't responsive is almost like having sex with a mannequin.

In Matthew 19:12, Jesus, in His reference to eunuchs, implies that some are born with an ability to let go of sexual desire, for some circumstances bring about the necessity of a man not having sex, and in some cases, a man might feel led to live a celibate life.

Men have, at least, some tendencies to feel that if they are not having an active sex life, for whatever reason, that at least much of their manhood has been taken from them. Men seem to be created wired to desire sex more than women are. That makes them neither inferior to nor superior to women. Just different. In 1 Corinthians 7:5, Paul advises couples not to go too long without sex, or it can create problems. This passage is difficult to apply to the husband caregiver.

Jan became increasingly disinterested in any form of affection, including simple hugs and kisses. I had become used to doing things she might not care for, such as giving her medications or bathing her. I grappled with the matter of giving her affection. I felt that that too was something she should have, even if she expressed no desire for it. It was along the same rationale as taking her places to give her a fuller life. At the same time, I realized that my desires, even needs, were also part of the picture. I made attempts to talk with her about affection. As her condition declined, that became impossible.

Within a year of her passing, I discovered a new connection, a very special connection, with Jan. As she lay on her hospital bed in our family room, I would bring my face to her, and she would open her mouth. As I came close to her face, she would pucker up for a kiss and hold it until after the kiss was over. Then she would smile. And this was the one affection we could still have with each other. This kiss was different than the romantic kisses that make the heart beat harder and faster. It was different than the bedroom kisses that, throughout the body, make the blood pump stronger. And there was something about it that made it more special, even far more special, than those other kinds of kisses. They reflected a special bond that we developed as Jan lost her ability to talk audibly. As our ability to converse, go places, and do things together declined, the Lord gave us a special connection with each other and with Him. A connection without and beyond any words.

I have wondered just what it was that made these kisses so different and so special. I believe the reason is because they were goodbye kisses. That might seem to have made them very sad, but they were not. Instead, they were precious because they went with her to heaven.

I continued the practice of kissing Jan before I went anywhere. Renee told me that on several occasions after I kissed Jan, and then walked away, she would see Jan with her lips still puckered up. Jan was clearly interested in more kisses. Unmistakably, in the last weeks of her life, there was still, in her, an affection for me. That meant more to me than I can express in words.

One day, about three months before Jan died, I kissed her, knowing the number of days left for us to kiss were limited. As we kissed, I had a grief cry. Afterward I looked at her, and she was smiling, more than her usual smile after we kissed. As it appeared to me, what she saw was not my tears but our closeness.

One morning, I put my lips to hers, and her lips did not respond. At that point, I knew without question that her time was very near. Early that afternoon, she died.

I think I have reached an age where my memory is not as sharp as it used to be. It is a normal condition that goes with age. Someday I might even begin to forget many of my memories of Jan. But there is one thing I will always remember—we kissed!

Temptation to Infidelity

People who are grieving are in a state of strong emotions. Any emotion affects our thinking, including our rationality. This certainly includes feelings of grief. Our emotions are God-created and can be instruments for great good. But grieving people can also be vulnerable to doing wrong.

The Jesus described in the Gospels was a very emotional person who could express intense grief. He was tempted in every way humanly possible (Hebrews 4:15). That would include the temptation to be carried by His emotions in a negative direction.

A prime example of this was Jesus at Lazarus's tomb. He was the officiating rabbi at Lazarus's funeral and ended up weeping deeply (John 11:33–38). Such behavior by clergy would be unprofessional conduct. Jesus could have made the situation worse instead of better. Fortunately He expressed what He felt while having control over those feelings.

A caregiver of a spouse with dementia no longer has the marriage he once had. He will long for what is now gone. While still loving his wife deeply, he can easily find himself caught up in longing for a relationship with closeness and a sense of connection. He may become involved in a relationship that he tries to maintain as a healthy friendship. But his emotions make that problematic. He tries to keep his feelings for that person to himself. But it doesn't take much for them to become apparent to others. He is very aware that his wife is going to die. Someday he will be able to pursue a new relationship very legitimately. He has a longing for that day while dreading the thought of his wife's death. His thoughts and emotions are full of conflict. Under these circumstances, a friendship can become an affair that is romantic and, perhaps, sexual. But the relationship is not about sex. It is about deep desires, emotions, and needs.

There was a time when I struggled with a friendship with a woman. It did not become, in any way, sexual. It was enjoyable to be able to have a female friend, simply to be able to converse with in a "normal" fashion. There was something satisfying in being able to share thoughts and emotions with someone who could verbally respond and could also share her thoughts and feelings. The problem was my inability to keep romantic emotions from emerging.

The friendship and all contact with that person ended. I continued to care for and love Jan. All my longings and loneliness continued. They were part of that rough road I was traveling on my spiritual journey. I spent time reflecting on what drove me, as a caregiver of a spouse, into this relationship. I do not claim that what follows is any complete explanation. It certainly does not excuse anything. I think it gives some insight.

First, being married to someone with dementia means missing what one once had and will never again have with that person. However, with her death will come the possibility of a new relationship. When circumstances are difficult, hoping for a better day is inevitable. Hope is good. It can prevent despair. It can also be the framework for temptation. Hope can stimulate impatience. That which is good can be lost by pursuing it too soon.

Second, having a spouse with dementia creates loneliness. One can have many other friends, but it's not the same. It can be enjoyable to have friends of the opposite gender, but that can easily create temptations. And it can be unrealistic to avoid the opposite gender altogether.

Third, more than I had realized, my relationship with Jan had, for decades, given me a great source of security. Life is full of circumstances that make us uneasy. Having someone with whom there is a special friendship can help handle things with much greater confidence. In a good healthy marriage, each partner will find security in the other person. If they don't, the marriage may have serious problems. I was struggling to maintain a connection with Jan and the confidence that went with it. I didn't realize that the enjoyment and benefit I had from this friendship was the confidence it provided. But since it had the flavor of what I wanted with Jan, the romantic emotion was lurking nearby and eventually raised its head.

Later I found security in close connection with the Lord and numerous other people, including connecting more deeply with people in general. In this way, I could have close ties with women as well. Most importantly, I worked on developing a close connection with Jan that I had not realized was possible. In the past, that hope created much longing. I affirmed even more strongly that God was using hope to create patience in me and trust in Him. Finally the Lord enabled me to consider that my hope might not necessarily be for marriage but for a fulfilled single life. And perhaps the single life could include a special friend but not necessarily a wife.

How does one protect himself from the temptation to infidelity? The usual answer is to set up certain precautions. These include not forming any friendships with anyone of the opposite gender, except within the family. Keep relationships with women distant, formal, or professional. Don't ever be alone with any woman other than his wife, sister, or daughter.

I have noted being aware of the prospect of someday having a new relationship. It might seem logical to have a precaution that says don't be thinking about having a new relationship someday. Having a rule to not think about something is to be thinking about what I am not supposed to be thinking about.

We live in a society where genders are not separated. Trying to keep this distance can be unrealistic. Setting up a set of rules of conduct can give a false sense of security. Therefore, one needs to do more than set up a list of precepts to follow.

It has been my observation that extramarital affairs only happen when there are difficulties in a marriage. It just doesn't happen that a marriage was doing fine until one of the spouses takes a notion to have an affair. Affairs are wrong. But affairs do not ruin marriages. Instead, damaged marriages create temptations for affairs. The best protection for marriage is carrying out a commitment to constantly building one's marriage.

Yes, this is something that needs full engagement by both partners. However, the focus of the married person should not be on whether his wife is doing her part. Instead, he needs to concentrate on his doing his part, regardless of how much effort she is making. Even if she is making no effort to improve their marriage, even if she is doing things that harm their relationship, he needs to do all he can to make their relationship as solid as possible.

Let me suggest the following. I do not pretend it is complete, but I will contend that these recommendations will go far to make for a solid, enjoyable, and affair-proof marriage.

- Be solidly committed before God and to your spouse to stay in the marriage.

- A solid commitment to being open and honest with your spouse
- Resolve not to say or do or be any place with any one of the opposite gender that you could not be comfortable sharing with your spouse.
- Commit to spending the rest of your life seeking to know and understand your mate (let me suggest that this is usually harder for the man but certainly a challenge for both).
- A solid commitment to oneness where whatever happens to one has, in a very genuine sense, happened to the other
- A dedication by each one to love the other in the manner described in 1 Corinthians 13
- A solid commitment on the part of the husband to love his wife sacrificially, and likewise on the part of the wife to respect her husband (Ephesians 5:33)
- Strive to build an intimate bond of oneness such that there develops between them a communication beyond words (more on this in the next chapter)
- Last, and by no means least, develop and maintain a romantic emotional attachment to your spouse. I place it last because often, it is placed first to the neglect of everything else. It's great when one can, and with their spouse, experience all that Dean Martin sang in "That's Amore." Romance is important. Deliberately cultivate romantic thoughts and feelings for your spouse. Pray to have those thoughts and feelings. They do enhance and protect marriage.

But the truth is, there is a lot about marriage that isn't romantic. High on the list is working through conflicts.

Putting together a good marriage is like cement workers lay-ing out a sidewalk. A lot of work needs to be done to smooth out the rough spots. Yet if people will look for it, romance can even be found here and in washing dishes and cleaning toilets.

It is true that since we are all members of a fallen human race, nothing will guarantee a healthy preservation of any marriage until death do us part. For starters, no married per-son has ever been entirely faithful to his/her spouse (Matthew 5:27, 28, which applies to man generically).

No one can ever say I would never engage in any num-ber of behaviors that could, or at least in some manner, ruin a marriage. Examples are addictions, workaholics, sports, hob-bies, churchaholics, political engagement, parenting, or any numerous other activities, many of them very commendable.

Part of the Lord's Prayer states, "Lead us not into temp-tation." I have thought this a strange part of the prayer. Does God lead us into temptation? Satan certainly does. The sec-ond part made good sense to me. "Deliver us from evil." There is evil all around us, and I can certainly use some deliv-erance from it.

In praying for this request, I acknowledge that God is aware of and sovereign over all things. It is true that if I have a temptation, God can and could keep me from it. He does allow us to have temptations. And He doesn't just passively allow temptation. There is a reason He permits us to be tempted. Recall that temptation can also be translated as "test." And God gives us tests for a good purpose—it can make us stronger and better.

We see greatness in Jesus, not only that He endured the cross but that He faced and overcame the temptation to not go to the cross.

Looking at this mysterious request, I certainly prefer not to be tempted. I see this prayer as an expression to God of my desire. In that way, it is like Jesus praying in Gethsemane, "Lord, take this cup from me." Jesus's desire was not to be crucified. And He, with deep passion, prayed to be spared. Yet He knew, beyond any doubt, that He would have to go to the cross. Gethsemane was where He faced and fully and finally accepted that reality.

In praying "Lead me not into temptation," I am acknowledging to God my weaknesses. I admit I can be taken in by temptations, including doing things I desperately do not want to do. I am expressing and confessing my awareness of my weaknesses. I'm saying to God that I know His Word says He gives me the strength and means to overcome temptation (1 Corinthians 10:13), but I don't feel confident in my ability. I admit that I lack trust in Him to enable me to overcome temptation. I need to pray daily, "Lord, I need You to protect me."

Despite this part of the Lord's Prayer, no one has ever been free from temptation. Even Jesus had temptations. Why doesn't God keep us from being tempted? Theologians have a lot of answers for this. Usually it has to do with the assertion that we have free will. If God were to take away all temptations, He would be taking away our capacity to exercise free will.

It can well be that it is part of God's plan that we are tempted. In my case, what if I had never met this woman? What if this relationship had not happened? The desire would have still been present. Then I would not have faced the issue of temptation to infidelity as squarely as I had to do. This conclusion is not, in any way, to excuse my behavior. It is saying that God used, and that it was in His plan to use for good, what I did.

Connection

As Jan's capabilities declined, and she became increasingly childlike, I sensed her becoming more distant from me. It felt like she was fading away from me. It reminded me of an occasional scene in a movie, when one person become increasingly out of focus for the other person. During this time, I progressively realized what I was losing. I longed for even the slightest experience of connection with her. It meant a lot one day when she called to me and, with tears in her eyes, thanked me for taking good care of her.

In time, I realized that I sensed God calling me to connect with Jan as best I could. It would have to be without the verbal sharing, going places, doing things, and facing life together that we had done for decades. As she came to lose her ability to say anything audibly, I gradually came to see, if not understand, that the connection I might potentially have with her would be a connection without words.

We use the right side of the brain for visual and spatial orientation and our emotions. The left side of the brain is for language and logic. The right side develops first. The connection and bonding with another human being in a baby starts in the right side of the brain. Using it, a baby bonds with others before language and certainly before logic develops in his brain and mind. As I was thinking about all this, I held our most recent grandchild, Jax, born just a few days earlier. At that moment, I realized that he and I had a connection beyond words. We can learn a lot from babies.

With the process of dementia, the left side of the brain deteriorates before the right. The person loses logic ability, and then speech, but can still feel and perceive. Any connection with anyone else must be without words, but the capacity for emotion and bonding is still present. But as a child's left side develops, he typically, if not inevitably, changes how his brain functions. The left side becomes more prominent.

Jan connected with me on a right-brain level in her latter days, unencumbered with the left side. The challenge was to relate my right brain to her right brain so that my very functional left brain would not encumber this connection and, hopefully, even enhance it. I invite all couples to take on this challenge.

Our most profound communication with God is sensing Him and His presence that is not a matter of our physical senses. As a result, we may have some physical sense of comfort, relaxation, etc., and emotions of peace, joy, love, etc. Two people in a close relationship can experience this with each other. It is best when the two people are together in a relationship with God. Note that God used Jax in service to Him. The Lord used Jax to help me experience and understand this communication without words.

We may recognize prayer as a close connection with God. Most typically, it consists of the person saying words to God. But more meaningful prayer is communication with God. The communication may use words but is far beyond words. The practice of praying in tongues, of course, uses verbalization. There are many different opinions about what constitutes this practice, often called glossolalia. But in its best usage, it is a communication with God in which typically the person praying doesn't know the content of his prayer, nor is it necessary. He simply has a profound experience of communication with God.

In John 3, Jesus, in His discussion with Nicodemus, speaks of being born again. In verse 6, He refers this to a being born of the Spirit. This birth is something that happens outside of the physical. However, its effect may be seen physically. The believer's awareness of his connection with God is every bit as authentic to him as all the physical connections he might have.

We live in a very physical world. Our soul, the eternal essence of our being, is inseparable from our physical body. Every thought, emotion, attitude, action, and all the five senses of physical perception are closely interrelated with activity in the brain. Our very physical brain connects inexplicably to our very nonphysical mind. Scientists, philosophers, and theologians through the ages have unsuccessfully grappled with this connection.

People who have a similar traumatic experience, good or bad, understand and connect where others without that experience cannot. Examples are caregivers, addicts, addicts in recovery, the married, the divorced, knowing the death of a spouse or child, having an unfaithful spouse, fighting in a war, etc. Such people can share in ways they cannot communicate with those without those experiences. Among the couples one sees in a restaurant, it is often easy to identify the married. They are not talking with each other. If this is because they are giving each other the silent treatment or are texting, that is most unfortunate. But it can be that they know each other so well that they do not have to talk. They have a connection without words.

People with dementia who cannot otherwise verbalize can often enjoy music and even sing. This ability makes sense when we consider that music involves much of the right brain.

Finally for believers, in heaven, we will have a heavenly body that connects to our heavenly mind and spirit. We will connect with our Lord and with each other in a myriad of ways far beyond anything we could ever imagine or think to ask. Yes, we will understand it better by and by, and marvel at how naive we were during our life on this earth.

It is not unusual and is understandable for people to both physically and emotionally withdraw from someone who is dying. The loss from death is painful. Separating oneself from that pain is natural. People commonly feel awkward around someone who is dying. They would often ask me what they should say when they were with Jan. My response is that it doesn't matter. Say whatever you feel like saying. The important thing is that you are present where she is.

I deliberately took the opposite stance. First, I had a conviction that this is what the Lord would have me do. Then there was the wedding vow to take seriously. Her condition meant I had to take up being with her in sickness and in health to a much fuller level. Finally I was confident of the thought of green pastures and still waters on the other side (Psalm 23:2). By faith, I had hope for the future.

Jan was unable to talk, to say even a single word, for the last year and a half of her life. Obviously I greatly missed being able to have two-way conversations with her. Employing a little humor, I would sometimes joke that at least this way, I won all the arguments. I would have loved to have been able to argue with her. I would have gladly settled for one where I lost.

My last fond memory of Jan speaking was in church. During the worship service, we sang a hymn she knew well. As we were singing, for a moment, our eyes connected. It was the fourth verse of "Amazing Grace." It begins, "When we've been there ten thousand years."

With all our past doing together now gone, going places, conversations, taking responsibilities of life together, sharing, etc., then all I had of Jan was Jan. She couldn't give to me by giving, doing, talking. She gave to me by being. I did a lot of giving to her by doing for her. But then, I felt that what meant most to Jan was who I was for her. Our kiss was not so much something we did but who we still were.

Connection with Jan became a matter of presence. There was little we could do together in the sense of both of us interacting. I could talk with her, although she did not talk in return. I could pray with her, although she spoke no words of prayer. I could take care of her, but she could do nothing for her care. I could be present with her, and she was present with me.

While Jan still had some speaking ability, there were things she said to me that had special meaning. The meaning pointed to something more. They brought out the connection beyond the words that we had. Here are some examples.

Jan's emotions had been flat for several months. One day she called to me. When I came, she was teary-eyed and said I was taking good care of her. She could see the emotional response in me and said, "You're going to be okay." Another time, after cleaning her up from a mess, she said, "That's really being a loving husband."

One day, Jan asked, "How can I encourage you?" I told her just asking that question was a great encouragement to me.

After Jan was diagnosed with dementia, she told me, "You didn't sign up for this." I understood what she meant. Yes, I vowed to be with her for better or worse and in sickness and in health. At the time, I had no idea that it included caring for her with this disease.

One day, Jan asked what she did right on our first date. I understood her to be asking what she did that caused me to want to continue seeing her. I responded that all she did was to be herself, and that was more than enough.

During a Sunday morning church service, I started to hold her left hand (she was sitting to my right). Then she took my right hand with her right. That initiative of affection from her meant a lot to me (incidentally she was right-handed; I am left-handed).

I took her to a Burger King. I bought a kid's meal for Jan. It was a good size for her. Several times, she pushed her Coke to me and said, "Share."

At night, as we lay in bed, she sometimes put her arm on me. I sometimes found this annoying when I had been asleep. I later came to appreciate what she was doing.

Jan once commented, "You must be ashamed to have me as your wife." I had a long talk with her, assuring her that I was not ashamed or embarrassed to take her anywhere with me, no matter who was there. She seemed content with that response. This incident caused me to want to make more effort to show her my love.

Putting Jan to bed, she could only walk a couple of steps from the couch. But as she was sitting while I was preparing the bed for her, she started to get up. I noted to her, "You don't walk when I want you to and then walk when I don't want you to walk." She looked at me and gave a mischievous grin. The best connection I had with her for weeks or longer.

These days with Jan were great lessons in learning to communicate from both the heart and the head. As a counselor advised me, the head gives the content while the heart provides the impact.

I pondered why I couldn't have learned this more before Jan's speaking ability declined. The truth is, it wouldn't have happened. I didn't realize the need. For this to happen, something, namely words, had to be taken away. Then I could recognize the need to relate in ways that were more than words. Then I could talk with her, and it didn't matter if she mentally understood what I was saying. We could have a connection just by our presence. I even came to know her presence when not physically present with her. But it took the Lord taking much from her to give much to us. The Lord takes away, and the Lord gives.

Philippians 2:6, 7 states that "Christ Jesus, who, though he was in the form of God, did not count equality with God a thing to be grasped, but emptied himself, by taking the form of a servant, being born in the likeness of men." In Revelation 1, Jesus appears to the Apostle John in His full divinity. For most of us, this manifestation of Him would be more than we could handle. For Jesus to connect with us, much of the demonstrations of His divinity had to be taken away. Appearing as an ordinary human being, people could relate to and connect with Him.

I highly recommend seeking connection with others, especially with loved ones, particularly with a special loved one. It is a worthwhile enrichment of one's life. Be aware that it is not a simple pursuit. It is never complete. Some find it more difficult than others. It does not preclude times of solitude. There is a need for balance in all aspects of life. Jesus was the master in making a deep connection with others. He also pursued times of solitude.

If you do want to pursue this, I offer the following suggestions:

- Decide how important this is for you.
- Decide how much you are willing to sacrifice to reach this goal, and then go further.
- Don't wait until one of you is disabled. Start now.

- Realize that if you do this, and she departs from this life first, it will make her departure harder for you, but it will be worth it. You will be glad you did.
- Make it a lifetime goal to fully know and understand your loved one, even though it is an impossible task, especially for men.
- Listen to her. Converse with her. Whatever you don't understand, ask. You will still lack a lot of understanding, but it will draw you closer and closer to your goal.
- State to her understandings you have of her and ask if they are accurate.
- Go places and do things together. Laugh together.
- Take an interest in her interests, even when they are not your interests.
- Constantly observe her. Try to learn something new about her daily.
- Especially look for what you like about her.
- Pray with her. It can be more intimate than sex. That may be why couples generally don't often pray together.
- Be a totally open book with each other (This also ensures fidelity. If you don't want to tell her what you're doing, then don't do or even think it.).
- Be aware of her, including when you are not in her presence (this is not the same thing as constantly thinking about her).
- Be aware of your feelings for and about her. Express them, especially to her.
- Realize that increasing closeness to her points to increasing closeness to God.

- Return to your first love. Do, think, and feel what was you then (Revelation 2:4, 5).
- Finally consider this warning. Connection and the closeness it brings is also a catalyst for conflict. I find I seldom have conflicts with people that I have only casual contact. I haven't researched this, but I would venture that most people have the most significant portion of their conflicts with their marital partner. The most common sources of contention seem to be money and sex. No doubt because these are very personal subjects.

The Lord's Supper

Searching for ways to connect with Jan, I found a special connection in worship. As Jan became immobile, I took her in her wheelchair to the Sunday morning worship service. The ushers were very good to us. They would take a chair out so that she didn't have to be sitting out in the aisle. And people would greet her even when she was unable to respond. Most of the time, she appeared to be oblivious to what was happening in the worship service. She would pay little attention to the songs, worship team, or the preaching. She spent most of her time looking around at the other people. Something did remain of her old extrovert nature.

The music in the services was a mixture of contemporary songs and traditional hymns. Jan paid no attention to the contemporary music. She also ignored the traditional hymns if they were sung in a more modern style. But when one of these songs was sung, and in at least basically a traditional manner, her face would light up. Her mouth moved. She was singing! She clearly knew all the verses, even the third verse (If worship leaders wanted to shorten the singing time, they would tell the congregation what verses to sing. Usually the verse left out was the third verse. I have no idea why.).

As she was singing, I would look at her, and she would briefly look back at me, and we had a special moment together. I felt the connection I so wanted with her. However, it was only for a moment. Then she would look away but continue singing. It appeared that there was a limit to how long she could handle that contact between us. Nevertheless, I was grateful for that moment. I also learned to watch her out of the corner of my eye. I enjoyed seeing that life in her.

I found participating with her in the Lord's Supper to be especially meaningful. I can't explain this. As with most of the worship service, Jan showed no awareness of the Communion service. I would feed her the elements. She appeared to assume that I was giving her a pill and something to drink to wash it down.

Various church traditions have had a myriad of explanations about the presence of Christ in the Communion service. I will not get into a theological discussion about whether He is present in some way in the elements or if the whole service is symbolic. Theologians have written a myriad of books on this subject.

We know that the Lord is always with us. Any time or place we enter into worship of Him, He comes closer to us. Christians worldwide and over many centuries have personally known His unique presence as they participated in the Lord's Supper.

In those days, as Jan and I took the elements of Communion, I sensed that together, we were taking in Jesus Christ in a very personal way. It meant a lot to me to experience an assurance of Christ with and in Jan.

In March of 2016, I took Jan to a local community Good Friday service. It consisted of scripture readings and music about the crucifixion. During the service, people were invited to the front of the sanctuary. There they could take Communion by intinction, dipping the bread in the cup. It became overwhelming for me. I tried to serve Jan the elements, but they ended up on the floor. I then took a smaller piece of bread and got it in her mouth. The difficulty in serving her Communion was very stressful. I knew whether Jan could take the elements was not a problem with the Lord. But somehow, it was important to me. Of course, I knew the day would come when I would not be able to serve her at all. After we returned to where we were sitting, a woman came to me, put her arm around me, and prayed for me. I don't know who she was and never looked at her enough to recognize her if I were to see her again. But I appreciated it and thanked her. I also felt someone else's hand on my back while she prayed. I have no idea who it was. Might it have been the Lord? And about that woman who prayed for me, I noticed, when she walked away from us, that she was clothed entirely in white. Was she an angel?

I'm not clear about the emotions I had at such times. *Sorrow* is not an accurate term, although there was discomfort. Nor was it tears of joy as the emotional happy ending of a movie. *Overwhelming* might be a good term. It would be best just to let myself fully feel it and not try to understand it.

Reflecting on this experience, I realized that Communion with Jan, in her state of dementia, was usually a challenge. It occurred to me that the first Lord's Supper was hours away from Jesus's death. He knew it was His last meal before His execution. I have mentioned how a person to be executed is traditionally offered the dinner of his choice for his last meal. Jesus chose to have the Passover meal before His death. The first Passover meal was just before massive deaths in Egypt. Every Lord's Supper I had with Jan could easily have been the last. I would want it to be a very personal time for us together. But she acted like she was indifferent. I understood, but that hurt. But perhaps she had more important things on her mind than something I am trying to put in her mouth. How did Jesus feel as He expressed His longing to be with His disciples for this last very personal meal, and they didn't get it (Luke 22:15)? It was the early part of the suffering of His crucifixion.

Reflecting more on that Good Friday service, I recalled my earnest desire to take the Communion elements *with Jan*. Then the Holy Spirit gave me a deep conviction. In my desire to partake of the Lord's Supper with Jan, I failed to think about something much more important. I had needed to focus on participating in the Lord's Supper *with the Lord*. What was a good desire had taken dominance over what was far more significant. While I was feeling very convicted of this, I sensed the Lord smiling on me and saying, "Elton, I already forgave you for that a long time ago. But now, understand what you did and what I have done."

In response to this, I prayed, "Lord, forgive me for what You have already forgiven me."

Since all of this and more, the Communion service has continued to have special meaning for me. I put together a list of the various aspects of the Lord's Supper that I experience. I do not pretend that this list is complete.

In the Lord's Supper, I have:

- An experience of Jesus at the last meal before His death.
- A distinct sense of the presence of Christ that is unique for this occasion.
- An awareness that I am celebrating the Lord's Supper with the entire body of Christ in all the earth and in heaven. There is only one body of Christ, one church. There is not a church on earth and another church in heaven. I am taking part in the Lord's Supper with Jan and all the saints everywhere.

- A profound encounter with the death of Christ, the death of people we especially love, and my impending death.
- A remembering of all my experiences of the Lord's Supper with Jan.
- Both the emotions of missing her and gratitude for my life with her.
- A sense of intimacy with my new wife, Linda, in celebrating the Lord's Supper with her.
- Gratitude to the Lord for giving me more than I even asked to have.
- The Lord furthering Linda and me on our journey together.
- Perhaps the shortest sermon ever preached consisted of the following sentence, "It's Friday, but Sunday's a-comin." Communion helps me get a deeper grasp of this statement.

To sense all this is overwhelming. It's beyond what words can express.

When the time comes to partake, I find it is better just to take part.

Intimacy

My experiences with trying to have closeness with Jan as she declined, the complete loss of her with her death, and then with a new wife, Linda, led me to consider a closer relationship beyond connection. As I lost and was losing Jan, I realized how much more I could have had. I feel deeply grateful to have that opportunity again with Linda. I pray I may, to a much greater degree, embrace that opportunity.

That relationship is called intimacy. The following are a formulation of my thoughts and limited understandings of this relationship. But first, you might like to go to the end of the chapter and read a poem I wrote on intimacy. However, I do think the poem will mean more to you after you have read this chapter. So I leave the choice to you.

Two porcupines are together on an unbearably cold winter night. To get warm, they come close together. Then they give each other too much pain to handle. So they put some distance between each other. They get cold again and repeat, trying to come together, but with the same result. They spend the night in an accordion-back-and-forth relationship.

Human beings are much like these porcupines. They have a great desire, a longing, to be close to someone. But when they do get close to someone, there is hurt. The saying "you always hurt the one you love" rings true. So they back off from each other. But then that drive revives, and they repeat the process. And they do so over and over.

That longing is called a drive, a need for intimacy. The thesis of this chapter—and it could be said of this book—is stated in two parts: First, the greatest desire, even the greatest need for every human being, is for intimacy. Second, the greatest dread and fear of every human being is intimacy.

Intimacy is being known and understood. To say to someone, "You don't understand me," may be to express sorrowful distance from that person. To say, "No one understands me," may be a statement of painful loneliness.

People sometimes divide the word *intimacy* into sections that together say, "Into me may see." To be known and understood may give the most excellent possible satisfaction and gratification. But on the other hand, it may be an extremely painful exposure, dreaded beyond all other hurts.

There is a difference between connection and intimacy. Before the pandemic restrictions, I did some volunteer chaplaincy work at a local hospital. Usually I went from room to room and introduced myself as a chaplain to each patient. I could tell almost immediately if I would be able to connect with that patient. It is possible to establish a connection very quickly. An intimate relationship takes time, even, sometimes in particular, for couples that fall in love at first sight.

Intimacy is more than learning about another person. That can come with a connection. It is more than communicating well and even beyond words of connection. It is knowing that person on a much deeper level. Connection is a relationship with the person. For example, there can be a relationship with a connection between two people who have an antagonism to each other. In intimacy, the relationship is a bond that drives them to stay together. A connection can be with several, even many, people. However, deep intimacy is only with one other person and with God.

Connection itself is safe, even if the other person is dangerous and a threat to one's physical safety. A connection can be enjoyable and beneficial, but it does not have the fulfillment of intimacy. Intimacy can be threatening. It is being vulnerable. Being vulnerable does not mean something wrong will happen, but it could. With intimacy, there is always the question, do I really want that person to know me? There is also the question of how much I really want to see that person.

Why We Desire Intimacy

An infant and his mother have had the experience of being one, one inside the other. One is utterly dependent on the other for its existence. That could be considered as an even greater intimacy and oneness than that of sexual intercourse. And the very creation of human life, the connection of an egg and a sperm, is a unique nonverbal union.

Then there is the traumatic event of birth. After being shoved through the birth canal, the baby is thrust into the wide-open world of light and noise. It's uncomfortable. It helps some to have their eyes closed, but the baby can't do anything about the noise. Being wrapped up in a swaddling clothes outfit also helps some. It makes him feel a little more like he felt in the womb. I have a picture on the refrigerator of one of my grandsons, taken shortly after his birth. His mother is enjoying holding him close to her. However, the look on his face suggests that he would like to say something like, *Hey, guys, I was doing fine where I was. Why couldn't you just leave me there?* It does help to be held and held close to someone's heart.

It is not difficult to surmise that there remains, in every human being, a desire to return to the security and intimacy of the womb. When I worked in Child Protective Services, we would observe that neglected babies, in particular, who were not often held, did not develop normally. The term *failure to thrive* seemed to come from this phenomenon. Thus it seems evident that the drive for closeness, for intimacy, is innate in everyone.

The innate drive for intimacy goes back much further. It had its origin in creation.

Genesis 2:18 states, "Then the LORD God said, 'It is not good that the man should be alone; I will make him a helper fit for him.'"

The term *alone* in Hebrew, according to *Strong's Concordance*, means separation; for example, a limb separated from a branch or even a human limb separated from the rest of the body. Unquestionably it is not healthy for anyone to have that kind and degree of separation. Thus this verse would be saying that there is, innate in all human beings, at least a need for companionship.

The question then is what will take care of that need. Adam had a relationship with God. But Adam was created with a need for a relationship with something also created. God gave him the opportunity and capacity to examine all the creatures of the earth. He found that none of them could address his need.

Then God created Eve, a woman. Verse 23 has Adam say, "At last." He realizes that this is the answer to his search. He speaks of her as being "bone of my bone and flesh of my flesh." He recognizes that she is different than all the creatures he had examined earlier. He is aware that she has come from him, and she, it can be presumed, is conscious that she has come from him. Note the parallel to a mother knowing her baby came from her, and the baby, we can surmise, is aware that he came from his mother.

Verse 24 speaks of marriage. If that verse relates to verse 18, then it says this intrinsic need in all people can only be wholly satisfactorily met in marriage.

That is *not* to say that everyone needs earnestly to pursue marriage. There are those—yes a minority, and I will not speculate as to what percentage—for whom God has a calling for which He, in His grace, enables the person to live a whole, meaningful, and gratifying life yet in the state of being single. The Apostle Paul speaks to this in 1 Corinthians 7:6f. And in Scripture, we do have the examples of the prophet Jeremiah, the Apostle Paul, and Jesus Christ Himself all being single.

In Matthew 19:9–12, Jesus addressed the possibility of someone not marrying. I take the term *eunuch* to mean more than someone who was castrated, even though in that day, that was the usual meaning. I suggest the following broader meaning of verse 12, with its list of various ways certain people become eunuchs. First, people have different personalities, including relational capacities, positive and negative, innate from birth. Some have such inherent characteristics that they are not good marriage material for anyone unless there is a radical change in their fundamental character. Second, due to how some people were treated as children, they cannot form a positive marriage relationship. Third, some experience a call of God to live a single life, at least for some significant period of their life (Jeremiah 16:2; 1 Corinthians 7:7, 8; 9:5). Finally I think it was nice of Paul to acknowledge that not everyone is gifted to do what he, Paul, could do.

There is, in Scripture, the description of a special bond between David and Jonathan (1 Samuel 18:1–3). Jesus had a special relationship with Lazarus and John. There is no indication in Scripture that these were sexual relationships.

As the result of the fall, we live in an imperfect and unfair world. There are many people well suited for marriage, but circumstances make marriage unavailable to them. Others are married and with their spouse but unable to have the intimate interactions usually available in marriage. Such was the situation for Jan and me. I explored ways to still relate to her as intimately as possible. Being in our fourth marriage decade gave us a base for a sense of still having an intimate relationship with each other.

Was Adam's experience of aloneness an experience of loneliness? I will contend that it was not. Loneliness is the result of the fall and the consequent universal presence of sin. Aloneness, or perhaps a better term is *solitude*, is good because it leads to something even better, namely a better relationship with God or other people, or both. So it was good that Adam, for a time, was alone. But Genesis 2:18 is saying that it is not good for Adam, man, to remain alone. Because of the fall, everyone experiences loneliness. But the goal for everyone is to move from loneliness to solitude, from which can go deeper, and even the deepest relationship.

Why We Fear Intimacy

As strong as is this desire for intimacy, there are reasons why we also fear it and will make efforts to avoid it. Generally regarded as highest on the list is the fear of rejection. If I do what is required for intimacy, namely letting someone see me as I am, my partner might not like what she sees. That rejection can tell me that I am not good enough and bring me to think of myself that way. How reassuring it is to realize that God sees every aspect of me just as I am. With that perspective, He not only accepts me, He loves me. Knowing that can give me a positive image that can take away the sting of rejection.

Second, since intimacy means exposing myself, it means allowing me to be vulnerable to someone. That makes it possible for that person to take advantage of me and to hurt me. There is also the possibility that if that other person lets me see into her, I could be tempted to take advantage of or hurt her.

For intimacy to happen, there needs to develop a relationship of trust. But no human being is entirely trustworthy. I cannot even trust myself constantly to be trusted. To have an intimate relationship with another human being, I need that relationship with God, who is always reliable. I can even trust Him to bring me back in line when I am not trustworthy. If my intimate partner violates my trust, God will take me through the hurt my partner caused.

The closer we are to someone, the greater the potential for conflict. We usually don't have conflicts with casual acquaintances. As two people get to know each other, they become aware of their differences. Some differences may provide a good balance. Others are fodder for conflict. Conflict brings up the desire to win. Intimacy means letting the other person know my weaknesses and my strengths. That gives the other person material to help her win.

Guarding yourself, keeping to yourself your weaknesses that might make it more difficult to win arguments, is a poor way to engage in conflict. A healthy engagement happens when both parties open themselves to the possibility that they are wrong, at least in part. Both partners need to be willing to realize and acknowledge where they are wrong when conflicts arise. Neither partner should engage in disagreements to win the argument. The purpose needs to be to discover truth, a best course of action, regardless of who was the initiator of that position. That requires humility or what Scripture calls meekness (Matthew 5:5)

Finally—and I fully acknowledge there could be other possibilities, even though I make every attempt to be who I really am before my partner—she may still misunderstand me. She could come to see me more positively than I do. She could put me on a pedestal. If this continues to develop, both the top and bottom of the pedestal could continue to get smaller. At some point, I will either fall off or be knocked off. Then my partner gets a new image of me. We need the Holy Spirit's guidance to help us know ourselves and present ourselves as we are to other people.

Marriage

Unless someone has a special calling of God, it is the human relationship most desired. Yet because it is the most intimate human relationship, it is the one that causes the most anxiety. It is the strongest possible bond between two people. Yet it is the most fragile, the most easily hurt bond between two people. Marriage can bring out the best in a person. But conversely, it can bring out the worst in a person, especially if it ends in divorce.

There is a "two become one" that is uniquely possible in marriage. It is life together, even when circumstances cause them to be physically separated for a time. They are still united. Any living together produces knowledge of each other not otherwise possible. Other relationships can be very close. But they are not a marriage. It is a relationship where whatever affects one affects the other. Whatever one does, says, thinks, or feels is, in some manner, participated in by the other.

Sexual intercourse is the most physically intimate act possible between two human beings. That is because it primarily (from a physical standpoint) involves the most intimate parts of the two human beings. In intercourse, the man goes into the woman. The woman receives the man. Genesis

2:24 states that "the two become one flesh." God clearly designed the male and female body for this intimate act to be possible.

In Genesis 2, the woman's origin is from within the man—his rib. And for every person, conception and the first stage of his life is inside someone else, his mother. That is the first experience of intimacy for a person (what effect would the production of a total test-tube baby have on its ability to be intimate, i.e., the *Brave New World* scenario?). Thus intimacy is at the very core of the beginning of our existence.

Marriage is a lifetime process of coming closer and closer to totally knowing each other in every aspect. God designed it to be ended only by Him, not by human action (Matthew 19:6). Marriage does bring out some further challenges on the path of developing intimacy.

Intimacy is hard work. It often demands effort when we don't feel like making it. The rewards of that effort can be very gratifying, but they are down the road. Intimacy is a process. In marriage, becoming one is not instantaneous at the wedding altar or the consummation of the marriage. Becoming one, becoming intimate, is a lifetime process.

In my single life, I did not have to be deeply involved with others. Life can be more straightforward and relatively predictable. With intimacy, there is always an unpredictability about the other person. There is always more to learn about the other person. That can be fascinating, but it also means there is always the unknown about the other person. All this brings out new things about oneself. That too can be either fascinating and good or threatening or both. Intimacy can be the way to find out both the best and the worst in oneself.

Intimacy means a change of identity. Before, my primary identity is in myself with God. Now a second and vital addition is added—being in a relationship with another person. Thus intimacy involves change. Change can bring good but also result in loss and grief, even when losing something we need to lose. Intimacy means I will be changing as the other person changes. And I don't know how the other person will change, nor do I know how I will change. So even very positive change can bring anxiety.

Relationship to God

Scripture asserts the truth that God created human beings to have a relationship of love with Him. Therefore, the most intimate relationship a person can have is his relationship with God. Given the nature of intimacy, it is what we most desire and, at the same time, what we most fear.

God, and God alone, knows every aspect of us (Psalm 139). He knew us before we existed. He loved us so much that He wanted us to be living beings and enjoy all the benefits of being alive. He loves us enough not to let our existence end. With death, He profoundly changes the nature of our existence. He loves us enough to let us go if we so choose.

The most frightening relationship we can have is with God. With another human being, I can hide much—if not most—of what I don't want that person to know. Even in the closest human relationships, there is always something hidden from one's partner. With God, I can't hide anything. Yet I can know little of God, no matter how close I am to Him. The alternatives are either a fear of God, using denial to avoid God, ignoring God, or a profound trust in God. The desire for intimacy is, most fundamentally, the desire for God, and the fear of intimacy is a fear of God.

God is addressed in Scripture as Father. The classic Lord's Prayer begins with "Our Father." Notice the father-child imagery of our relationship with God. A child knows very little about his father and knows much less than his father. The father knows much more about his child and everything else (disregarding teenagers for the moment). But that is not a concern to a child who is wholly trusting his father. Also a child is accountable to his father for his behavior and attitude. His father can punish him for his behavior. For this reason, he may hide some of his behaviors from his father. That is what Adam and Eve did in Genesis 3.

There are several well-known reasons people reject the Christian faith or any form of relationship with God.

a) The hypocrisy they see in the lives of believers. They see people not living what they profess to believe.

b) They have a negative experience with people who are part of a church.

c) Something unfair happened to them, or they see unjust events happening, and God lets it all happen.

d) There are philosophical questions: Is there God? If He is a good and powerful God, why does He allow evil? Is the Bible true? The list goes on.

e) Then there is the most profound reason—the fear of intimacy with God.

God and Marriage

1 Peter 3:7 speaks of how a husband is to treat his wife. The verse ends by stating that he is to do this "so that your prayers may not be hindered."

When Jan and I went to the pastor, who officiated our wedding, for premarital counseling, he focused our attention on this verse. It brought home the vital role of prayer for a good marriage. Jan and I did pray together, and it helped us. However, we could have done more with prayer, and it would have done more for our marriage.

I have found that it is common among Christian couples, including pastors, that they do not have an active prayer life together. Why might that be? I suggest that the answer lies in the nature of prayer. When a married couple prays, we have two people in the most intimate human relationship relating to God in the intimate manner of prayer. That is a lot of intimacy for any two people to handle.

Given the human tendency to fear intimacy, it is not surprising that we resist prayer. To go to a prayer meeting involves becoming closer to other people while coming closer to God. That can be very threatening. That easily results in prayer meetings being the church activity with the least attendance. The most intimate prayer is to pray with one's marriage partner. So naturally, the most dedicated Christian couples can find in themselves a resistance to praying together.

Scripture states that the most important commandment is to love God and love other people (Matthew 22:37–39). We have here two commands inseparably bound together as one command. The marriage relationship is designed to be a model or representation of the relationship of Christ and the church (Ephesians 5:32). The Greek language in which the New Testament of the Bible was first written has several words for love. The love to which God calls us in 1 Corinthians 13 is agape love. That is the love of God for people and the love people are to have for God. And it is the love people are to have for each other. Engaging in this love is challenging.

It is good to note here that there is a distinction between love and intimacy. The greatest commandment is not to be intimate but to love. It is possible to love without intimacy.

We are called to love whether or not there is intimacy. It is not possible to have intimacy without love.

The greatest possible intimacy with another person is only possible in conjunction with an intimate relationship with God. The closer two people come to God, the closer they come to each other. And coming closer to each other in a godly manner will draw them closer to God. Conversely drifting from God can hurt their marriage, and the onset of marital distance can distance each of them from God.

A couple who are not with the Lord has a ceiling boundary to their intimacy. But when the Lord is in their relationship, the limitations to their intimacy are infinitely expanded. So I needed the Lord to be able to pursue intimacy with Jan throughout her dementia.

What if one partner is closer to God than the other? 1 Corinthians 7 and 1 Peter 3 note a marriage where one partner is a believer and the other is not. It asserts that the believing partner can have a spiritual effect on the unbelieving partner or the partner not as close to God. Not being on the same page spiritually will affect their relationship with God and each other. It can make for a difficult marriage. Part of what Job suffered was his wife's spiritual perspective (Job 2:9, 10).

Scripture is skeptical about the prospects of a Christian bringing a non-Christian spouse to the Lord (2 Corinthians 6:14; 1 Corinthians 7:16; 1 Peter 3:1). There is data readily available online that bears this out.

There are a couple more reasons we tend to fear intimacy brought out in the marriage relationship. One is the realization that an intimate relationship will almost always involve sacrifice. Intimacy invokes love, and love calls for sacrifice with no guarantee of reciprocation. Ephesians 5:25f is another description of the role of the husband in a marriage. It is a call to be prepared to sacrifice himself for his wife as

Christ sacrificed Himself for the church. Note that Christ's sacrifice was crucifixion. To keep all this in balance, note that the earlier call in this text is for the wife to obey her husband. That can certainly qualify as a sacrifice.

Where was intimacy in a situation like I had with Jan, especially in the unresponsiveness of her last months? It was found in the tender moments that still happened, in the sharing of the Lord's Supper, in a kiss that was the only thing she could share, and in her presence.

It was discovered in the sense of loss and mourning, the expression of grief. It was present in times of talking about her or thinking about her, and all words ended.

Finally there is the fear of losing the person, of separation. Is it a good idea to invest in an intimate relationship that is going to end? Parents bring a child into this world and heavily invest themselves and all their resources with no guaranteed results. Parents raise their children with the goal that they will leave and go out on their own. Yet the greatest joy of parenting is to see their children go out into the world as responsible mature adults.

For children, their greatest fear can be abandonment, where at least one parent doesn't stay with him or even with the other parent.

The divorce rate of marriages amply demonstrates that marriage carries no guarantees. The fear of intimacy can drive someone to an affair. An extramarital relationship can keep someone "safe" from intimacy. Even apart from infidelity, most marriages have stresses that can pull them apart. For every marriage ending in divorce, I often wonder how many end up without affection and love, much less intimacy. How many couples do no more than coexist?

No relationship remains static. In the long run, it either grows or declines. For it to grow, effort is required. Some couples have no difficulty doing what brings them closer together. Others require deliberate, conscious, intensive struggle that can be very uncomfortable. No effort is needed to make a relationship decline.

Except in the movies such as *The Notebook*, one partner dies before the other. That makes it almost a given that anyone in an intimate relationship will either lose their partner or subject her to the same situation. So people fear intimacy because of a dread of its loss.

I, nevertheless, deliberately made a conscious decision to be as close to Jan as possible until the moment of her death. I knew it would be hard. When it happened, it was very hard. Afterward, looking back, I am, without reservation, grateful that I did. It was a most precious experience yet one I would never want to have again nor wish on anyone.

Jesus knew what it was to lose intimate relationships. At the Last Supper, He sat down with those He was closest. They were all emotionally distant from Him. They had, on several occasions, heard Jesus talking about dying and dying by crucifixion. It made them uncomfortable. Perhaps it was dawning on the disciples that this could happen. But they were also in a state of denial.

At Gethsemane, He wanted His closest disciples near Him. Instead, they fell asleep. No doubt, they were exhausted. But sleep was a means of avoiding the reality that Jesus was trying to prepare them to face.

As He hung on the cross, they left Him. Two left Him even earlier. On the cross, Jesus yelled, "My God, My God, why have You forsaken Me?" Jesus had known intimate relationships, but now He was stripped of all of them. There can come a time where a loss of intimacy is a participation in the sufferings of Christ.

Although this is one of my longest chapters, I conclude that I have come nowhere near adequately covering the subject of intimacy. Nevertheless, I will be audacious enough to propose that it gives some insight into this matter. I will not be so foolish as to suggest that someone reading this chapter now knows intimacy for what it is. One can understand when he has it, doesn't have it, or has it to a degree. In any case, words are an inadequate means for describing what he has or doesn't have.

The only way to even approach a grasp of intimacy is to engage in it. Perhaps this chapter does help us understand why we are reluctant to do that. It is much easier and more comfortable to reflect on and write about it than to engage in it. Sometimes what cannot be expressed adequately in prose gains at least some expression by putting it in the genre of poetry. The following is in poetical form of what I have tried to express in the last several pages.

Intimacy

our greatest desire.
our greatest fear.

total exposure.
total coverage.
the greatest security.
the greatest insecurity.

the greatest fear of loss.
the greatest sorrow from loss.
the best way not to know loss.

conflict creator.
conflict resolution.

the place
one is most influenced by another.
one is most himself and no other.

change
stability

No one
can see it,
can say what it is.

Everyone
knows what it is,
knows it when he sees it.

Talk about it?
First, be a poet.

Jan's Death

Bill's Death

Jan was the oldest of four children. She had two sisters and a brother, the youngest sibling. About two and a half years before Jan passed, her brother, Bill, developed severe health problems. One of her sisters had him hospitalized. It became apparent that he might not live much longer. That was another grief journey for me.

I took Jan to see Bill. He was in the critical care unit, hooked up to life support, and unconscious. He was barely recognizable. I asked Jan if she knew who that was. She replied, "Bill." I was visibly moved by what I saw. Jan showed no emotional reaction either to Bill or to me. That was hard, but I understood.

In less than two weeks, the medical personnel determined that Bill could not recover. Jan's sisters decided to have the life support removed. Bill died shortly after that.

Jan was more affectionate for a short time after I told her Bill had died. I took that as a reaction to her brother's death. When I asked her if she knew where Bill was, she said, "Heaven." Otherwise it was hard to read much emotional reaction in her.

I took Jan to the graveside and funeral services. Renee was with us, and Jan did well. Again it was hard to read her emotions. That evening, we had a family gathering at my daughter Lori's home. She and her family live nearby, here in Turlock.

Jan's World

I have mentioned that it is not unusual for a dying person to withdraw from others. I noted the examples of my mother and Elijah, in Scripture. They can be in a different world from others. When Jan was diagnosed in April 2011, we both understood that she would die from this disease. Jan could state very casually but meaningfully that she was going to die. That made a significant difference between us. I have never been in that state where I was facing my death as she was hers.

Almost six months before my father passed in 2002, he told me that he was ready to die. He was comfortable with his relationship with God in Christ, and with that, he had prepared for death. He kept a very positive spirit during his last months. I had been close to my dad and was still closer those final months.

I was not prepared to hear Dad talk that way. I didn't share my reactions with him. I could and did share a lot with Jan, and she could see my grief. I was in a world of the grieving. I didn't feel that she understood my world. As an old popular song said, "We live in two different worlds." Although we were very far apart, we were very close. It was a difficult time, and it was a most precious time. We lived facing death in our separate ways. In different worlds, we lived together. Not understanding each other, we were intimate.

Jesus knew the world of grief. He wept at Lazarus's tomb. At His triumphal entry, He wept over Jerusalem. He also knew the world of the dying. He understood early on that He was going to die. He even knew how and when He would die. He lived in a world of grieving and a world of dying. Living, embracing both worlds, He lived and was alive in the fullest possible life.

For several weeks, about four years before her death, Jan would either say she was about to die or had died. There were incidents where, as I was about to take her someplace, she would advise me not to be upset if she died while we were there. There were several incidents, during that time, of her telling someone she was about to die.

One evening, she told me she had died that afternoon. She said she was going to the mortuary. Her body would be there, but she was going to heaven. I asked her how she knew she was dead, and she said she wasn't breathing. The following morning, I asked her if she was still dead, and she said, "No."

On a few occasions, Jan would say she was dead or dying when I wanted her to do something she didn't want to do. After all, if she was dying, I shouldn't expect anything of her.

When Jan said she was dying, I found that the best response was to reply, "It is the Lord who decides when you will die." That seemed to satisfy and to settle the matter, at least for a while.

Sometimes her reference to dying was indirect. Several times, she said she thought we had lost a day. I suggested we could get along without it, and she seemed satisfied. She sometimes responded by saying, "I think we should get on the same day as the world." For a while, she was concerned we might get Ebola. That was when there was an outbreak in Africa. Fortunately she accepted my assurances that that wasn't likely.

On several occasions, Jan said she did not want to die alone or be in heaven alone. She wanted me to go to the next life with her. I couldn't adequately explain to her that I was unable to arrange that. My best response was to tell her that she would not be alone. Jesus would be with her. That seemed to reassure her.

One could attribute these statements from Jan as coming from her dementia. The state of her brain did affect how she communicated. At the same time, I am confident that she had come to where death was present for her in a way that it had not yet been for me. But what she said did help draw me into her world with at least some grasp of it. Interestingly it didn't pull me into a further grief state. I felt it drew me closer to her. I do wish I had entered more deeply into what she was saying.

Rehearsals

One morning, Jan was sitting at the kitchen table, eating breakfast. Suddenly I could see her fading away. I could see she was not falling asleep. I had not seen this in her before. But I had seen it when I did orderly work. Her eyes had a faraway look. She was unresponsive. I was hesitant to call the medics. I was afraid she would end up in ICU, and I knew she didn't want that. She appeared to be dying. It didn't matter that she would be going to a better place.

I took her to the bedroom. As I laid her on the bed, she slapped me. It was not as strong as usual. It was the first time I was glad to get a slap. Debbie had called Renee, who came right over. We decided to take her to Same Day Care that connected with Family Medical and our doctor.

Jan had developed a urinary tract infection (UTI). Our doctor had prescribed a medication for it. I had given her a pill for it about twelve hours earlier and then again that morning, as specified. It turned out that the medicine was too strong for her. Our doctor changed her medication to something milder, and she was fine.

There were other times when I thought she might be dying very soon. She would enter a decline but then bounced back. However, she did not fully come back to where she was. She was like a bouncing rubber ball. Each time it came back up, it wasn't quite as far as the time before. I came to see these events as rehearsals for the day she would die. They were not pleasant. I found myself praying, "Lord, please, no more rehearsals." At the same time, I could see that they were a preparation for when Jan died.

The last few months, Jan kept getting closer and closer to death but was still alive. It was like a line on a graph that kept getting closer to zero without reaching that point.

The last three or four months before Jan's death, she seemed to smile more. Asleep, she often had a smile on her lips. It was hard not to have the thought that the Lord might be giving her glimpses of heaven, and she was smiling at what she saw.

One day, about three months before her death, I found myself crying as I kissed her and put my arms around her. Then I looked at her, and she was smiling. It was different than the smiles I usually saw on her. It seemed that what she saw was not my tears but our closeness.

Bedfast

In August 2016, I agreed, in consultation with hospice, that it was time to have Jan on complete bed rest. Hospice supplied a hospital bed for her. I wondered, at that time, if she would live until our fortieth anniversary in November. On July 4, 2017, the hospice doctor made a home visit. He commented that a year earlier if someone had told him that

Jan would be alive a year later, he wouldn't have believed it. Jan passed one week later.

Her bedfast condition meant I would not be taking her anywhere. What affected me the most was not being able to take her to church. I could have obtained someone to be with her while I attended. I didn't feel good about that because my attendance would keep someone else from going. The church we had been part of for decades had a radio broadcast of the service (this was before the live streaming of services that became common during the pandemic). On a Sunday, when the church observed the Lord's Supper, I used whatever was available for the elements.

One Sunday, our daughter Lisa, from Seattle, came for a visit. She offered to be with her mom while I attended a service. Listening to the service on the radio had worked fine, but I realized how much better it was and how much more it meant to be there. Toward the end of Jan's life, people from our Sunday morning class began watching Jan so I could go to church.

A hospice nurse advised me that with Jan's bedfast condition, I should turn her every two or three hours to prevent bedsores. That included at night, which was not a problem. I didn't need to set an alarm. Being a middle-aged male and with prostate problems, I would wake up at least twice. I had a routine. First, I checked that she was still breathing. Then I checked to see if she needed cleaning. Third, I turned her to prevent bedsores. Then I rekissed her good night.

Our daughter Lori gave Jan her pregnancy pillow. It was a U-shaped large pillow that Lori used while pregnant. Jan was very comfortable with it. It helped hold her in place after I turned her.

I attended an Elvis impersonation concert. I was enjoying it when I started thinking, *It sure would be nice to have*

Jan with me, even in a wheelchair, unable to talk, and not able to take in the concert. It caused tears.

Those days required that I put much more time and energy into caring for Jan. I had the means to get more help. The long-term care insurance would have covered the expense. I was asked if I would place Jan during her final days when she could no longer swallow food. My response was, "What for?" I saw no reason to do that. I was confident that Renee, Debbie, and I could continue to take care of her at that time. I wanted to have that extra involvement with her.

A friend pointed out that sometimes families prefer to place their loved one when death is imminent. They don't want the memories of their loved ones dying at home. I knew that home was where Jan and I wanted her to die. I never regretted that decision.

Eating

As Jan declined, her food intake also declined. Naturally with less activity, she needed less food. Her energy also declined. She could be too tired to eat. Sometimes she simply didn't want to eat. She would clamp her mouth shut, and nothing was going to go in it. Later she would be ready to eat. I learned to be careful about feeding her. She would not have a good sense of when she was full. There were times when she would "pocket" food. That is when someone in her condition would place food on the side of her cheek because she wasn't interested in eating. That could result in her choking on food. Toward the end, her digestive organs begin shutting down, and she was unable to digest food. With all this, I learned not to be overly concerned about getting her to eat.

Increasingly Jan had to eat only very soft food. After a while, I had to puree all her food. Chewing was beyond her capacity. She lost the ability to put food to the back of her mouth to swallow it. I had to place it back carefully. There was always the possibility of choking. In time, she could not drink water. A thickener had to be added to any liquids to enable swallowing.

As Jan's brain continued to deteriorate, her medications became less effective. Her brain no longer knew what to do with them. Pills to slow down the symptoms of her dementia had no relevance. The only appropriate prescriptions were for relieving discomfort. That included opiates. Some caregivers of a loved one are not comfortable giving such drugs. At this stage of Jan's life, I had no concerns about her becoming addicted. My focus needed to be on making her as comfortable as possible.

Making Funeral Preparations

About a year and a half before Jan passed, I decided to prepare for her funeral. Jan had already stated her desires. She wanted to make sure the Gospel message was presented. She anticipated there would be relatives there who were not Christians. She was concerned that they knew what it was to embrace Christ. She wanted to have the mortuary located near where she grew up. The service would be in the church we attended. Burial would be near her parents. There was another nearby cemetery where several of her relatives were buried. She reminded me, joking that she did not want to be buried there because she might argue with them. A friend of hers, Marlene Bauch, was an excellent soloist. Jan wanted her to sing and chose the songs for her to sing. She did not wish for any donations of her organs. I thought that would have been a good cause, but it was more important to honor her wishes.

I sought to and did fulfill all her desires except one. She wanted Pastor Stensether, the pastor most of the years we attended Crossroads Church, to officiate at the service. I couldn't fulfill that wish because he died before she did. It was a nice thought that he was the officiating greeting pastor as she entered heaven.

I found myself having anxiety about what would happen when Jan died. I discovered that making preparations could decrease that anxiety. That might not work for everyone. It is a personal decision. Many people might ask, "Why not just enjoy her while she is still alive?"

My response was, "Why not do both?"

I anticipated, and when the time came around, that having most preparations taken care of made her death much less overwhelming. Facing the grief from the loss of a loved one, plus having to make a lot of preparation decisions, can be too much to bear. After my initial reaction to Jan's passing, I spent time calmly letting people know of her death and the funeral plans.

I contacted the funeral home and arranged the services they would provide. I picked out a casket and flowers. I went to the cemetery where she would be buried and purchased a plot. I contacted Jan's friend about singing at the service. I also arranged for Renee to sing a solo. I asked Lois Johnson, one of Jan's sisters, and our daughter Lori to prepare a PowerPoint of her life. They did an excellent job.

I wrote an obituary for the local paper. When the time came, I gave a copy to the funeral director, and he arranged for its publication.

I decided to have a viewing of her. Some people don't want to have such a viewing of their loved ones, feeling that they don't want that to be their last memory. In seminary, we were told that viewing has a positive purpose—helping people face the truth that the person has passed. I decided that it would remind me that she had fought the good fight, finished the race, and now was receiving her reward (2 Timothy 4:7, 8). Viewing was not mandatory.

The church had a coordinator of weddings and funerals. I first met with her almost two years before Jan's passing. She was very helpful. As I met with her, we reviewed the plans I was making. When Jan passed, she took care of many matters that made it much easier for me. She saw to it that the funeral service and reception afterward ran very smoothly.

I knew I wanted to speak at the service. I was questioned as to whether that was advisable. I knew it would not be easy. Most widowed people wouldn't attempt it. The obvious question was, what if I couldn't complete my presentation? I considered that. I had decided to speak from a manuscript. I arranged for a close friend to have a copy of my talk with him. If I was unable to continue, he could come up and complete it.

I was reminded that a funeral is a service to minister to those who attend, including myself. So at the service, I should be receiving instead of giving. I concluded that I wanted the service to allow me to express what Jan meant to me.

I did not have a difficult time preparing what I wanted to say. It was personal and stirred my emotions. But having spent years writing my journal and other writings, I had enough experience to handle this writing assignment. The challenge was to be prepared to deliver the talk.

I started by reading it out loud. I was soon able to handle that emotionally. I continued with reading it to one or more close friends, including Jan. That was a different matter. In every case, I was able to present it without a problem. But as soon as I finished, I would break down. After doing this at least a dozen times, I was able to be composed when I finished. And the composure was genuine. I was not stuffing any emotions.

It occurred to me that I had been reading this paper primarily as a grief catharsis. It did serve that function. Then I discovered that it was also an expression of thankfulness to God for the marriage he gave me with Jan and for the support from other people. The paper was a thanksgiving for good memories. That added perspective gave me a new strength to present my paper.

Besides making all these funeral arrangements, I also took care of our financial and legal matters. In consultation with a lawyer, I drew up a will. I had our accounts put in trust. I mentioned earlier having a form specifying Jan's end-of-life directives. After Jan passed, I had no problems accessing any of our financial accounts.

During the last weeks before Jan's passing and knowing her end was near, I realized how accustomed I had become to caring for her. I had ideas of what I would do after Jan was gone. Yet I felt anxiety about how I would handle the freedom I would then have. Again change of any kind produces anxiety. It's not unlike what many people are experiencing as I write this chapter. Our country appears to be coming out of the pandemic. Many are experiencing anxiety about going back to work, socializing, traveling, going to church, and other "normal" activities.

I composed a poem during Jan's final weeks. I think it addresses and even gives an answer to this anxiety.

But Still

We are doing well, but still…
We know it's all working for good, but
    still…

> We know God will take us through to
> what He has planned, but still...
> We know that He has a beautiful, won-
> derful plan,
> but still...but still...but still...
> And then He says to us, "Be still."

It just occurred to me that I used *we* instead of *I* in this poem. I think I was aware, more than I knew, how much of this same anxiety was in other people, especially our families and Debbie and Renee, my caregivers.

The Last Day

On Monday, July 10, 2017, I had cataract surgery. Those created concerns. Would she die during the surgery or when I was still not fully conscious? But it had to be done. The surgeon had arranged for an extension of my license until the surgery would enable me to pass the eye exam. It quickly improved my distance vision. But would I be able to read my paper at the funeral?

By Tuesday, July 11, Jan had eaten almost nothing the last two days. She was on oxygen all the time. A hospice nurse gave Jan three to five days, possibly a week. I called Lisa in Seattle, and she arranged to come down with her kids as soon as possible.

On Wednesday, June 12, I could not get a reading on the oximeter, even with the oxygen on her. I gave her some morphine. That helped her breathe more comfortably. I kissed her. Her lips gave no response. I told her Lisa was coming and asked her to hang on until she arrived. No response.

As I stated earlier, I had decided not to try to be with Jan the moment she died. If it happened, that would be good.

If not, that would be okay. That took away a lot of stressful waiting. At 1:07 p.m., I was in the living room talking with a hospice social worker. Debbie came in and said that Jan died. I came to the family room and instantly saw that was true. I had been prepared to be unprepared, and when the time came, I was unprepared.

I broke down in a tidal wave of grief, as though it was something unexpected, even though all day, I was expecting it to happen. All of Greg's and Lori's families and several hospice people came over, but I was virtually unaware of them. I remember seeing a hospice worker leaving and noting that I had no idea she was there. My son-in-law Brad later told me that I was in "utter grief." My family stayed until 11:00 p.m.

Debbie called me the next day. She said that just before Jan died, she called out, "Mom, Mom" several times. On several occasions in the past, when something meaningful happened, Jan would say, "I wish I could share that with Mom." I couldn't help but think that perhaps Jesus had come for Jan and brought Jan's mother with Him.

Regardless of what happened, it was a remarkable event. Jan had not uttered a sound for at least a year and a half. With her disease, over time, the brain develops cavities and shrinks to about one-third of standard size. So how was she able to articulate anything at that time?

Lisa and her children had been here about a month earlier. All of them contacted an infectious virus. So Lisa didn't go close to her mother. Jan passed about four hours before Lisa arrived. After Lisa had an opportunity to see her, the mortician came. I helped put her body on the gurney, holding her head and upper body. Two years earlier, I had decided I wanted to do that.

He put a blanket over her. It bothered me when he put it over her head, but I understood.

I have wished Lisa had gone ahead and gone close to, hugged, her mother. Would it really have mattered if that caused Jan to die a few weeks earlier? But at the time, it clearly seemed to be the right thing to do. There are no easy answers. We did the best we knew to do at the time.

That night, Lisa and her children slept in the guest bedroom. I was alone; Jan was gone. The next day, workers came and took the hospital bed and oxygen equipment. The large couch, TV, a rocking chair, and a table were still in the room. Pictures were on the walls. The room was empty.

Funeral

The funeral service was one week after her death. During that week, I was able to have a good time with Lisa. We did some shopping. We took the kids to the county fair. I enjoyed it, even though I went through a lot of emotions. I agreed it was wise to have Lisa do all my driving for me. My emotional state had a physical effect. I became acquainted with Imodium.

The viewing of Jan went well. Several people came, and I enjoyed greeting them. It was hard emotionally. I spent some time standing beside the casket and touched her body. It was hard. I kissed her lips, and they were soft but, of course, unresponsive. I don't think I said anything to her or tried to. I was present.

We had the graveside service before the funeral service. I was pleased with it. It was a good turnout and went as I had hoped. All my family was present, including my brother and sister, all my children and their families.

After the service, I touched the casket and broke down. Renee asked if I would be able to speak. I felt confident, not even nervous, that I could. I had had enough grief expressions that I was not concerned with how long they might last. Also I knew that if I didn't speak, I would always wish I had.

I was also pleased with the service at Crossroads Church. Renee and Marlene did excellent solos. Lois, Lori, and Lisa had excellent PowerPoint presentations. The officiating pastor was a good friend. His wife also died of dementia. We used to get together and compare notes. He spoke of our hope in heaven and certainly brought out the Gospel message.

I was able to deliver my entire presentation. I felt relaxed. Someone later told me I looked like I was enjoying myself. The congregation even laughed at my humorous sections. I had Debbie come up toward the end of my talk and share her experience of hearing Jan calling out to her mother.

The reception afterward also went well. I enjoyed greeting people. Again the funeral coordinator did a fine job. Toward the end of the reception, when most people had left, I sat down and relaxed. I was wearing a long-sleeve shirt. I pulled it up to check the time. I discovered that I had a bright-red rash on both wrists. No doubt, I had been operating on adrenaline. But no question, it was an act of God that got me through.

That night, I felt intense loneliness. Lisa and her family slept in the guest bedroom. But I felt very alone. I had the thought that I could get a bottle of scotch and chug it down. I could medicate all my emotions. But I knew that was not the answer. I knew it wouldn't help at all but only make things worse. I stayed in bed and fell asleep.

A couple of nights later, as I fell asleep, I heard a female voice speak to me, saying, *You have to take this. You have to go through this.* I understood. I had to go through the grieving process and adjust to life completely without Jan. I needed to accept that I would be going through a time of loneliness. With a bit of thought, I realized it was the Lord speaking to me. He used a female voice. God can use any tone He chooses.

I became aware of my emotions after the service. I felt like eating but felt full. I was tired, but it was difficult for me to rest. Grief was still present, but I didn't feel grief unless I focused on it. I wanted and enjoyed social interaction but wanted it deeper than anyone could give. I was fully confident that God was getting me through this, but it was still hard and created anxiety. I was concerned about all I needed to do; I was apprehensive about having too much empty space-time. The mix of emotions seemed to never end.

A New Normal

Shortly after the funeral, I spoke to the hospice staff at their regular staff meeting. I thanked all of them for their help. I noted that several of them had become part of Jan's and my family. While talking, I took off my wedding band.

I also shared with the caregiver support group, thanking them for their support. Without comment, I took off my wedding band while sharing. I continued to attend several more support group sessions. It did help make the transition. Other people in the group had done that as well.

One Sunday morning, I shared with the Sunday morning class that Jan and I had been part of for many years. While sharing, I removed my wedding band.

Taking off my wedding band might seem strange. Some people continue to wear theirs for some time after the death of their spouse. The reality of death's separation must be faced. It is a process. Each one has his timetable. Mine started while I still had Jan. When she died, it was time to engage in the process of moving on.

Well before Jan's death, I gave thought to what I might do after Jan died. I had a full-page listing of possible involvements. I did not attempt to do all of them. Having done this, I did not lack things to do. I avoided being at loose ends and the depression that can result.

Planning did not mean forgetting Jan. I still felt loneliness. I understood that activity would not take that away.

Nothing brings down grief except grieving. Grief is never gone, but in the acceptance of it comes joy.

I continued to meet with my counselor and spiritual formation coach. I met with friends. I took care of all the legal matters regarding finances and assets. I resumed volunteer work that I had been doing before Jan passed.

I made several visits to Jan's burial site. After a while, grass would start to grow over her tombstone. In time, there was a release as I viciously pulled out that unacceptable grass. Nearby was a tree for me to sit under, my grief tree. I continued to make trips to the living room. One chair in that room was my grief chair. I continued journaling and other writing. In all this and more, I met with God.

In the fall, my church had a clothing drive for victims of fires in Northern California. Until then, I hadn't given much thought to her clothes. Finally I decided to donate them. She had a lot of clothes, some of which I had never seen her wear. Giving those away was not a problem. Then there were clothes that I had put on her numerous times. I did not hesitate to donate them, but it was stirring.

February 24, 2018, was the first date of Jan's birthday after her death. We had a family gathering at my house. I gave Jan's wedding ring to Lori, our oldest daughter. My wedding band went to our son, Greg. Our daughter Lisa was not able to come. I announced that I would give her a ring I gave Jan for our thirty-seventh anniversary. In addition, I gave Jennifer, our daughter-in-law, a special necklace I had given Jan.

Someone suggested I get a dog for companionship. We had not had pets since the children were young. Jan was not fond of pets. I could have enjoyed a dog or other pet, but I knew a pet would not fill the hole in me. Having a pet would have been just another activity. Like Adam in Genesis 2, I needed more than an animal for companionship.

I endeavored to balance my needs to be with people and be alone, be active, be still, take care of business, and contemplate. Writing this book has led me to meditate on a myriad of things. It has made composing it much longer. Each person has to find his balance in these matters. As it is stated in Ecclesiastes 3:1, "For everything there is a season, and a time for every matter under heaven."

As part of Jesus's giving His all and going through it all for our salvation, He experienced extreme loneliness. I have discussed how Scripture says everyone left Him (Matthew 26:56). John 19:26 speaks of the disciple John and Jesus's mother, Mary, standing by Him. Any mother can only take so much without being overcome. John would have had to take her away. After that, Jesus yells, "My God, My God, why have You forsaken me" (Mark 15:24). Jesus could not have been more entirely alone.

There have been times when this verse has been particularly significant for me. In my loneliness, I still believed that God was present, but it seemed like He was far away. During those times, I felt like I could identify with Jesus and what He said.

Regret

It is impossible to go through life without making mistakes and without doing wrong. That means anyone's life will have events that one will wish he had done differently. Everyone has regrets.

Being a caregiver compounds the probability of committing regretful acts or having regretful attitudes. The caregiver faces myriads of emotions and mixed emotions, ever-changing situations, and situations with no clear answers. That can make one think he could have done better, even when he did make the best choice.

The solution is to accept the reality that we will make mistakes, and we will do wrong. Biblically this is to say that we are sinners, and sinners do wrong. Sin affects how we think. That distorts our judgment and results in making mistakes and bad choices. There is no reason to beat ourselves up over past actions. Accepting this reality can eliminate a lot of anxiety and regret.

Part of accepting that we will make mistakes is taking responsibility for our deeds. We may attempt to understand our actions, but we don't make excuses or blame others. Accepting responsibility where we have done wrong means repentance. Repentance is much more than being sorry for what we did. It means a sincere desire and commitment not to repeat that action. The most effective repentance is to confess before God, receive His forgiveness, and go forward living under His grace.

It is possible to feel guilt or regret over actions we took that did not include any wrongdoing. Confess and repent of those actions as well. It can bring comfort and release to us as we realize that God is not angry at us for those actions.

Taking responsibility for our actions means addressing how they may have affected others.

The ninth step of the twelve steps in the AA program states, "Made direct amends to such people (that we have harmed) wherever possible, except when to do so would injure them or others." And where our actions have affected our own lives, we do what we can to clean up our mess.

It is possible to receive God's forgiveness and the forgiveness of anyone we have wronged and still have a forgiveness difficulty. Often the most formidable challenge of forgiveness is to forgive ourselves.

If that is the case, consider the following question: if God has forgiven you, who are you not to forgive you? God is willing to forgive you. On the other hand, if you do not forgive yourself, are you holding yourself to a higher standard than God's?

If that is your situation, let me suggest the following exercise. Stand in front of a mirror, preferably a full-length mirror. Look directly at yourself in the mirror. If I am doing this exercise, I say the following, "Elton, God has forgiven you. So, Elton, I forgive you." Using your name, say this slowly and thoughtfully and as many times as needed. I think you will find it to be a powerful and helpful exercise.

Living a godly life is much more than doing what is right and good. It is just as much a matter of how one handles himself when—not if—he does wrong. When one does wrong, he can: (a) fully confess, (b) he can try to hide it, or (c) try to shift blame. The first alternative is hard initially. Alternatives *b* and *c* are harder in the long run.

All this is especially important for the caregiver both before and after his loved one's death. A healthy addressing of regret will make for a better relationship with his loved one, God, other people, and himself.

Perspective on Death

Death is what we are least able to prevent but try hardest to prevent. It is what is most certain but hardest to discuss. That is particularly hard in speaking of those we especially love. Hardest is our death. The exceptions are a terminal illness or life becomes so miserable that someone considers suicide. Even then, it is not easily discussed.

Death, with regard to life on earth, means the ultimate separation. The opportunity for closeness, intimacy with that person, is gone. Death is the ultimate attack on our drive for intimacy. And so, the dread of death becomes a fear of death. Hebrews 2:15 states that the fear of death can put us in a state of slavery.

In 1 Corinthians 15, Paul covers what is most important—the Gospel. And the critical feature of the Gospel message is that through Christ, there is victory over death. Death does not have to be feared. Paul was in constant danger. In 1 Corinthians 15:31, Paul speaks of dying every day. To interpret that as daily dying to sinful desires is to take the verse out of context. Paul was in constant danger of being killed and, ultimately, was killed. Yet he could be content, even with death always hanging over his head (Philippians 4:11).

I do not claim any special explicit knowledge about the next life after death. However, if what we most desire is intimacy, then the worst thing that could happen to us in the next life is to have no opportunity for intimacy. Jesus speaks of being "cast into outer darkness" (Matthew 8:12; 25:30). So hell would be ultimate aloneness, even if—especially if—one is around other people. In the existentialist Sartre's play *No Exit*, he is usually understood as saying hell is other people. Then we may see heaven as complete intimacy with everyone. That makes death to be either what we might most fear or most desire.

As Paul said, the Gospel gives us the message that "to die is gain" (Philippians 1:21) for the Christian. The day of his death is the best day of his life. Yes, there is victory over the sting of death (1 Corinthians 15:55). However, to have a new life, there must be the death of the old life.

So what have I learned from my care and love for Jan during this last year of her life? First, I came to realize how true it was that Jan could die at any moment. In the womb, where we are conceived, a mortal imperfect body is developing. From that point on, the capacity for death is always with us. With Jan, it was apparent that she was dying bit by bit. And so are we all. With the Apostle Paul, we "die daily" (1 Corinthians 15:31).

Even well before the last decade of her life, Jan may have had a profound realization of this reality. I noted that she made efforts to fix up the house, supposedly to be in good order as we got older. She got the house painted inside and out and had a new roof. At the time, it felt like she was preparing to die. It seemed like a negative mindset to me, although what she did was good.

Perhaps she had a subconscious premonition of what was ahead. It could also have been that the Lord was using her activities in those days to give a prophetic message to me. Unfortunately, however, I didn't get or, at least, didn't carefully read the memo.

So we all live with the certainty of death and the uncertainty of when it will happen. I have heard more than one person give a morning prayer that began, "Thank you, Lord, for another day that was not promised to us." The pandemic age vividly drove this truth home. Anyone we met at any given time could be the carrier of a deadly virus that could potentially be transferred to us. Or we could unknowingly be the carrier of a virus that may be a transfer of death to someone else.

Since death is inevitable, it might seem obvious that we all need to prepare for our death and prepare ourselves for the deaths of those we care for and love. However, there is, in us, the innate drive to live and for our loved ones to continue to live, even if we believe strongly in a beautiful life to come after death. So no matter how much we prepare, the drive to live keeps us unprepared. But as I noted earlier, we can even prepare to be unprepared and, when the time comes, be unprepared.

In light of this, as Francis Schaeffer said, *How Should We Then Live?* The Apostle Paul wrote that everything we do should, in some sense, be done for the Lord (Colossians 3:17, 23). The goal for Jan was to help her live as fully as possible for as long as possible. That would be a worthy pursuit for all of us. Paul expresses this principle when he advises us to "redeem the time" (Ephesians 5:16). The ESV translates this as "make the best use of the time." Will I always know the best way if I take the time to consider all the options to use at a given time? Of course not. I trust God that He will guide me to make good decisions, that He will even use my bad decisions for good, and I don't have to waste time worrying about whether I have made the best choice.

We can live as fully as possible as we realize that all people were created with a purpose, and as long as they are alive, their life has meaning. According to Scripture (Psalms 138:8; Philippians 1:6), a person does not die until that purpose is fulfilled. There are undoubtedly many circumstances that can challenge this assertion, and it has many ramifications. I will mention that this is not an argument to use all possible means to keep everyone alive as long as possible. However, it does mean that no matter the circumstances, I can be confident that my life and the lives of others have a purpose.

At least from the standpoint of probability, most, perhaps everything, that I do on this earth will not be remembered by future generations. I know, for example, very little of my great-grandparents. However, everything I do does have a lasting impact, whether any other human being gives it any recognition. Furthermore, how I live each moment of my life on this earth will affect how I live in the life to come (Romans 14:12; 2 Corinthians 5:10). Thus how I view death and how I view life are inseparable. I often hear that when people tell their stories, it impacts both others and themselves. And that will impact how they impact others still. So I write, not knowing what the result of this book will be. I trust God to do with it as He will.

In pondering death, we naturally consider what life will be like after we die. We naturally prefer to contemplate how it might be to live in heaven. We often think of it as an ideal existence to have and enjoy any and everything we could want. That frequently reminds me of an episode in the old *Twilight Zone* series. In that episode, a man who had had a rough life dies. He wakes up to a setting where a guide introduces him to an environment where he gets whatever he wants, and everything goes his way. He lives in a Las Vegas-like atmosphere, where he always wins at any of the games he plays. When he plays pool and breaks the rack, every ball goes in a pocket. If he wants a fast car to drive, it is readily available. Needless to say, he can get anything he wants from the most beautiful women. His initial reaction is that this was heaven beyond his wildest imagination when he was on earth.

However, after a while, this life did not work so well for him. He grows weary of this life of getting whatever he wants with no effort. Finally he gets so sick of it that he tells his guide that he wants to go to the other place. In response, the guide gives a devilish laugh and informs him that he is in the other place.

I can be backed by Scripture that the life we live now prepares us for the life that we will have after we die. So what kind of life might this man have lived to prepare him better for the next life? Let's presume that he had lived his life constantly thinking about and striving for what he wanted for himself. That is, he lived a selfish self-centered life.

Living this way had not brought him joy and satisfaction on earth. Then after he died, he thought he had, at last, come to a life where he could fulfill all his self-centered ambitions. Then he came to a sad realization. The living of a self-centered life is hell. Hell is populated by selfish people.

Scripture tells us that "It is more blessed to give than to receive" (Acts 20:35). This man had no awareness of this principle. 1 Corinthians 13:5 tells us that love does not insist on its own way. Heaven is not where we get to indulge in our selfish desires. Heaven is where there is whole, complete, perfect love for God and other people. It is where people constantly and gladly give of themselves to others. To prepare for heaven, live as Jesus lived, a life given for others.

In this life, out of our pain and suffering, we tend to be hard on one other. I gained an insight on this one night with Jan. Putting Jan to bed one night, she started slapping me. I let her know my disapproval. There was a look of hurt on her face. Then I said, "Jan, right now, this is hard for both of us, and we are hard on each other. But someday, we will be together where we are good for each other. And we are good for everyone, and everyone is good for us. The Lord will decide when that is to be. Jan, do you know where that is?"

And she said, "Heaven."

As for seeing loved ones in heaven, for me, that will particularly be my first wife, Cindy, Jan, and my present wife, Linda.

I would not wish on anyone the life of being a caregiver for a loved one. It is heart-wrenching to care for one who is dying and there is often suffering and certainly debilitation in the process. But caregiving is an excellent opportunity to learn to live a life for others and experience the joy of so doing. It is one of the finest opportunities one can have to prepare for the life to come.

Jesus said that there are no marriages in heaven (Matthew 22:30). But in 1 Thessalonians 4:13f, Paul assures us that all who know the Lord will meet again in heaven. And heaven, being what it is without the limitation on our abilities brought on by sin, particularly the constraints of connection we have in this life, we will connect perfectly with everyone. We will have fulfilling relationships with everyone far beyond the most satisfying relationship of the best possible relationship any married couple has, or could have, here on this earth. The best relationship any married couple has, or ever will have, on this earth will be trivial, superficial, and unsatisfactory compared to every one of our relationships in heaven.

Here on earth, we, at best, know God imperfectly. We pray, wondering how effective are our prayers. We long for a sharper response from God. In heaven, we will see, know, and interact with the Lord in a manner we cannot even imagine (1 Corinthians 13:11–12).

So in the years to come, what will people remember of Jan.? Of course, I have no way of knowing. But I am sure that people who knew her would agree that she was always caring and concerned for others. I know that that is how I remember her. I certainly know that I will never forget her. Perhaps this book will help, at least, some people have her in their memories for a more extended time. For Jan's funeral, I composed a poem expressing what might always remain of Jan. Dementia might have hidden these aspects during her last days. Death took her from this life but did not take from this earth who she was.

The poem is as follows:

It's What Remains

She no longer had quite the same physi-
    cal appearance of her youth,
But the beautiful woman God created
    always remains.
She was a great cook whose skills declined
    and gradually left,
But the nurturing woman God created
    always remains.
She could no longer be friendly, outgo-
    ing, caring, loving,
But God's love in her always remains.
She could no longer reach out to others,
But the Lord's loving arms around her
    always remain.
Her business sense with finances, prop-
    erty, and assets was gone,
But her investments for Heaven always
    remain.

> So to Jan and all—*Vaya con Dios*. Which
> is to say, go with God.
> And let it ever be true that God with you
> always remains.

Relief

People generally look at death in terms of loss and grief over the loss. They recognize it as, at least usually, the most brutal event human beings must face. We have a sense of foreboding about our own death. Even if we believe there will be a life after death for us that will be good (heaven), people generally dread the process and prospect of dying. Sometimes someone fears the possibility of a life after death that is bad (hell), but I think that percentage is small.

We recognize that for the person who has died, there is often a great relief. We talk of him being in a better place. The physical pain that he may have had is gone. He now has a restored body that is free of disease. Mental and emotional torments are gone. Relational conflicts are over. In the next life, we will even get along with our in-laws and people of that other political party!

People will often try to comfort someone who has lost a loved one to death by pointing out areas where they can now experience relief. They no longer must see their loved one suffering physically, mentally, emotionally, or in any other way. They are now free from the myriad of chores they had to do over and over and over in the care of their loved ones. There are no difficult decisions to make, etc., etc. The problem is, in missing our loved one, we often miss doing even these unpleasant tasks, and we have that longing to see our loved one again, even in her frail state.

With the death of a spouse, one is sometimes told, "There are other fish in the sea," as though one could replace a spouse as one might replace a car or appliance that is no longer working. A surviving spouse might indeed remarry, but he will not see a new wife as a replacement for his former wife if it is a healthy new marriage.

But a question remains—is it acceptable to have a sense of relief from the death of a loved one? Or perhaps more accurately, is it appropriate to talk about having a sensation of relief. There is a natural tendency to think that if one has a sense of relief in the death of a loved one, he didn't have that much love for his loved one. That can create all kinds of guilt emotions.

But if one is relieved of a whole set of unpleasant tasks, sights, and interactions and, therefore, experiences the emotion of relief, is there anything wrong, or a problem, with that? Relief is a pleasant sensation. Loss can have two simultaneous components: grief and relief. While I treasured having Jan with me in her last days, there was a lot in her presence that was not just unpleasant and uncomfortable but painful. It is hard to describe what it is like to see her decline bit by bit by bit. And every decline brings on new grief. One never gets used to it. It is like lifting a certain weight until it is relatively manageable. Then more weight is added, and the process starts all over. The process never ends as long as the one loved one is still alive. Grief and relief might be classified as contradictory emotions. But does that mean they can't exist side by side as mixed emotions, along with many other mixed feelings?

Relief does not dissipate grief. I missed the Jan I no longer had. The Jan I could talk with, share everyday experiences and the deep things of our hearts. The Jan I connected with relationally, emotionally, spiritually, physically, and beyond the best of words. Even the Jan I would argue with, was sometimes distant from, was so different from me and who made no sense to me, or I to her. And when she died, I missed the Jan who was dependent and, with that dependency, totally trusting. And relief would not take away any of that. So even though I had been grieving for over six years, and even though I experienced tons of relief, there was still a grieving process to complete. And I understand that even a beautiful remarriage would not, in itself, make that loss go away. The completion of a grieving process does not ever completely take away the loss.

What about the death of a spouse where it was a difficult marriage? But then, the difficulties of that marriage are over. Both are relieved of all that conflict. But if the death occurred without resolution, reconciliation, and closure with the loved one who died, all that conflict can remain inside the survivor. Does death in this circumstance bring any relief, or does it only bring the anguish of unresolved emotions? What will need to happen for the survivor is a spiritual journey to forgive one's departed of all the wrongs one feels he received from that person, and repentance and experience of forgiveness from God of what one did wrong, or feels he did wrong, to his loved one. But one cannot confess and repent to his departed. True, but it doesn't matter for the departed. For her, it's over. She is in a different life now. She is free from what happened to her on this earth. The survivor does not have to make amends to his departed. The Lord has provided that with the new life He has given her.

The better solution is always to build and maintain a good marriage relationship and not face such a situation.

Remarriage

I have described how I grieved Jan's decline and, finally, her death for years. At the same time, I pondered the possibility of a new relationship. I have heard married people say they could not consider anyone else if their spouse were to die. I have described how I carried with me these two emotions that many might regard as incompatible.

I decided that if I remarried, it could be a tribute to Jan. My reasoning was as follows. Suppose the situation was reversed, and I had taken ill, died, and Jan was widowed. Let's presume that she felt she had a good marriage with me. Furthermore, she didn't just miss me. She missed the state of being married. So she decided that she would like to pursue being married again. I would consider her remarriage to be a compliment to me.

On the other hand, suppose Jan had found being married to me to be a horrendous hardship. She decided that she did not want to get into a situation like that again. Consequently if any man showed any interest in her, she would tell him to get lost. I hate to think that that could have been Jan's reaction to having been married to me.

There are several considerations to resolve before pursuing a new relationship. The first is that it is essential to recognize that one's former spouse is gone. That is the process of grieving. There must be a letting go. That does not mean one is entirely over that loss. One is never absolutely over the loss of a loved one. I still know my loss, as a teenager, of my friend Johnny. But I have gone on to form numerous other close relationships.

In the traditional wedding ceremony, each one vows that he goes into the marriage "forsaking all others." Neither one is to have a former romantic relationship that they still long to have. That does still allow for fond memories of another relationship. A precaution in a new relationship is to make sure it is not used to cover over the grief one still feels.

Another important realization is to understand that the new person will be different. She will look different, will have different tastes, ways of doing things, responses, and other political views. That means there will be a lot of adjustments. She will not be a replacement. Any expectations that she will be like the last spouse will spell trouble.

In any marriage, there is the possibility of one partner becoming disabled and having to be cared for by the other partner. That possibility increases with a senior citizen couple. It causes many widowed people to dismiss considering remarriage. They don't want to risk having to repeat the caregiving process.

I don't relish that thought either. But because of the special-connection-without-words bond I had with Jan, the caregiver experience was a very precious, meaningful, and fulfilling one for me. I am very grateful for that experience. In all honesty, I don't think it would have happened if Jan had not had that disease.

Yes, it seemed to me that it would be great to have that relationship of connection again. This time, it would be with a woman that I could also talk with, go places with, do things with, etc. But it was also possible that the will of God was for me to live a single life. In that state, I might have a special relationship with a woman but with the boundaries of what is not God-honoring outside marriage. And even then, it could be a fulfilled life but without the fulfillment of an intimate marriage. It would be a life that is content to forgo that relationship.

But what if I were to remarry and then become a caregiver again? I did not want to glibly say that I would readily submit to that as being the will of God. But if I could have that complete unspoken and spoken deep bond with this new wife, then when she was in the brain-decline process, my relationship with her might be even more profound than it ever was with Jan.

In the traditional wedding vows, the couple promise to take each other "for better or worse." I suggest that this means each one is saying to the other, "I'd rather be worse off with you than better off with someone else." I resolved that if I remarried, and she became disabled, I would do all I could to provide for her. I wrote a poem that was my best effort to express my thoughts on this. It is titled "You Ask."

You Ask

You ask,
If the doctor gives that pregnant word,
    dementia,
What then?
Her brain shrinks; my heart grows.
Each new day, a day not promised.
As it's possible, we fully live each day.
The date unknown. The end certain.

You ask,
And if she cannot speak, hear, think, feel,
    be?

Let that day and days come.
No dread, no fear.
In love, we are more near.
For, the Lord takes away, and the Lord
     gives.

You ask,
What are you saying?
Listen to the silence! Hear us talk.
No need for sound, sight, taste, touch, or
     fragrance.
Free of all that and more,
Taking up time and energy.
Freedom I now know only in part,
Can't be expressed in human words
But deeply true and oh so real.

You ask,
What about the pain? You're in denial!
On that day and days
My pain will flow.
Sorrow, anguish. Oh God, I know!
     But with us a unity
     enjoyed far more abundantly
     than any could think or show.

So ask,
Will I not grieve my loss and Loss?
As and when she is no more?
In those days and when that day comes
Oh yes, you will see
My grief, all that, and more.
I pray, "Please God, No!"

But if the Lord gives her and takes
    her that way,
I will treasure her forever and all
    those days before.

I ask,
May I offer this prayer?
Now she lays in peace asleep,
Into your hands, I pray you keep.
And if she dies before we wake,
I trust you, Lord, her soul to take.

I have also considered the prospect of my getting dementia. I found it much more challenging to ponder and resolve. Perhaps having experienced it being Jan brought that setting clearly before me. Unfortunately, I haven't experienced it being me.

One cannot adequately write what it is like to experience what one has not personally experienced. All of us have experienced injuries and diseases that, for a time, limited our activities. Others have experienced a mental condition that limited their ability to think clearly. But except in the very early stages of the disease, none have experienced dementia and then shared with others what they experience.

You might wonder why I care to ponder such a thing. It isn't easy. There is a profound saying that the unexamined life is not worth living. We are creatures that will die. An examination of oneself has to include facing our death. Likewise, we are creatures that are vulnerable to debilitating and terminating diseases, such as dementia. Hence the personal need to address the prospect of having this disease.

I have expressed the thought that as this disease strips enough away from a person, it leaves the core of what one truly is. Dementia often brings on a personality change. The result can be positive or negative. To the extent that that is true, my conclusion has been that it is wise, while I am of a sound mind, to develop, as best I can, that core of my being.

I have also learned that dementia can change a person to act and speak differently from his true nature. That means that I have limited control over what this disease might do to me. I hope and pray that whatever it does, I do not become someone who makes life miserable for those who love me. I want to be as pleasant as possible for those who must care for me.

I have noted that as the disease makes one increasingly more dependent on others, one becomes increasingly less mature. I have spent all my life seeking and working to be an increasingly mature person. I don't think my most significant difficulty will be accepting help for what I can no longer do myself. But what will it be like to act, think, and be increasingly less mature? Jesus admonishes us to be as little children (Mark 10:14). Is it possible that this condition might make me a more spiritual person, closer to the Lord? Thus in declining, I will be growing.

I am fortunate to have long-term care insurance on myself. That will enable Linda to afford to have help in care for me. I also have a portfolio to draw from if she cannot care for me at home and needs to place me. Unfortunately, it is increasingly difficult to get long-term care insurance. That made it not feasible to get such a policy for Linda.

A remarriage by two senior citizens inevitably carries complications not present in a first marriage and at a younger age. I will mention three primary issues. First, I have already noted the matters of loss and grief from a previous marriage that need to be addressed and sufficiently resolved. Second are the feelings and attitudes of children and other relatives.

They may have their issues to settle before someone new comes into the family. The third is the matter of finances and other assets. How will the assets and incomes of each one be used to handle living expenses and discretionary spending?

There is also the matter of two people who have each had decades to develop their particular habits and preferences. No matter how much they may be suited to each other, each one will have to adjust to the other one's way of doing things. We have been sharing cooking duties. But that has meant still another woman coming into my kitchen. Of course, she had to have her own ideas of where things should go. So I had another adjustment with one more woman coming into my kitchen. And this time, it was part of the kitchen becoming our kitchen.

Pondering all this brings me to a much greater realization of the importance of trusting in God in a new marriage. Whatever happens to me, I am in His hands. I take comfort in that. It gives me the confidence to face what lies ahead. That may sound naive. The future is always filled with uncertainty. It helps to develop with God's grace a sincere trust in Him.

Having said all this, if one is single and has a definite sense of calling to be single, then he should fully develop his life as a single person. He will form deep personal relationships but not anything leading to marriage. The Apostle Paul notes that the single person has freedom for service to God that the married person doesn't have (1 Corinthians 7:32–34).

He has to accept that he will not have any human relationship with a marriage's depth. As a Christian, he needs to make sure that his decision results from divine calling and not avoiding the trials present in a marriage relationship. He needs to realize that to do the latter is to take the "easy" out of "not taking a chance on love."

If one has a definite sense of calling to be married, he should pursue that and in as godly a manner as possible. Most single Christians do not appear to have that clear sense of calling in either direction. For them, the right course of action is to be open to both possibilities. Develop a deep perception of awareness of the advantages, difficulties, and challenges of both. Know that any close deep relationship will inevitably bring some hurt and pain. The person of his love will disappoint, and the deeper the love, the deeper the potential hurt. He needs to develop the principle that to love is to experience hurt, but it is worth it. On the other hand, if he elects marriage, he needs to make sure he is not doing so primarily to escape the pain of being alone.

In 1 Corinthians 7, Paul suggests a man having a female companion, but they are not married. He expects that to be a relationship without a sexual relationship. He admonishes that if that isn't working, the couple should marry and be free to have a marital sexual relationship.

Many senior citizen marriages are made primarily for companionship. There is not the expectation that they will form a deeply intimate relationship. I see nothing in Scripture that prohibits such a relationship. They can enjoy the presence of and interactions with each other.

In this relationship, both people will have a lot of freedom for the pursuits that they are called. Each one needs to be clear to each other about what they want in their relationship.

I had a clear sense of what I wanted in a woman I might marry. It was a given that she be a person of faith in Christ to give us spiritual unity. Beyond that, the primary criteria were: First, someone I could bond with deeply, a soul mate, someone where she and I are as open as possible about our past, thoughts, feelings, and hopes. Second, we would have an active prayer life together. Third, when—not if—conflicts arose, we would work them out thoroughly. There would be no sweeping under the rug. Her housekeeping, cooking, bed performance, and physical appearance would be secondary. That is not to say that I would be disappointed if those qualities were present as well.

In my wedding service with Jan, we wrote our own vows that we spoke to each other. In my vows, I said that I knew she would have a profound influence on me. I vowed that I would be open to that happening. Over forty years of marriage, she certainly did. I knew that in a remarriage, I needed to consider the impact my new wife would have on my behavior, attitudes, emotions, and thoughts. I also needed to reflect on what impact I might have on her.

I considered the distinction between forming a relationship with a deep bond compared to a very romantic one. Without defining either one, I'll distinguish them as romance focused on feeling, while a bond is an awareness.

I thought about the following. Suppose I had two girlfriends. With one, we were creating the bond relationship that was my desire. With the other, we were developing a romantic relationship. Which lady would be better for me? Would I be confident that the bond relationship would also become romantic, or would I hope the romantic would also become a bond? All other factors being equal, my rational mind would opt for the former, but my emotions might well be for the latter. With Jan, I acknowledge that it started as romantic and moved to a bond. I think that is true for most marriage relationships, including the best ones. A good marriage needs both. A union with just the bond will last. One with just romance will not.

I met Linda about three months after Jan's passing. People might consider that relatively soon. However, I had been grieving for Jan for over six years. We dated steadily for nine months and then married. She moved into my house, and it has become our home.

Being married to Linda gave me everything I had hoped for and more. She was the right person to allow us to develop the bond, the connection beyond words, and the intimacy that I had wanted to have. It is still far from perfect. It is still challenging and, at times, uncomfortable. And in that bonding development has come romance.

One afternoon, as we were dating, I was at her place. She was raking leaves in the backyard, and I was doing the same in the front yard. I couldn't see her, and there was a house between us. But I was with her. We were present with each other. I was alone but with her and not lonely.

We have a good prayer life together. That has been particularly meaningful when we have a conflict. On numerous occasions, we have been at an impasse. Then we finally get our act together and pray. In all honesty, neither one of us feels like it. The prayers are anything but refined. But the results are impressive. Invariably then we can resolve things quite quickly and thoroughly. I will share that without prayer, I'm not sure if we would even have married.

Linda was also widowed after a long marriage. That gives us an understanding of each other. She will always miss her husband Jeff, as I will always miss Jan. We accept that in each other. We can easily talk with each other about the one we lost. It has helped us develop more love for each other. Love is not to be confined.

We have found a lot of common interests. It is accurate to say that we are very much alike. However, we come from notably different families and have very different histories. Furthermore, she is an artist, particularly in the areas of poetry and painting. Getting to know her as an artist has been a very broadening experience for me. I would describe us as very much alike, except that we are very different. I have thought of writing a book about my experience with Linda. The subtitle would be *What Does It Mean to Be Married to an Artist?* With the significance of prayer in our relationship, the primary title might be *We Prayed.*

As for those areas that I listed as secondary, I will simply note that we eat well, the house and front and back yards are much neater and improved, and we enjoy private times close together. She is attractive, a few years younger than me, and is very young in my heart. God has been good.

This chapter would not be complete without me making a special acknowledgment. Linda has had several publications of her poetry and shown her paintings in numerous exhibits. She has received several awards for her work. As I completed this book, I asked Linda to design the book cover. She carefully considered this project and created the painting you see on the book cover. My sincere thanks to you, Linda, for this act of love.

Grace Guilt

For years, I experienced a sense of guilt over how fortunate I was. I realized that I had a fine set of circumstances for which I could take no credit. I am relatively secure financially, in good health for my age, and had great support, through the years, in caring for Jan. My history of poor and foolish decisions got me into relatively very little trouble, and I had good spiritual training and education.

Why me and not others? It is the same dynamic as the soldier who returns from the battlefield unscathed, when many of his fellow soldiers were severely injured or killed. Is it just that I should have such an unfair advantage over so many others who are so unfortunate? We say such a soldier has survivor guilt. We might also say that I have had grace guilt.

Many others have much less and have more arduous lives. It's not that I am more spiritual, behaved better, or worked harder. So I must credit either good fortune or the grace of God. I take it to be the latter.

I have finally realized I can enjoy all that I have without experiencing guilt. For reasons I can't explain, God chose to give me what I have. It's not a cause for pride nor is it a cause for shame. It is a cause for thankfulness.

I realize I have been guilty of feeling guilty over what God has done. Harboring that feeling is saying God did wrong. But who am I to judge what God should or should not do? Doing that is walking into a very imprudent territory. God does whatever He wants to do. And He does not owe me any explanation, much less justification for what He does.

Having made the decision not to engage in grace guilt, I still felt that emotion. What I felt deep inside had not caught up with what I decided in my head. That was all right. In time, my heart caught up with my brain.

Scripture says, "To whom much has been given shall much be required" (Luke 12:48). This verse certainly applies to me. I am blessed so I can be a blessing to others. But it would be wrong to serve Him out of obligation for all He has given me, or even to serve as a thanksgiving to Him. To do so would be to attempt to be worthy of what I have received.

Instead, I trust, or at least hope, I serve Him out of love for Him. I often need the Holy Spirit, in both His teaching and convicting ministry to remind me of that (John 16:8–13).

The parable of the talents makes it clear that one cannot use lack of ability and favorable circumstances to avoid service to God (Matthew 25:14–30). With the Lord's guidance, we do what we can as much as we are able. We help others where we have the opportunity and are free to enjoy what we have.

Finally and, no doubt, most importantly, I need to constantly dwell on the thought that there is the most profound reason why I am treated so unfairly well by God. It is precisely because Jesus was treated in such a bad, evil, unjust, and unfair manner. In blatant contrast to my always-prepared inclinations, He accepted this treatment without any resentment. And there were absolutely no grounds to make any case for balancing the wrongs He received with any wrong He had done (Hebrews 4:15). He embraced even His brutal crucifixion, out of love.

I have mentioned how once, after having gone through a particularly difficult time, I had the audacity to offer the following prayer, "Lord, I deeply thank You for taking me through these very difficult times. And I thank You for how You used these times to teach me and to develop me to be more of what You would have me to be. But in the future, when You want to teach me, if You could do so in more pleasant circumstances, I would greatly appreciate it."

And the Lord responded to me, saying, *Elton, I would love to teach you in more pleasant circumstances. But you don't learn during the pleasant times. You only learn through difficult trials.* And of course the Lord, as always, was right.

I have a sense that these good times are also a trial, or test, from the Lord. The test is to see if, this time, for once, I can learn and grow while the going is good. And of course, Satan is present, tempting me to be complacent and neither learn nor grow. I hope and pray that during this good time, I will have the maturity to move forward.

It has been my experience that a good period will, at some point, be followed by a period that is, at least, challenging. And the trials of life that come are often more challenging, or at least different, than those of the past. The Lord has given me no indication of what my next set of challenges will be. That is no surprise as He has never forewarned me before. I have no giftedness in foretelling prophecy. So I seek to simply trust in His grace to be teaching and developing me for whatever lies ahead.

One day, Jan was sitting quietly on the couch in the family room. Then she said, "The church is floundering." I had no idea where she got that or what she meant.

I decided to respond by asking her, "What do you think we should do?"

She replied, "You need to take some leadership."

I could tell I wasn't going to get anything more on this from her. I often think of this incident, feeling it does have some meaning for me. I still have no idea what. Life is full of interesting mysteries.

About the Author

The author graduated from the University of California, Berkley, in 1965. He has a degree in mathematics and has an informal minor in philosophy. He received a master of theology degree from North Park Seminary in 1969. He is ordained in the Evangelical Covenant Church. He has served in pastoral ministry and social services, including Child Protective Services. He served as a chaplain at a Teen Challenge Christian-based chemical dependency recovery program for men. He is now retired.

Elton and his wife, Jan, raised a son and two daughters. He has nine grandchildren and a great grandchild. He was very involved in the care of his parents during the last six years of their lives. His mother developed dementia during the last years of her life.

His wife was diagnosed with dementia, a brain-injuring debilitating disease for which death is the only cure.